WHEN HEARTS COLLIDE

VICTORIA LUM

ETERNAL HEARTS PUBLISHING

When Hearts Collide

By Victoria Lum

Cover Design Copyright © 2024 Y'All That Graphic

Editing by Theresa Leigh and Amy Briggs, Proofreading by Michele Ficht

Print ISBN: 979-8-9900169-1-0
EBook ISBN: 979-8-9900169-0-3

Author's Note

Author's Note: Please note this story may contain areas that may be sensitive to some readers. For a list of potential areas of sensitive content, please visit: https://www.victorialum.com/sensitive-content-information

DEDICATION

To my ladies who like to read about assholes with a tortured soul...this one is for you.

RELATIONSHIP TREE

THE KINGSLEYS AND EXTENDED FAMILY
(LA HEARTS SERIES)

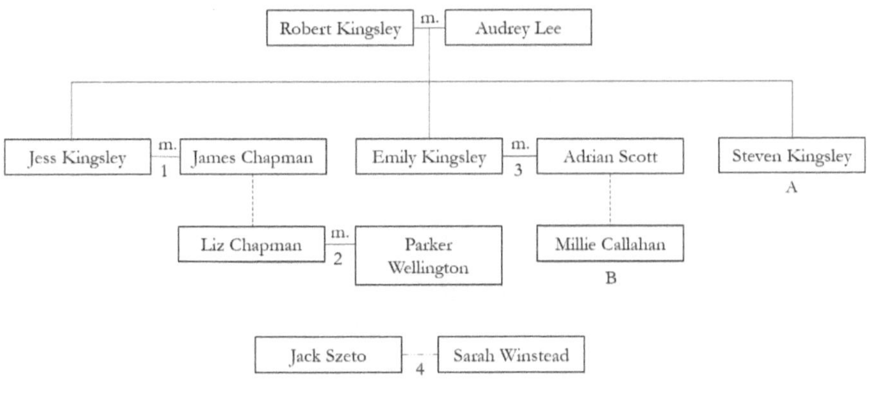

THE ANDERSONS AND FRIENDS
(THE ORCHID SERIES)

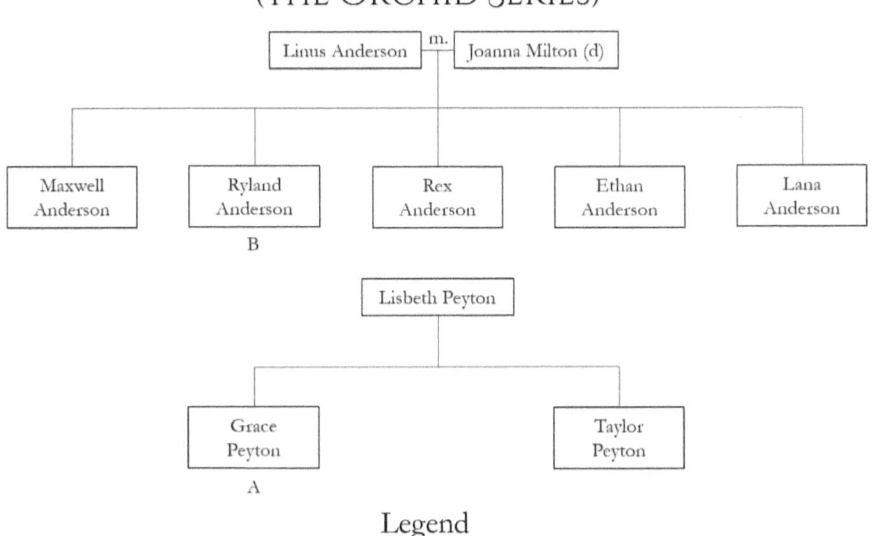

Legend

—— Family ----- Siblings --·-- In Relationship   m. Married   (d) Deceased

Books

1 – *The Sweetest Agony* 2 – *The Coldest Passion* 3 – *The Harshest Hope* 4 – *The Brightest Spark*
A – *When Hearts Ignite* B – *When Hearts Collide*

Disclaimer: Only main characters are included. Awesome side characters including children are not in this tree.

Chapter 1

The gunshot is deafening.

The sound echoes in the quiet morning just before the screeching cries from a flock of quail fleeing the scene of a murder pierce the eerie silence.

I'm still standing.

For the brief millisecond as the rifle ricochets in my hands, time freezes, the seconds suspending in an alternate dimension. My breath lodges in my throat as goosebumps prickle my forearms, already glistening with a thin layer of sweat.

The damp fog in the waning twilight, the skies lightening from dark navy to pale blue as the sun announces its arrival, all seem sharper and more visceral.

In this instant, I stare at nature in its eyes, not knowing if I'll be the person left standing.

To conquer or be conquered.

But I feel so damn free. Alive. Unapologetically honest.

A wide grin splits my lips. I savor the high streaming in my veins and I can finally *breathe*.

The beast inside me roars. For a few blessed minutes, it's uncaged, unchained, untethered. It can run, it can escape, it can raze the fields to its heart's content.

This motherfucking boar, with an impressive set of razor-sharp tusks, a beast twice the size of the normal wild hogs I've hunted in the past, is now a dark clump in the distance.

"Good job, Ryland. Waking up before dawn paid off, eh?" Jerome, my trusted hunting guide of fifteen years, gives me a terse nod before raking his weathered, tanned hands over his shaggy blond hair. I flew him out here to California from back home in New York just for this hunting trip; a rare escape for me.

My lips twitch in a half-smile, sweet satisfaction flooding my insides, mixing with the heady rush of adrenaline. It's a sensation a man can be addicted to.

The hunting. The freedom. The danger of the chase.

The stress I've accumulated in my tight shoulders slowly leaches out of me.

"It's satisfactory," I reply.

"It's good to see you smile finally. I was beginning to think you forgot how to do that."

Jerome and his assistant, a stocky guy who looks no older than twenty, follow me as I amble toward the fallen beast to see if my shot hit front and center.

Two blurry shapes of blue and yellow catch my attention. I glance at the low-hanging branches, finding a curious bird, the sialia currucoides, the mountain bluebird, staring at me with sharp eyes, its vibrant blue feathers a sharp contrast to the browns and greens of the muted valley landscape in the fall. Its partner, the sturnella neglecta, the western meadowlark, with its captivating yellow chest, breaks out into a sweet, melodious song.

The birds cock their heads in unison as we observe each other. They don't seem to care they're in the presence of danger, or how the rules of nature dictate they should flee as I step closer to them. In fact, the meadowlark's song grows louder.

It's as if they're here to say, *fuck the rules.*

The thought brings another small smile to my face. If I had more time, I'd take out my camera and capture the sighting on film.

The birds fly away, soaring into the free skies. My heart pounds at the flap of their wings.

Riiing.

The shrill sound jolts me from my reverie. After taking the satellite phone out from my pants pocket, I stare at the screen, my grin slipping off my face.

Maxwell.

Swallowing the lump in my throat, I feel the real world sweeping in with the lethality of an assassin, and the invisible tie around my neck choking me again. The duties of being an Anderson offspring, bound to live by the terms of the perpetual family trust set by our forefathers, all shove their way into the forefront.

The gilded cage. The hundreds of years of impeccable Anderson legacy.

But you don't need to answer the phone, Ryland. Technically, I have fifty-three more minutes of freedom left.

But family always comes first.

Jerome whistles, ignoring my buzzing phone. "Look at this motherfucker." His black boot toes the hog on the ground. "Dead center, Ryland. Perfect shot."

He crouches down and eyes the animal. "Too bad for you, buddy. Can't escape fate."

My heart plummets, my fingers shaking as I hold the vibrating phone in a death grip.

Can't escape fate.

Life has a way of curling invisible chains around your hands, dragging you off to a predetermined fate, and no amount of kicking and screaming will set you free.

The thought sobers me, and I blow out an exhale, my breath coming out in a white plume. The wild boar, a large beast that terrorized the rest of his herd and strutted around like the king of the grasslands a little while ago, is still, its beady eyes unfocused toward the clear blue sky, facing a freedom he'll no longer experience.

It's another futile attempt for me to rewrite history.

The small scar on my right eyebrow flashes in phantom pain. A reminder all freedom comes at a cost. There are often unforeseen circumstances.

I stare at the dead hog.

I won. You lost. Again.

The victory is hollow. For the first time, the thrill of the hunt is short-lived. Muted. The sharp, serrated knife has finally dulled at the edges after years of use. It still cuts, but with more effort and energy, the satisfaction of the knife slicing through thick slabs of meat like butter no longer there.

The buzzing of the phone stops and begins again.

I shake my head to dispel the thoughts. Breathing deeply, I press answer. "Miss me already? I've only been gone for two weeks."

Maxwell's deep chuckles come across the line and I crouch down, pull out twines of rope and other supplies, and prepare the hog for our descent back to base camp. My fingers deftly tie the rope around the boar in a combination of clove hitch and square knots, the motions as natural to me as breathing. It's a ritual I have every time I make a kill. I need to be the one to prepare the carcass, to pay my respects, the least I could do to honor the fallen prey.

He murmurs, "Just checking to see if the wilderness has finally gotten to you. I don't understand your fascination with hunting. It's barbaric, not to mention dangerous."

"Says the man who regularly risks his life racing motorcycles and fast cars. Pot calling the kettle black, don't you think?"

Finishing up, I step back and motion to Jerome and his assistant. They can do with the meat whatever they want. I don't care. It's always about the thrill of the chase for me. I know they will redistribute the meat to other people as they always do after each hunt. Slinging my sleek Christensen Ridgeline FFT rifle over my shoulders, I hike back toward base camp.

Maxwell stays silent, no doubt reflecting on something I said. We may be fraternal twins, but we're two sides of the same coin. He's the silent, stoic one—a man of a few words, heavier burdens, and I'm the outward face of the family, the epitome of wealth and success.

All smokescreens, fake smiles and even faker charm for press junkets, when all I want to do is snarl at them. But the public eats it all up.

"How's LA treating you? Things aren't the same without you here," Maxwell asks.

I hear the faint sounds of classical music echoing in the background, a song from Puccini's *La Bohème*, the melody rich and heartbreaking, with the unique scratchiness of the vinyl record playing from our vintage phonograph, and I smile. Maxwell is predictable this way. He must be at the estate, his preferred place of solace.

"I'll be back before you know it. The company will survive without me and the IPO isn't for another year or two."

I kick a pebble on the ground. "And Edmund only needs me to cover for him for his courses for a few months at ULA while he steps away for his family emergency. I'm happy to help. Is everyone doing all right?"

I'd stay behind to teach full-time if life allowed me, if I could shed my heavy cloak of responsibilities. The intoxicating rush of satisfaction when I see my students' eyes sparkle with newfound knowledge is unparalleled.

Academia was a dream I shared with Mom; a woman cruelly taken away from us too soon. And now it's a dream I carry alone.

"Same old shit. Rex is partying it up with some flavor of the week. Ethan is brooding over something, but he's tight-lipped about it, and Lana is in Paris for a business trip. We had a family dinner at the estate last week."

My chest briefly warms as I think about my younger siblings. Despite my resentment toward the obligations of being an Anderson, I love Dad and my siblings with all my heart.

I close my eyes and breathe in the crisp air, which carries a hint of earthiness mixed with fresh morning dew on golden grasses and fallen leaves. *The smell of freedom.*

I'll never be "just Ryland," but out here, somewhere near Bitterwater Valley in Central California, I'm as close to him as I can be.

I clear my throat. "You should go out more, Maxwell. Stop holing yourself up at the estate or The Orchid. We're only thirty-five, not eighty-five. Live a bit for yourself."

The phonograph clicks off and silence fills the line. His voice is quiet when he replies, "You know I don't get a lot of choice in my life. Solitude is the one thing I get to choose for myself. I'm happy, Ryland, all things considered. And Fleur is successful, isn't it? Even if the CEO is in the shadows, our profits have doubled over the last five years and will only continue to grow after the IPO."

"But you aren't truly living." A weight settles firmly on my chest. *You're a fucking hypocrite, Ryland.*

"I'd say the same for you, hypocrite," he whispers back.

Damn twin-sense. We may be separated by miles, but I swear there are moments when I think he can still hear my thoughts.

I force out a chuckle, my fingers playing with a twig from the ground. "What on earth are you talking about? I *am* living. Ryland Benedict Reginald Anderson, famous second son and face of the affluent Anderson family, chief operating officer of Fleur Entertainment Holdings, the largest hospitality conglomerate in the world by day, adjunct professor by night, impeccable reputation, women fawning over me left and right. The world is at my fucking fingertips."

The twig snaps in my hand, and I swallow the bile making its way up my throat.

My fingers trace the dark leather bracelet around my wrist, knowing its twin is on the same arm of the caller on the phone. "I'm the fucking opposite of you."

"Why the public fawns over you with your surly ass personality is anyone's guess."

"It's part of the charm."

He snorts. "But you aren't happy. Don't bother lying to me. I only wish you'd tell me why."

"You think too much."

He laughs. I can imagine his smug smile, a rare expression transforming his cold face into something resembling a living being. His Majesty is the beautiful frigid king, his nickname from the press, even though they don't have any interactions with him despite their attempts. Even so, they want to know all about the mysterious CEO of our family business.

Clearly sensing I won't tell him anything else, he changes the subject. "You ready for the press conference tonight?"

"As ready as I'll ever be. The jet is waiting for me now." *I wish you could take on the press sometimes. It's fucking exhausting. This entire life is fucking exhausting.* But I don't say the words aloud.

"Good luck. I'll be tuning in. Don't fuck up, brother. We need all the good press we can get for the IPO. You know what's at stake. Counting on you."

A rustling sound interrupts my conversation and I turn around. Jerome and his assistant grin as they haul the large hog, now hanging from a sturdy stick. My chest pinches as I'm ensnared by the lifeless eyes of the dead animal, bringing up a faded memory of another beast in my past, one that almost took my life if it weren't for Maxwell.

I owe it to him. In more ways than one.

The scar on my eyebrow pinches again.

A lump forms in my throat and I close my eyes, letting my mind drift back to the time I got the aching scar.

The large boar charging toward me, its tusks gleaming in the sunlight, its eyes cold with fury.

Dad's loud holler which echoed from far, far away.

Maxwell darting in front of me, pushing me out of the way as the boar hurled itself at us.

Screams. Echoes. Pain. So much pain.

Gunshot.

I owe *him*. Be brave.

I reply to Maxwell, my voice hoarse, "Never. It'll be another win for the family."

Family first. Always.

CHAPTER 2

"Mr. Anderson!"

The throng of reporters rises to their feet, their hands waving in the air, all clamoring for attention like a bunch of overzealous pigeons scrambling for breadcrumbs thrown by tourists in Central Park. I wish for the thousandth time to be back in the serenity of the grasslands from this morning.

Flashes of blinding lights dot my vision as I paste on my fake smile for the camera—unfortunately for me, smiles are necessary at these events—my hands curling around the podium in the large conference room inside the Kensington Hotel in downtown Los Angeles. I spent the past twenty minutes announcing our IPO plans to the public.

"Mr. Anderson, please! Over here!"

A shrill-voiced reporter separates herself from the crowd and I squint, eyeing the familiar curvaceous blonde in the front row, my loyal fan from CBC News, who apparently has followed me here from New York City.

I point to her. "Maggie, fancy seeing you here. Yes?"

She flushes a pretty pink, clearly surprised I remember her name. Little does she know, before every press conference, I'm given a small dossier containing the names and photos of the reporters and cameramen who'll show up. As the face of the company, I'm here to answer their questions and dance the tightrope between being friendly enough and standoffish with the press, who can change their opinions like a toddler's random meltdown.

"Mr. Anderson, why did your family suddenly decide to go through an initial public offering for the nightclub branch of your business? Isn't that divesting some control from your family?"

My fingers adjust the cuff links peeking out from under the sleeves of my navy Italian bespoke suit. At least this isn't a stupid question for once.

"This isn't a sudden decision and there's significant work to be done before we take Fleur Twilight, our nightclub subsidiary, public."

I grip the sides of the podium. "Fleur Twilight is twenty percent of our overall business and is rapidly expanding as consumers clamor for unique nightclub experiences where they can frequent the same location and expect a different atmosphere each time. We offer them that. No two nights at our nightclubs are the same. An IPO allows the public to partake in this exciting venture and will also let us grow at a quicker speed to better serve our consumers. It's a win-win situation."

The success of the IPO is life or death for Fleur Twilight, but there's no way I'll volunteer that information.

More clicks of shutters and bright flashes, the furious scratching of notes on notepads, and the cycle begins anew, another annoying chorus of "Mr. Anderson."

"When will we see Maxwell or your father in public?"

I arch my brow at the question, which should come as no surprise since it always comes up at every press conference. My answer remains the same each time.

"I'm not their keeper. Your guess is as good as mine." I soften the barb with a quick smile before glancing away.

"What about you? Any girlfriend in the works? When will we see you settle down?" a loud voice hollers from the back, followed by a smattering of laughter.

A muscle twitches on my forehead and I fight the urge to loosen the crimson tie around my neck. Gritting my teeth, I level a glare at the reporter in question, Brad something from *Gossip Times*, the premier gossip channel and website in the country. Why the fuck were they invited to this press conference in the first place?

"It's better to control the information than to let them make up their own," Lana's voice whispers in my mind. My sister is a PR genius, but fuck, I'm the one who has to deal with these inane questions.

"You should know better than to ask me that, Brad. No comment on my personal life. Let's focus on the IPO instead."

My nostrils flare as I keep my eyes pinned on his and while his complexion pales at whatever he sees on my face, he doesn't back off.

"You're practically American royalty, the prince of the USA. The public has the *right* to know. Are you hiding a lady somewhere? Or a boyfriend? Or a secret family?"

And there go the rest of the reporters, all predators seeking their next kill, and right now I look like defenseless prey under the glaring spotlight on stage. Sweat gathers on the back of my neck and a sticky heat crawls up my spine. I fight the urge to snarl and give them a piece of my mind.

I live my life with precision and control so I'll never have to feel powerless, and yet, in moments like this when I'm forced to play a role for the sake of my family, I feel like a rabbit cowering in the presence of a hawk.

I *refuse* to be the prey.

"If there are no other questions about our IPO plans, I bid you goodnight."

Spinning around, I button my suit, my free hand fisting at my side and I stride off the stage toward Cedric, my assistant, who's waiting by the staff corridor, his face paling as he takes in my foul mood.

More questions are hurled at me as I disappear into the hallway, knives thrown at a retreating back. Zero sportsmanship. *Fucking cheaters.*

"Do a better job at screening reporters in the future. This is fucking ridiculous," I bark at Cedric, who nods, his eyes widening with fear, as my blood heats further. The predator in me always senses the fear inside the prey, and with humans, it's no different.

A few minutes later I'm whisked away in a town car to my temporary oceanfront condo in Manhattan Beach. I crack open a window, my lungs sick of the circulated air of the AC.

The clouds are thick tonight; the news reporting the first storm of the season may be upon us soon. I feel the dampness and restrained energy in the air. I love storms—nature's ultimate light show and demonstration of unleashed power.

Unchained. Untethered.

The secret I've carried in the back of my heart makes a reappearance. *I want to live for myself.*

Tugging my tie from the choke hold around my neck, I take a deep breath before unbuttoning my dress shirt. *You fucking hypocrite, failing to live the advice you've given Maxwell before.*

My fingers grasp the small platinum pendant and my mom's parting words ghost in my ears. *"Live for yourself, Ryland. Be brave."* A heaviness settles in my chest.

My phone pings with an incoming message. Letting out a deep breath, I crack the joints in my neck.

Steven

> American royalty? Prince of the USA? Man, they have shitty standards. And yes, CBC telecasted your press conference live and, of course, I had to tune in and watch you flounder.

I smirk, my tight muscles relaxing slightly, and I type a response to my good friend, Steven Kingsley, a Wall Street titan at Pietra Capital, one of the top investment firms in the nation.

Ryland

> Why do you think my family calls me "Your Highness" as a fucking joke? You can have the title if you like.

Better you than me. Press conferences are bloodbaths disguised in suits and good lighting. But seriously, you looked like you were about to murder that reporter. Did he hit on a nerve? Is there a woman none of us know about?

I scoff, shaking my head.

Women. Love. They have no place in my carefully curated life. A life that was planned for me like the lives of every Anderson offspring in the last several hundred years. I have zero interest in the useless emotion, especially after experiencing the gut-wrenching pain of losing Mom from the damn family curse hanging over our heads, the curse dooming the women the firstborn men of our family love. Not to mention, I saw what Maxwell went through with his high school sweetheart, Sydney.

Mom used to say love was having your heart live outside of you.

I can't do that. The vulnerability. The never ending loss when they inevitably leave, and they always do. The Anderson men aren't lucky in love. Plus, I can never put a woman's needs first, and if I ever love someone, that's what they would deserve, isn't it?

So, no. Love is the *last* thing I need.

My jaw clenches. A flash of wispy blonde hair and beguiling, innocent eyes rises to the forefront.

Fake. All of it. The cheating snake. But I'll take that secret to the grave.

No woman. Hell will freeze over before I fall for any of them.

CHAPTER 3

 Millie

Dear Mom,

I miss you. I hope you're watching down on me from heaven. Wish me luck today. It's my first day of class at ULA. It's nice being back in LA after so many years. I'll let you know how it goes.

Love, Millie

THE ESPRESSO MACHINE isn't working.

A tiny sliver of panic crawls under my skin. *I need coffee to function, especially today of all days.* I press my finger on the blinking blue button again and wait, my foot tapping an impatient rhythm in the kitchenette.

I shove several gummy bears—my snack of choice—in my mouth. *Come on, please.*

Nothing. *Dammit.*

"You have to jab it harder. Think of it as the eye of an ex and you want to poke it out when he smirked at you after hurling insults about your weight," a sardonic voice drawls from behind me.

I stifle a grin before thinking of the annoying smarmy smile of Lloyd, my one and only ex-boyfriend. *"Ask your brother for me. I just need a small business loan. You'd do it for me, right? You want me to succeed, don't you, hot stuff?"* Even though this was two years ago, the sharp flame inside my chest still burns hot whenever I think of the opportunistic bastard.

Gritting my teeth, I stab the blinking blue button, pretending it's any part of Lloyd's body.

Whirrr...

The machine resurrects from its comatose state and the life-giving smell of coffee soon fills the room.

"Yes!" I whisper before turning around, finding my new roommate for the year, Jocelyn Song, standing there with a smug grin on her face, her arms crossed over her chest.

She lifts a brow as if to say, *see, what did I tell you?*

"Thanks, Jocelyn, I mean, Joss."

Jocelyn and I only met last week after I moved in. She had posted an apartment-mate listing on the University of Los Angeles's student portal and I applied. Adrian, my older brother, complained the entire time because I refused to move into his beautiful penthouse apartment in downtown LA. Let's just say I really didn't want him hovering over me like a hawk.

She shrugs and rubs her eyes as she retrieves my thermos from one of the basic white cabinets and hands it to me. I pour the piping hot coffee from the espresso container before starting the frother for the milk.

I shake out my tight shoulders. Bouncing on my feet, I gnaw on my lip.

Bounce. Bounce. Bounce.

"Damn, you look like you're trying to psych yourself up before going off to war. It's only the first day of class. Nothing's going to happen other than introductions and reading the syllabus. Not to mention the weather doesn't look so great, so everyone will probably be late. We Angelenos can't drive in the rain. Plus, you're only here one year, so you're just like an exchange student. You can treat this as a vacation."

Laughing softly at her quizzical quirk of her brows, I reply, "I'm the kid who usually can't sleep before the first day of school. I don't think I slept at all last night."

"You don't have class until three, right? Why are you up now? It's only noon. I, on the other hand, have to leave for my first lecture now, so I don't have much of a choice."

She yawns and rubs her eyes again, her shoulders slumped, before she lets out a deep, exasperated sigh. I don't know her well enough yet, but she looks sad and exhausted—dark eye circles marring her otherwise pale, unblemished face, her long black hair in a shaggy bun. Her orange ULA T-shirt is wrinkled and her jeans have a weird, dark stain on it. She looks like she needs the coffee more than I do.

Tentatively, I reach out and put my hand on her shoulder.

"Um...I know we don't know each other well yet, but are you okay? If you need to talk to anyone, I'm here and I'm a vault. Just FYI."

Jocelyn bites her lip, her brown eyes taking on a concerning wet sheen, and she shakes her head.

"Thanks. Life is tough right now, but I'll let you know if I need anything."

She clears her throat and forces out a smile. "So, we're in the same class together, right? Three p.m. Business Ethics with Professor Kristoff?"

"Yep. But I got an email saying Professor Kristoff has an emergency and needs to be away for a bit. They have someone else guest lecturing instead."

Her eyes take on a sharp glint and she leans in, as if to divulge to me the secrets of the illuminati. "You're new here, so you don't know, but *everyone* is excited about Professor Anderson. He guest lectured every so often at ULA in the past, but never for such a long stint. The classroom is going to be *jammed packed*, mark my words, *even* with the rain."

"Why? Is he a celebrity or something?"

She *tsks* and shakes her head. "I'm glad we're having this conversation before you walk in unaware. Professor Ryland Anderson is from the New York Anderson family...you know, *the* Anderson family." She pauses for dramatic effect.

I frown. The name rings a bell. "I've seen his name on the news before. Doesn't that family own half of New York? I don't really follow the gossip rags."

"They do. They are the definition of old money, right next to the Kennedys, Vanderbilts, and the Rockefellers, and equally, if not more, mysterious. They own Fleur Entertainment Holdings."

Seeing my nonreaction, she adds, "Tell me you're a nerd without telling me you're a nerd. Fleur owns all the big night clubs and many top luxury hotels in the world, not to mention The Orchid in NYC."

This sounds very familiar. Adrian may know more, now that he has worked his way up from our humble beginnings to being a self-made billionaire. He recently came back to LA from New York after we moved there when I was seven and he was nineteen.

And everyone knows about The Orchid, the exclusive establishment for the rich and famous renowned for its secrecy. Rumors abound as to what's inside the large fifty-plus story building in Manhattan, where it's said anyone can get anything their heart desires within those walls.

Apparently seeing the light dawn in my eyes, Jocelyn waggles her brows, her earlier sullen mood disappearing.

"Yep, I see you know who I'm talking about. He's the face of the family, the one most often featured in the press other than his playboy younger brother, Rex. And more importantly, he's *hot*, like movie-star hot."

Her eyes take on a dreamy, faraway look as she lets out a wistful sigh. "I've seen him from afar before and I'll never forget those cheekbones, that jawline, and those broody eyes. A man has no business looking that good. He's not even human. He's a *god*. So what if he's a cold asshole."

I blink, trying to hold back a snort at the lovestruck expression on her face. "I'm sure he's just a man, not some kind of higher power."

Jocelyn shakes her head and gapes at me, her mouth dropping open.

"Have you been listening to *anything* I just said? He's definitely not just a man. But seriously," she leans closer, "word of advice from his past students... He's a stickler for the rules, as serious as Sunday school. He's strictly a 'look, don't touch' type of guy. He's *completely* off-limits. So, keep your hands to yourself. Rumor has it some girl cheated on an exam and then tried to 'make it up to him' by taking off her shirt during office hours and he not only lit into her, made her cry, but also got her expelled. He *hates* cheaters."

Chuckling, I shake my head. "You guys don't have to worry about me. Men are the last thing on my mind right now," Especially after my douchebag ex, Lloyd. "I just want to ace this class since it's one of the funnel classes to the Education Honors Program at NYUC."

"NYUC?"

I nod. "New York City University Carlisle. Most everyone outside New York calls it NYU, which gets confusing because of the other NYU in the city."

"Huh. I didn't know there were two NYUs."

"See?" I smirk.

"So, what's with this special education program thing you're talking about?"

"Their honors program is the best program for education majors in the country because it merges business and education curricula together and focuses on real world, practical applications of the education degree."

I bounce on my feet again. "It's a big deal for my major. If I do well in this class, I have a very good shot of getting into that program when I go back home next year."

If the professor can write me a letter of recommendation, that'll go a long way too.

And I'll be one step closer to accomplishing my dreams to first be a teacher then work my way into education policymaking, so I can make a difference in the lives of the many disadvantaged youth in the country or perhaps even in the world.

The sky is the limit, really.

I, of all people, know how critically important a good teacher is to students in poor neighborhoods and unstable family backgrounds. After what I went through when I was younger, when Mr. Roberts showed me the importance of counseling and family support services, which are sadly lacking in disadvantaged neighborhoods, I realized the only way for me to make a difference is through policymaking.

So, the last thing on my mind is men. Distractions from my goal. No, thank you.

But tiny wings flap inside my heart when I think of my parents' romance, one that withstood time and surpassed Mom's death. Maybe with the right person at the right time...

Glancing up, I see Jocelyn already moving about, pouring herself a coffee, and getting ready to head out the door.

I holler just as my phone rings in the background, "Thanks for the heads up, Joss. I'll see you in class later today!"

She flashes me a peace sign before slamming the door with a bang, the walls shaking from the force.

I scramble to my bedroom, push aside my current knitting project, something I enjoy doing in my free time, to pick up my phone on the desk before it stops ringing.

"Hey, Adrian." I huff out a big breath, a little winded from leaping over piles of books by the entryway of the kitchen and scrambling over the laundry basket in the tiny hallway of our two-bedroom apartment.

The space is small and bare bones, but I love it—even though I'm sure my brother would much prefer I live in somewhere fancy with around the clock security.

Adrian's face appears on the screen. His normally stony face, one completely befitting his moniker by the press, "The Shark," relaxes a smidgen, and I swear I can see the beginnings of a smile on his lips.

"Why are you out of breath?"

"Well, hello to you too, brother. You look great today. Why thank you, dear sister. Did you have lunch yet? No, I haven't. Ah, I see. Excited for your first day of school? Defi—"

"Very funny."

I grin, watching his lips twitch as he sits back in his chair, the workaholic in his office, his fingers playing with a...seashell?

"Why are you holding a seashell?"

A mask falls over his face and he puts the shell away on his desk out of sight as he straightens up and adjusts his tie. "You haven't answered my question yet."

I roll my eyes and let out a sigh. "I ran in here from the kitchen. Don't worry, Adrian, I don't have a secret boyfriend and I'm not having fantastic, out of breath, mind-blowing sex."

Adrian turns green and holds up his hand. "I don't need that visual...ever. And any men you ever date, you need to make sure it's for the right reasons," he begins, and my earlier good mood vaporizes instantly.

"I don't go around advertising Adrian Scott is my brother. Not anymore." Not since my god-awful ex. "Plus, our last names are different. It's not like anyone will automatically make the connection Millie Callahan is the much younger sister of reclusive billionaire, Adrian Scott."

I shrug and stare at my fingers. "You don't have to worry about me. I'm nineteen and have been taking care of myself for a very, very long time," I whisper before my eyes flicker back to the screen, a nagging ache settling on my chest at the mention of our past.

Adrian has been obsessed with rising from our barely solvent childhood to crafting an empire so no one will dare to look down upon us anymore. As part of his revenge plan against everyone who stomped on us at our lowest, he even changed his last name.

He winces and releases a ragged inhale, clearly fighting to tamp down his emotions.

His voice is rusty and thick when he says, "I'm sorry I haven't been there for you before, Millie. I know you had to grow up far quicker than any girl should. With Mom gone and Dad a mess, you took care of him when I was away and even though you wouldn't tell me, I'm sure things weren't easy for you."

A lump forms in my throat as the backs of my eyes burn. *I've waited years for him to say this.*

All the days of me pretending everything was fine when I was drowning inside. All the tears I had shed in the dark under my thick comforter on my bed to ensure no one could hear me because life was difficult enough without me adding to his burdens.

His eyes darken into a stormy blue, and he continues, "But I-I'm proud of you, Millie, of the young woman you've become today. I know I didn't have a hand in it. I should've been there for you more, I—"

"Took care of us and put food on our table when Dad couldn't work. You picked me up from school and checked my homework when Dad was in his cups. You tried your best, Adrian. I don't blame you."

I can't blame him.

I cover my hand over my mouth so he doesn't see the slight trembling of my lips and suddenly, my eyes feel very heavy as if the lack of sleep from last night is finally catching up to me.

I'm so tired. In more ways than one.

Flashing a forced smile, I whisper, "I love you, Adrian. I only wish you wouldn't be so hard on yourself and so angry at the world. You deserve happiness, just like all of us."

He clenches his jaw, his eyes flashing. "I'll be happy when the bastards pay for what they did to Mom and our family."

"We didn't have everything, but I was happy. I don't need all the materialistic things. I just want my family to be happy...the family I have left."

It's something Adrian has never understood and something that pains me every time I talk to him and watch him work himself to the bone trying to add more zeroes to our bank account. Then there's the hatred in his eyes when he talks about taking revenge on our rich grandparents, who abandoned Mom when she married Dad because he was poor, and how they didn't even care we were on food stamps at one point or their daughter didn't have money for cancer treatments. They didn't even come to her funeral when she passed away when I was seven.

From outward appearances, it seems like he has the world in his hands now—the fancy suits and nice cars. But he's miserable inside. Mom wouldn't have wanted that for him.

Adrian slowly unclenches his fists. "Let's not talk about it. I called because I wanted to wish you a good first day at ULA. I'm glad you're spending a year here so I can see you more often than if we're on opposite coasts. But I guess I fucked up the well wishes call too."

Tamping down the heaviness in my chest, I smile brightly, something that comes second nature to me, even though I don't feel an ounce of positivity inside.

He needs me to be happy. It'll make him feel better. "I know you care, Adrian. And thank you for calling. I'm very excited."

He forces out a smile and before long, we disconnect the call.

I rub the familiar ache in my chest. Sitting back in my chair, I look at my minimally furnished room, taking in the heavy tan drapes drawn over half of the windows, blocking some of the gloomy daylight streaming in from the outside, the simple full-size bed with a fluffy white comforter, which suddenly looks very inviting, even though I tossed and turned in it the entire night, the potted purple pasque flowers, an understated yet beautiful member of the buttercup family, on the nightstand.

Exhaustion weighs on my eyelids. I yawn and look at the time again. Twelve-thirty. I still have a couple hours before I need to get on campus. A nap won't hurt.

A nap always makes me feel better afterward. Then I'm going to go to class.

Starting today, things will be better, and maybe I won't have to hide anymore.

CHAPTER 4

THE SUDDEN BOOMING OF thunder wakes me up.

I jolt up on the bed, my breathing coming out in rapid pants, my skin damp from a dream I can barely remember as a flash of lightning blankets the room in blinding white light.

Slowly, my senses come alive, my ears registering the hammering of rain against the windows, the sounds of tires screeching against wet pavement five stories below at street level, my nose taking in the moisture and earthy smell of the first storm of the season. My lips are parched as I mindlessly reach toward my nightstand for a cup of water, my brain still disoriented.

Where's the water? I usually put a cup of water here at night before taking it to the kitchen in the morning—

Holy shit.

I grab my cell phone from the nightstand, noting the time. Three p.m.

Shit. Shit. Shit. I'm late for class, the most important class this year. I can't believe this. Why didn't I set an alarm? I thought I set an alarm—

My fingers swipe to the alarm app and I realize I mistakenly set the alarm for two a.m.

Fuck! How am I so stupid?

Leaping off the bed, I grab my messenger bag, stuff my laptop in it, praying it still has enough battery to last me through three lectures.

I dart into the bathroom for a quick glance at the mirror, letting out an "Ow!" when I stub my toe against the door frame, and take in my ragged appearance—messy, long brown hair, blue eyes, a pale blue tank top and black leggings. I hastily run a brush through my long strands. *No time to change, this will have to do.* Grabbing a cotton blazer from the hook behind the door, I quickly dart out of the bathroom and leave the apartment.

Fifteen minutes later—thank goodness I don't live too far away from campus—I throw open the sturdy metal door of Kepper Hall room 201. My lungs are on fire from the mad dash from the parking structure to the building in the pouring rain. It's a deluge out there—a scene from apocalyptic movies.

The door swings open with much more force than anticipated, making me lose my momentum. My messenger bag slides off my soaking wet body and lands on the floor in a loud *crash*, the textbook, laptop, and some supplies spilling over the dark tiled floors like blood splatter in a crime scene.

My heart leaps to my throat as my skin heats, and I feel several dozen pairs of eyes on me as the classroom falls into an abrupt hush.

Fuck my life.

My hands shake as I kneel to pick up the things which have fallen out of my bag. Students murmur, no doubt talking about the idiot who, not only is late on the first day of class but has also forgotten her umbrella and looks like a drowned rat in the New York subway system.

Then, the hairs on the back of my neck prickle to attention.

"Students, this is an example of what *not* to do in life if you want to succeed. Preparation is the key to success, in the real world, and *especially* in this class." A booming, deep masculine voice echoes in the room and the hushed whispers immediately silence as a chill befalls the classroom.

Heavy footsteps sound closer and closer, each *thump* a jolt to my heart, which is already careening out of control. My fingers tremble as I hurry to pick up the pens on the ground.

A pair of pristine, gleaming black leather shoes comes into my vision.

Blood drains from my face as I slowly look up from my squatting position on the floor and perhaps it's the sheer panic from the last fifteen minutes finally catching up to me, the heated embarrassment of making a scene in the middle of class, the fact I forgot to eat breakfast or lunch earlier, or something equally innocuous, but the world literally blurs when I take in the tall, imposing man standing steps away from me.

My fluttering heart stops mid-thump. My lungs forget how to breathe. Goosebumps form on my skin that have nothing to do with how cold I was a moment ago from the rain and the wet clothes.

Perfectly tailored dark gray pants, struggling to hide the muscles underneath them.

Crisp white dress shirt under a slim-fit vest molded to what clearly appears to be a muscular chest.

Strong forearms crossed over said magnificent chest, the thick, mouthwatering veins amidst the light dusting of hair practically begging me to trace them.

Corded neck, an Adam's apple rippling, leading to a cleanly shaven, angular jaw that seems to have one of those dark shadows even the sharpest razors cannot tame, slashing high cheekbones, and aquiline nose.

A thick head of tousled dark hair that looks effortless, like he rolled out of bed appearing like the god he is with no effort.

And startling, stormy eyes rivaling the thunderclouds outside. Eyes currently blazing with bloody murder.

Shit. Jocelyn wasn't kidding earlier. The person in front of me is all man and brimming with power.

The seconds turn into minutes, or perhaps I've entered an alternate dimension.

My heart restarts, the rioting beats loud inside my ears and I find myself helpless and ensnared by those intense, searing eyes, my body frozen in place.

Professor Ryland Anderson.

"Are you done being a *complete* fucking distraction?"

His words are an icy cold bucket of water dumped onto my strangely heated body.

I quickly close my mouth, not even aware my lips were parted until then, and stammer a response, "S-Sorry, Professor Anderson. I d-didn't sleep last night and overslept and forgot my umbrella when I ran out the door and—"

"Save it for someone who cares." His eyes are stormier, murky pools of tar.

"Psst. Here," a dark-haired guy sitting next to the aisle whispers as he hands me my laptop, which apparently is by his feet, but I barely notice him.

I nod my thanks before scrambling up, the sudden motion combined with everything that has transpired leaving me weak in the knees and a sudden wave of dizziness hits me.

You've got to be shitting me.

I sway on my feet as the world swirls around me, black dots blinding my vision, and before I make an even bigger fool of myself and fall flat on my face, a strong hand clasps my arm, steadying me.

Suddenly, I can't breathe, every nerve ending focused on the small spot where he grips me. The sensation is akin to a live wire shocking my system, wreaking havoc inside. His touch singes me, boiling my blood within a split second, and everything...*everything* feels sensitive and alive.

My lips part, emitting a barely audible gasp, and I look at my rescuer, finding my professor staring at his hand on my arm with a shocked, inscrutable expression on his face. His grip tightens on my arm.

His eyes skim over my wet clothes, flaring slightly at whatever he sees, before he quickly lets go as if I'm contagious with Ebola.

He whips his head toward me, his voice taking on a hard edge. "Tardiness is unacceptable in this class. Three strikes, and you're out. This class is only for serious students who want to learn and achieve something in their future. There is no room for excuses, no room for lies, and *absolutely* no room for distractions."

His words are lashes from a barbed whip across my skin, flaying me alive. I flinch and clutch my messenger bag tightly against my body to stem the sudden trembling of my muscles.

"Miss..." he prompts as he backs up a few paces and pins me with another chilly glare.

"C-Callahan. Millie Callahan."

"Miss Callahan. One strike. You have two more left. Now *scram* and find a seat so the rest of us can go back to learning," he barks, and I flee, my legs shaking, my heart racing, my breathing quickening.

Amidst the insanity and my irrational thoughts, one in particular rises to the forefront and at that moment I know deep in my gut, everything is about to change.

CHAPTER 5

I FIND A SEAT five rows from the front, sandwiched between a guy who is probably a linebacker and taking up half of my chair, and a girl who is discreetly reapplying lipstick. My heart is still racing from the embarrassment moments ago.

Squirming in my seat from the discomfort of the wet clothes sticking to my body, I peel off my sodden jacket and drape it over my equally disastrous messenger bag. The AC churns on in the background, the cold air burrowing deep inside my bones. I shiver, my hands rubbing my slick forearms, but it's no use. I'll have to wait until I get back home and take a scalding hot shower.

I blow out a calming breath and try to focus on my surroundings. Looking around, I frown, unable to find Jocelyn. Isn't she supposed to be in this class too?

"We've already covered the syllabus, important exam and project dates, and my grading scale. This class covers the fundamentals of business ethics. And before you think this is going to be an easy A, let me disabuse you of that notion. It. Won't. Be." Professor Anderson's voice vibrates in the room, his speech measured and direct, clearly someone who's used to getting the attention of everyone in the vicinity.

"I'm reminding you again, half of the material in papers and exams will be from class lectures and *not* from the textbooks. So, Godspeed if you think you can skip class and get by. Now, I want to discuss the theory we'll spend the next two weeks discussing ..."

A flurry of sounds rustles through the classroom as students start typing on their laptops or frantically scribbling notes on their thick notepads. I hurriedly pull out my dinged-up laptop from my soaked messenger bag, grimacing at the new scuff marks on the silver surface, and flip open the lid. Swiping at the water droplets on the black screen, I press the power button to turn it on.

Black screen of death. Not even a blinking monitor or the familiar electrical buzzing.

I scrunch my nose and close my eyes, muttering a silent prayer.

Weather gods, have I wronged you somehow? What's up with me and electronics today?

Gritting my teeth, I poke at the power button again, trying the "imagine this is an ex" trick from this morning.

Stab. Stab. Stab.

Absolutely nothing.

"Arrrrrgh," I growl as I continue to inflict violence on my laptop. The rainwater probably started its demise and the impact on the hard floors most likely finished it off.

"This is such BS," I mutter and shake the uncooperative machine, a last-ditch effort to revive it.

Suddenly, the hairs on my forearms stand at attention and the air thins around me.

I feel him before I see him.

A whiff of woodsy cologne with hints of citrus hits my nose and I can't help but take a deep inhale, wanting to savor the scent.

"Is there anything you want to share with the class, Miss Callahan?" The smooth, lethal voice which will probably appear in my nightmare tonight questions from my right.

I close my eyes and grimace before slowly turning to look at a fuming Professor Anderson, whose countenance has only gotten darker and angrier with time.

Biting my bottom lip, I shake my head and whisper, "Nothing to share."

His nostrils flare and a muscle twitches in his forehead before he whirls around and strides back up to his throne in front of the classroom.

The thumping in my chest intensifies and suddenly, my skin is hot to the touch and I'm no longer feeling cold.

"We'll be going over ten business ethics theories with roots in philosophy. Now, one might ask, why go through all the fuss to dissect ethical decision-making in the business world?" Professor Anderson pauses, his torso hunched over the redwood podium, his hands gripping the sides.

There's an energy about him—intense and captivating—which beckons you to drop everything you're doing to listen to him. He surveys the class, lasering everyone in their chairs as the collective room suspends their breaths in anticipation.

His lips, pressed into a thin line, twitch, like he's satisfied with our response, and he leans forward even more as if to divulge a secret.

"Imagine a world where the main goal of small businesses is to grow into large corporations and because of the laws of capitalism, there's a mad race to capture market share, to increase the bottom line, where dollars and cents matter most above everything else. Where the pure definition of success is driven by how padded your pocketbooks are, how much return you can bring to your investors, and how high you can get your market valuation to be. A pay to play type of world."

Slowly, he steps away from the podium and paces back and forth on stage. Smirking, he gestures wildly in the air as he commands the room. "Don't have to imagine too hard, right? Because that's the world we live in. But without ethical guidelines, these businesses could run amok, shattering the very bones of our infrastructure. When money becomes the *sole driver* of success and decision-making, the edifice of society and the world is already on the verge of collapsing."

He shakes his head, as if knowing something we all don't know, and I find myself clutching my broken laptop, wanting to know what'll happen to this world we're living in.

"You might think, isn't this hypocritical of you, Professor? Your family owns one of the largest corporations in the world, one of the beasts reigning over the fray."

His lips tip up in a derisive half-sneer and he stops his pacing. "And *that's* precisely what makes me the best person to teach this class. To explain why companies need appropriate ethical frameworks in place. Capitalism is wonderful within defined regulations."

I can't see his eyes clearly from here, but I can see the brightness in his gaze, the muscles in his chest and arms rippling with energy like he's bursting at the seams, his hands swiveling in the air as if he's presenting a theory that'll change our lives and the future of mankind.

The way he comes *alive*.

Living. Breathing. Breathtaking.

My pulse beats a heavy drum in my ears and I release a breathy exhale, every inch of me mesmerized by the rising and falling of his voice, the fiery passion emanating from his entire being, the myriad of expressions fluttering across his face, like they're desperate to escape the cold facade he usually has them buried under.

"God, he's so hot," the blonde next to me whispers. "Imagine all that energy and passion focused on you."

I nod, completely entranced by my professor, wanting to absorb every ounce of knowledge from him. I don't even want to pay her any attention.

She continues, clearly undeterred by my lack of response, "My dad is a member at The Orchid and there are rumors he's a beast in bed and gets off from chasing willing women in their sex club. I totally wouldn't mind him hunting me down."

Chasing? Hunting? Her words unwittingly bury themselves in my brain. Lewd images loom in my vision. A brimming masculine power hovering above me, a deep, raspy voice whispering in my ear, taking the control away from me. I gulp, my thighs clenching at the sudden ache appearing low in my belly.

This is ridiculous, Millie. You're nineteen, not a friggin' thirteen-year-old who just discovered her hormones and is experiencing her first crush. Snap out of it.

Shaking my head to wake me up from this strange haze I'm in, I focus my attention back on the powerful man on stage, determined to learn the recipe to his secret sauce. If I'm going to become a good educator one day, I want to captivate the room like he does.

Strange bodily reactions? That's basic biology toward novelty. Fleeting and will fade in time.

Giving myself a quick mental pat on my back for listening to logic, I turn on the recording function on my cell phone. I'll just have to transcribe this lecture to notes later when I get back home.

The next hour blows right by as Professor Anderson paints a startling realistic picture of the current business climate, where inflation is at an all-time high and corporations are struggling to survive while the public is weary of the future of the economy. He claims this is the perfect environment ripened for bad corporate decisions.

I can't tear my eyes away for one minute.

Our gazes meet twice during his lecture, and each time, I see his eyes narrow before darting away.

A trickle of unease pools in my chest as I think back to the disapproval radiating from his glare. I'm unused to this blatant distrust coming from a professor. I'm a hard worker, a straight-A student, because my brother has taught me the way to climb out of poverty is through education. I'm determined to make something of myself without depending on Adrian, and it's unsettling to see Professor Anderson's apparent dislike of me.

It feels wrong and I *need* to correct whatever this is. It's a necessity, like how my lungs need their next breath of air.

"Read chapters one through three before class on Thursday. Be prepared for your first debate. Don't be late."

His words are as effective as an alarm clock, waking up everyone from the spell he has placed us under. Excited whispers and hushed conversations fill the room as students quickly filter out the door.

I slowly pack up my things as my breathing quickens. I *have to* apologize to him. To tell him my tardiness and everything afterward were unintentional. I need him to understand I mean no disrespect, so I can begin this class on a good footing. I want him to like me, so he'll write me a recommendation letter later on.

This urgency drives me to hastily climb out of my seat and make my way to the front of the room, where he's adjusting his cuff links before putting on his suit jacket in one smooth, sweeping motion, clearly someone who's very familiar with these formal threads. His long fingers grip his papers as he stuffs them into his black folio.

Wetting my lips, I carefully approach him, my fingers twitching at my sides. My clothes are much drier now, but my hair is still wet, and this level of dishevelment makes me uncomfortable, like I'm standing naked before him.

Vulnerable. Heated. Jittery.

He freezes, his muscles tensing the closer I approach him. Then he resumes packing his belongings and decidedly *not* look at me.

"P-Professor?" My voice comes out shaky. I curse myself for sounding like a little girl cowering in front of some deity.

He's only a man, not a god. Somehow, that's not reassuring at all.

He doesn't look up, his fingers clutching his phone on the desk. "Yes?" A low grunt.

"I want to apologize again. My tardiness earlier today was very much unlike me. I take your class very seriously and want to assure you this won't happen again. Please forgive me."

My fingers tangle with each other, trying to generate the power to remain standing before him, this man with tethered energy rolling off him.

Professor Anderson's attention snags on my fingers, his frame stiffening before he slowly meets my gaze.

Chilly gray eyes remind me of the swirling clouds at the eye of the storm and pin me in place. They're penetrating, seeing through my defenses.

"Your future is not my responsibility, but your own. Make the right choice for yourself. It doesn't matter to me." His voice is barely above a whisper and yet echoes in the quiet room, much louder than the rain pattering against the floor-to-ceiling windows.

He straightens to his full height, and I let out a small gasp when I realize how tall he is, how big his presence is, and how small I feel standing before him. He frowns, a crease forming between his brows, and I have an irrational urge to smooth out the lines, to ask him what's wrong.

Without another word, he strides out of the classroom, turning off the lights along the way. The door slamming shut echoes in the dark, and I suddenly find myself bereft without his heated presence.

Nothing makes sense. After all, I've only met the man a little over an hour ago.

I stand there in silence, listening to my heavy breathing. My hand travels to my chest and rubs the tenderness forming behind my rib cage.

I must be delirious from the lack of sleep and food. Or maybe Mercury is in retrograde.

Lightning flashes across the sky, singeing the room in a burst of light. The hairs on my forearm stand up straight and I don't know why, but I feel compelled to look outside. My feet carry me to the windows, where I witness nature's tantrum in full force.

The rain is falling down so hard, it almost appears invisible unless you're looking at the light from the streetlamps. The university must have turned them on early because of the dark skies. The thick thunderclouds, gray and heavy, sink low in the sky, smothering everyone underneath its wrath.

And a man. A lonely silhouette of a man. Tall. Defiant. Unrelenting.

Professor Anderson stands in the middle of the gravel path a few feet away from the windows, his body seemingly frozen.

I place my hand on the glass pane, my breath fogging up the surface as I stare at him.

He slowly tilts his head up toward the sky, letting the rain wash over him, like it's cleansing him. His eyes are shut, his lips tilting up in something resembling a smile.

A heartbreaking smile.

My chest spasms in pain, my muscles coiling in tension, and every atom of my body pulls me toward this man, who looks so hauntingly alone while he stands out there in the pouring rain. He looks cold, like he hasn't felt warmth in ages.

Nonsensical. Madness.

After a moment, he shakes his head as if mad at himself, and clenches his fists.

Then, for some unknown reason, he suddenly straightens up, his posture defiant once more, and he slowly turns around.

Our eyes meet in the distance, through thick glass and drowning rain, and I let out a shaky exhale. I want to withdraw, to step away from the window, but I can't seem to make myself move.

I'm held immobile by the intensity in those dark eyes.

Lightning streaks across the sky, followed by a loud rumble of thunder, the flash of electricity illuminating every masculine angle of his face, how the rain has rendered his hair into dishevelment, the raindrops clinging to his skin like a lover's caress, soaking through his shirt and suit, but he doesn't seem to notice.

The muscles in his jaw twitch and he takes a few steps forward, as if compelled to do so. I press my palms harder against the glass, my body wanting something I can't name. My heart kicks against my rib cage, wanting to escape, to hurl itself toward the man below.

Logic ceases to matter. Inexplicable insanity.

Our connected gaze is a sizzling live wire and neither of us can look away. I wonder if I'm seeing a side of him he doesn't show anyone else, and I have no idea what I did to deserve this intimacy, this honor.

After a few seconds, he jolts, like he has been dragged out of a trance. His nostrils flare and those beautiful gray eyes take on a harsh glint before he tears his gaze away from me. He turns around, his hands fisted tightly by his sides, and promptly strides away, carrying with him more tension and charged intensity than the storm raging around him.

I watch him until he becomes a tiny dot in the distance, my fingers clutching my chest.

Later that night, I sit at my desk in the bedroom and take out a piece of stationery from the drawer. Floral stationery, in honor of Mom's green thumb. I scribble another letter to her.

Dear Mom,

The skies are crying today and perhaps because I'm near you again, I feel its tears most intently. I don't think there's a timeline for grief or a way to fill the hole in my chest.

Seeing how Dad still misses you so much, even after all these years, should warn me away from love. But my heart is conflicted because I still want what you and Dad had. Star-crossed lovers who went against the world and married each other, in love until the very end…and even beyond.

Do you know I've never seen Dad go on a date after you? We still celebrate your birthday and I still make hot chocolate with mini marshmallows, the way you used to make them for me. I remember how you described your romance with Dad. You called it a whirlwind. I didn't understand it back then. I just remembered thinking this was a funny word, like the wind was dancing, twirling, and whirling.

But now...I want to experience it. The whirlwind.

I miss you.

Love, Millie

As I set my pen down, a startling image forms in my mind. A lonely man standing alone in the rain, a soul feeling colder than the wind, more broken than the fallen branches from the storm. A gaze so electrifying it's like two kindred souls are set alight because of each other for the first time.

Professor Ryland Anderson.

CHAPTER 6

THE HEAVINESS CONSTANTLY LIVING in my chest slightly lessens as I walk across Hannigan lawn before the next class, careful to avoid the fresh puddles accumulated overnight from the rain. Buildings and schools in LA are not designed with good drainage systems in the land of the drought.

The infamous California sunshine makes a reappearance, as though yesterday's storm was a hallucination. Students greet me as I pass by, and I respond with a few curt nods.

With each step taking me deeper into the university, and my lungs raking in the lingering smell of rain in the air, I feel the stress slowly escaping from my body. My mind fights the daily battle to compartmentalize, to shove my unwanted thoughts regarding my role in the family business into the back of my mind.

When I stood in the rain after the first class, feeling the wetness soaking through my clothes, spreading over my skin, and witnessing the light show in the murderous skies, I felt free. In another life, I would be doing this for the rest of my life—teaching and watching those young eyes light up in the room. In that moment, I felt a tiny sliver of happiness, like my heart was waking up after a long slumber.

I felt cleansed in the rain. I felt minuscule. Insignificant. Like the world wasn't depending on me, my family wasn't relying on me, and the rules of the family trust binding every Anderson, whether by birth or by marriage, to the family business weren't there.

Under the judgment of the brilliant skies, I didn't have to contend with the guilt over the repercussions if I branched out on my own, how my *entire family* would lose our company and wealth to third parties under the damn irrevocable, perpetual trust set up by our forefathers.

In the pouring rain, Ryland, both the man and the professor, was enough, and I didn't need to be Ryland Anderson, the COO, the public face of the family, the one taking on those duties because Maxwell preferred the shadows and because I was the glue that held everyone together.

Given everything he had done for me, and the twist of fate that allowed me a freedom he could never experience for himself—simply because I happened to be seven minutes younger than him, thus escaping the constraints of the curse—how could I complain? What right did I have to feel suffocated by life when he was the one to get the short end of the stick?

But in the rain, in the eye of the storm, with nature howling around me, its power unyielding, terrifying, yet breathtaking, I felt entitled to my thoughts and emotions. I could scream and yell my frustrations into the void, and no one would hear a thing.

No one would know my selfish resentment.

Except her.

The young woman with soulful eyes.

Millie Callahan.

She saw me from the windows. When my eyes caught her looking at me, my body lost its ability to move. It was a lightning strike, singeing my insides, shocking my senses back to life. Her piercing gaze sliced through my carefully crafted armor. I couldn't explain it. I just knew she saw me somehow...the real me behind the suits. The burst of emotions—too many to name—left me reeling, and as I forced myself to walk away from her, I settled on the one I recognized the most.

Anger.

Furious at myself for responding so inappropriately to my student, mad at her for being temptation embodied.

It made no sense. It was impossible and ridiculous.

I quickly shove the thoughts aside.

Releasing a deep exhale, I see the five-story stucco building of Kepper Hall in front of me. A heat simmers in my veins as I anticipate the first debate in class and hear the students' arguments.

Ping.

I pause on the front steps, taking out my phone and opening the new incoming email.

Subject: Important Reminder: University Policy on Faculty-Student Relationships

Dear Faculty and Staff,

As a new academic year begins, we wish to remind you of our university's policies regarding faculty-student relationships within our community. It is critical to uphold the highest standards of professionalism and ethics in our everyday interactions.

1. Faculty-student relationships: All romantic or sexual relationships between faculty members and students are strictly prohibited.

2. Consequences of non-compliance: Failure to adhere to these policies will result in investigation and disciplinary action, which may result in termination of employment.

We trust you will continue to contribute to our university's reputation for excellence by upholding these standards.

Sincerely,

University of Los Angeles Human Resources Department

This must be related to a sordid scandal between a TA and her much older, married professor during the summer session that rankled the academic community. Why would anyone risk their reputation for a quick lay is beyond me.

Unbidden, an image of Millie appears in my mind again.

Large, doe-like blue eyes, the color of the brightest sapphires, framed by the lushest lashes, long espresso hair curling around the heavy swells of her chest, partially hiding the protruding nipples plastered against her thin, wet shirt, which left little to the imagination. The plump, pillowy lips parted on a gasp when she saw me approach her after she barreled into class like an act of God, the beautiful meadowlark lying at the foot of a beast.

A water nymph. Seductive yet innocent at the same time.

Heat rushes to my groin as my senses relive the sensations of seeing Millie Callahan at my feet on Tuesday. The woman whose penetrative gaze sees too much, whose aura is innately seductive at the same time.

I remember my sharp anger and frustration at the latecomer crashing into our class halting abruptly when my eyes took in the vixen bringing the elements indoors. My lungs froze mid-inhale, my eyes unable to drag themselves away from her.

The brief minutes between us seemed heavy, ripe with tension, the thumping in my heart intensifying, my skin sizzling when I grabbed her wrist when she looked like she was about to faint after standing up. The bolt of anger that seared me when I saw the jock flashing a smile at her as he handed her the laptop lying at his feet.

I clench my fists at the barrage of unwanted sensations churning inside me and lock my jaw.

Fucking insane. Completely inappropriate.

She's over fifteen-years younger than you.

She's forbidden.

She's your fucking student.

It was an off day, that's all. Effects of the electrical storm.

———— • ————

"How many of you have worked as a delivery driver? InstaEats? Delivery Dash?" I unbutton my suit jacket and lay it over the back of the wooden chair by the desk in front of the classroom.

The class is silent as I prowl back and forth, waiting for a brave soul to answer. I know my reputation—hard-ass, cold, stickler for rules. The real world is much harsher. They might as well get used to it now.

"Are you all deaf this morning? Too hungover from partying?"

I pause my pacing, my eyes skimming over the sea of orange and white—there's a school rally today, but the party began yesterday, and the collective hangover of the students is starting to royally piss me off. They're here to learn, to understand their roles and responsibilities in society, not to cruise through education and expect the world to be handed to them later.

A few hands raise in the air. Finally.

I try not to look at her. The woman who saw through me in the unrelenting storm.

She's a girl, barely a woman. Get your fucking shit together.

She's sitting in the second row today, her posture ramrod straight, eyes bright, like she's excited to be in class, like she's so fucking happy to be here, to listen to me. Her hair, no longer the wet mess from Tuesday, is a tapestry of browns and caramels, the silky strands long, shiny, and thick. My groin twitches as I admire those luscious locks.

Perfect for grabbing onto after I chase her in the woods, feeling the wind on my face, the exhilaration in my veins. Then I'd wind them around my hand and tug, jolting her to a stop. I'd put them against my nose and take a whiff because I'd be craving a hit of her sweetness. Then I'd haul her toward me—

Fuck. Fuck. Fuck.

I flinch, my eyes darting away at the nonsensical, *completely* inappropriate, intrusive thoughts. I need to get my ass back to The Orchid and book a scene. I've been without sex for too long and it's messing with my brain.

I point to a redhead with her hand raised in the front row. "You. What's your name?"

"Ashley," she replies, her voice raspy as she bites her bottom lip in a motion I'm sure will bring many boys to heel. It just fucking annoys me.

"Tell me, is your pay mostly from your wages or your tips from customers?"

"The tips, of course. I do pretty well for myself once the guys see me when I drop off their takeout." She gives me a wink and thrusts out her ample chest.

I pinch the bridge of my nose and fight the urge to roll my eyes. I *love* teaching, but this incessant fawning rankles. I can already imagine the coy glances and sly invitations these girls will give me after they get their exam results to see if I can give them "extra credit" to help them pass the class.

Cheaters thinking they can get ahead and not put in the work beforehand.

Cheaters with ulterior motives.

Sydney's face floats in front of my mind and I grit my teeth, shoving the image away. "Do you get medical benefits from your company?"

"No. Not that I need them. I'm very healthy." Ashley lets out a breathy laugh, her voice heavy with innuendo. "Professor, I'm strong...and healthy. Ready for anything, really."

The frat bro next to her, someone who resembles an extra for lifeguard movies, shifts in his seat, his eyes raking over her body with interest. I bite back a sigh. This is going nowhere.

"Do you know why you don't get benefits from your company?"

I try again, stuffing my hands in my pockets. Anything to keep from reaching out and shaking her and any other student who is treating this class like a date with a billionaire instead of taking it seriously.

Ashley shrugs, staring at me with those annoying stars in her eyes. I pinch my nose again and raise my voice, the impatience seeping out in spades. "Does anyone have anything *meaningful—*"

"It's because they classify us as contractors instead of employees," a sweet voice replies from my left.

The voice I've heard only once before, but I know I'll recognize anywhere.

My chest tightens, and the pounding pulse quickens in my ears as I turn toward Millie. She still has her hand raised as if she's asking for permission to speak, but her sapphire eyes glint with knowledge, with eagerness. She's not asking for permission. She's making her presence known.

My heart skips a beat. *Will she be different from the others? Or will she be a disappointment?*

I clear my throat. "And why do you think they do that?"

"Minimize costs and maximize profits for them, of course."

I nod. "If you're an investor of InstaEats and you infused capital into their fledgling company five years ago, and now they are rewarding you with increased dividends because they were careful with their cost management, that's good, right? The right thing a company should do for its stakeholders."

"But not the right thing for its workers though."

She leans forward on her desk, her hands clasped in front of her, deepening the shadow of her cleavage showing above the round neckline of her unassuming red T-shirt. Renewed heat circulates in my body and I force myself to drag my eyes back to her sapphire gaze again.

"Precisely," I begin, my voice sounding hoarse to my ears. "This is just one example of business ethics. What's ethical to one group of people may not be the correct thing to do for another group, even in the same situation, like in this case, investors versus workers. Should the company give a livable wage and correctly classify workers who have accumulated a certain number of work hours as employees, thus giving them full benefits?"

I pause, taking in the furrowed brows of the students. "But if they do that, they'll decrease their bottom line to their shareholders. Or should the company maximize profits at a cost to the workers, who now have to sustain on something as unpredictable as tips in a turbulent economy while finding other ways to get medical benefits, if they can even afford it?"

"There's also one more group of people affected in your situation."

I cock my brow. "How so?"

She swipes her tongue on that distracting plump bottom lip of hers, the innocent motion much more captivating than what Ashley did moments ago. The energy radiating from her is so effervescent, it's the bright beacon of a lighthouse shining through the torrents of rain in a stormy sea.

Millie replies, "The customers are impacted as well. The ethics of the situation aren't black and white. When you presented the case as you did right now, it seemed like the company was unethical because they took from the wellbeing of the workers to pad the pockets of their investors."

Her tentative voice becomes stronger and more confident. "But that's not completely true. If the company treats these workers as employees with additional benefits and a higher wage, despite their competitors not doing the same, don't they still have a fiduciary duty to their investors? What about their corporate employees with pension plans that'll be worth nothing if the company goes under or if their stock tanks?"

My breathing quickens and before I know it, I find myself standing in front of her, my lips threatening to quirk into a smile.

"What does this have anything to do with the customers?" My voice is deceptively quiet, but every cell in my body is pulsing with energy, every nerve ending sizzling with anticipation.

Millie's eyes widen and she swallows, her delicate throat rippling. "To do the right thing for their investors, the company will want to pass the higher costs to third parties, in this case, the restaurants or the customers in question. But is that ethical? To have the mom-and-pop shops and us customers pay for a broken system? Isn't this a lost cause? Everyone loses."

She stares at me, her plush lips parted, like she's waiting for my approval, for my praise.

Fuck. She'll look so good on the ground beneath me.

A bolt of heat slices through my body and I stagger back half a step, lust warring with the curl of satisfaction at her thoughtful answer and provoking questions.

Shit.

My voice is rough when I reply, "Exactly. You're exactly right. This is why having a solid understanding of business ethics is important before you step into the cutthroat world out there. Because once you're swimming in the thick of it, it's hard to keep your eyes on the shore. It's difficult to know if you're paddling toward land or toward your demise."

A murmur ripples through the class as other students shoot their hands into the air, clearly affected by Millie's passionate analysis and wanting to share their thoughts on this moral quandary. I tear my gaze away from her and step away, resisting the impulse to look back.

But I feel the heat of her gaze boring into me. A sensation so visceral it's almost physical, and I crack the stiff joints in my neck, my hands clenching in my trouser pockets.

"Under the utilitarianism theory, what should InstaEats do in this case?" I turn back to the rest of the class and the thumping in my heart intensifies.

More. More. More. It clamors for more.

CHAPTER 7

Millie

Dear Mom,

I think he hates me and I don't know why. But my eyes can't help but look at him and the way he stares at me...it sets my body on fire. And sometimes, I sense admiration in his eyes. Why are we drawn to the forbidden? Sometimes, I wonder if I have a masochistic streak in me.

Love, Millie

"SO HOW'S LA? It's been a while, right?" A pair of bright gray eyes reminding me of a certain brooding someone meet mine on the computer screen.

Munching sounds also filter through the speakers. Taylor Peyton, my best friend from home, is chewing on carrot sticks as we meet up for our weekly video chat.

"Yeah. It's nice to be back here after so many years."

I sit back in my chair, my body wrapped in a pink, fuzzy robe after a quick shower. My fingers fiddle with the half-done shoddy attempt at mittens and begin unraveling the yarn. *How do those videos make them look so easy?*

"What did I miss? Hey, Millie. We miss you already. Why are you taking your project apart?" an energetic voice says from the background.

A flurry of bright purple flashes across the screen and settles next to Taylor, who's rolling her eyes at her sister and squinting at the ill-fitting sweater she has on.

"How do you have so much energy, Grace? You've been up since five this morning and it's eleven at night now and you still act like a fucking Energizer Bunny."

Grace grins and waggles her brows, her brilliant eyes, so blue they almost appear violet, flashing in humor. "I think I took all the energy between the two of us. And you definitely sleep enough for the two of us."

"Your positivity is revolting," Taylor spits back, but I can see the fondness in her eyes.

The two of them are Irish twins, with Grace being one year older than Taylor, and their personalities can't be any more different. Grace is the positive, go-getter older sister and Taylor is the grumpy, "the sky is falling, and the apocalypse is around the corner" younger sister. They are the most loyal girls I've ever met and are my family outside of Adrian and Dad.

"Millie was saying it was nice to be in LA," a new husky voice joins us and another monitor flickers on, showing the last of our quartet, Annabelle Law-McKenzie, known to her friends as Belle. "Sorry, I crept in there silently and didn't want to interrupt your daily bickering."

I snort and unwind the towel wrapped around my hair and shake out the wet strands. A deep warmth fills me. "I miss you girls a lot. While I'm glad to be back in LA after twelve years, it no longer feels like home. Home is where you guys are."

A chorus of "awwws" echoes and Taylor scrunches her nose, her skull-shaped piercing glinting under the lamplight. She once said her body piercings are expressions of her art and her mood. I guess someone must've pissed her off today.

"You're going to make me cry, woman," she grunts. Grace laughs and shoves her gently.

I show them my knitting disaster. "And this project needs to be scrapped and restarted. This looks ridiculous."

"You're such a perfectionist, Millie. Those mittens look fine to me! Anyway, what did you do so far? How was your first day of class? Any cute guys? How's Hollywood?" Grace rapidly fires her questions as she leans eagerly toward the camera.

"Oh God," I mutter.

"What? I'm living vicariously through you. It's not like I'll be able to travel across the country for a vacation of my own."

She grimaces before exchanging a solemn glance with her sister, who gives her a comforting pat on her shoulder. I gnaw on my bottom lip.

"Not for long, Grace. Once you graduate and kick ass in the finance world, you'll be able to afford grand trips around the world and do everything you've always wanted to do," Belle gently suggests, giving her best friend a wink.

The Peyton sisters have had a rough go in life. Their dad is a no-show and they live with their mom in a seedy part of Bronx. But Grace is smart and has a full ride to NYUC, where she met Belle a few years ago, and Taylor, likewise, has a full scholarship at her dance academy. I have a feeling their days of pinching pennies will end soon.

Grace waves Belle away, her face flushed, no doubt from the compliments. Taylor pops another carrot in her mouth, the crunching noise loud over the speakers.

She swallows and says, "And if Grace can't hack it, we'll always have you, Belle. When you guys have those fancy ass New York or Paris fashion shows, I'll provide free labor in exchange for room and board."

Belle laughs and ties her sleek black hair in a messy topknot.

Our quartet is a strange bunch. Grace is the spunky, smart one determined to make something out of her circumstances. Taylor is the grunge-makeup-wearing, multiple-body-piercing ballerina. Then there's Belle, the old money, high society heir to a fashion empire and also the only child of an international supermodel from Asia, and me, the girl who is "just Millie," trying to pursue her dreams of becoming a teacher with no one knowing my connection to one of the most reclusive billionaires in the country.

That's right, the girls don't know my connection to Adrian. I met them shortly after Lloyd broke up with me and I didn't want any of my future relationships to be tainted in the same way. But now, several years in, I can't help but feel guilty I've been withholding part of myself to my girls, because they aren't Lloyd. But it's hard to open up and tell the truth after years of secrecy.

"Anyway, spill. Tell me all about sunny California."

I snort and set aside the yarn on my desk. "Not so sunny. There was a storm a few days ago and my first day was a disaster." I tell them what happened with my oversleeping and my face-planting entrance. My skin heats thinking about that day.

"That sounds horrible and so unlike you! You're Ms. I'm prepared for anything! Did you get in trouble?" Grace asks, her eyes wide.

"I don't think my professor likes me. And that's putting it mildly. But it could be worse. I could be having one of my horrible periods and dealing with this crap at the same time."

Letting out a sigh, I brush my damp hair. *It's true.* Or at least, that's what I tell myself, imagining how much worse my encounter with Professor Anderson would be if I were dealing with stabbing cramps and cold sweats.

I change the subject, not wanting to discuss him further when I barely understand my feelings myself. "But other than that, things have been good. The campus is beautiful, and I finally got to visit the exotic blooms exhibit at the LA Arboretum and Greenhouse last weekend. Those beauties were a sight to behold."

I smile, thinking of the delicate white petals of the ghost orchid, the vibrant colors of the middlemist red, the striking blue green of the jade vine.

Mom would have loved it if she were here. When I was younger, she was too busy with her two jobs to take us to the Arboretum, not to mention the price of admission for a family of four was staggering and we didn't have the funds to spare.

Someday, I want to open a greenhouse for the public so everyone can access these flowers for free.

I look down, my eyes prickling as a lump forms in my throat. It's been twelve years since I lost Mom, and there are some wounds time cannot heal. Deep down inside, I'll always be the little girl missing the warm hugs from her mom and wishing she can feel protected in her embrace instead of pretending to be brave in front of everyone else. A wetness trickles down my cheek and I quickly swipe my hand to hide the evidence of my tears.

I whisper, "But being back here has been more difficult than I expected. I miss Mom."

Glancing up, I see three frowning faces staring at me in concern and I twist my lips into something I hope resembles a smile. I don't want them to worry about me. "It was nice. I feel closer to her than I've ever had in over a decade. These are happy tears."

I grab the packet of gummy bears from the corner of the desk—my little pieces of happiness—and plop one into my mouth, savoring the sweet flavor. Food makes everything better.

"Aw, Millie. I'd hug you if you were next to me," Taylor whispers, her eyes taking on a wet sheen, "And I don't fucking like to hug people. Gives me the hives," she gripes, earning snickers from all of us, effectively breaking the strange tension.

"So, any guys? Hotties on campus?" Belle grins and waggles her brows.

My mind automatically flashes to a pair of slate-gray eyes, the color of molten quicksilver, a tall, arresting man in a dark suit, and I flinch. He's definitely not a "guy" but all man. Tingles appear in my lower belly.

Nonsense. He's your professor, Millie. He's forbidden.

"What's that look on your face?" Grace peers quizzically at me, her face plastered up against her screen.

I blink and look around, my skin feeling warm once more. Dammit. I twist my hands on my lap. "What face?"

"That face. There's someone, isn't there?" She's like a vulture hovering around a dying animal.

My bedroom door squeaks open, and Jocelyn traipses in with my insulated mug. "You left this in the kitchen," she whispers, before waving to the girls on the screen and dashing out of my room.

I take a sip of the hot chocolate, nearly spitting out the scalding contents. *Darn insulated mugs for keeping contents boiling hot.*

I need to throw some salt over my shoulders or sage the room or something to ward off more mishaps in the future.

I shake my head, my eyes watering. "There's no one. Absolutely no one. I'm here to kick ass, get good grades so I can get into the honors program when I'm back. That's it. No distractions." And definitely no distractions with *professors.*

"You have to go out and enjoy yourself, Millie. Life can't only be about studying and getting ahead. We never see you date, and I think you've only mentioned that asshole ex of yours before, who I very much want to beat up based on what you've told me about that chauvinistic lecher."

She sighs. "Or if I had a pet, like a good guard dog, I'd find him and set it on him. I hear dogs are good at sniffing out assholes." Belle cracks her knuckles, her eyes taking on a murderous gleam, and I bite back a laugh.

"The dog thing again? Why don't you get one, Belle? You've been talking about getting a pet forever."

Belle's eyes turn sad. "Still living with my parents. They don't like animals."

She blinks and shakes her head, clearly trying to dispel her melancholy. Belle is the kindest, most down-to-earth person I know, despite her privileged upbringing. She doesn't talk about her family a lot, but I have a feeling they have her on a tight leash and deep down, she's very lonely in that large mansion of hers.

"I mean, Belle has a point there. You're studying abroad in a way. It's the perfect time to be in a casual fling," Grace comments.

Taylor scoffs. "You're one to give advice. You don't date either."

"Neither do you!"

"All of us are going to die as spinsters. When we're old and wrinkly, we can buy a big house with a nice garden and live together with fifty cats and a few dogs," Belle drawls, her lips twitching in humor. "And maybe...we can also adopt some children and raise our own family. I've always liked kids." Her voice turns soft at the end, the smile now seeming a little more forced on her face.

I furrow my brows, wanting to ask her about the loneliness in her eyes, but she smiles and gives me a wink. *Maybe I'm thinking too much.*

"No distractions. No men. Not right now," I repeat. Too much is at stake. "I need to focus my energy on class and applying to the honors program. Less than point five percent of the applicants get in. My grades must be excellent, my resume stellar, and my reputation spotless, if I even want a shot of getting in. There's no time for unreliable men."

Who'll probably want me because I'd be a steppingstone to get to Adrian.

No, thank you.

"Ugh. No fun," Taylor grumbles.

"But hey, Millie." Belle snaps her fingers to get my attention. "If anyone can do it, it'll be you. Remember what you told me? 'The best way to predict your future is to create it.' That's what you're doing now." She gives me a saucy wink.

I smile, the strange unease from earlier today almost dissipating.

Almost.

A pair of haunted stormy eyes floats to the forefront, and my chest clenches.

CHAPTER 8

AFTER DISCONNECTING FROM THE call, I let out a satisfied sigh. Leaving New York and the girls behind has been harder than anticipated. While it's nice that Adrian is close by, things just aren't the same without my girls around.

Belle's parting words reverberate in my mind as I slowly rise from my chair and traipse toward the bookshelf in the corner of my room.

I pull out a thin volume, my fingers tracing the worn glossy cover of my seventh-grade yearbook, flip it open, and gingerly take out the yellowed pages of my handwritten essay nestled there. I smile at the scribble on top of the page, the words bringing back a fond memory during a dark time.

Excellent job, Millie. "The best way to predict your future is to create it." Even if the road is hard and the skies are gray, you're bravely walking forward, one step at a time, and one day, you'll find yourself on top of the mountain, the sun shining on your face, and you'll look down and be amazed at how far you've climbed.

I looked up at Mr. Roberts as he handed me back my paper at the end of English class. The topic was to write a personal essay about a difficult life experience that had a significant impact on us.

I remembered feeling the burst of anger when I received the prompt. When was life *not* difficult for our family? For Dad? For Adrian? For me? Especially in the last five years, with Adrian at Cornell and barely at home, Dad doing marginally better than when we were in LA, when he buried himself in photo albums and video recordings of Mom with the bottle as his best friend.

When I got back to our cramped apartment on the outskirts of Brooklyn after school a week ago, my notebook in my hand, because we couldn't afford a laptop, I angrily scribbled the darkness living inside my heart on the yellow, lined pages. The festering, molding darkness which was growing into a monster of its own.

I wrote about how unfair life was. How my life turned upside down when Mom was diagnosed with cancer ten years ago. How I barely, just barely, remembered the good moments when everyone was happy. And how I'd hold on to those memories like they were a lifeline.

Mom and Dad dancing in the kitchen to some song on the radio when I'd clap in glee because they looked like the princes and princesses from the fairy tales Mom read to me at bedtime, the stories that always ended with "and they live happily-ever-after." How Adrian would make a puking sound when Mom and Dad threw their heads back and laughed before Dad planted a loud kiss on Mom's mouth. How Mom would blush and giggle afterward. Our apartment was small, the linoleum already peeling on the kitchen counters, the bathroom door had a broken lock, but we were so happy back then.

Beautiful, bittersweet memories of the past. Colorless, hopeless gray of my future.

My essay was a mess of graphite on crinkled paper, angry slashes nearly digging holes into a sheet which was dotted with the dried spots of my tears. I poured my heart into it and told whoever was reading I hated my life.

I hated how I had to put on a brave face every day at home so Dad wouldn't worry about me or feel guilty about his sadness. After all, how could you ever recover from losing the love of your life?

I had to pretend life was great whenever Adrian visited from Cornell, because I wanted to see my older brother happy, but even that seemed impossible because he only turned more withdrawn after we left LA.

I knew he tried his hardest to pretend everything was fine whenever he came home, but I also knew the anger I felt inside me was twenty times more in him, because he was older and he knew a lot more about our situation, and how could two angry people comfort each other?

So, I had to be brave. I had to pretend everything was awesome, that I wasn't sad or missing Mom like I'd missed an amputated limb.

When we had our first school dance earlier this year, and my friends were dress shopping with their moms, complaining how their moms wouldn't let them buy this or that, I had to stifle the burning anger and aching sadness in my gut because I didn't want any dress. I didn't need the fancy shoes. I didn't even want to go to the dance.

I'd give *anything* just to have one more day with her. To feel her wrap her arms around me and tell me everything was fine because she was here.

I ended the essay saying school was pointless. Life was pathetic. The future was hopeless. This essay was ridiculous. For one insane moment, I didn't want to pretend anymore. I didn't want to be the good student, the perfect daughter, the sweet sister.

The fucking caregiver.

I. Just. Wanted. To. Be. Angry. He could give me an F on the paper for all I cared.

"Mr. Roberts, I-I wasn't expecting—"

He smiled, his eyes crinkling at the corners, his pale hand, freckled with age spots, brushed the thick clump of gray hair on his head. "You thought you were going to get in trouble?"

Wordlessly, I nodded, still clutching the paper in disbelief.

He sat down next to me.

"My dad died in a boating accident when I was twenty years old."

I squinted at him, trying to imagine a much younger Mr. Roberts.

He chuckled. "I know. It was when dinosaurs roamed the earth."

I stifled a grin.

"He was fishing. It was something he loved to do whenever the opportunity came up. A few days home from school, summer vacation, a special Friday or two when he'd 'call in sick' for me." He winked, fondness in his husky voice.

"But that day, it was a Saturday during Labor Day weekend. I had a barbecue to attend with my friends from college so I couldn't go fishing with him. He went anyway. The weather suddenly became unpredictable, and his little boat capsized. He washed ashore two days later."

Mr. Roberts's voice was sullen, his pale blue eyes taking on a faraway glint, and for a moment, I could see the shadow of a young man who found out his father wasn't coming home.

"I was devastated and angry at myself. I thought, if I went with him, perhaps I could've saved him. I was younger, stronger, a better swimmer."

He glanced at me and gave me a sad smile. "A million what-ifs. I was mad at life, the world, everyone, and everything, even though I knew this was a freak accident. Even though I knew being upset wouldn't change my reality. I thought, what was the point of everything if life...fate...whatever you wanted to call it, could suddenly turn you upside down?"

He turned to me, his voice raspy, and said, "What I'm trying to say is, and this took me years to come to terms with, as an *adult* no less, that we live life as best as we can, to prepare for a tomorrow that is uncertain. We put one step in front of another and go on this beautiful hike that will be full of ups and downs, rough patches, and smooth pathways. I've lived a long life, Millie, and yours is just beginning."

Mr. Roberts covered his mouth as he coughed. "I've had a lot of rainy days, but also my share of sunny, beautiful ones. And while you may feel like everything is wrong with the world right now, that some-how, there's no hope for the future, you're still shaping your future, step-by-step, little-by-little. What you're experiencing right now, includ-ing writing this essay, is part of creating and molding that future...your journey. This isn't permanent, and if you continue to put one foot in front of the other and envision a tomorrow that's different from what you're going through right now, it'll come to fruition."

"But what if life continues to beat me down?" I whispered.

I didn't know how long I could continue being strong for everyone around me.

"From what I read in this essay, young lady, you *are* strong. *A fighter.* You're still standing, aren't you? And that quote on top of the paper is from Abraham Lincoln. He, too, went through his share of traumas and became the president of the country. Put one step in front of the other, create your own destiny, your own future. And one day, you'll look back and realize you're already there."

I got an A on the paper.

Then he'd make it a habit to ask me how I was doing every day after class. He told me he wished there were family services or counseling available in our district, but our neighborhood wasn't wealthy enough and the funding was cut a few years ago. So instead, he took it upon himself to be there for students in need.

Students like me.

He taught me to channel my anger and emotions into something more useful—reading, writing, gardening, a hobby to honor Mom's memory. He told me he'd still go fishing on holidays, something he liked to do to honor his dad.

It was then I decided I wanted to become a teacher. Just like him. To make a difference to other girls out there who may feel life was hopeless. Then someday, I would work my way into policymaking and hopefully put back those much-needed family and counseling services in underserved school districts.

The paper crinkles in my hand as I re-read my hasty scribbles, the pencil marks almost faded over the years. I swallow the lump in my throat and expel a deep breath, trying my best to dislodge it.

That girl is still inside me. Still faking it to the world to the best of her abilities. Still trying to be the happy daughter her dad won't have to worry about, still trying to be the positive sister for her older brother, who is still burning hot with rage.

But I'm stronger now. I'm brave.

I'm a fighter.

CHAPTER 9

"FLEUR TWILIGHT UPCOMING IPO Indicative of Problems with Industry Titan's Cash Flows?" The name of the article hits too close to home.

An anvil sits on top of my chest and my stomach roils as I scroll through the news articles on my phone while waiting for my driver to pick me up and take me to the airport for my trip back home to New York City.

They're not wrong. This IPO means life or death for Fleur Twilight. The economy is in the pits and people are more careful with how they're spending their hard-earned money. Nightclubs tend to be one of the first items they cut from their budget. Fleur Twilight is still profitable, but with the way it's burning through cash to maintain our signature bespoke, luxurious experience, it won't be for long.

"Prince of USA's Impeccable Reputation Carrying Upcoming IPO Plans."

My tie feels like a noose around my neck as a sticky heat crawls up my face and muscles bunch in my shoulders.

Unimpeachable reputation. Unblemished. Face of the family. Hundreds of years of history.

It all falls on me, the reluctant pawn in the game of chess I'm playing.

I can't escape.

The silence in my condo is deafening. Letting out a deep sigh, I stride toward the full-length mirror by the door and take in my appearance.

Carefully arranged hair, the brown so dark, it's almost black, and steely-gray eyes. Classic Anderson traits. Slight under eye shadows that can't be helped with all the work I have to do remotely for the family business and for the university. Perfectly tailored suit from France, the dark navy offset by thin black pinstripes. An expertly knotted tie.

Perfection. Faultless.

All lies.

The flush from minutes ago darkens and I resist the urge to tear off my tie, throw something at the walls, and let the scream bottling up inside me finally rip out of my lungs.

Family first. Everything else second. *You can't be so selfish.*

The thin, jagged scar on my right eyebrow flashes in pain and I wince. My fingers tremble as I lightly touch the evidence of the carelessness of my youth.

The price of freedom.

The sun was bright that day, its golden rays highlighting the lush green trees on the Adirondack Mountains. I jumped over a fallen log, a fiery buzz in my veins. I couldn't have cared less about the beauty of the forest. It could have been barren for all I cared.

Dad chuckled as he walked a hundred feet ahead of us. It was a rare long weekend when he didn't have to work. He wanted some manly bonding time with his two eldest sons before we headed off to college. Maxwell grumbled behind me, muttering some nonsense about how he preferred to stay home and paint or hang out with his girlfriend, Sydney, instead.

Stay home when you could run free in the woods, taste freedom on your tongue, and feel like you'd conquered the world? What a load of bullshit.

"Stop complaining, bro. I just made my first kill, Maxwell. My first! And what did I tell you? This detour is so much better than the main trail. Aren't you glad you guys listened to me instead of going on the same boring route again? The game is so much better here."

"It's a *pigeon.* Don't get your panties in a twist. And trails are there for a reason. They're boring because they're safe."

I rolled my eyes and whirled around to face my twin and best friend, all the while walking backwards without a care in the world. "God, you act like you're eighty sometimes. At least I hunted something. What did you get, nothing? What's the gun on your belt for? Decoration?"

"I prefer to capture nature on canvas, not actually kill nature," he deadpanned.

"God, how did we even share a womb?" I muttered while trudging backwards.

I whistled some song I heard classmates talking about in eleventh grade English. I raked in a deep inhale of the sweet scent of maple and birch trees mixed with the earthiness of the damp soil. This was a high I could get used to.

A noise crinkled behind me but I barely noticed, my mind still reliving the excitement of firing the shot from the rifle and feeling the satisfaction of the bullet hitting the pigeon. It was nothing I had ever experienced before.

This exhilaration. This freedom. This other side of me I never knew I had.

I found myself wishing I packed my philosophy books with me. If I could have curled up on the wicker chair in front of the lodge with my books, life would have been perfect.

Suddenly, I heard a loud thumping behind me.

"Look out, Ryland!" Maxwell screamed, his eyes widening in terror.

I frown, and mouthed, "What?"

Maxwell charged forward, his eyes taking on a determined glint, and in that moment, it was like seeing myself in a mirror. Even though we weren't identical twins, but the piercing gray pools, the harsh cheekbones, the furrowed brows, were all features I recognized in myself.

Within seconds, he barreled into me, tackling me to the ground in a half twist and a sharp pain exploded in my eye, radiating to the rest of my face, taking the literal breath out of my lungs.

"What the fuck—"

"Oh my God!" My father's harsh yell sounded so far away.

Maxwell laid above me as another weight landed on top of us, and he released a guttural groan. I gasped when I saw a wild boar lodging its tusks into Maxwell's side as my brother fought to cover me with his own body.

"Maxwell!" I gasped, and the boar snarled before Maxwell wheezed and twisted his free hand, somehow holding a gun, and finally pulled the trigger.

The *boom* echoed among the trees and burrowed straight into my heart. Maxwell collapsed on top of me as the boar fell over sideways. I heard Dad's pounding footsteps as he tried to reach us as fast as he could.

I rolled out from under my brother, my eyes widening when I saw the warm, sticky crimson liquid on my hands.

Maxwell's blood.

No. No. No.

Maxwell coughed, his face as pale as a sheet of paper, and I ripped the hem of my favorite gray Metallica T-shirt and pressed it over his wound, my heart pounding, clamoring for its womb mate.

"Please, please. Maxwell. Stay with us. Please. Oh my God," I chanted repeatedly under my breath as Maxwell grabbed my hand.

"Ryland, you okay? It didn't get you, did it?" He groaned and his eyes took on a wet sheen.

Shaking my head, I pressed on his wound, watching the blood seep through the shirt. "I-I'm okay. Hang in there, Maxwell. Hold on, help is coming."

"Couldn't let my favorite brother get mauled by a wild pig," he whispered, his dark hair pressed against his sweaty forehead. "I'm fucking cursed, anyway. Better me than you."

"You asshole. Don't you dare. Fuck the curse. Maybe it's me that's cursed. We're twins, after all."

Maxwell wheezed in half-laughter, half-pain. "Seven minutes. I'm older than you by seven minutes, so the damn curse is mine. Don't you dare forget it. My life is not my own, so this is probably the most heroic thing I could've done...and you would've done the same thing for me."

He trembled on the ground and his eyes rolled to the back of his head before his body fell still.

"No!" I screamed. "Maxwell! Stay with us, please."

Dad reached us and barked out instructions into his satellite phone as I helplessly watched my twin bleeding on the ground, a pool of dark red staining the damp earth underneath him. Shaking my head, I pressed harder on the wound, my mind in chaos, my body swept up in bone-chilling fear.

A crimson river suddenly flooded my eye, and I winced from the belated flash of pain. My fingers trembled as I touched my face, feeling a deep gash on my right eyebrow.

I should've paid attention to where I was going.

I should've been more careful.

I should've stayed on the trail, followed the plan.

Freedom always comes at a price.

The thought echoes in my mind as I trace the faint scar on my eyebrow, the streak of pale skin almost invisible from far away. After all, it has been almost twenty years ago.

The scar is a reminder of the steep price to pay when you go off the beaten path. My path is with my family, toiling away in the family business, not in the wild, not in academia, not in anything else.

Ping.

I glance down, noting my driver's text stating he has arrived.

A ball forms in my throat and I take one last look at my reflection before walking out the front door without a backward glance.

CHAPTER 10

ON THE SURFACE, the various theories of business ethics are contradictory. Utilitarianism suggests the correct ethical decision should maximize net benefit or minimize the costs for all parties. The Rights Theory dictates a decision should be evaluated based on the impacts to the individual and basic human rights of the stakeholder.

I want to offer an alternative argument. Aren't these two theories two sides of the same coin? The right to autonomy, to make decisions for ourselves, for example, is a crucial factor to our happiness. Without considering individual happiness, how can we achieve happiness in the group?

My fingers smooth over the pendant nestled above my navy cable-knit sweater as I reread Millie's first paper. The topic is to argue for a prevailing ethics theory.

"Without considering individual happiness, how can we achieve happiness in the group?"

Her words are arrows to my chest. She's speaking directly to me, peering under the thousand-dollar suits, the shiny facade of a fancy title and a rich last name, and jabbing her weapon into the tender flesh of my heart, opening wounds no one else has ever seen before.

I clutch Mom's pendant tighter in my grip, the metal edges digging into my palms before letting go and looking out the airplane window forty-plus thousand feet in the air.

"Mr. Anderson, we'll arrive in New York City in one hour. Would you like any food or refreshments?"

"No, thank you. Are the arrangements ready when we land? We're already running late."

"Yes, sir. The helicopter is on standby and will take you straight to The Orchid," the flight attendant replies before returning to the attendants' quarters.

I settle back into my seat and close my eyes, but Millie's words keep echoing in my ears. I can hear her dulcet voice whispering those sentiments to me then following with, *why aren't you living for yourself, Professor?*

It's madness. The thoughts are a disease corrupting my mind, attempting to obliterate my control, my morals. Why am I thinking of her?

I shouldn't be noticing the way she fiddles with her fingers before she speaks in class. Or the way the swells of her chest move when she releases a deep exhale after delivering her answers with passionate ardor. Or how her eyes trail me as I walk around the room.

I shouldn't notice the way her pale skin flushes a pretty pink when my eyes catch hers in the middle of lecture, her tongue flicking out and swiping her plump lips as if she's nervous.

I shouldn't live for the moments when she lingers after class to ask me follow-up questions on lecture topics, her pupils dilating when I mutter back a response. Or memorize the way the tips of her ears flush when she makes a comment that'll make my lips twitch with repressed humor.

Gnashing my teeth together, I open my eyes and stare at the dimming skies, an endless stretch of dark blue, a thick blanket of clouds underneath us. I'm literally soaring above the earth, a sensation I used to revel in when I was six years old, when Dad took me on the jet for the first time.

Back then, as I stared at the great beyond, my face pressed against the windows, I felt like life was filled with endless possibilities. I could become a superhero like Dad, who I'd hear from classmates how many people worked for him, how he was a very important man.

I could become anything.

But now, as I behold the endless skies before me, the freedom it represents, suspended in midair with technology not making sense to me even as an adult, the elation I used to feel is long gone. Instead, the dark expanse out there seems to taunt me.

You can look, but you can't have.

My phone pings with an incoming email with the heading "Congratulations to our newest tenured professors at ULA" and it's a dagger digging into the bleeding wound in my chest.

What I'd give to be on the shortlist for tenure track, instead of dealing with IPOs, investors, and reporters. To spend my days buried in research, my specialty being corporate governance and ethics, something rising in importance in a world that is increasingly focused on the bottom line at the expense of morals and ethical standards.

But I can't, because of the damn trust. *The fucking prison.*

All legal Andersons, defined as legitimate Andersons through marriage or bloodline, *must* work for the family business if they choose to work. Failure of one person to do so will cause the entire family to lose a significant portion of our wealth and control over Fleur. The funds will go to an array of government organizations.

Our forefathers thought this was a way to tie the family together, to ensure the wealth gets passed down the generations. It was an idea they brought with them from regency England back when the estates and fortunes of the aristocracy were entailed.

It's archaic. It's ridiculous.

If it were only my wealth we were risking, I'd have no qualms in stepping out from the fold and pursuing my dream of being a full-time tenured professor, but this isn't the case. My actions will cause everyone I love to lose everything.

And I can't be that selfish.

My hand finds its way back to the paper I was grading, my eyes roving over the last paragraphs like a madman, my heart beating against the prison of my rib cage.

I want to be free. A tiny voice whispers from deep within. A voice I haven't dared listen to for so many years but is louder and more incessant these days. One can only hide its darkest nature for so long.

My stomach swoops and falls, cold sweat breaking out on my back. I press a button on the controls to turn on the air. *I can't breathe.* My lungs attempt to rake in more oxygen, but the effort is exhausting.

I can't breathe.

"Why aren't you living for yourself, Professor?" imaginary Millie murmurs and my head falls back on the headrest.

I press another button on the controls, closing all the shades simultaneously.

Darkness. Much-needed relief.

"Happy Birthday, Dad." I stride into a private room inside Kobayashi, a Michelin-starred Japanese restaurant, one of several equally lauded fine dining experiences offered within The Orchid.

"His Royal Highness has arrived, better late than never," Rex snickers from his seat on the traditional *tatami* flooring. "The food is getting cold."

He slides his hands behind his head, unleashing one of his devil-may-care, shit-eating-grins at me. I roll my eyes and smirk. I don't even bother correcting him on his nickname for me, which has spread like wildfire to everyone who knows us, only to be made worse by the press's moniker of me as the Prince of the USA.

"I know this might sound shocking, Rex, but sushi is usually cold," Ethan, my youngest brother, offers, twirling his empty sake cup in his hand.

"You're so boring, Ethan. How the hell are you younger than me? *Fine.* The food is not as fresh as it was, then."

"From when it came *ten* minutes ago?" A skeptical rise of a brow from Ethan.

"Unlike you, he had to travel thousands of miles to be here," Maxwell murmurs to Rex. "Cut him some slack, won't you?"

He flashes me a small grin, his dark eyes twinkling, a rare moment of levity for my twin. He reaches for his drink on the table, the metal clasp on his leather bracelet flashing in the dim light.

"You boys will send me to an early grave," Dad says as he stands and pulls me into a tight hug. "You didn't have to fly all the way out here for a dinner."

"Of course I do. It's not every day your old man turns sixty-five. It's only a jet ride away. Sorry for being late. There were some inclement weather issues, and the flight got delayed by traffic control."

He waves me away and takes a seat at the head of the long table, already filled to the brim with a scrumptious rainbow assortment of thinly sliced fish, from ahi tuna to jumbo scallops, artfully crafted hand rolls, which look more like pieces of artwork than food, unique creations of Chef Kobayashi, who has won multiple accolades in his long illustrious career.

The door bursts open and in wafts the soft scent of roses.

"Ryland, you're here!" Lana, our youngest sister, breezes in. Her long brown hair, partially covered by a thick scarf, is flying behind her.

We all stand at her presence—chivalry is decidedly not dead in the Anderson family, the manners passing down for generations with roots from our titled ancestors in England.

Technically, we still have a dukedom with Dad and a marquessate with Maxwell, the eldest son of a duke, but they don't have active duties in England since they are not elected hereditary peers. But regardless, the family has inherited hundreds of years of tradition and the infamous stiff upper lip of the British aristocracy.

"If only men outside this room had the manners you all have." Lana grins, flying into my outstretched arms, and burrows her head against my chest. "I miss you, B."

My chest warms at the inside joke, and I press a soft kiss on her hair. As another tradition, our family gave us middle names in alphabetical order according to age. It was said there were too many of us to keep track of. Maxwell's middle name is Angus, mine is Benedict, and the rest of our siblings' middle names follow the same pattern.

"It's only been a few weeks. And you have three other older brothers to terrorize you."

"You're my favorite," she whispers into my ear before pulling back and giving me a sassy wink. "Don't tell the others I said that."

"I heard you loud and clear," Rex complains with a mock scowl on his face, "don't come to me with your men troubles later on."

"Oh please, I'm the one who usually mops up after your women troubles, not the other way around."

"If the press gets a whiff that the members of the C-Suite of multi-billion-dollar Fleur Entertainment Holdings are all behaving like squabbling six-year-olds, our stock price and IPO plans will tank," Maxwell mutters, but his eyes are soft as we watch Lana and Rex bicker with each other. "Why anyone will believe us is beyond me."

"I think you guys got my birth year wrong," Ethan quips.

While he's the fourth child in the Anderson pecking order, he gravitates more toward Maxwell and me than with Lana and Rex, who were as thick as thieves growing up.

"The IPO plans are still going well?" I ask Ethan, who is our chief financial officer, and will be doing most of the heavy lifting on the accounting and financial reporting side of the offering.

"The Board of Directors is formed for Fleur Twilight. We just engaged with an accounting firm to audit the financial statements. You know the partner."

I cock a brow. "Who?"

"Jess Chapman."

"Steven's oldest sister?"

Ethan nods. "She flew out here two weeks ago with her husband, James. We met up with them and Steven here. So, we have that going for us. At least it's someone we know and like who'll be digging into everything, not that there's anything interesting in Twilight's books."

"No more shop talk, you guys," Lana interjects as Rex nods beside her. "If you start talking about the IPO, then I'll need to start gushing about how Ryland is making my job as chief of PR easy with his impeccable public image, and Rex will then make everything about him and his latest marketing efforts."

"They are *groundbreaking* campaigns because I'm a genius. Investors are lining up at the door because of them." Rex narrows his eyes at her.

Lana arches her brows as if to say, *See?*

I shake my head. My siblings are a rowdy bunch, but I wouldn't trade them for anything in the world. If only Mom were here to see us now.

Lana brings up her phone and says, "I know the press thinks everything is hinging on you, B," she looks at me, "but you know we have your back, all jokes aside, okay?"

"I know." *But I'm still the only person the press focuses on.*

"I'm not going to insert myself into this. I'm retired and leaving the madness of the company to you five." Dad polishes off the sushi on his plate before he reaches for another helping of the stir-fried udon on the table.

"Enjoying retirement, Dad?" He retired three years ago after handing over his position to Maxwell. "Still gardening?"

Dad smiles, his eyes glazing as if reminiscing about the past. He nods, his fingers twisting the silver ring on his left hand. "I feel closer to your mom in the gardens."

A heavy silence blankets the room as my eyes dart to Maxwell, finding his brows furrowed, a heaviness in his tall frame. I clasp one hand on his shoulder and the other on Dad's, giving them both a soft squeeze.

They're the biggest victims of the curse, their burdens are the hardest to bear. Not to mention, they're subjected to the same family trust I'm trapped in. *And you think you're living in a cage? You haven't lived in their shoes before, you ungrateful bastard.*

"I'm sure she's looking down on us and is happy at what she sees," I murmur, my voice thickening as the pendant weighs heavily under my sweater.

Faded memories of Mom float through my mind—her kind green eyes, bright smile, playing hide-and-seek with us in the large backyard gardens of our estate. Rex was screeching at the top of his lungs, alerting everyone to his position, and Ethan was babbling nonsense as the nanny shushed us because baby Lana was asleep.

It's one of the last memories I have of her before she died.

"Anyway, retirement has treated me well. I think my hair has stopped graying." Dad chuckles, pointing to his mostly gray hair streaked with the dark strands prevalent in our family.

We laugh and I look around the room, taking in the people I love more than anything in this world, the very people I can give up my life for without a second thought, the reason I've dutifully followed the footsteps planned for me since I could walk and take my rightful place within the company.

I take in Lana's bright smile, her cheeks flushed at whatever Rex is saying, Rex's arrogant smirk, something the ladies love him for, Ethan's exasperated sigh at the new ruckus at the table, Dad's face, finally not creasing from stress when he was at the helm of the company, and my twin and closest friend, Maxwell, who's smiling softly at the same scene before me.

Family first. Sometimes, it's best not to travel the road less taken.

CHAPTER 11

Toward the end of dinner, Dad stands up and raises his glass. "To your mother, who'd be very proud of you all. She's here celebrating every milestone as she's always in our hearts." He stares at us, his eyes suspiciously red.

My chest clenches, and I roll my lips inward before taking a sip of sake. Maxwell clasps Dad's shoulder and whispers something in his ear, a smile on his lips that doesn't quite reach his eyes.

Maxwell murmurs, "And to Dad, the man we all look up to. Happy Birthday."

We follow his lead in sending well wishes to our dad. I do my best to tamp down the sorrow threatening to bubble up in my throat.

Of all the siblings, Maxwell and I had the most time with Mom. She passed away when we were nine from what the press reported as a "freak accident," a sudden heart attack after falling off the stairs in our family estate, but we all know better. It wasn't an accident at all.

It was the family curse.

The one that befalls the women the firstborn sons of our family love. The mysterious and strange deaths. The ominous fates. The suspicious lack of women in the Anderson lineage, except for Lana. It's the reason arranged marriages or marriages of convenience are prevalent in our family. All part of the secret burdens everyone in our family carries, especially Maxwell.

Back when I didn't know any better, I used to scoff at the legend, unwilling to accept something as *ridiculous* as the truth, despite Dad's solemn face when he sat Maxwell and I down in the library after Mom's funeral to tell us the dark secret. Then there's the hoarseness in Grandpa's voice when he clutched Maxwell's hands on his deathbed, telling Maxwell he was strong enough to bear this curse just like the men before him.

Even so, Maxwell and I refused to believe in the curse. It wasn't scientific. It felt superstitious. It seemed fantastical, something out of a horror movie.

But then, who could fight the evidence presented in front of us? Generations of untimely deaths, including Maxwell's high school sweetheart, Sydney, the girl he foolishly gave his heart away to and eloped with when we turned eighteen?

And now, as I look at my brother, the eldest of the family by a mere four-hundred-twenty-seconds, the seven minutes which changed the course of his life and mine, the heaviness sinks deeper into my chest. What right do I have to live for myself when the choice has been taken away from Maxwell just because he exists, simply because the doctor pulled him out of the womb moments before me?

Maxwell and Dad share a laugh before Dad says, "Don't need to leave early on my part. John will take me back to the estate. Enjoy yourselves tonight."

We hug Dad goodbye before Lana announces she's leaving to meet with her friends at the ladies' lounge upstairs, followed by some foreign-sounding innovative medspa treatments at one of the few specialty luxury spas on the upper floors.

Five minutes later, the rest of us gather in one of the coveted private rooms in the gentlemen's club, usually reserved for weeks in advance.

The space is large, with floor-to-ceiling windows decorated with thick, velvet drapes, a dining and work area separated from the lounge. The decor is tasteful and masculine, dark woods interspersed with glass furnishings—a mixture of modern with traditional. From the Tiffany floor lamps to the modern pendant lights, luxury drips from every aspect of the room, and the few others in the club are similarly furnished. There are definite advantages to being the owners of The Orchid—one room is perpetually earmarked for us.

Rex plops down on a sofa with an audible sigh and starts swiping on his phone, a wide grin on his face. Ethan heads to the wet bar and pours a few drinks for us. I nurse my whiskey and sit in my usual navy armchair by the roaring fireplace, watching the flames dance on top of the embers, emitting a warmth I don't quite feel inside me.

"Who are you texting?" Maxwell asks Rex before he walks over to the windows.

"The other guys. They're nearby and are heading up right now."

As if on cue, a crisp knock sounds from the door a few seconds later, and Charles Vaughn steps through, his gleaming blond hair shining under the warm overhead lights, every inch the Scandinavian royalty stock photo nickname he has earned from friends. While he isn't royalty, he is close, with his family owning the Bank of Columbia and him at the helm.

Steven Kingsley follows him inside, dressed in his three-piece gray suit, like he came directly from a work meeting, which wouldn't be surprising, considering he's a fucking workaholic.

"Ryland." Steven steps up and smacks a hand on my back, a rare smile lighting up his usually serious face. "Crawling home with your tail between your legs already? Scarred the students at ULA for life?" He rakes his hand over his perfectly coiffed black hair.

"Oh please. The students are getting the education of a lifetime. Not only from books, but also from practical application."

"I saw the replay of your press conference a few weeks ago. *Gossip Times* got on your nerves, huh? But I must admit, there's some truth to what they're asking. We've *never* seen you with a girlfriend. And the women from your scenes at Noire upstairs on the Rose floors don't count. They're sexual outlets, not the real deal." Charles sinks into the sofa next to Rex, who perks up in interest as the gossipmonger within our group.

"I heard something about the Rose floors?" Rex grins, seeming all too interested in the several floors within this building infamous for a variety of adult entertainment.

The Rose floors have everything from luxury suites equipped with specialty furniture and toys, to kink rooms, burlesque clubs, and even a faux-outdoor club, Noire, which lets folks engage in various scenes or fuck "outdoors" without worrying about the prying eyes of the paparazzi. They are forbidden to enter this high-security building except on rare occasions.

Our companionship services, paid escorts for everything ranging from innocuous dates for galas to things of a more lustful nature, also operate within those floors.

It's a fine legal line we straddle, but with some influential lawmakers and even a few Supreme Court justices as members here, people look the other way. This is also why the personnel for the Rose floors are handled by Elias Kent's legitimate business front. The notorious and enigmatic crime boss has ways of handling delicate matters we don't want to know anything about.

Plausible deniability.

Our only requirement is the employees of the Rose floors must be here of their own free will and be allowed to quit like any other job.

The Orchid is a haven for the rich and famous who are lucky enough to undergo multiple rounds of interviews, pay an exorbitant annual fee, and secure an invitation only membership. It's a place where the power makers can mingle and relax without worrying about public image.

It's a place where *any* wish can be granted. Thousands of influential deals are brokered within this building. There's a reason it's the crown jewel of Fleur Entertainment.

"They're fishing for gossip. There's no one," I reply.

"You're not a monk, bro," Rex retorts, "I find it hard to believe there's absolutely *no one* piquing your interest."

Dark brown hair, a heart-shaped face, and stunning blue eyes seeming to see all too much materialize in my mind. My heart skips several beats and heat rushes up my neck.

You're a sick man. I shove the image away.

"Where will I find time to date these days? The company takes up my entire life and any extra time I have is spent teaching." I throw back my drink in one gulp, wincing at the burn.

"You don't have to teach, you know. I think the family reputation can survive without the Prince of the USA spending time in academia. We give back in many other ways—our charities, volunteering, scholarships," Rex comments, his brows furrowing as he scrutinizes me. In this moment, the playboy is gone and in his place is the concerned brother.

"I want to continue teaching." It's the one respite keeping me going.

"Something else is going on then. I don't know what," Rex replies. "You're quieter than you usually are. And I've been monitoring the Rose floors activities. You haven't booked a scene in at least half a year. Is this a health issue? Something wrong with your dick?" Fucking bastard.

"How did you get that information?" Steven asks, sitting up straighter on the other black sofa across the room. "Doesn't Elias keep that info under lock and key?"

Rex waggles his brows. "I have ways of making all people open up to me...including the coldest of bastards."

He swivels his head toward me. "Don't think I let you off the hook. Tell us what's going on. Maybe we can help. You have the smartest people in the city here, especially me, of course."

I roll my eyes, a spark threatening to ignite in the chilly cavity of my chest. "My health is perfectly fine," other than the increasing difficulty in breathing sometimes, but that's neither here nor there, "and my cock is functioning fine. I just don't feel a need to frequent the floors these days."

And frankly, no one has captured my interest.

But is that really true, Ryland?

Fuck.

"Red flag for sure," Ethan quips. "I agree with Rex this time. You used to run around in Noire playing predator and prey at least once a month. What did you say the last time we asked? It was freeing to your soul, and you felt in touch with your primal self. 'Crucial to your mental health...' I think was the phrase you used. Why haven't you been there for half a year or are you getting some action on the side, which circles back to the original question... Do you have a woman?"

I shake my head, my fingers gripping my empty tumbler tightly. *Stop asking me questions I don't want to answer.* The sensation of not being able to breathe is returning and a vein pulses on my forehead. I fight against the urge to stand up, throw the glass against the wall, and break open a window to let the cool fall air in.

"I haven't heard him mention anything about spotting strange birds these days, either. That was one of his old-man hobbies, bird-watching," Charles murmurs as he strides to the fireplace, his aristocratic features harsh with the roaring fire behind him.

Steven cocks his head to the side. "At first, I thought this was just a joke, but now I think there's some truth to these questions."

He taps his finger on his chin and muses, "Something's going on. I can't place it. But Ryland, whenever you want to talk, we're here for you. But in the meantime," he addresses the others in the room, "let's lay off of him."

I chuckle halfheartedly, the pressure on my chest easing as I set the tumbler on the imported coffee table made from the finest dark oaks and glass. It looks like these idiots won't press me.

How can I explain to them the discontent simmering in the background for the last decade, which suddenly threatens to explode and incinerate everything in its path? Even I don't understand it well.

"Anyway, how are you doing, Steven, with your father and TransAmerica?"

Misdirection. The best way to stop their incessant questioning is to turn the spotlight on someone else.

My friend's face darkens. His family is based in LA and is at the helm of the large conglomerate, but for some reason, Steven never wanted to take over the company, and opted to move across the country to make a name for himself on Wall Street. "There may be a situation brewing on the horizon. I'm monitoring it."

"Anything I can help with?" Charles offers, and the men break into a serious discussion about warding off takeovers and working with bad actors who are resorting to using shady tactics to get what they want.

I get up from my chair and stride to the large windows, staring at the enormous park in the middle of the city, punctuated by the warm glow of streetlamps, with the bright flashes of headlights from cars and buses whizzing by.

The city never sleeps. It has a heady energy that used to make me excited, but now can't seem to eke out a thump in my heart.

"Hey," Maxwell murmurs as he stands next to me, gazing out the window. "Don't think I don't know what it means when you slink off and stare outside. You're feeling trapped somehow, right? Guilty perhaps?"

His words pummel my chest and I clench my jaw, not wanting to answer him lest I give anything away in my voice.

He always knows what I am thinking.

Maxwell slaps his hand across my back. "You don't need to tell me anything until you're ready," he murmurs.

I stare at our reflections on the glass windows, silhouettes almost identical, but with distinct differences—he's taller than me by two inches, slightly leaner, his hair longer, the jawline a little more refined and aristocratic and a tall, Roman nose instead of my curved one.

"I just want you to be happy, Ryland. Don't feel guilty. The curse is random luck. I'm not jealous of you."

He clears his throat. "I'm glad you can be free to live and fall in love. I've accepted my place in life and made the best out of it. I only wish you'd release yourself from whatever's holding you back. I want you to be happy, and so would Mom."

Wetness prickles my vision as the pendant weighs heavily on my chest and the light leather bracelet suddenly feels like a fiery brand around my wrist.

What have I done to deserve this unconditional love? I'm a selfish man deep inside. Secretly resentful of everything that was given to me, the good fortune Maxwell would probably die to have. The good fortune most people in the world would cry tears of joy for.

Ugly. Dark. Corrupted.

Ungrateful.

"Let it go, Ryland," Maxwell whispers as we stare into the night. "Let it go."

CHAPTER 12

"You like it, don't you, baby girl, when I give it to you hard and rough, you little sl—" the low, raspy voice of Theo Andrews, my favorite audiobook narrator, erupts from the speakers of my laptop and cold sweat breaks across my skin.

Shit! Someone kill me now before I die from mortification.

The classroom erupts into laughter as my fingers fly to the mute button on my laptop. My heart clogs my throat, my face surely turning as red as a tomato, and I want the building to collapse and bury me alive.

Damn these social media websites for automatically playing when you open the browser. Last night, I was watching the latest audio teaser clip of a spicy dark romance novel and obviously forgot to close out of the tab.

The snickers continue and I bury my face in my hands, not wanting to face the world.

"Shut it guys. It's just an audio book clip online. Don't pretend you guys don't watch them too," Jocelyn says from next to me and I peek out from between my fingers and flash her a grateful smile.

Despite the dark circles rimming her eyes, which seem to have gotten worse in the last few weeks, she looks fierce, unkempt hair and all.

Jocelyn has become a good friend to me and just last night, she cooked me dinner when she heard my stomach grumbling at ten p.m. because I was so buried in my studies, I had forgotten to eat.

She gives me a wink and continues, "At least Millie reads...but if my audiobook narrators sounded like *that*, I think I'd give this reading thing a try too. Maybe I'd actually pass this class if I read more." A grimace flashes over her face before her expression smooths to one of nonchalance again.

More chuckles echo around us and a few guys shoot their brows up on their foreheads, their eyes giving me the elevator glances, making me want to crawl back into the hole I desperately need to be in.

Utter mortification.

"Who's he?" a cute redhead next to me whispers while eyeing my laptop.

I blow out a breath. *Embarrassing moments happen to everyone.* "He's Theo Andrews and he—"

"Laptop working today? Nice to see you're finally prepared for class, Ms. Callahan. If it's *okay* with you, I'd like to begin," a deep voice rumbles.

The classroom abruptly silences as our attention focuses on the imposing man standing at the threshold.

Oh. My. God. How much did he hear?

Professor Anderson's eyes pin me in place. His scathing remarks are ropes binding my hands and feet. My body heats up again.

He's leaning against the door frame, his posture deceptively casual, but his demeanor is anything but. His tailored gray suit and white dress shirt stretch over his body, an expertly knotted navy tie cinching his neck, but not hiding the muscles rippling in his throat.

My heart skips several beats as my breath leaves my body. God invented suits for this man.

He narrows his eyes at me before lifting his brow.

I blink and take a fortifying breath. "Yes, Professor, please begin."

Class technically starts now, so my little incident before isn't a disruption to class, and I won't apologize.

His stare holds mine, as if he's waiting for me to say something else, like stammer "I'm sorry," but I remain silent.

The pulse, which had calmed down moments ago, erupts into chaos. I straighten up in my chair and tilt my face up, my lips curving into what I hope is a confident, composed smile.

His eyes flash with something, but his expression quickly shutters. Looking away, he strides to the podium and sets his laptop bag down before unbuttoning his suit jacket.

Leaning forward, a muscle twitches in his jaw, and he grips the sides of the podium. "I want to discuss a serious matter today. Fanny Reardon, can you come up to the front of the room?"

A brunette from the back stands up, her face as pale as a sheet of paper, her hands trembling as she slowly makes her way toward the front.

"Hurry up! We don't have all day," he barks, and I can't help but flinch.

Quick footsteps echo in the quiet room, the tension thick in the air, and the temperature drops at least ten degrees. A sense of foreboding blankets the atmosphere and people shift in their seats uncomfortably.

"Y-Yes, P-Professor?" Fanny trembles before Ryland, a defendant standing in front of a judge for sentencing.

"Can you tell me where you were last Monday during our first exam?"

"H-Here, of c-course. Taking the exam."

Professor Ryland's lips curl into a snarl, the whites of his teeth flashing. "Do you want to revise your answer?"

Fanny cowers before him, her eyes darting to all of us sitting before her. Sweat mists her face.

"N-No. I was here."

A stack of paper flies in front of her, landing at her feet in a haphazard pile.

"Gregory Timmons, get your ass up here!"

"P-Professor, I-I..." Fanny begins, her face crumbling, and she slaps her hands over her mouth, muffling the sobs tearing out of her throat.

A lanky blond guy stands next to Fanny, his fingers pulling at his hair.

"The two of you have the exact answers, down to every incorrect answer. Your essay responses, while the phrasing is different, share the same sentiments, again, including every single correct or incorrect response."

Professor Ryland slowly walks around the podium, his steps slow and measured, a lion circling his prey before digging his teeth into their flesh. He cracks the joints in his neck, the sound echoing in the room as we sit frozen in our seats.

He hates cheaters. Jocelyn's words before our first class reverberate in my mind. Oh shit.

"I can tolerate stupidity. I can tolerate ineptitude. But there's one thing I can't tolerate."

The muscle twitches in his cheek as he leans down over them, even though Greg is almost the same height as him.

"I fucking *despise* cheaters. People who think they can take shortcuts and use underhanded methods to get ahead, to further their ambitions. *Pathetic.*"

My pulse riots in my ears as I watch my two classmates shrivel before him.

Fanny whispers, "P-Professor, we have reas—"

Revulsion drips out of every word from his mouth. He points to the door. "I don't care about your reasons. It's all bullshit. You both are the scum of the earth and I've reported your cheating to the dean and the disciplinary committee. Now, *get out of my classroom!*"

Fanny whimpers, her tears streaming down her face, and Greg shakes like a leaf before he ushers her out of the room.

The door closes with a resounding *bang*. My pulse is loud in my ears as the room falls silent, the quiet so eerie I can hear myself breathing.

Professor Anderson keeps his back toward us, his tall frame shaking almost imperceptibly, his hands fisted tightly to his sides.

Slowly, he turns toward us. "Let this be a warning to any of you who have funny ideas about cheating. Your futures will be ruined. No. Exceptions."

His eyes sweep the room before his gaze lands on mine. "Am I making myself clear?"

I flinch under his withering glare. My heart rate skyrockets to the roof.

"Yes, Professor," all of us respond.

"I'll repeat what I said on the first day. This class is reserved only for serious students, no cheaters, no liars, and absolutely *no distractions.*"

He stares at me, a harsh fierceness reflected in his eyes, and I find myself breathless, with anticipation or fear, I don't know. His gaze roves over my face like he's memorizing every freckle on my skin or peering into my mind to wrench out every single chaotic thought fluttering inside me. I feel like a bird at his feet, and he's staring at me like I'm his next meal. I should be scared, worried. My fight-or-flight response should be activating.

But instead, a strange heat flows through my veins.

No distractions.

My fingers curl into my palm, digging into my flesh, and I tear my gaze away.

"Today, we will go over…"

I hear his footsteps as he paces in front of the podium, but the words are muffled. I'm underwater, disoriented, trying to find my way to the surface, my lungs burning for air.

No distractions.

I feel his searing gaze on me for the rest of the class, each deep rasp and hoarse grumble prickling my skin, the air thinning every time he passes by my seat. A throbbing appears between my legs, and I fight the urge to clench my thighs.

My eyes dart up and our gazes connect. His nostrils flare and a muscle tics in his jaw.

No distractions.

I can't help but wonder, is his warning for me or for him?

CHAPTER 13

THE CRISP FALL BREEZE blows across my face as I walk through a thick grove of trees while juggling a cup of hot chocolate and a small ceramic pot of yellow daffodils in my hands, all the while balancing the phone tucked between my shoulder and my ear.

"I got the flowers from the florist right before they were about to close, Dad. I just need to make a stop at my professor's office hours, then I'll head out to the cemetery."

Dad's voice is rusty as he replies, "Thank you, Millie. I can always count on you."

He lets out a deep sigh, exhaustion clear in his voice. "I should make a trip out there. Give the flowers to Francine in person. But, after all these years, I...I still..."

I pause in the middle of the garden and sit down on the lone green bench. Carefully setting down my things, I smother the ache in my chest and hope I sound upbeat.

"Mom is with you always, Dad. It doesn't matter if you haven't been back to visit her grave since we moved to New York. With a love like yours, she never really left."

A lump forms in my throat. "And I'm sure she'd love the flowers. I read in her journals daffodils were her favorite. They're bright and cheerful, don't you think? I remember Mom liked to laugh a lot."

The memories are fading year after year, but the feeling never disappears. I can still feel her presence around me.

Loss is a strange thing.

Some days, you walk around and feel whole. The sun is warm on your skin and you notice bright butterflies fluttering about as you go through your everyday routine. Things feel peaceful. Content.

Then there are days when you feel winded. When the loss hits your head like a sledgehammer, and you wonder if you'll ever feel awe or happiness again. When the hole in your chest feels more like an abyss and you know you'll never stop missing that person.

Today is the latter. It's Mom's birthday. She would've been fifty-eight years old if lymphoma didn't take her away from us.

There are some things I guess you'll never get over, no matter the years that have elapsed. I'm sure if Mr. Roberts is still alive, there'll still be a hole in his heart for his dad. A hole that has never healed.

"Give her a kiss for me, sweetheart." Heartbreak lances Dad's voice, even after twelve years, the pain still sounds fresh and raw.

"I will, Dad. I love you." Swallowing the sharp needles in my throat, I disconnect from the call.

I stare at the beautiful shrubbery next to me, taking in the bright orange-red tubular blossoms of the California fuchsia, a sight that'll normally bring a smile to my face, but today, I just feel bereft.

A gentle breeze carries the scent of wildflowers as I sit in this small, private oasis, one of the many courtyards on campus. The small gust burrows deep into my bones. Instead of feeling comforted by the tranquil breeze, I feel cold instead; the chill causing me to shiver.

With trembling hands, I pick up the hot chocolate I purchased from the campus coffee shop earlier. I take a sip and grimace at the fake saccharine taste, one reeking of artificial chocolate flavor and sugar.

It doesn't taste the same as Mom's chocolate.

Do I still remember how it tastes, really? Or am I just hanging on to a faint imprint of the past, each memory a string slowly thinning on a rope as I hang over the edge of a mountain, trying to hold on for dear life?

Will I forget her someday?

My nose burns as I look across the courtyard, where I see the small blurry shapes of students walking to and from class. Girls laughing in groups, their eyes glued to something on their cell phones. Guys breezing by without a care in the world on their skateboards, backpacks haphazardly slung from their shoulders.

LA is beautiful in the fall, especially now, so close to Halloween. The leaves are turning brown, and other than the occasional bouts of rain, one can still wear flip-flops, shorts, and T-shirts out and about, unlike back home in New York where folks are bundled up in jackets and scarves.

I blow out a breath and brush aside my melancholy before checking the time on my phone. I need to catch Professor Anderson before his office hours end.

After quickly gathering my things, I stand up and hurry toward the stately red brick building with quaint black shutters—the faculty building for the business and accounting professors.

Minutes later, I stand in front of the closed door of the office used by adjunct professors and guest lecturers for office hours. My pulse kicks into an unsteady rhythm as my palms grow sweaty.

I can do this. He's just a man. A regular person.

But a regular person doesn't make my heart sprint circles in my rib cage whenever he stares at me in class. A regular man doesn't invade my dreams at night, dreams involving him standing in the pouring rain, all coiled tension and leashed energy, dark eyes teeming with intensity and unsaid emotions.

And heartache. Something I can feel like a punch to the chest.

In my dreams, we're always standing a few feet apart, the rain drenching my hair, my face, my clothes, but my feet are encased in cement blocks, and I can't move, walk toward him, or put my arms around him to offer him my warmth.

When I wake up, my body is drenched in sweat.

Fevered dreams of an unattainable man.

Misplaced emotions, Millie. You're looking for someone to protect you, and a mysterious, tall professor is the perfect target for your imagination. It's not real.

Squaring my shoulders, I raise my hand and rap on the door.

Knock. Knock.

"Come in." A terse command. A deep voice. Goosebumps bead on my forearms.

I rake in a fortifying breath and open the door, finding the literal man of my dreams frowning at a stack of papers in front of him, brandishing a red pen like a weapon. His desk is sparse, with nothing on top other than a laptop and a ULA mug with a bunch of pens and pencils jammed into it.

His dark hair is disheveled, his blue tie tugged slightly loose around his neck. A thick lock of hair has fallen over his face. My fingers twitch. I wonder how his hair will feel against my skin.

His white shirtsleeves are rolled up, once again offering a tantalizing view of his muscular forearms. A dark navy suit jacket hangs on the coat rack in the corner of the small office. A seductive scent of the woods mixed with citrus permeates the room.

His frown is now a scowl as he slashes angry red marks on the paper, his head shaking in apparent displeasure. He plucks another paper from the pile, his eyes roving over the document in concentration.

It's like he's lost in his own world, completely forgetting someone just stepped into his office.

He's in his element.

"Professor Anderson, is this a good time?" I ask softly, clutching my drink and the potted flowers closer to my chest. Like a shield against what's about to come.

His head snaps up, his sharp eyes widening a fraction and something imperceptible flashes in his gaze. The gray pools darken as he immobilizes me with his searing stare. He rises to his full height, the motion seeming automatic, like the rest of his aristocratic breeding.

No potted plant can save me from the lasered focus of his attention on me.

"Mill—Ms. Callahan," he murmurs, his voice raspy. *Millie.* He almost called me by my first name. I want to hear him call me that. "Yes?"

I adjust the flowers and drink in my hands and use my hips to close the door behind me. The soft *click* sounds loud.

Carefully, I walk toward him and find his imposing frame tensing, the muscles bunching in his shoulders as he sits back in his large leather chair, warily eyeing my approach, like I'm going to destroy him.

Setting my things on his desk, I take a seat and clasp my hands on top of my lap. "I want to ask you to write a letter of recommendation for me. If you're open to it."

"For?" He cocks his brow, his frame relaxing slightly, as if relieved at the topic I'm bringing up.

"The Education Honors Program at NYUC. I'm only at ULA for one year. I'll be back at NYUC next year and the honors program is notoriously difficult to get into. Your class here is one of the funnel classes to the program. I'm sure it would go a long way if you wrote me a letter of recommendation."

Professor Anderson sits back, his posture deceptively relaxed, but his eyes remain shrewd. "And you think you deserve a recommendation from me?"

"I know we didn't start off on a good foot, but I hope I've proven to you in the last few weeks I'm serious about your class. My grades are stellar. I have a lot to offer, and it's my dream to get into the program."

"Why?"

I tug my fingers and sit up straighter. "I want to become a teacher or a professor. Travel the world and teach those less fortunate. And maybe in the future, a policymaker advocating for equal education amongst all socioeconomic classes."

He steeples his fingers in front of him and stares at me, his gaze unwavering.

My fingers twist and tangle, my tongue darting out to wet my parched lips. His nostrils flare and he swallows, the muscles in his corded throat rippling.

Ignoring the flutters percolating inside me, I soldier on. "I want to be a guiding light and teach the leaders of our future. I want to make a difference, like how a teacher in my childhood made a difference for me when times were dark. *I want this to be my legacy.*"

He stills as he listens to my words, his eyes never leaving mine. His gaze is penetrating. Unforgiving. A muscle pulses in his jaw and slowly, I see his hands curl into fists on top of the table.

Seconds pass by, but he says nothing. Doesn't acknowledge my story. Doesn't answer my request.

"I...I want to honor my mom's memory...to make something out of a tragedy, I...I..." More words threaten to tumble out of me, but I hold them in, the rest of the sentence practically choking me.

He just sits rigidly, as still as a statue, his face free of any expression, and yet, I feel emotions pouring out from him in torrents. The vein throbs on his forehead now. A heat crawls up my body, and I'm sure my face is flushed. *Why is he looking at me like he's seen a ghost?*

My pulse dives off the cliff, and my hands shake on my lap. *This is a mistake. He hates me. He has since the first class. There's no way he'll write the recommendation for me. This is so embarrassing.* I quickly scramble up, the chair scraping the floor in a loud *screech.*

This is a mistake.

I pick up my bag from the chair, my hands mindlessly reaching for the hot chocolate and flowers on his desk. "I-I'm sorry to disturb you, Professor. I can see this isn't the time for it. Or perhaps you need more time to evaluate my performance. I'll go. I'll—"

Crash.

The pot of daffodils falls on the hardwood floors, the pot shattering into a thousand pieces. Just like my fragile heart today. In my haste to make a quick escape, my uncoordinated hands dropped the first flowers

Dad got for Mom in over twelve years, the ones symbolizing his love for her.

A sob escapes my throat, my vision blurring instantly.

My hand flies to my mouth as I turn away, trying and failing to look at anything other than the imposing man before me. With his laser eyes. Eyes that seem to see *everything*.

CHAPTER 14

MY MIND IS A scramble of sadness and embarrassment, my breathing quickening into short bursts. My vision is blurry, the tears welling up rapidly, and I bite my inner cheek in a last-ditch effort to halt my inevitable meltdown.

I don't want to break down in front of him. This cold man. This oxymoron. A man who makes me feel so warm with a simple gaze.

But why am I falling apart in front of him...after holding everything in all these years?

A thousand thoughts skate through my consciousness as I give up the fight and wipe my sleeve over my wet cheeks.

"I-I'm sorry, Professor," I stammer, my voice thick. "This is inappro—"

Suddenly, a solid wall of heat appears in front of me, the enticing scent of the forest and citrus enveloping me completely, almost like a tender embrace. I stare at his chest, his heaving chest, like he, too, is struggling to breathe and make sense of this. His muscles flex under his crisp shirt and tailored vest, and he lets out a ragged exhale.

The sound is rough. Anguished. Completely masculine.

My body shakes. I don't know if it's from the emotions of the day or from everything I've bottled inside me for so long.

Or perhaps it's from him. This fortress of a man who can make me feel so out of control just from his mere presence.

Wordlessly, he lifts his hand and brushes his thumb gently over my cheek, wiping away the tears there. My eyes flutter shut of their own accord, my skin blooming under his caress. I lean into his palm, relishing the slightly rough scrape of his skin against mine, and his warmth against my chilled skin.

I whisper, my voice shaky, "I grew up poor, so poor we were barely keeping the electricity on. All our money went to Mom's health care when she was diagnosed with lymphoma. At first, the doctors were optimistic, but I remember so little of that time. I was too young. Then, she went into remission. And for a while there, we were happy again. There was laughter and dancing in the house, trips to the park, and cookies for breakfast. I got snuggles and bedtime stories."

I don't know why I'm telling him this, but the cork bottling it all, forcing me to be the responsible, cheerful person for the people around me, has finally popped, and everything comes tumbling out.

Perhaps it's because he's silent, offering nothing except for his heated presence radiating with so much intensity, standing a mere inch away from me. His large hand is still cupping my cheek, his thumb smoothing soft circles, igniting a flurry of sparks at the light contact.

I continue, "Then, I remember one day, Mom's eyes were red when she picked me up from school. When we got back home, she gave me a tight hug before locking herself inside her bedroom. I heard her sobs. Gut-wrenching sobs. They weren't something a seven-year-old would ever forget. From that moment on, we were sad again. It turned out the cancer came back."

More tears slip out and he carefully wipes them away, still not saying a word, still a mountain of knotted tightness in front of me. He feels like a haven, blocking the storm raging around me.

"The battle was hard fought, but we lost her in the end," I choke out the next words. "My family moved to New York afterward, but we were barely holding on, you see. But a teacher saw *me*. He looked after me and saved me when I was drowning in pain."

My hand slowly lifts from my side, my fingers unbiddenly reach for the buttons on his vest. I don't know why I'm doing this, but I want to touch him, to let him feel an ounce of what he's making me feel right now. The silent comfort is akin to carefully wrapping bandages around my bleeding heart.

I hear his sharp inhale, a ragged half-breath. I feel the slight rippling of his muscular chest from my touch. All man. Every inch of him.

I still don't look up as I whisper in this startling intimacy, "I wanted to become a teacher then. To make a difference in someone else's life like the way he made a difference in mine. You see, it's the ultimate way I can honor my mom...to make something out of a tragic situation."

My exhales are loud in the office, which seems smaller than before, or maybe the man in front of me has a presence filling the entire room. Unable to stop myself, I continue to fiddle with his buttons—little elegant squares of tortoise pattern rimmed with gold—they look expensive, unattainable, unapproachable, just like the rest of him. *What am I even doing?* But I can't stop myself. I want to lean on him, on this pillar of quiet strength.

I'm tired and he looks like he can be my respite. My oasis in the desert.

The silence stretches on, the tension thickening with each second. The tingles on my cheek where his hand is grazing me spread south to the rest of my body, the warmth chasing away the chill inside me.

A magical elixir.

"I lost my mom when I was young too." His deep, raspy voice pierces the silence, like he's talking to a lover in the dark. "I know the pain, the hole inside your chest that can never be filled."

My breath freezes as I listen to his quiet words.

"She'd sit with me in our rose garden and read me parables inherent with life lessons. Back then, I didn't understand them. They were just interesting stories with happily-ever-afters for a six-year-old." He chuckles and my eyes flutter shut as I imagine the little boy he once was.

"She had a way with words and could explain difficult topics in a way I could understand. I'd fall asleep with the sound of her voice in my ears, the warm breeze on my face, the taste of the sweet grapes on my tongue.

And later, I'd repeat the stories to my brothers, watching their eyes light up with curiosity."

Slowly, he drags his hand to my neck, his touch still barely above a graze, but feels like a searing brand. I let out a gasp and his fingers squeeze ever so slightly before releasing. It's almost like he wants to feel my vitality, to see how I'll react.

I feel a pulsing heat in my lower belly. He trails his fingers to my chin, the sensitive scraping eliciting a shiver in me, and tilts my head up.

My lips part on an exhale as my eyes finally meet his. Mesmerizing slate, rimmed with dark blue, the hue so imperceptible, it's almost black. They're the color of the turbulent skies. His brows are angry slashes on his forehead, completely at odds with the gentleness of his fingers. He looks furious at himself.

"It's why I'm a professor now." He swallows before his thumb lightly touches my bottom lip, like he's testing the texture. "It was her dream to become a tenured professor...and now, mine."

His last words are wistful, as though he can never live to see his dream come true. It makes no sense.

"Are you going for tenure?" I want to ask him more, but he distracts me by lightly caressing my lip once more.

"No, sometimes, dreams remain what they are...dreams. They'll never be reality. And I'm needed elsewhere." He scoffs, a low, rumbly sound drawing me closer. "These dreams are not for someone like me."

"Why?" I whisper.

His thumb is still on my lip and his gaze darkens as he drags his eyes up to meet mine. "Because my actions affect others. Because I can't be so selfish."

"It's not selfish to want something for yourself." I swallow. "You owe it to yourself to live for you. After all, we both know how short and unpredictable life can be."

His nostrils flare, and his thumb resumes the seductive motions against my lips. Teasing. Grazing. Dipping slightly, just the tip, into my mouth.

A bolt of heat travels to my core. A faint voice in the back of my mind says, *this is wrong.* But everything feels decidedly *right.*

The thick tension in the room changes nature and turns sultry, heady...or perhaps, the elements were there all along, simmering in the background and today is a match to the gasoline.

Tentatively, I close my lips around his thick digit and press a soft kiss on his thumb. The room swirls around me, this invisible dance of seduction making me drunk. My heart pounds against my rib cage.

"You're a fighter too, and I see you." My quiet words are uttered on an exhale, but they come straight from the burgeoning flames inside my chest.

His eyes dart to my lips, which are still parted, to the way his thumb is swiping the lower lip like it's the answer to his problems, the problems no one has ever seen.

Until now.

Kindred spirits. Kismet. Fate.

Our breaths mingle and seduce, and he leans in ever so slightly. His hand travels to the back of my neck, his fingers digging into the nape. My eyes flutter close.

Riiiing.

We jolt apart, the pulsing in my chest an earthquake within me. He pants heavily, his eyes fevered, darting around the office, shock making a late appearance. I clasp my hand over my heart. Everything feels so hot, so sensitive, so *everything. I want more.*

He strides back to the desk and picks up the phone. My body feels bereft without his heat and touch.

"Anderson here. Yes, I'll be at the meeting in half an hour." Professor Anderson stares at me as he speaks on the phone, his voice even and calm, completely at odds with the sharp intensity on his face.

Letting out a breath, I quickly pick up my things, my fingers trembling from the residual jittery energy. A sudden *crash* of pens on the wooden desk forces me to look at him again. He empties the mug he has been using as a penholder.

"If he has a problem, he can come to me himself," he replies while he walks around the desk and slowly kneels before me, his strong back muscles straining against his shirt and vest as he bends down to the floor.

I frown. *What is he doing?*

"I stand by my decision. There's no room for cheaters in my class." He deftly picks up the daffodils scattered across the floor and puts them in the mug, then he scoops up the larger chunks of potting soil and arranges them in the cup as well.

He's restoring my flowers for me. Fixing all the broken pieces. The thumping in my heart intensifies, no longer satisfied with running sprints, and is full on free-falling off the cliff.

He hands me the flowers and returns to his seat. I quickly make my escape, eager to leave this room, my insides churning with many tumultuous emotions and inappropriate feelings.

My body feels feverish. Scorching. Completely opposite from the chilled state I was in when I walked in here fifteen minutes ago.

I twist the doorknob, desperate to take a deep breath of fresh air, to make sense of the riot of sensations inside me right now.

"I'll write you a recommendation."

I turn around, finding him staring at me, his eyes dark and stern, still glittering with unsaid sentiments. His hand covers the receiver on his phone. He swallows, the Adam's apple bobbing in his throat.

Wordlessly, I nod and offer a small smile.

He looks away, the icy mask of indifference slipping back on his face, as if the last fifteen minutes of interaction didn't happen at all.

I shut the door, leaning against the cool oak for support. Anything to help me regain my senses. Turning around, I look at the silver placard on the door. *Professor Ryland Anderson.*

"Ryland." I test out the name under my breath, the wings flapping wildly in my stomach and I realize I've never called him by his first name before.

A strong name. Just like him.

Ryland.

CHAPTER 15

Millie

Dear Mom,

I think he's the special someone for me, the man I told you before whose gaze sets me on fire. He's someone I feel an undeniable connection to. Someone worthy of the word "whirlwind." I think he hides his tattered heart behind a suit of armor, but he's hurting, just like me. And for the first time in my life, I want to heal him, because I think I understand him.

He sees me. The real me.

We're all types of wrong. But you'd understand, right? After all, you left your entire world behind to be with Dad, forsaking your wealth, status, your disapproving parents, all for the sake of love, a love that was a whirlwind.

His name is Ryland..and I think..he's my whirlwind.

Love, Millie

I WATCH THE SKIES dim, the clouds slowly encroaching on the blue. It's dreary and gloomy outside. The weather app says it shouldn't rain yet, not until this evening. But the view outside the classroom windows begs to differ. *Dammit. Isn't it supposed to be sunny all year round in LA? I must've forgotten how temperamental the weather can be during storm season.*

I stare at my dry clothes—a pair of dark blue jeans and a soft cream sweater that'll be a pain to wash. *Ugh. I should pack an umbrella in my bag from now on.* El Niño is no joke.

Students filter in, excited chatter erupting around me. My prime seating in the center of the front row offers me an unobstructed view of the small stage.

Of him.

"You're early." A wry drawl captures my attention.

"Of course," I wink, "and I saved you a seat too."

Jocelyn plops down heavily on the seat next to me. She has been half-present in class and at the apartment, but she hasn't told me why, and I don't want to pry. But if her dark eye circles and sallow skin are any sign, she must be going through something intense and personal.

"Want some gummy bears?" I take out a small packet from my bag and hand it to her. Maybe the sugar will perk her up.

She yawns and grabs the bag from me before slouching in her seat. "Thanks, girl. I'm so tired. I just want to sleep."

Turning to her, my brows crinkle with concern. "Seriously, Joss. Is everything okay? I'm worried about you. You didn't get home until close to midnight the last few days...not that I'm trying to be a stalker or anything."

She gives me a sad smile. "I'll be fine." She lets out a fake chuckle. "I'll be even better if I can pass this class."

"You can do it! I have faith in you. Did you get the notes I emailed you? If you have questions, just let me know."

"Thanks, girl." She glances away and scrutinizes her phone.

I frown and turn my attention toward the door, wondering when his tall, imposing frame will cross the threshold.

A nervous energy slithers through me at seeing him for the first time since after office hours last week. My skin feels sensitive, and the fabric on my sweater tickles my skin. The air smells like chalk dust mixed with wet earth. I sit up straighter and glance at the clock on top of the chalkboard. One minute before class begins.

As if on cue, and always on time, the door slams open and the room abruptly silences. Ryland storms in, a burst of crackling lightning and rioting winds, his steps faltering ever so slightly when he sees me. The slight halt to his hurried gait is almost imperceptible.

But I see it.

And my heart skips a beat. The connection from last week. It's still there.

His eyes flare and his lips part, a muscle feathering his beautiful jawline. He abruptly looks away and walks to a small desk and chair in the middle of the stage. He looks every inch a prince from the fairy tales...or perhaps, the villain, with his tall, dark looks and angry features.

Ryland shrugs out of his suit jacket, dove-gray today, and proceeds with his daily routine of taking out his cuff links, pocketing them, before slowly rolling up his shirt sleeves. It's like watching arm porn in slow motion.

I wet my lips and sit up straighter, trying to ignore the pulsing between my legs. My laptop is turned on, and I wait with bated breath for what he'll do next.

Will he address me? Acknowledge what happened in his office last week? Or will he pretend like it was nothing when it was *everything* to me?

"Class, I'm disappointed with the last papers you turned in." His stern voice sends ripples over my skin.

Ryland leans forward on his desk and scowls at us. "The average grade was a D, with only two papers earning As. If you can't even do well in this class, how will you do well in the real world?"

The room is silent, and I see students hang their heads in apparent shame.

"You may believe otherwise, but I don't wake up each day intending to fail you in class. I'm not here to 'get' you."

He frowns, his head swiveling to take in every one of us. "I want to prepare you for the future when the stakes are much higher. If anything, I want to leave a lasting legacy...for you."

Legacy.

My heart races at the mention of the word, reminiscent of the conversation we had in his office. *I want this to be my legacy.*

Ryland's eyes snare on mine, as if he too remembers our conversation. As if this is a slipup on his end. His jaw locks, and I see his hands clenching into tight fists.

He drags his gaze away and releases a deep breath. "And so, for the first time and most likely the last time, I'll give you another chance. Rewrite your papers and if you can turn in something more profound, something to change my mind, I'll use those grades as your final grades for the assignment."

He walks around the desk and props himself up against it. "Don't. Disappoint. Me."

The classroom is quiet as he splits the tall pile of essays on his desk with his TA and they walk around the room to hand out the papers to us. Tracking his movements with my eyes, I twist my fingers on top of the table, gnaw on my lip, and wait for my turn.

The stack of papers thins out over time until he is left with one. He pauses at the end of my aisle, his forehead pinching in concentration, his shoulders taut and raised. He runs a hand over his thick, luscious hair and finally turns toward me.

Our eyes catch and hold, intense grays against dark blues, stormy clouds hovering over deep cerulean seas, and I swallow, my breathing quickening with each step he takes, each step bringing him closer to me.

Hushed chatter fills the background as students talk amongst themselves, no doubt about their grades or comments on the papers, but I don't really notice. All I see is this hulking man striding toward me with the lethality of a predator in the woods who has identified his prey, his next meal.

"There are rumors he's a beast in bed and gets off from chasing willing women in their sex clubs. I totally wouldn't mind him hunting me down."

My classmate's words from the first day of class whispers across my mind and sharp heat shoots between my legs.

Tangled limbs. Sweat and bites. Having the control taken from me.

My lips part and my face feels warm. My sexual experiences with Lloyd had been forgettable. Lackluster. The man couldn't get a woman off if his life depended on it. Somehow, I don't think that would be the case with the towering man in front of me.

Ryland sets the paper face down on my desk and hovers above me briefly. He releases a deep exhale, one I can hear above the noise in the classroom. I put my hand on top of the paper to take it away from him before he stops me, his much larger hand pressing against mine, his pinkie grazing my thumb.

Leaning in ever so slightly, he whispers, his voice a gravelly seduction, "Good job...*Millie.*"

My name on his lips. A bolt of heat shoots straight between my thighs.

Unbidden, my tongue darts out to wet my lips and he freezes, his eyes glued to the motion. They darken and smolder, and in that instant, the rest of the room fades into darkness and my world is only him. The tempestuous charcoal pools holding me in place, drawing me closer. The heavy raggedness of his breathing. The small but distinct pressure of his little finger pressing against my thumb. The spicy citrus tinged with a masculine scent of the outdoors that's uniquely him.

This can't only be one-sided. My mind is groggy, drunk from the presence of Ryland Anderson.

After another second, he straightens up, his lips curled in a half-snarl, in disgust. *Danger.* He shoves his hands in his trouser pockets and stalks off, taking the maelstrom away with him, leaving me breathless all the same.

I flip over the paper and see his elegant, masculine scrawl on top.

"Strength is the morality of the man who stands out from the rest."

- Friedrich Nietzsche

Thought-provoking analysis of ethics and the greater good. I look forward to witnessing your accomplishments in the future. Your mother would be proud. After everything, you're still standing. Remember, you're a fighter too, and one day, you'll achieve your dreams.

- R.

My eyes prickle and burn. *He sees me. He understands me.* I look up, finding Ryland leaning once more against his desk, the heat of his gaze firmly on me.

Biting my lip, I smile shyly at him, only to watch his face darkening. If he didn't hand me back the paper himself, I'd think someone else wrote those comments.

Someone nudges my shoulder, and I'm tempted to ignore her.

"Psst. Millie, *Millie!*" Jocelyn whispers urgently next to me.

My mind still on the man before me, I answer, "Yeah?"

"What did you get?"

"An A."

She falls silent and I turn to look at her.

Jocelyn's eyes well with tears and her lips wobble. "I'm so going to fail this class."

She shows me her paper with a D scrawled on top.

My forehead pinches. "I'll help you study, Joss. You can do this. We still have time."

She shakes her head sadly and stares into the space in front of her.

Letting out a sigh, I turn my attention to the front of the room, where his fiery gaze meets mine once more.

Ryland's attention is unwavering, a solid beam of spotlight in a dark room. I can bask in the warmth of his presence, and I'll never be cold again. My eyes dart to his message on the paper before returning to his face. I arch my brow. *Do you mean it? What you wrote?*

He narrows his eyes, like he's reading my mind before tilting his head slightly to the side and returns a brief cock of his dark eyebrow, the one with the small scar. *Of course I do.*

He then flattens his lips and crosses his arms before tilting up his head, so he's literally looking down at me as if to say, *don't overthink this. You're not that special.*

Squaring my shoulders, I thrust my chest out, determined not to cower underneath his scrutiny.

Fragments of our interactions sift through my mind. His gentle caresses. Whispered words. My kiss on his thumb. My fevered dreams and chaotic emotions. *This can't only be one-sided.* This intensity. This pulsating chemistry between us. The palpable tension. Things that should never appear between a professor and his student, with over fifteen years of life between us.

I shouldn't encourage this. I shouldn't test him. My reputation is at stake. The honors program, my future, everything.

But the whirlwind.

A spark of deviousness tears through me. I want to see what he'll do next. Leaning forward slightly on my desk, I unleash a vixen I didn't know was inside me all along. I smooth my fingers over my long, thick hair, and slowly twirl a lock around and around, winding it in circles, curling it over my delicate wrist, imagining it is him doing it.

His eyes focus on the movement, the graphite turning almost pitch black in the distance. Then, I wet my lips again, a move that was subconscious before, but this time, it's a deliberate slow, sensual lick, feeding into the fire burning in my veins, slithering between my legs.

His eyes flare and the muscles in his arms flex and ripple as I see his fingers dig into the desk behind him, his knuckles stark white. A flush creeps up his tanned skin and his strong chest rises and falls like tumultuous ocean waves. The throbbing vein on his forehead makes a reappearance.

Feminine pride sweeps through me, and I lower my eyes, gazing at him through my lashes, and break into a smile, a warmth spreading through every atom of my body.

"Thank you," I mouth.

He flinches and falters before swallowing again, the vein still rioting against his forehead. A muscle pulses in his cheek and he gives me the barest nod.

It's not one-sided.

I smile, and suddenly, the incoming storm doesn't feel too gloomy anymore.

CHAPTER 16

It's wrong.

This craving, bordering on obsession.

But like an addict, I can't stay away. And it's getting worse, lecture after lecture, the temptation taking on a life of its own.

My eyes unwittingly find her in the sea of students. My ears automatically pick up the light, sweet voice, just like the meadowlark's song. My fingers...well, they itch to be near her, to feel her soft skin, which blooms into a pink flush in my presence.

The students are clustered in small groups today, preparing to present an argument on a case study, where I'll poke holes in their positions.

Why? Because that's what the business community will do to them when they're out in the workforce. To succeed, not only do you need to make the best choice for the situation, but you also need to defend your position against critics.

My attention is captivated by her, this water nymph who seems so delicate and vulnerable and yet so strong at the same time. A mesmerizing contradiction. Life has been rough to her, if what she told me in the office before was true.

My mind drifts to the most erotic and anguish-laden fifteen minutes of my life again for the thousandth time this past week. The way she brought in the sunshine from the outside and yet seemed so cold. How her soulful, sapphire eyes were so sad, but she tried to hide behind a practiced, fake smile, one I recognized immediately because it is something I often wear myself.

Then she told me about the loss of her mother, a pain I felt viscerally because at that moment, we were the same person, both trying to mend a hole in our hearts, a hopeless, fruitless task. And her tears...the liquid marring her brilliant eyes...they were speared into my chest, and I could feel its impact wrenching the air out of my lungs.

Nothing could prepare me for the burst of possessiveness, the burning compulsion to protect her at that moment. The ethics of the situation, our age gap, the complete power imbalance, all reasons I'd repeat to myself every time before class, before I knew I'd see her, flew out the window, merely mist vaporized into thin air.

This has to stop. This madness. This rumination.

I stare at her right now, knowing I shouldn't. She's laughing at a group mate, a slim Asian girl I've seen her sit next to from time to time.

There's a lightness in her frame now. She is still standing before me, head held high, her effervescence not dimmed one bit. In fact, she seems even more determined to prove to the world nothing can snuff out her spirit.

It's a beautiful sight to behold.

Her fingers absentmindedly trail over her cheek and curl a lock of wavy hair behind her ear, and my own fingers twitch.

I remember every little thing about our interaction in my office—how soft her cheeks were, the creamy skin tinged with swaths of pink, which darkened with every second I kept my hands on her under the guise of wiping those tears from her face.

How, even during her pain, she was able to comfort me when my darkness leaked out. How she seemed to truly understand and wanted to set me free. Then there was that tentative swipe of tongue on my thumb, the sharp pleasure shooting straight into my veins.

I wanted her then. To wrap her in my arms and protect her from the elements, from the rain, so she'd never have to be a water nymph again.

Every moment in class with her ever since last week has been torture.

I want to wind those luscious strands around my hand, much like she did earlier last week when she was teasing me with her coy smile.

Then there was the incident with the erotic sound clip she was listening to, and fuck did I want to act out that scene with her. I want to pull her head back to expose her throbbing pulse, then—

This is wrong. Forbidden. You're a fucking ethics professor. Stop it, Ryland.

Her eyes flicker to me, as if sensing the darkness in my thoughts, and whatever she sees causes the smile to slide off her face. Her chest swells and falls, and that enticing pink flush is spreading across her skin once more.

Tearing my gaze away, I check my watch and clear my throat. "Time's up. Group one, you're first. Who have you chosen to represent you in this debate?"

The cluster of students in the first row all turn their heads and stare at Millie. She does the twisty fingers thing again, but this time, her eyes hold a spark of deviousness, like she knew the darkness of my thoughts just moments before.

"I'm representing group one, Professor." She steps away from behind her desk and stands up tall.

A fire churns in my gut and I fight every impulse to step back or stalk toward her. With a flick of my hand, I motion for her to proceed. "The floor is yours, Ms. Callahan."

"The case study revolves around the pricing of a new medicine that'll stop the progression of kidney disease in patients and can decrease the likelihood of patients needing dialysis or a kidney transplant in their lifetimes," she begins, her voice wavering as we all focus our attentions on her. Her fingers continue to pull and twist with each other.

"Gentech Pharmaceutical has been criticized about the exorbitant prices of this lifesaving, miracle drug." She looks at her teammates, who are nodding in apparent encouragement.

She turns back to me, her voice stronger and louder. "We're here to argue pricing the drug at such a high cost is immoral and unethical. Under Kantianism, as members of society, we should focus on Gentech's underlying duty to patients. They have a moral obligation to treat these patients ethically, which includes allowing them fair access to the drug. If the price is too expensive, Gentech is condemning these patients to death."

I bite back a smile. I expect this argument from her. It's one I've heard from many students before, young people with an interminable amount of hope with little to no experience with the ugliness of the real world, where sustaining on hope by itself will starve you.

"In addition, based on the Rights Theory, human beings have the fundamental right of access to health care. Excessively high prices for this drug will violate this essential right. And after all, as a pharmaceutical company, what is Gentech's mission statement? According to their website, it's 'To better mankind by innovating with integrity, and to deliver medical treatments that will help patients prevail over diseases and improve patient outcomes.' How can they achieve that if they aren't even allowing lifesaving medicine to land in the hands of those who need it the most?"

Millie pauses, excitement pouring out of her in spades, her eyes brimming with passionate fervor.

The heat simmering in my veins burns through me and I begin my rebuttal. "Pharmaceutical research is expensive and takes years to complete. Thousands of man hours, hundreds of failed projects, many revisions, before a viable product can be put out. You say a pharmaceutical company's purpose is to help ease the suffering of the common man from diseases. How can they do this without recouping their costs?"

She furrows her brows, her mouth parting to respond, but I hold up my hand. "You talk of Kantianism's focus on duty and the Rights Theory's focus on fundamental patient rights. What about the duties and rights of Gentech to themselves and their employees and shareholders? Should they license their patent for cheap to other companies so the price of the drug will drop, knowing that'll be at a significant cost to them, one that might threaten the company's wellbeing and viability, and endanger the livelihood of the thousands of employees working for them? Don't they have a right to their intellectual property?"

"But those are only monetary and capitalistic concerns," she retorts, her eyes flashing in anger. "How can that measure against the value of human life? How are those two things even *remotely* comparable?"

God, the fire in her eyes is fucking intoxicating. I want to bathe in it and control it. I want to let it wash over me, curing me of my darkness.

There's a hush in the classroom now, everyone avidly watching the debate.

No, they are watching her.

This luminous nymph clearly out of her depths on dry land, yet still attempting to wield the currents of water around her, brandishing her only weapon the best she can.

Heated blood travels to my cock, the discomfort quickly becoming clear by the bulge in my pants, but I find myself not caring. Instead, I step closer, entranced by her.

Fuck, I should step away. Stay back. But like a Siren, she lures me closer with her song.

But I'll only hurt her in the end. My abyss will snuff out her flames. My prison will clip her wings. My darkness will corrupt her light.

"You know, pharmaceutical companies are typically working on multiple research projects at the same time. Including medicines to cure *cancer.*" I can't stop the poison from seeping out of my voice—to punish her, to punish me for this insanity brewing between us.

You're an asshole, Ryland. Fuck, you're a grade A prick.

She flinches, no doubt thinking about her mom.

I continue, "If we went with your theory of making the medicine readily accessible to everyone at a cost to Gentech, then they won't have the funds to continue their research for their cancer drug and tens of other drugs for other human diseases."

I take a few more steps forward, but she refuses to cower before me even when I loom above her. Instead, her eyes are chilly swirls of treacherous seas, threatening to level me with her glare.

Pressing further, my voice hard and low, I ask, "What about utilitarianism? Don't we want to focus on the greater good? Are we saying we'll forsake the lives of millions with other life-threatening conditions such as cancer or lung disease, diabetes, or other plight, just so folks with kidney disease can all get the aid they need at a cheap cost?"

Her lips curl, and a mist appears in her eyes. Millie fists her hands by her sides. Somehow, I don't think these are tears of sadness.

She's furious.

The anger leaching off her body is the most addictive drug. Fucking intoxicating. I can't get enough.

I lean forward, the last vestiges of logic pulling me back just enough, so we maintain the barest respectable distance between us. "Do those other patients' lives not matter to you? What about their families? Or maybe *a little girl missing her mom?*"

She flinches again, her mouth parting in shock.

I'm such a fucking bastard. I want to bash my head against the wall, but like a sadist, I continue.

I rasp, my voice heavy and thick. Almost guttural. "How can we be so selfish and only think about the individual or small groups of people and not for the greater good, the rest of the population?"

We can't be so selfish. I can't be so selfish.

She delivers a blistering blow, which in my twisted mind, seems more like the pleasurable pain of a lover's nails digging into your back during a rough night of fucking.

"You *bastard*," she seethes, the insult a quiet scathing whisper only I can hear.

I smile, the sight causing her to recoil. *That's right, Millie. Stay away from me. I am a bastard. One that'll ruin you, and one that is fucking hard for you right now.*

Clearing her throat, she straightens up even more. She tilts her chin up in defiance, and responds, "How do you measure the price of one patient's life versus the other? Who made you God? When human beings give themselves the right to value one sick patient's life over another, that's when society is corrupted beyond repair."

Her backhand is forceful, a powerful liver punch, and I stagger back, my hands shaking, my lungs stealing the air from around me, the heat in my veins now a full boil, scorching me from within, charring my insides beyond recognition.

And yet, I savor the pain, the burn, the sharpness of her eyes on me, slicing me to pieces.

It makes me feel alive and free.

"If we can't empathize with the individual, our sorrows for society's plight are just *bullshit* and plain lip service." Her heated gaze softens, the rest of the words unspoken.

"*Without considering individual happiness, how can we achieve happiness in the group?*" Her wise words from her first essay in class.

Suddenly, the air feels thin in the room, her attention too raw. I feel exposed. Naked. The horrid dream of showing up to work without a stitch of clothing on.

She sees me, just like I see her.

Kindred spirits.

"What if the individual wants something inappropriate for the greater good? And shatters the society's rules for right and wrong?" I murmur, staring at her plump lips.

So soft. So inviting.

I crave a taste.

Millie's eyes widen, her pulse feathering her slender neck. She exhales. "Maybe it's time to redefine the rules then." Her reply is as light as air but is taut with meaning.

I swallow, my gaze capturing hers again, watching those blue eyes darken, the pupils slowly encroaching on her irises, her breaths quickening, each movement causing her chest to swell and tremble.

Someone coughs in the background, the sharp sound shaking me out of my trance. I clear my throat and step back, the cool air of the room finally knocking some sense into me. "An enticing argument, Ms. Callahan. Well done."

Looking up, I find the other students sitting with rapt attention, the spark of insight appearing in their eyes. A few teams gather around and whisper passionately amongst themselves, clearly wanting to amend their argument with whatever new ideas the debate just now generated. My chest hums in satisfaction. This is why I want to teach.

I feel the heat of her gaze on me as I walk back toward my desk, needing distance from her, this woman who threatens to unravel everything I stand for.

My temptation.

The rest of the class passes by quickly, with each group ardently defending their opinions. Ultimately, we realize there is no black or white in this situation, no win-win solution.

Millie is quiet for the rest of the period. The variations of her—the flirtatious vixen from the beginning of the lecture, the nervous student finding her voice, the quiet seductress passionately defending her opinions—have receded into the background. In their place is someone contemplative, and I can sense the myriad of thoughts coursing through her mind.

Every quirk of brow, every rippling of her throat, every scrunch of her nose. Her thoughts are written clearly on her face in a language only I can read.

Confusion. Lust. Admiration. Excitement. And so much hunger.

My hands fist behind my back. I want to satiate that hunger, so she'll never be wanting for anything again.

A timer buzzes and class ends.

"Excellent discussion today, class. Remember, the revised papers are due by Friday."

The students hurry out of the classroom, excitement seeping through their voices as conversation topics range from weekend plans to college sports. I see the Asian girl, Jocelyn, I believe, dragging Millie out of the classroom. Keeping my eyes away from my temptation, I pack my materials in my briefcase before restoring my sleeves and cuff links.

Then I slide on my suit jacket, grab my umbrella, and head toward the stairwell.

The mood of the sky has taken a dreary turn during the last hour, the storm drenching the pavement and courtyard when I finally make it to the entrance.

The trees rustle as an icy breeze kicks up in the air. The alluring scent of jasmine with a hint of vanilla reaches my nose from the open doors.

Her scent.

The hairs on my forearms stand at attention, my body already attuned to the woman I'm sure is standing outside.

I can feel her presence like a hunter sensing his prey.

Snapping open my umbrella, I step onto the small patch of pavement covered by the cement overhang of the building. Sure enough, Millie stands there, her hands rubbing her arms as she stares forlornly at the rain.

She shivers and blows out a deep breath, like she's trying to psych herself up to run into the elements, returning to her state as a water nymph after an excursion on dry land. Visions flood my mind—the first day when I met her, when I found her on the floor of my classroom drenched head-to-toe and when she looked so cold and lonely standing in front of my desk in my office, clutching the pot of daffodils.

The same overwhelming need to protect her fills me, an inferno blazing my insides.

I don't want her to become a water nymph again. I want to see her fly in the skies like the meadowlark.

I know I should ignore her and walk away. But I can't.

Wordlessly, I stride up to her and place my free hand on hers. Her tempting lips part in surprise as she looks at me and for a moment, a brief, selfish moment, I stand there before her, my larger hand on top of her smaller, chilled one, and just look at her.

My eyes rove hungrily over her features, committing them to memory—the thick, shiny chocolate strands billowing in the wind, sending a stronger current of jasmine laced with vanilla toward me, her special brand of magic, the eyes like tranquil waters soothing the ragged edges of my soul, the heart-shaped face, her nose already tipped pink from the elements.

The cool breeze sweeps by, and a lock of hair falls over her face. Wetting my parched lips, I gently brush the strands to the side and tuck them behind her ear. Millie's eyes widen, her pupils dilating. Her breathing quickens, the pulse thudding rapidly in her throat.

I feel the mirrored frenzied beats inside me.

Step away, the wind whispers. *Do the right thing. Be the bastard.*

But my nostrils flare and I tangle my fingers with hers, my soul allowing for one more selfish moment, one more taste of freedom. My long fingers glide over hers and a thousand sparks light up my skin, sending heated blood south, the simple touch far more erotic than anything I've experienced in the past, with nameless, faceless women.

I don't remember any of them.

I only see her.

Giving her hand a squeeze, I open her palm and curl it around the handle of my umbrella. She won't need to be cold again with me here.

Turning away, I walk into the rain, letting the elements soak my body once more. I feel her stare on my back, but I don't turn around.

Instead, I let the rain wrap me in her embrace. A sharp gust whisks by, an icy front shocking to the senses.

I should be cold, but for the first time, amidst the pouring rain usually making me feel alive when the icy chill settles into my veins, I'm not. Instead, I'm kept warm by the heated intent of her gaze on my back, and my soul has never felt freer.

CHAPTER 17

A KNOT FORMS IN my stomach as I stand before his closed office doors once more. This time, it's not from nervousness. It goes beyond that. It's like I feel the verge of something monumental happening and these are the few precious moments of calm before it hits. My heart is rattling like a runaway train behind my rib cage, and I clutch the small paper box tighter in my hand.

Heaving out a breath, I knock.

Knock. Knock.

"Come in." His voice is terse and serious, as usual.

I used to think it was cold and unfeeling, but now I know better. The baritone holds a hard edge but is filled to the brim with banked emotions. The icy man with the warmest touches and gentlest caresses. The one who wordlessly gave me his umbrella so I could stay warm while he walked into the frigid rain.

The quiet, selfless giver.

Opening the door, I find the man who's been haunting my dreams in a state of undress. Ryland faces away from me and I see his naked back, just for a brief second, before he deftly dons a fresh shirt. My mouth runs dry at the quickest flash of tanned skin and corded muscles, the ones I've suspected are underneath his tailored shirts and bespoke suits all along. He's so huge, all coiled power and banked energy.

He can easily overpower me. My thighs clench at the thought coming from nowhere.

"Sorry, I'm running late for a gala." His voice is a tendered scrape on my fevered skin and my core pulses, a bolt of heat settling in between my thighs.

"Professor, it's me, Millie." I'm proud of how steady I sound. Completely at odds with the roiling of my gut.

He freezes for a beat before turning around, his fingers quickly buttoning his shirt, hiding his broad chest from my view. I catch a glint of silver, a pendant of some sort, before that gets hidden from me as well.

"Yes?" His face is aloof. I shove the box toward him, and he frowns before taking it from me. "What's this?"

"Thanksgiving is coming up, and I was doing my holiday shopping earlier and saw this and thought of you...to thank you for your tutelage this semester and your support." *When I was crying in your office. When you offered me your umbrella.*

For seeing me.

I fiddle with the hem of my jean jacket. "I was going to give this to you before winter break, for Christmas, but with the weather and everything, I figure you can use it now."

Ryland stares at the package in his hand, his brows pinched, before opening the lid. He takes out the scarf I spent hours knitting—a navy cable pattern with a thick center twist. This is my third attempt. I started on the project after the disaster with the mittens.

I slide my fingers into the pockets of my pants to hide the redness on my fingertips. I poked myself so many times with the big needles as I hurried to finish it last night.

"I-It's cheap. Just a small token of thanks. For e-everything," I stammer and lie, watching his long fingers curl around the soft yarn, kneading the material.

"I figure it's cold and rainy and sometimes I see you without an umbrella." *Standing so lonely in the rain, so I hope this gives you warmth.*

I don't say those words. I know we can't cross this line. Unlike many things in the real world, this isn't remotely a gray situation. This is black and white. We *cannot* get involved. His reputation and mine, his career, and my future.

It's a nonstarter.

"The rain makes me feel alive," he murmurs, his fingers slowly stroking the scarf.

My heart hiccups at the longing in his eyes. "And you feel you aren't alive right now?"

He stills for a beat before resuming the stroking. "No. I'm merely living." He doesn't stare at me. "I sound like an asshole, don't I?"

"No. You're only human. Perhaps people from the outside only see your name, your net worth, but wealth doesn't equate to happiness, and sometimes..." I pause and bite my lip, waiting to see if I've offended him. He doesn't speak or move. "Sometimes, I think wealth comes with a price, with responsibilities and shackles average people don't see."

Ryland's nostrils flare and he slowly lifts his gaze. Penetrating. Haunting. Aching. The heat of his stare on me, like I'm the center of his universe, is so intoxicating. My fingers twitch with the need to touch him, to smooth the furrow of his brows, the lines around his mouth.

I whisper, "So, no. I don't think you're an asshole. I think you're someone who's tired of paddling in the deep ocean and wishing there was a life raft near you."

His eyes darken and glitter. He swallows, the Adam's apple of his throat bobbing up and down.

Maybe I can be your life raft. My pulse riots at the thought.

He clears his throat and sets the scarf down.

"Thank you," he replies, his voice gruff.

Ryland's gaze remains on me as he grabs a long scrap of black silk from his desk and wraps it around his neck—a traditional self-tie bow tie. His face is impassive, but his fingers tremble slightly as he attempts to fashion the fabric into something presentable. His motions are stilted, uncoordinated, and those piercing gray eyes of his flash in frustration, in anger.

I walk around the desk and stand before him, tentatively reaching out.

"M-May I?" I motion to the thick silk ribbon he's murdering with his hands.

Another second passes by, and those eyes of his grow darker as he gives me a curt nod.

Stepping forward until I'm a few inches before him, the first time I'm so close to him since that day in his office, I'm hit with his unique scent of nature and oranges, mixed with his own manly fragrance, and a hint of minty aftershave. Goosebumps form on my skin as I slowly loop the silk around his neck, my fingers grazing his heated chest, feeling the tension radiating from it.

We're standing so close and yet it feels so far apart. Our breaths mingle in the tiny sliver of space between us and my pussy throbs. I feel my nipples prickling underneath my thin bra, and I pray they aren't showing through the sweater. His breathing is harsher, louder, like he too is having a difficult time with this proximity.

I finish knotting the silk into a perfect bow and press my hands on his hard chest, stealing a quick touch from him. His muscles ripple underneath my palms and I quickly let go before stepping back.

Looking up, the expression on his face takes my breath away. His charcoal pools are pitch black and affixed to my lips, his cheeks and forehead are tinged pink. Those perfectly refined lips are parted. A tongue dips out. It's almost like he's imagining how I taste.

My core clenches, and I feel wetness seeping into my panties.

"How do you know how to tie a bow tie?" he rasps.

I still haven't stepped away. We're as close as two people can be without touching.

"I had to do it for my brother from time to time. And I enjoy doing it for people I..." *care about.* But I can't say those words out loud. Instead, I quickly amend, "People who need the help."

More heated looks and heavy breaths, each of us on standing on a tightrope suspended between two skyscrapers, hoping we won't plummet to our deaths.

"You look good." I wet my lips and flash him a tentative smile.

"I hate dressing up in penguin suits, but it's part of my job." A boyish grin appears on his face, an expression making him look years younger, and my heart swoops and falls to the floor.

"What would you prefer to do if you had free time?"

"Hunting. Reading in my cabin in upstate New York." He rakes his hand over his thick, tousled hair. He grimaces, and a flush spreads to his neck. "Birdwatching."

I try and fail to stop a giggle from escaping my mouth.

He bites his lower lip. "What's so funny? An old man like me can't like birdwatching? I've heard it's an old person hobby."

I shake my head. "No, it's not that. I'm laughing because you look so happy when you talk about your hobbies. I'm glad you have an escape. Everyone needs one. Mine is gardening. I like to nurture the plants and flowers, to feel the life at my fingertips. It's why I prefer potted plants over bouquets."

My fingers tangle with each other. My eyes dip down to his chest and a heat crawls up my face. "And I also like knitting," my gaze darts up to his as I stammer, "n-not that I knitted the scarf, of course." Heat rises to my face, and I curse my inability to lie. "Some say knitting is an old person hobby too...and you're *not* old."

A few seconds pass by before he answers, the lightness in his voice moments ago nowhere to be found. "I'm at least fifteen years older than you." It's a warning, but it might as well be foreign language to my ears.

"Age isn't only measured by years but also by experience." *Does a mere number matter when I feel my soul calling out to you?*

A muscle pulses in his jaw before he tears his eyes away from my face and steps back, shrugging on his formal jacket. "Thank you for helping with the bow tie and for the gift."

He doesn't look at me now and my heart pinches at the rejection.

I turn back at the doorway and find him holding my blue scarf in his hand, slowly looping it around his wrist.

Around, and around, and around.

———— ✦ ————

I come home later that day to the sound of gut-wrenching sobs.

"Joss?" I call out as I set my keys and bag on the glass dining table and head toward her room.

The sounds are muted now, muffled sniffling from behind her door, which is cracked open. Quietly, I enter her dark, musty room and find her sitting on her bed, her face buried in her palms. Her beautiful, shiny black hair is in disarray, like she has spent the last ten minutes pulling at it.

"What's wrong?" I ask gently as I take a seat next to her and place my hand on her back, rubbing soothing motions on her tensed muscles. "Tell me. Maybe I can help."

She shakes her head. "No one can help me. Not even God is listening."

"You can talk to me. It's better than bottling it up inside." *And I should know that since I'm an expert at burying my emotions.*

Jocelyn murmurs into her hands, "I'm failing Anderson's class. I know I shouldn't be surprised, since I haven't been in class half the time. Even my revised paper was a D."

"I can help you study. And worse comes to worst, you can take it again next year. One bad grade won't affect you."

"No. You don't understand," she turns to me, her eyes teary and bloodshot, "I'm doing poorly in *all* my classes this year. Anderson's class is the closest I have to passing. If I fail his class too, I'll be put on academic probation, and I can't do that. I can't disappoint my mom like that."

Jocelyn grabs my hands and clutches them tightly. "Millie, please help me. You have to help me. Don't you see? Millie," her voice pleading and desperate, "the reason I haven't been in class a lot is because my mom is in the hospital. She has breast cancer."

Tears are streaming down her face now, but she makes no move to wipe them. "Things don't look good, Millie. The doctors don't think she'll last the holiday season."

My heart plummets and the old ache, one I thought had scabbed over a long time ago, splits wide open.

"Mommy?" I bury my face on top of her chest as Dad cries in the background. The machines beep and hum in the hospital room. Everything smells strange. Sterile. I hate this smell.

"Sweetie pie," Mommy whispers, her thin, bony hands stroking my hair. "Don't be sad. Mommy is going to heaven. It's beautiful and Mommy won't be sick anymore."

Dad makes a choking sound. He called Adrian a few minutes ago. He's coming from his job at the supermarket.

Tears spring from my eyes as I clutch her skinny body. She doesn't smell like Mommy anymore. She's barely warm. I shake my head hard. "No, Mommy. I don't want you to go to heaven. I want you to stay with us. I want more bedtime stories and kisses."

Her voice is weak, and she coughs, her entire body shaking, like coughing is making her very, very tired. "I...I want to stay here with you too, sweetie pie," her voice is thick, and I hear her sniffle, "but...it's my time to go. My turn. Just like you do at school, right? Take turns. But I'll be watching over you, Adrian, and Daddy, and I'll love you forever and ever. Be brave, Millie. Take care of Adrian and Daddy for me. They need you to be strong. Give them the kisses and smiles, okay, honey?"

I cover her with my body and press kisses on her chilly face. Please don't leave us, Mommy.

Jocelyn's weeping brings me back to the present but the memories of Mom's last day on earth are sharp, the pain so cutting, so painful, it feels as if it happened yesterday.

"We'll get through this, Joss," I murmur, my voice thick as I'm assaulted by the memories of the past. "Have you talked to your professors? Maybe they'll give you an extension?"

"I asked! They all said there was nothing they could do." Her face crumbles. "Apparently, too many students used family emergencies as excuses in the past, so now they're no longer able to give out extensions."

Shit. There must be a way to help her.

"I'll help you study. We'll cram the knowledge into your brain if it's the last thing we do."

Jocelyn shakes her head, her shoulders slumped. "I-I don't know if I can do this."

Swallowing the lump in my throat, I grab her hand and pull her off the bed before dragging her to the living room. *I need to help her...to help the little girl who is crying by her mother's bedside.*

I gently push her onto the sofa and grab my bag from the dining table. "You *can*. For your mom. You have to do this. We have no time to lose."

Pulling out my notes and textbooks from the class, I heave out a deep breath. *She can't disappoint her dying mother. It'll be her biggest regret.*

She slouches on her seat, her posture defeated.

"Joss! We got this, okay?" I lean down and hold her clammy hands in mine. "We got this."

She nods and she whispers, "Yes. I got this."

I walk through the first set of notes with her. Her eyes are glazed over, but I see her trying to pay attention.

"The most important theories he'll probably cover are these..."

We spend hours reviewing the materials and taking practice exams online and from the back of the textbooks. By the time midnight rolls around, I've polished off two cups of coffee, a sandwich, and a bag of gummy bears. Jocelyn nibbles on her sandwich as tears slip down her face. She shakes her head in defeat.

She isn't doing well. Her best score has been a C minus so far.

"What am I going to do? I can't do this, Millie. I might have retained a third of what you just went over with me." Her face crumbles and she sets aside her half-eaten meal.

I fist my hands on my lap and take a seat next to her. "Try your best. Just try your best. We'll continue studying. Pull an all-nighter. We can do this."

Jocelyn pleas, her watery eyes staring into mine, "I don't want to ask this, but I'm desperate, Millie." She takes a deep breath. "For the exam, can we sit in the back? You take your test and I take mine, but if I need to...and I'll try not to, maybe I can peek at your answers?"

What? Shock tears through me. Seeing my frozen expression, she sits up, her voice urgent. "But I'll try not to...I really will. But I need help, Millie. I have no one else to go to."

"But that's wrong, Joss. It's not right. Isn't that cheating?" And *he* will be so angry. He hates cheaters and rule breakers.

Jocelyn shakes her head vehemently. "It isn't cheating! Well, not completely, right? If anything, I'm the cheater and not you. You aren't taking the test for me...but I might need help with a question or two. It'll be a safety net for me."

Her brown eyes light up for the first time since I got home earlier. "Maybe I won't need help. But please, I need this safety net, Millie. There are two hundred of us in the classroom. No one will focus on us. No one will know."

Her bottom lip wobbles and she repeats, "And you're not taking the test for me, right? You're taking the test for yourself. Please, Millie. I wouldn't ask this of you if I wasn't desperate."

It's not really cheating. I'm just taking the test for myself and she's doing the same for herself. Maybe she won't need the help. Her words bounce around in my brain. My heart thuds in a rapid rhythm.

Somehow, I don't think he'd see it this way. Shame washes over me and curls around my gut. I can't believe I'm considering this. I'm the rule follower, the straight-A student.

Taking in her teary eyes once more, I'm hit with a sharp pinch of pain as I remember the little girl inside me, the one who cried herself to sleep after Mom passed away in the hospital, the girl with the broken heart which has never truly healed.

I pray Jocelyn won't need my help during the test.

I curl my arms around her and wrap her in a tight hug, my eyes wet with tears, an aching hole in my heart. "Shh... Let me think about it, Joss. Shh..."

I'm good at hiding myself from others around me. I have a lifetime of experience, after all. His intense eyes flash into my brain and I shake my head, my chest feeling heavy. *He won't know. And maybe she won't need my help.*

Jocelyn shakes in my arms, her sobbing loud in the room.

I rub circles on her back, feeling all the bottled-up pain and sadness pouring out of her body. "Shhh... I'm here, Joss. I'm here for you."

CHAPTER 18

Something is wrong today.

I can't place it, can't pinpoint it, but I feel it deep in my gut, and my gut is never wrong. It's what makes me a good businessman.

The class is quiet as the students focus intently on their exams. It's the last exam of the year before the final paper is due mid-December. It's weighed the heaviest, but by now, after a few months of debates, policy papers, and hours of coaching in office hours, I'm hopeful the class will perform well.

She isn't sitting in her usual spot today, front and center a few feet away from me, my temptation within arm's reach. Instead, she's sitting in the back with her friend, Jocelyn, in a shadowed corner of the classroom, like she's ashamed of something and wants to be invisible. But how can she be invisible? It's impossible. She shines brighter than the sun cutting through the clouds on a rainy day.

Jocelyn coughs and I see Millie glancing up, her teeth savagely attacking her bottom lip. She sneaks a quick look at her friend before shuffling in her chair. Then her eyes dart to mine and quickly flicker away.

Something is definitely wrong.

Quicksilver slowly seeps into my veins, and a foreboding heaviness settles on top of my lungs. My stomach flips.

It reminds me of the dread I felt at the playground right before school was dismissed the day Mom died. The sun was shining brightly, the usual New York humidity in the air. Friends were running around playing tag or kicking a ball across the lush, green lawn, not caring if they were making their uniforms dirty. It was a normal day. But my hackles were up. Something felt horribly wrong.

The hour passes by quickly—a strange, eerie calm—and instead of being one of the first students to hand in her paper, she's one of the last, along with her friend.

Millie keeps her eyes down as she walks up to my desk, her shoulders hunched, and a thin layer of sweat beads on her forehead. Her test paper is crumpled at the corners from her tight grip. She lets out a soft sigh before placing the paper on top of the stack of exams on the table.

A nervous energy filters through me, and I stare at her bowed head, silently beckoning to her. *Look at me, little lark. Tell me what's wrong, so I can fix it.*

She doesn't look up, doesn't try to catch my eyes, or flash me that sweet smile of hers. Instead, she and Jocelyn slip out of the classroom, as quiet as phantoms.

I release a stale breath. I want to go after her. To fight and defend her against whatever is plaguing her. To be her avenging warrior.

"Professor Anderson? I have a question regarding next week's class," a student asks.

Giving the closed door one last glance, I turn to the jock in front of me. "Yes?"

It's for the best. The distance.

But why does it feel so wrong?

"Professor Anderson, here are the top ten scorers on the exam as you requested." Johnny, my TA, who helps me with grading sometimes, hands me a small stack of papers.

I always skim through all the graded exams, but I like to read the top scorers in detail. The insightfulness in them usually has my heart pounding, and a warmth filling my veins.

They're a reminder of why I love this job and how I'm shaping my legacy. They tell me to continue, despite Fleur taking up my entire life, leaving me little to no time for myself. No hobbies other than the very occasional trips to the forest to birdwatch or hunt. No women other than mindless fucks in Noire, a way for my body to satiate the beast inside me. But despite everything, I still carve out the precious hours for academia.

"Thank you, Johnny. You can go home now."

He nods before slinging his messenger bag over his shoulders and walking out of my office, leaving me in blessed silence.

I flip through the pile of exams, wanting to see what my little lark has come up with.

My lips tilt in a smile as I take in the familiar feminine script, beautiful like art, on one of the papers. *Of course, she's one of the top scorers.* A thrill sweeps through me, and I eagerly grip the pages and begin reading. Every answer is immaculately thought out. I can feel her passion in her words. *God, she'll become a damn good educator someday.*

Setting aside her test, I take the next exam in the stack, noting the name *Jocelyn Song*. Interesting. Jocelyn hasn't been doing well in the class. I wonder if Millie helped her friend study.

My eyes skim over the responses—some are clunky, but the correct sentiments are there. Nonetheless, I'm impressed, since this is a significant improvement compared to her past assignments and exams.

I'm about to set the exam aside, but something stops me...something small and insignificant but raises my hackles.

Frowning, I pick up Millie's test once more. I scan through the answers, noting the phrase that prickles my mind.

One must consider individual happiness in order to achieve happiness in the group.

She made a similar sentiment in her first paper, the one I read on the plane while traveling back to New York for Dad's birthday dinner.

Flipping to the same question in Jocelyn's exam...there it is. *Verbatim.*

A breath lodges in my throat as the warmth inside my chest quickly roils and churns, changing flavor. The thumping in my heart becomes a chaotic riot.

Sweat gathers on my upper lip as I review their exams side by side, including the multiple-choice questions. There are differences, a few questions Millie gets right that Jocelyn doesn't, phrasing of sentences that are slightly different between the two of them. But they express the same sentiments, the same opinions.

I shake my head in disbelief and fall back into my chair.

The furtive glances between her and her friend. Her sitting in the back of the room. Every little innocuous move from this morning. The complete one eighty in Jocelyn's performance on this test.

Something is off. This doesn't make any sense.

My lungs ache. My breathing comes in heavy pants. I can only come to one conclusion in my mind.

Cheating.

The word echoes in my mind. But it can't be. *She can't be a cheater.* She can't be the same as the others. She can't be the same as *her*.

"You're a fucking cheater, Sydney." I staggered back as I stared at the beautiful girl in front of me, the girl of Maxwell's dreams...and of mine.

"Ryland, please. You don't understand. I...I love him too. But we married too young. I don't think I realized, but I've learned it's possible to love two people at the same time. I can't get you out of my mind, Ryland." She stepped forward, each movement a betrayal to my brother, her *husband*, the man she eloped with after high school graduation.

I'd never seen Maxwell so happy before. The sparkle in his eyes. His usually rare smile not leaving his face. It was like he stepped into the sunlight from the shadows, and he was warm for the first time.

He told me the other night, before we went back to our rooms at the estate, "I'm so happy, Ryland. This curse is bullshit. Look at us, we're still standing. Sydney is still alive and well. We beat the curse. And one day, in a few years when I'm older, I can tell Dad. I'll tell him I don't need to marry some girl I don't know. I already have a wife I love, and everything is fine. All fucking superstitions."

Tears fell from her lush green eyes, marring the soft cheeks I'd admired from afar. She stood an inch before me, my back plastered against the wall in front of my bedroom, which was right next to Maxwell's room.

"I've thought about it. Long and hard. And I realize, if I have to choose, it'll be you. All along, it has always been you, Ryland. You were the one I first saw at the art exhibit. I remembered losing my breath over you, at the way you smiled at the patrons and gestured to the art. I thought you were Maxwell, that it was *your* exhibit."

"Then why did you start a relationship with him?" My heart slammed against my rib cage and I wanted to throw up.

I could've loved you. Her sweet smiles, her kind heart. The way she brought light back into the house. The way she'd tease me and make me smile when I had a bad day. The way she was a sore loser when we played Scrabble. How she'd laughed when I brought her a bowl of ice cream as penance. Then Maxwell started losing on purpose, doing everything he could to please his angel.

They were all fucking lies. A disguise hiding an ugly, corrupted heart.

There was no satisfaction in her confession. I'd thought about it before, in the middle of the night, when images filled my mind of the only girl who made my heart skip a beat, even though it wasn't the thrashing against the rib cage sensation I'd heard about. But it was happiness, a coveted taste of joy. *What if she was with me instead?* And then the heavy guilt would eat at me, a corrosive acid burning a hole in my gut. Maxwell was so happy with her. He found the happily-after-ever he wasn't supposed to have. How could I feel this way?

And now, as she stared at me with the eyes I used to love, the tears which should've torn my heart into shreds were turning my stomach with revulsion instead. No. This was *not* what I wanted. I shook my head. I was absolutely disgusted.

"You said your vows, Sydney. For better or worse," I growled.

"I regret them! Ryland, don't you see? I can't go on living like this. You feel something for me. I see it in your eyes. This," she motioned between us, "this is right. The right thing to do. Stem the bleeding now before it hemorrhages. We can't help what the heart wants!" she cried before throwing herself on me and pressing those soft lips of hers onto mine.

I froze for a second before wrenching her off me. "Excuses. All of it. You *disgust* me!"

And worst of all, for a moment when her lips touched mine, my body reacted. My heart skipped a damn beat again.

I was disgusted with myself.

Shoving the memory away, I crinkle the exam in my hands, lava flowing hot in my veins, but my eyes are no longer focused on the beautiful writing in front of me. It's a blur of gray against white.

Sydney died a week later. A boating accident. Maxwell was devastated, withdrawing into his cold, hard shell once more. The curse is real...and there's no way on God's green earth I'll ever let him know his wife, the woman he once loved, made a move on me mere days before she passed. That she wanted to leave him. I'll never do that to him.

I stare at the exam in front of me, my breathing rapid, a thin layer of sweat coating my skin. *It can't be. She can't be a cheater.* But the lead sinks deeper inside my chest.

I need to get to the bottom of this.

My phone pings with an incoming text.

Maxwell

Sorry, Ryland. We need you back here. There are some issues with the IPO and it'll take all hands on deck. When can you get back?

My hand grips the phone, wanting to throw it against the wall and see it shatter into pieces. Time to go back to the real world where hundreds of years of Anderson history falls on me to uphold.

But first, there's something I need to do.

CHAPTER 19

THE MOMENT I STEP into his office after his terse email, I know it's over. *He knows.*

He motions for me to sit across from him, his brows furrowed, his face serious.

"Millie," he murmurs and slides my exam over to me.

My breath lodges in my throat and cold sweat breaks out over my skin. Jocelyn ended up fake coughing and nudging me during the exam, desperation in her eyes. The test was harder than expected and there were questions we didn't cover the night before.

In the end, I couldn't do it. I couldn't ignore the little girl trying not to disappoint her dying mom. And so, I leaned back in my chair, nausea churning in my gut, and let her look at my answers before we turned in the exam.

"Yes, Professor?"

He slides Jocelyn's test next to mine, and he has circled in red phrases and answers that are identical on the two packets. Damning evidence of our deceit. A chill sweeps through me, and I want to throw up. *Damn it, Joss. You couldn't have varied your answers just a little bit?*

"I'm concerned your friend has cheated off of you on the exam."

His words draw my attention to him. There's a hesitation in his words, a thin thread of hope, like he's holding his breath.

"Did Jocelyn cheat off of you? You seemed troubled in class. Is there anything I need to know about?"

My lips tremble and I open my mouth to speak, but no words come out. I twist my fingers on my lap. I try again.

"P-Professor, what are you going to do to her?"

Ryland's eyes narrow, the concern in his slate irises shifting into something colder. His nostrils flare. I can feel the temperature of the room dropping by ten degrees.

"If she cheated, I'll report her and she may get expelled."

"No! Please don't do that." I look down at my lap. "I-It's not what you think it is. W-We have reasons."

The silence in the room is heavy and suffocating. I pull at my fingers, afraid to look up at the man before me. *I can't let Jocelyn take the fall for everything. I can't let him report her. She'll be so devastated. And her mom?*

After a few seconds, I gather my courage and look up and my heart plummets to the floor.

The harshness in the slate eyes, as sharp as a steel blade. The twitching muscles in his jaw. His perfect lips curled up in a hard sneer.

The absolute *hatred* pouring out from the man standing behind his desk, every inch of him straining against his perfectly tailored black suit, every inch the powerful billionaire the press has mentioned in the papers.

My pulse skitters and grows thready. Acid churns in my gut.

"You were in on it, weren't you? You're a *fucking cheater* too. You thought I wouldn't find out." His voice is a low, guttural whisper, lethal in its quality.

"You thought I was *stupid,* didn't you, Ms. Callahan?" *Ms. Callahan.* A sharp ache slices across my chest. "You thought you could wind me around your pretty little fingers, bat those lovely eyelashes on your face, and maybe shed some tears and I'd just let you go?"

"R-Ryland." His name slips out automatically and he flinches, his eyes flaring at my usage of his first name, something I've done a thousand times in the privacy of my thoughts but never aloud.

"It's *Professor Anderson* to you, you cheating, deceitful little girl."

"P-Professor, I...I—"

"You what? Trying to buy yourself some time to spin more lies? You thought you could take advantage of my feelings toward you, didn't you?

Treat me like a fool?" His face is chilly, his eyes flashing—the fiercest lightning in the dark skies.

Tears spring into my eyes as I hear him acknowledge out loud for the first time this invisible yearning between us. "Your feelings?" I whisper.

"Stop!" His command is terse, his anger so palpable, the betrayal clearly cutting deep inside him.

Going into the exam, I knew if I got caught, it'd be over, because he hates cheaters. Everyone in the school knew it. I saw the way he berated Fanny and Gregory in front of the classroom. Rumor was, they were expelled.

Ryland has never told me the reason he hates cheaters so much, but I know it to be true from the venom in his voice when he's said the sentiment in the past. But I never expected his hatred to stab me in the core, leaving me a bleeding mess before him.

I never expected it to hurt like this.

But I didn't have another choice, did I? I'd walked in Jocelyn's shoes before. Intimately. Felt the sadness and helplessness of not being able to do *anything* as everything fell apart when Mom passed away. I experienced anger and depression in the years after.

I know *personally* how exhausting it is to pretend everything is fine for the sake of uplifting everyone around me.

How could I deny Jocelyn? How could I let her disappoint her mom in what looks to be the remaining few months they'd have together?

There wasn't any other choice.

My vision blurs as I stare at Ryland towering before me, every inch the livid, vengeful god about to exact revenge or punishment on the mere mortal. The disappointment and anger radiating from him are knives to my heart.

My tongue is furry and thick. I pull and twist my fingers. "I...I had a reason for it."

His silence is foreboding.

"Jocelyn's mom is dying of breast cancer and she hasn't been able to devote more time to class and studying. She was going to be put on academic probation if she failed your class. I helped her study. We pulled an all-nighter trying to get her caught up on the material, but there was simply too much for her to absorb in such a short time. And so when she nudged me to glance at my test...I let her."

I look up at him, my fingers twitching with the need to take his hands, the hands currently knotted to his sides, white knuckles, and all. "P-Please understand. I went through what she did. I *had* to help her. Please don't punish her. If you need to punish anyone, punish me. Report me instead."

My cheeks are wet with tears as I let go of the dreams I had—the honors program, graduating at the top of class, honoring my memories of Mom and Mr. Roberts. The repercussions for cheating are severe: a big black mark on my transcript and I might get expelled. But I couldn't do this to Jocelyn.

I couldn't do this to the little seven-year-old girl crying on top of her dying mom deep inside me.

Ryland is still silent, his chest heaving large breaths, loud in the chilly room, which used to be so warm, so heated because of him, but now feels as frigid as the arctic.

I whisper, "It's the right thing to do."

He flinches, his eyes widening, darkening, his glare even sharper and slicing at my words. His lips twitch and sneer, the whites of his teeth flashing.

"Excuses," he angrily spits out, "Excuses, all of it. I've heard everything I need to hear. Now get out of my office!"

His command shatters the rest of my heart and pulverizes the fragments to pieces. I'm gone from his eyes, his soulful, cold eyes. Instead of the intense passion I usually see in those swirling charcoal pools, I now only see revulsion reflected in them.

I swallow the lump in my throat and choke on my sadness. My face and nose are a mess of tears, but I don't care. It doesn't matter anymore.

"I'm sorry, Professor," I whisper. "I'm so, so sorry."

I leave the room, feeling his wrath singeing my back, and know that life will never, ever be the same again.

He left without notice.

Johnny, the TA, announced to class this morning he'd be taking over the lectures for the last month of the calendar year with the dean of the business school supervising. Apparently, Professor Anderson had to take care of urgent business back in New York.

"Thank you so much, Millie," Jocelyn whispers as she pulls me into a hug after a home-cooked meal. She said it was the least she could do to thank me for doing something she knew violated my morals for her.

"I'm going to be fine because of you. Even though I did well on the exam, I was still a little shy of passing the class. However, Professor Anderson sent me an email with extra credit before he left. It was a simple exercise, something anyone could do. Between that and the grade on the test, I'll skate by...just barely. It wouldn't have happened without you, Millie!"

She hugs me tightly before traipsing back to the kitchen and turning on the faucet. I hear her humming happily under her breath and the dishes clinking in the sink.

Ryland didn't end up reporting me or Jocelyn, much to my surprise. I don't know whether to laugh or cry at that. My dreams are still intact and I can still graduate. But of course, this means I'm not getting the recommendation from him and will need to get one from my other professors.

I stare at her, the shadow of the little girl inside me, the ghost of the woman who's still in hiding today, and my heart twists inside my chest.

A bittersweet pain.

I did the right thing. It's unethical, but the right thing, nonetheless.

But we're over. Irrevocably so. But then again, we never started, did we?

It was a tragedy written in the storm to begin with. An anomaly. And now, it's gone.

There's a new chasm in my chest, one I'm not sure I'll ever fill.

Later that night, I sit in front of my desk and take out a piece of paper. With a heavy heart, I write another letter to Mom, the woman I know would love me unconditionally, the woman who'd wrap me in her arms right now and comfort me if she were still here.

I sniffle, moisture misting my eyes, and begin.

Dear Mom,

The thing you never told me and I never realized until now is...whirlwinds, by definition, aren't permanent. And when they leave, they leave a sea of debris and devastation in their wake.

He left, Mom. I betrayed him. It was for the greater good, but it was still considered cheating. It was something he hated, and I did it anyway.

Is it possible to truly fall in love and be in a relationship without the other person acknowledging it? Why does this feel like a breakup when nothing has ever happened between us? Why does my heart hurt so much, the pain waking me up in the middle of the night?

I wish you were here with me. You'd tell me what to do.

If the stars align and one day my path crosses with his again, I hope I'll get another chance to prove myself to him, to be deserving of his love. I hope our story hasn't ended yet because, despite the pain gutting me to the core right now, the whirlwind was so beautiful, Mom. Utterly breathtaking. And I'm not ready to leave its madness yet.

Love, Millie

CHAPTER 20

Millie

ONE AND A HALF YEARS LATER

Dear Mom,

It's finally happening. The senior year Education Honors Pro-gram. I've worked so hard to get here. I know I'm lucky to have gotten in despite what happened at ULA. All the late nights and long weekends, spending my hours in the library instead of partying it up with friends have paid off.

I've never forgotten him, you know. Him. Ryland. Mom, when does the whirlwind end? When do I stop spinning? Why do I find myself still looking for his tall, dark shadow every time it rains?

Love, Millie

I stuff the letter and pen into my tote on top of the bench in our rooftop garden. The sun is in full blaze today and the air is muggy, even though I'm thirty floors above street level in the trendy SoHo apartment building Belle and I live in.

Wiping the sweat off my forehead with one hand, I pinch my navy NYUC T-shirt with the other and attempt to fan myself. It's useless against the heat of a New York summer day.

Blowing out a breath, I grab a handful of gummy bears from the open bag in my tote and stuff them into my mouth. I examine the planter full of geraniums in front of me, making sure the soil is evenly spread and sufficiently moist for the colorful blooms of magenta, purple, orange, and red.

It never ceases to amaze me how one type of flower can have so many colors. So vibrant, as if they have personalities of their own.

Mom would've loved our rooftop garden.

After I moved back to New York after spending a year at ULA, instead of living in the dormitories on campus at NYUC, I moved in with Belle instead. Her family bought her this beautiful apartment in SoHo, walking distance to shops, restaurants, nightlife, everything my family couldn't afford until Adrian struck gold in his business. Much to her chagrin, the apartment building doesn't allow for pets, which is her biggest regret about living in this spectacular space.

I finally told the girls about my relation to the elusive billionaire, Adrian Scott. Between how broken my heart was with the way things ended in Los Angeles and the incessant guilt loitering inside me, I couldn't keep this from them anymore. Deep down, I hoped they wouldn't look at me differently, and it turned out I was right. The girls rolled with the news like it was a weather report, making fun of me for being so secretive, then went right on with life. Nothing changed between us and for that, I'm thankful.

The best thing about this apartment building is this glorious rooftop space. Belle's family paid a premium for the exclusive use of the large rooftop area, which was barren and unassuming when I first moved in. But I saw the potential right away.

And so, I began spending hours cultivating a garden of my dreams, one I knew Mom would love if she were here. Thinking back to Mr. Roberts's words, this is a way for me to honor her, doing something she would've loved to do.

Standing back, I survey the multiple planters—large rectangular ones, smaller square boxes, thin rail planters, all filled to the brim with an assortment of flowers that bloom in the summer—geraniums, lavender, petunias, marigolds, and daylilies. The scent is heavenly, almost enough to cover the city smells of car exhaust from the street far below.

I also planted small trees of various heights and installed wooden trellises now filled to the brim with lush climbing vines. It helps mute the loud ruckus of cars, buses, and pedestrians, the classic New York City soundtrack.

This is my oasis in the city. A place where I can hear myself think. A place where I can get lost in memories of Mom, of the past...

Of him.

When I came back to the city after finishing my sophomore year at ULA, I tried looking Ryland up. I wanted to apologize again. I wanted to make him understand why I had to do what I did, why there was no other choice. I wanted to let him know the situation was like the ethical cases he taught and like the real world, not everything was black and white.

I wanted him to forgive me and look at me with heated passion in his slate eyes once more.

But it was near impossible to access the elusive billionaire, with his security team and the fortress at Fleur's headquarters or The Orchid.

I could ask Adrian to grant me a guest pass, but then I'd have to tell him, and even though Adrian had mellowed a little because he finally succeeded in getting revenge against our grandfather and he also got back together with the one woman he had never forgotten, Emily, one of Steven Kingsley's older sisters, there was no way I'd let my overprotective brother know I was half in love with my much older professor.

And so, I've been suspended in limbo, waiting for an opportunity, perhaps after my graduation when I'm no longer a college student. When

I've redeemed myself. When we're no longer forbidden. But I miss him. Terribly so.

He felt like the warm, comforting sunlight, shining light into the dark corners of my heart. Even though I was pretty sure he couldn't see that about himself.

He still feels like the only person who has ever truly understood me.

But even as the chasm in my heart widened and darkened last year, my resolve strengthened. I couldn't let this derail my future, the one he left intact for me when he didn't report me to the school.

And so, with every waking moment, unless I'm in class or with my girls, I've dedicated myself to studying and working hard, hoping one day I'll be able to see him again and things will be different.

I have many regrets in life, but what I did in LA isn't one of them. At least Jocelyn is doing well now based on her email to me last week. Her mother passed away shortly after the quarter ended, but what I did saved both the mother and the daughter an additional heartbreak.

I would do the same thing all over again.

My phone *beeps* from an incoming text.

Belle

> Step away from the plants, Millie. Step away.

I wipe the sweat off my forehead with my arm again and bite back a grin.

Millie

> How do you know I'm in the rooftop garden?

Taylor

> You're always there, and I don't even live with you!

Belle

> What Tay said. I'm here to remind you to get your ass in the shower and get ready for dinner at

> Corazón. Reservation is at 7. We get to grill Grace about Steven! *snickers*

Taylor

> That fucker. I can't decide if I've forgiven him yet.

Belle

> Your doom and gloom lol. Get over it, Tay. It's true love. Even the blind can see that.

Grace

> You know I'm in this group chat, right?

I giggle at the rapid-fire messages between my girls and quickly type in my response.

Millie

> Fine. Fine. You got me. I'm going to get ready now. See you soon.

Two hours later, my stomach is filled with spicy tuna rolls doused in Valentina hot sauce from Mexico, my eyes watering and mouth flaming as I chase down the food with sake. I've come to realize, I'm drawn to things I shouldn't be attracted to, like flaming peppers which burn the roof of my mouth off or unapproachable, forbidden professors.

The mariachi band plays a lively tune in the background of this Mexican-Japanese fusion eatery in the bustling Chelsea Market, the restaurant packed to the brim with patrons enjoying Sunday night before the weekday grind begins anew tomorrow.

"So, I saw the cutest Pomeranian at the shelter going to his forever home yesterday," Belle exclaims, her voice filled with so much happiness. "I was worried about the little guy—I wish all shelters had no-kill policies."

Taylor nods. "I don't know how you do it, Belle, volunteering at those animal shelters. I may have a black heart, but even I can't take seeing these cute animals get euthanized if they don't get adopted."

In the last year, Belle has been spending her Saturdays at an overcrowded shelter in Brooklyn. It was her way of giving love to the less fortunate.

Belle's eyes well up. "That's why I do it. To help them find homes...as many as I can. Until I come into the rest of my funds, then I'll build my own no-kill shelter and move them there."

Grace sighs and pats Belle on the back. "Don't be so hard on yourself. You're doing the best you can for those little guys."

I nod. Belle would adopt them all if she could, but the apartment has the strictest no pet policy. The woman has so much heart to give, I sometimes find it hard to believe she is from the upper crust society families typically more worried about the brand of clothing they wear than the plight of the less fortunate.

"It's not enough. They deserve more." Her voice is thick, her pale face flushed with emotions she rarely shows. She sighs and takes a large sip of water before turning to me. "Ignore me. Anyway, first day of senior year tomorrow for you. Excited?" She nudges me on the side.

I nod. "Yes, and no. I'm also nervous about the Advanced Ethical Leadership course. It's a special part of the honors program and will stretch from the summer quarter all the way until graduation next spring."

"That's a mouthful. Why are you nervous? You always do well in school." Grace pats her nonexistent stomach and stretches her hands above her head, her dark hair piled high into a messy bun.

"I heard it's tough and they're switching the curriculum this year...new professor, syllabus, everything. I feel like my life is a series of levels in a freakin' arcade game and this is the final boss I need to beat if I want to get into the PhD program of my choice. I've already submitted my applications early and I'll be a shoo-in if I pass this program. If I do well, I get to have my choice of schools."

"Fuck, girl. Only you'd willingly go to more school. That's shitty hard work." Tay scrunches her nose in distaste, her black nose ring glinting under the lamplight.

I laugh. "You're working your way up ABTC, the *best* ballet company in North America. You work harder than me." She's going to be one of the prima ballerinas in the industry in the next ten years, I know it.

Grace throws her arm around me. "You'll do great, and we'll be rooting for you." She gives me a cheerful grin before letting out a satisfied sigh. "Life will be *great*."

Tay snorts. "*Everything* is rainbows and roses to you right now, you love drunk fool. Steven will need to work harder to get back into my good graces."

"Hey! He had a very valid reason for leaving me."

"I can understand his reasoning, but that doesn't mean I forgive him for making you cry. He's lucky I got a few more family members out of this ordeal." Tay tosses back her sake in one gulp.

She and Grace recently found out they were related to the infamous Andersons, but before the revelation, Grace thought she was actually related to her boyfriend, Steven Kingsley. It nearly tore the lovebirds apart. It was a mess.

"It's all water under the bridge. We're together and happy now and I also got a bonus family out of it." Grace has hearts in her eyes as she no doubt thinks about her boyfriend.

The two of them are living their happily-ever-after after weathering their dramatic whirlwind of a romance, and I'm thrilled for them.

Whirlwind.

Dark eyes. Leashed power. Aching soul.

My heart clenches as I shove away thoughts of Ryland Anderson. I bite my tongue to avoid asking Grace and Taylor about him. I'm not ready to let them know yet. They see him regularly now at family dinners since he's their half-brother. *After graduation, when I'm no longer a college student, I'll find him. We'll be on a more equal playing field then.*

"I guess Grace won't be moving into our large house with fifty cats and ten dogs later on," Belle comments, humor in her voice. "Tay and Millie, it'll just be us three. Well...maybe...if I'm lucky."

She clears her throat and picks at a piece of lint on her cream-colored couture sheath dress, her modelesque posture hunching over briefly. Her dark eyes shutter before she forces out a fake smile.

"Never mind. Good luck on your first day tomorrow, Millie!" She raises her cup for a toast and I down the sake in one gulp, hoping the alcohol will settle my frayed nerves.

———— • ————

Wesley Hall is buzzing with commotion when I walk past groups of students chattering excitedly amongst themselves, hands gesturing wildly in the air. It's a small room with large windows on the top floor of the building and will be my home away from home in the honors program for my senior year. Frowning, I adjust my French braid over my shoulder and make my way over to Chloe, who's sitting in front of the room.

Strong arms swing me around in a brief circle. "Hey, Millie."

"Shit, you scared me!" I laugh, greeting my friend Fred Carias, who gives me a wink as he saunters to his seat.

We met last year in sociology when we were assigned to a group research project together. Shaking my head, I sit down next to my friend, Chloe Lee, who is Belle's cousin, in the front row of the room.

"I tell you, girl, that guy has a thing for you," Chloe murmurs, her thumb pointing discreetly toward Fred, who's chatting with his friends.

I snort. "No way. Fred and I are completely platonic. He's like a brother to me." *If my brother were a harmless blond teddy bear and a ray of sunshine.*

"I'm never wrong," she singsongs and grins gleefully, her chocolate brown eyes sparkling with mischief.

I glance at Fred, finding him smiling at me once more. I give him a tentative wave. It seems friendly. Too bad I don't feel anything for him, my heart long snagged by a certain tall, brooding man it can't seem to forget.

The excitement in the classroom rises an octave. Classmates are huddled over their phones and giggling at something on the screens.

"What on earth's going on, Chloe?"

Chloe waggles her brows and beckons me closer with her curled fingers. "Psst. Hot off the press. Marissa works at the back office, and she told Ally, who told Sandra the news. Apparently, the faculty adviser for the new Joint Ethics Advisory Program is the professor for this class. And guess who the professor is?"

"Who?" My heart suddenly kicks up a rapid beat. I can feel the hairs standing up on the back of my neck, a harbinger of something monumental. A sixth sense.

"Eek! We're so lucky. The professor is—"

The door is thrown open and the world as I know it ceases to exist.

Because in steps someone I haven't seen in over a year and yet has haunted my dreams at night. The man I've compared all the interested guys to since him. The reason I'm still single, having only gone on two first dates in the last year and a half.

My breath catches in my throat as I'm rooted in my chair, a gasp tearing out of my lips.

You've got to be kidding me.

"Good morning, class, and welcome to Advanced Ethical Leadership, which will be combined with JEAP this year. I'm Professor Anderson and I—"

Ryland freezes when he sees me. His eyes widen in shock.

God, he has grown more handsome in the last year and a half, his presence larger, more encompassing. The sharp angles of his face are more pronounced. His normally clean-shaven jaw is covered in a short, sexy, meticulously groomed stubble, the perfect, perpetual five o'clock shadow. He's dressed in a slim navy suit, which encases his muscular body, a body which has grown bigger and stronger than I last remember. Those piercing eyes of his are twin flames of quicksilver.

My memory hasn't done them justice. I've forgotten the searing heat of his stare, the banked power in his eyes, and how it feels to bask in his attention. I've forgotten the way he sucks the oxygen out of a room with his presence and how the currents pulse between us whenever our gazes connect.

The same electricity crackles in the air now, and my heart skips several beats before sprinting in my rib cage. My hand flies to my chest, feeling the rapid thumping underneath my shirt. My face feels heated, my head heavy, as I stare at him.

Time has dulled nothing. The banked fire comes roaring back in an inferno.

The briefcase in his hand slips out of his grasp, clattering on to the floor, its contents spilling across the dark hardwood.

My heart hiccups. The reversal of the day we met at ULA when I was sprawled at his feet isn't lost on me.

The silence is loud as he glares at me, a myriad of indiscernible emotions flickering behind those passionate eyes. A chair scrapes across the floor, the sound slicing through the trance I find myself in. An awkward tension fills the room.

Ryland seems frozen in his steps, unable to move.

"What on earth?" Chloe breathes next to me as we stare at the imposing man, a picture of brimming power, who doesn't seem to notice the mess on the floor.

Unbidden, I leap out of my chair and kneel before him, helping him pick up his things from the floor—a black folio I recognize from ULA, a few pens, a slim laptop, and a—

I clutch the softness in my hand, my gaze darting up to him standing over me.

A navy, cable-knit scarf with a thick center twist.

My scarf.

It's summer though. Why is he carrying it with him?

"Ryland?" I whisper, gripping the scarf tightly in my hand. Never in my wildest dreams would I imagine reuniting with him like this, once again in a professor and student capacity.

My voice jolts him out of his stupor. He quickly bends down and snatches the scarf out of my hands before stuffing it back into his briefcase. His face is flushed and his eyes skate over my face desperately, like he's been starving in the desert and I'm his first sight of food and water. Then, as abrupt as a sudden cold snap in the middle of summer, his eyes chill and his jaw flexes. His hands curl into fists.

Slowly, I stand up, my fingers twisting against each other, my pulse shaking in my ears.

Whoosh. Whoosh. Whoosh.

Absolute chaos. Insanity.

"Ms. Callahan," his rasps, his voice thick and hoarse. "Please go back to your seat."

My legs trembling, I make my way back to my chair, my mind disoriented, my breathing rapid, like I've been hit with a blow to the head.

Or to my heart.

"What was that?" Chloe asks, "Do you know him?"

I stare at Ryland, who's stalking up the steps of the elevated stage, the intensity radiating off him like a category five hurricane, obliterating everything in its path, wreaking catastrophe in its wake...

Pulling me straight back into the eye of the storm.

CHAPTER 21

MY FIRST CLASS AT NYUC was a disaster.

I was distracted, unnerved, my mind a cluttered mess of emotions and restrained impulses.

Destructive impulses along the lines of striding to the front row, hauling a certain brunette from her chair, and dragging her to a dark corner of the room. Then I'd clamp my hand around her slender neck and find out how her plump lips taste, if they were as sweet as they look.

I'd bite it to punish her for invading my mind, searing a permanent brand there, such that even in her absence, a day wouldn't pass by without some thought of her, the person who saw through me when everyone else couldn't.

Fuck. This is all types of wrong.

Wrong. Wrong. Wrong.

When I left LA, I was going to stay away, far away from her, to protect her light from my darkness, to let the little bird fly high in the skies instead of shooting it down. I was going to respect the thick black lines separating my world and hers.

And now she's back in my life again because fate likes to fucking play me as a fool. She's once again my student and one thousand times more beautiful and enticing.

I fight the urge to loosen the black silk tie around my neck as I sit on the sofa of Dean Jacob Emery's stuffy old-fashioned office decorated with dark woods and so many fucking gold antiques and other gaudy displays of wealth and power. My eyes dart to the half-opened windows, noting the curtains fluttering in the breeze.

Why is it still so stifling in here?

Strong footfalls reach my ears before a hearty voice bellows, "Ryland. How was your first day at NYUC? It was on Monday, right? Students have been treating you well, I hope?"

Jacob was Mom's friend from college, a bona fide workaholic who refuses to retire, saying work is his life. He hangs his suit jacket on the coat rack before taking a seat across from me.

"Things are fine. Thanks for the opportunity."

He waves me away and smiles, his hazel eyes crinkling at the corners. He looks young for someone in his late fifties. Mom would've been his age if she were still here. "Julianna would be proud of you. She wanted to become a professor, you know?"

And she would have if her parents didn't arrange for her to marry my father and she had to give up all her dreams to become a dutiful Anderson wife per the damn trust. The women married into the Anderson family would either stay home and spend their time in charities, raise families, or would join the family business.

She'd probably still be here if she weren't entangled with the Anderson family and the curse which killed her.

The pendant weighs like an anvil on my chest. I clear my throat, my mind trying not to think of the generous, kind woman who left my life too early. It's a pain I don't think I'll ever recover from, an agony few people can truly understand.

Except her. My forbidden temptation.

Shit.

"I've heard great things about your classes at ULA. Unblemished record of students with a high passing rate and rave reviews," he begins, and my breath lodges in my throat.

Unblemished, my ass. I shouldn't be an ethics professor. If he only knew what goes on in my mind, he'd be appalled and fire me on the spot.

He clears his throat. "So, why do you want to meet today if everything is going well?"

"I want to switch classes."

"Why?"

Because I'm mind fucked over a certain vixen in my classroom. Because I've already violated my ethics for her and I'm afraid I can't withstand temptation the second time around.

I settle for BS instead. "With the IPO in full swing right now, it's requiring more of my time than originally expected, and the commitment needed for Advanced Ethical Leadership and JEAP is too high. I'm afraid I won't be able to dedicate my full energy into the year-long program."

Jacob settles into his chair, a pensive frown on his face. "You're the perfect candidate for this class. You and your family's impeccable reputation, your business prowess and knowledge, and frankly, I'm in a bind. There's no way I'll be able to find a professor with half your caliber on such short notice. This is the keystone course of our Education Honors Program, the reason our endowments increase year after year."

Fuck. I knew he was going to say this, and I can't disagree with him. It isn't easy to find a leader of a Fortune 500 company who doesn't have public scandals, who has brokered ethical deals benefiting all parties equally, leading to the growth of Fleur Entertainment Holdings at an unprecedented rate in the last few years.

Even I can't find another person to replace me.

He leans forward, a shrewd glint in his eyes. "If you told me this half a year ago, perhaps I could make arrangements, but now...it's simply impossible. But how about this? I know you wanted tenure when we approached you for the adjunct professor position. And you know we don't offer tenure track to part-time professors without doctorate degrees. Your accomplishments in the business community with Fleur are well-known and much deserving. So much our university can be persuaded to grant you an honorary doctorate."

I narrow my eyes, a heavy pulse thumping in my ears. Images float into my mind of me teaching full-time, no longer splitting my precious hours between two jobs, designing every aspect of my courses instead of teaching curriculum crafted by others, running my own research projects and teams, spending every waking moment doing the things I love.

Impossible dreams, and yet, seeming almost within reach. If I get tenure, maybe it's a sign I can approach my family about my discontent with working at Fleur.

"What do you mean? Are you saying NYUC will grant me a doctorate and put me on the tenure track?" I fight to keep my face impassive, because that is the number one rule in business negotiations and despite this being a dean's office at a university, *everything* is business and politics.

Something must have shown through, because he grins and sits back in his chair, his hands clasped on his lap. A position of victory because the damn bastard knows how much I want to be a tenured professor. "This program is important to us, and part of its draw is its distinguished lecturers and professors, including yourself. If you teach this course and take on the faculty adviser role for JEAP, then everything else will just be a formality."

Tenured professor.

He's dangling my dreams in front of me like meat to a starving bear fresh out of hibernation. A fucking shark through and through.

A muscle pulses in my jaw, and my nostrils flare. This isn't a fair game. He had a better hand all along.

Clearly seeing my inner turmoil, Jacob's voice softens to that of Mom's good friend once more. "Ryland, I've watched you growing up. I've seen how your eyes sparkle when you guest lectured here every so often in the past. I've never seen that passion when you talk about your work at Fleur. You're meant for academia, son. Frankly, I really need this year's revised curriculum to succeed, and I don't trust anyone other than you to take this seriously and carry it to fruition."

He clears his throat. "In the last two years, like many universities, ours has had its share of scandals—large-scale student cheating, sordid affairs, bribery in the admissions office, assaults happening on campus. In the past, these cases would have been governed by the Ethics Committee of the Board. But there's been increased scrutiny and criticism that the people in our governance committees are biased. In the last few years, folks have been clamoring for better representation. The students want to have a say in these cases."

"That's why you established JEAP." Everything makes sense now.

He nods. "So, this is much more than just a class. The media and our peers have their spotlights on us. And you, Ryland, are the perfect person for the job. Impeccable reputation. Respectable family, despite the blip earlier this year with your dad and your half-sisters."

My lips twitch at the mention of my half-sisters, Grace and Taylor, both lovely women I've come to know and love. Dad called a family meeting last year and told us a secret he had kept from us all these years. After Mom died, he fell in love with another woman and had a family on the side. He wanted to shield her from the curse, and so he never married her, but they broke up and lost contact when Grace was a baby and her mom was pregnant with Taylor.

It was a media shitstorm when the girls' lineage was brought to light. A rare black mark in the Anderson name. But our family embraced Grace and Taylor as our own and since Dad didn't commit adultery, eventually the press moved onto something else.

Jacob taps his fingers on his desk. "Your reputation is unimpeachable. Under your and Maxwell's leadership, Fleur is frequently lauded as one of the best places to work. Even your competitors have nice things to say about you. You're a leader of a remarkable dynasty in the country—that's how the press describes you, and that's what we need right now. So, I can promise you this: if you go through with the program this year, I'll make it my duty to get you the doctorate and secure your placement on our tenure track."

Impeccable fucking reputation. The very thing our IPO and apparently my dreams depend on. Our family can't survive another black mark, something like the high-profile son fucking his much younger student. Three hundred years of dead Anderson ancestors breathe down my neck. My lungs burn with the need for fresh air.

If they only knew what goes through my mind when I think of a certain student and the lines I've crossed already. How I should've reported her and her roommate a year and a half ago.

But in the end, I couldn't do it. I couldn't ruin the future she described to me before—the one where a little girl would finally honor the memory of her mom, where she would go forth and travel the world and be an inspiration to others less fortunate. The future where a beguiling woman risked everything because her heart was too big, too empathetic, such that she couldn't bear to disappoint her roommate's dying mother, because Millie understood how it felt.

Just like how she understood me.

"It's the right thing to do." Her words float to the forefront and a fresh torrent of flames burn my insides.

No. She's a cheater, no matter her intentions. All useless excuses. I knot my hands into fists and attempt to even out my ragged breathing.

If they only knew how filthy and dark the inner recesses of my mind are.

But I still want her and, like the fucking selfish bastard I am, I also want my fucking dreams, even if I can't find a way out of the family trust right now.

"Son, what do you say?"

My lips twitch and I clench my jaw. There's no other answer. "Fine, but I hold you to your word, Jacob."

I'm well and truly fucked.

———◆———

"In this class, there are no exams, no quizzes," I announce to the group gathered in the darkened classroom, a PowerPoint presentation displayed on the screen behind me.

There's a rumbling of excitement amongst the students, clearly excited at the prospect of not needing to study.

"Instead, you and your group mates will be tasked with developing a corporate whistleblower policy in the summer quarter, a leadership training plan in the fall, evaluating your policy against a 'plucked from the headlines' case in the winter, and evaluation and final presentations in the spring. The lectures will also include JEAP committee meetings, in which we'll preside over real-life cases within NYUC and come up with recommendations for the Ethics Committee. This is heavy on real-life education for you to apply the theories you've learned over the last several years."

My eyes sweep the room, noting the students rapidly typing on their laptops. Teaching seniors in the honors program has its advantages—folks appear more focused and serious about their work.

I try not to notice her.

And fail miserably.

Because it's impossible. Even in a room so dark, I can barely make out the faces of the students below the stage. But she glows brightly from within, beckoning all to look at her.

Her magic makes me weak.

Her thick, glorious hair is curled over her shoulders, a pensive pout on those sexy lips, her delicate brows furrow in concentration. Swaths of smooth skin lightly bronzed from the sun show around her simple white tank top, which clings to the heavy swells of her tits, her body seeming to have grown more luscious, her earlier innocence now laced with a heavy dose of feminine sensuality.

My imagination during the countless dark nights where I've taken my erection in my hand and indulged in fantasies of her, my cock having lost all interest in other women, does not remotely compare to reality.

The aching lust and want I've tethered away with my iron will come roaring back like a tsunami, attempting to obliterate the battered sea walls guarding my heart.

God, she takes my breath away.

My cock stirs in my pants, and I shove my hands into my pockets, hiding my clenched fingers and look away. *Stay away. Your reputation. Tenure. The IPO.* Fuck.

"Professor?" Millie's sweet voice drags my attention back to her. I give her a curt nod. "Will you give us details of the case before we start the project? That'll be helpful before we spend too much time on it."

"Yes. You'll receive your materials before you begin."

She nods and follows up with another question. "As with all ethical dilemmas, interpreting the case and its conclusions are very subjective. How will you evaluate our performance? Especially if you may not agree with our assessment, which doesn't mean the case isn't completed to satisfaction?"

Gone is the tentative honeyed rasp of the wide-eyed sophomore in ULA. In her place is a woman on the cusp of taking the world by storm, the posture and cadence in her voice strong. If I thought the innocent coed was attractive before, this version of her threatens to undo me.

She's a confident prey taunting a seasoned predator and fuck if that doesn't turn me on.

"Great question." A blond guy, someone who looks like he shows up to church every Sunday and plays bingo with seniors in his free time, stares at her with fucking hearts in his eyes. I want to grab him by his buttoned-up collar and toss him out of my classroom.

Shit.

"Everything will be listed in black and white in the instructions on the portal. Be patient."

My words come out harsher than intended, and she stiffens before tilting her head up.

"Thank you, but with all due respect, Professor, not everything in this world is black and white. In fact, most of the world is gray. I just want to ensure the beholder of said grayness is impartial."

Chloe, the girl next to Millie, nudges her sharply on her side, but Millie keeps her unwavering gaze on me, a hardened glint in her eyes. She's daring me to call her out on her impertinence.

Blood rushes south to my stiffening cock, which is now at half-mast. I'm fucking glad I'm standing behind the damn podium.

Leaning forward on the sturdy surface, I keep my gaze pinned on her. In the past, she'd flush and waver. The pulse would throb against her throat like her body was waving a white flag.

But no, this Amazonian in front of me meets my stare head-on and instead of cowering, she sits up taller, thrusting those luscious tits out and cocking her damn brow.

My fingers twitch at the challenge in her eyes. My lips twist in a half-sneer. "Are you *questioning* my reputation and impartiality, Ms. Callahan?" I ask, my voice a hoarse rasp.

The room drops ten degrees as everyone swivels their heads toward the Siren in the front row. All we're missing is the popcorn.

Chloe grabs Millie's arm, but I barely notice, my attention affixed solely on the bane of my fucking existence before me.

"No, sir," she murmurs, and the word, *sir*, out of her lips, her only sign of submission, has my dick roaring at full-mast, my body not registering how inappropriate my reactions are. "Of course not." She feigns a demure smile.

I want to snarl, my entire body aching, throbbing, needing to grab her, to pull her against me so I can feel her soft curves flushed against mine, and growl in her ear, *"Run, and don't let me catch you."*

Fuck it all.

Apparently, my body believes the right time to think about women and Noire is in the middle of a fucking class with someone who is completely inappropriate in so many ways. Someone who has the power to carve out my heart and decimate it when she leaves, or when I destroy her, leaving me a shadow of a man like Dad and Maxwell after losing Mom and Sydney, respectively.

My mind clamors for rational thought—a person drowning, flailing his arms, and trying to grab onto anything.

The cheater. Fucking cheater. *She's the same, Ryland. The same. Don't forget that.*

My nostrils flare and I tug at my cuff links. "Questions from anyone else?" I bark into the relative darkness.

The room is still and quiet, so silent I could hear crickets if it were nighttime. My body is on fire, my mind a beast trying to tear at the chains binding it into civility.

How will I last the entire year with her here?

CHAPTER 22

I watch the throngs of tourists walking on 5th Avenue from my office at Fleur. They look like clusters of ants, eagerly heading to their destinations, whether it be the large expanse of greenery that is Central Park, the luxury shops in the likes of Louis Vuitton and Bergdorf Goodman, or the impressive facade of the Metropolitan Museum of Art. The humid summer heat doesn't appear to faze them, and I can practically feel the teeming energy radiating seventy stories up from street level.

I wish I could feel an iota of excitement. Instead, unease slithers inside me like a phantom itch.

My fingers fiddle with the pendant around my neck, smoothing over the cool edges, then the indentations of the gem-studded key within the lock, and a weathered memory edges to the forefront.

"This is your grandparents' lock and key pendant," Mom said when I asked her about the necklace always affixed around her neck. "Let me show you its secret."

I leaned forward, my eyes widening. I loved secrets and as a first grader, adults would often say things like, "When you're older, we'll tell you," whenever I asked questions they didn't want to answer.

Never Mom though. She always treated us as though we could handle the information.

Mom fiddled with the pendant, and with a flick of her fingers, slowly detached the key embedded within the lock.

I gasped in wonder. I thought it was one necklace all along, but apparently it was really two pieces!

She whispered, "See? This is a pair that can be worn as one necklace or broken apart into two necklaces. You're supposed to give the key to the person you love. It symbolizes eternal love."

"Like forever?"

Mom laughed and pulled me toward her soft waist. I buried my face against her scent of roses. She made me feel like anything was possible. "Yes, my sweet boy. Forever."

"Yuck. I don't want to love girls. I only love you, Mom."

She chuckled and pressed a kiss on my forehead. "Someday, you'll want to give your heart to someone else. That's what love is, you know? To have your heart live outside of you. It's scary...but beautiful."

That didn't sound very good to me. Frowning, I stared at her. "Then why do you have both the lock and the key then? Shouldn't Dad have one of them?"

Mommy stiffened, the corners of her eyes drooping slightly. She looked sad. Why was she sad? She rubbed my back, and I snuggled back into her arms, listening to her reassuring heartbeat. *Ba-dum. Ba-dum. Ba-dum.* "It's only for true love, honey. One day, you'll understand."

When she died the following year, Dad gave me her necklace.

He was wearing it around his neck then.

True love. I've always scoffed at the phrase. There's no damn way I'll put my heart in someone else's hands. There's no fucking way I'll infect another person with my darkness, have them give up all of their dreams, and drag them into my gilded cage with me. It looks like half of this necklace won't ever find its owner.

But then, an image of *her* appears in my mind. So fucking tempting. My heart skips a beat.

It's physical, that's all. That's all there is to it.

Knock. Knock.

The sound at the door pulls me back to the present. I tuck the pendant back inside my pin-striped shirt and fix my sage-green tie. I walk over to the bookshelf next to the windows and peruse the volumes.

"Come in."

Maxwell strides in, his quiet presence somewhat calming. He stands next to me and stares out the windows, at the world at our feet, the city our family wields considerate influence over. "You look troubled."

"You think too much."

"You really need to come up with something better. You say that whenever I'm right about something and you don't want to admit it."

He peers at me, the identical charcoal eyes contemplative. "Is this about the IPO? Or something else?" Maxwell steps back and muses, "Or *someone* else?"

Fucker. Damn twin-sense.

I don't look at him, my eyes now surveying the glass fortress next door, The Orchid, our haven, the establishment opened by our great-great-great-grandfather when he emigrated from England because he missed the gentlemen's clubs like White's over there. It blossomed and grew from the moment the doors were opened.

"I think it's a woman. You've done well under pressure before, so this can't be work," Maxwell comments and chuckles softly under his breath. "I never thought I'd see the day when my twin is troubled by love."

"There's no one. Stop it." There can't be anyone. For way too many reasons. The IPO, our pristine reputation, my academic tenure, her dreams, and her future.

"Why? You're the second-born. You don't have the fucking curse hanging over your head. Why can't you fall in love? Live because you can do so when *others* can't." His normally calm voice takes on a chilly edge and my eyes dart to his face, finding his eyes darkened, his features glacial.

A vein throbs on his forehead. "Why are you wasting your life, Ryland?" *The life I wish I had.* The words are unsaid but heard, nonetheless.

A swift burn churns through me, a tempest out of clear skies. "You don't know *anything*, Maxwell. You don't know how much I gave up for the family. You don't know—"

"Well, tell me then! Because, for fuck's sake, I don't understand why you've become more and more of an unemotional rock in the last few years. *This* is the most emotion I've seen from you in two years! Two fucking years! You think I don't notice how you go through the motions at family dinners, at meetings? Your smile as fake as shit?"

He steps closer, his eyes ablaze with a rarely seen passion. "You don't go out. You barely step foot into The Orchid other than your damn apartment and I'm pretty sure you haven't had a fuck in years. You think the others don't notice? Even Steven texted me the other day, asking what the hell was wrong with you. Even he noticed and he just went through his own crazy shit storm when he got together with Grace. You were *that* obvious. We're your fucking family. Tell us so we can help!"

A frustrated growl tears out of my throat, and I swipe a few books off the bookshelf, the burst of violence loud in the room. The heavy volumes lay in a heap on the floor.

I'm fucking unraveling.

"I can't breathe, Your Majesty! Okay? Is that what you want to hear?" *I'm not allowed to have what I want in life. If I do, you and the people I love will lose everything. I'm trapped, lifeless, like the boar I killed in the past. This fucking guilt is snuffing the life out of me.* "For fuck's sake. Leave me the hell alone. Stop reading my mind. I'm already trying to live for both of us, dammit. I don't owe you anything!"

I don't owe you anything.

The words echo in the large office, and I'm thankful the walls are double insulated, which I hope means no one else outside of this room can hear my outburst. Maxwell staggers back, his dark eyes wounded, his jaw clenching.

Anguish slices through me. I owe him everything. I owe it to him, to my family, to wear my responsibilities with pride instead of suffocating resentment. Fleur is my life, my blood, my future, the Anderson legacy. My family always comes first.

Always.

Despite the twist of the knife in my gut and the coiling of the rope around my lungs. Loop, loop, loop, the binds getting tighter over the years.

He rakes his hand over his dark hair and lets out a frustrated sigh. "I can't deal with you like this, Your Royal fucking Highness." He sneers, tossing my nickname back at me. "I came to ask you if you had reviewed the draft S-1 filing for the IPO yet."

I huff out a frustrated breath. What the hell is wrong with me today? "What filing?"

Silence fills the room.

"The fucking registration document that gets filed with the SEC. One of the most important regulatory filings for the IPO. I've looked over it, and so has Ethan. Where the hell are your comments? They were due last week. You never forget this stuff."

Shit. Fuck this shit. I bend down, gather the books on the floor, and slowly stack them back on the shelf, one by one, sorted by topic.

How could I forget? Why did I forget?

You know why. Your mind is filled with useless, inappropriate thoughts of the one woman you shouldn't think about.

She's the one person who gets you tied up in knots like this, and you aren't even in a relationship. Imagine if you were in one, how she'd have the power to destroy you.

Maxwell walks toward the door, pausing before he twists open the doorknob. "I don't know what the hell is going on with you, but get your shit together, Ryland."

He slams the door shut behind him and I grit my teeth. I stare at the leather bracelet around my wrist as guilt threatens to suffocate me. I still clearly remember the day when Maxwell gave it to me during our trip to Dublin after high school graduation.

He made a huge and uncharacteristic showing of sentimentality and sat me down on a bench in St. Stephen's Green, Ireland's answer to Central Park, after a day of sightseeing and drinking too much Guinness. He shoved a package at me wrapped in parchment paper and tied with twine. Sweat rolled down my forehead from the summer heat as I stared at him quizzically, and he grinned and motioned to the gift.

I untied it and held up a sturdily braided leather bracelet, the deep brown almost black in some areas. It had a rectangular silver clasp on one end and, on the other, an intricate knot—one of those infinity knots I'd seen before.

"It's a Celtic sailor's knot. There's no beginning or end. Supposed to symbolize protection and eternal love and friendship. It was said the sailors gave it to their loved ones before they went to sea," Maxwell said as he pulled up the hem of his blue T-shirt and wiped the sweat rolling down his forehead.

A heavy punch of guilt threatened to unmoor me when I saw the large gashes on his torso, now fully healed, but the ugly, winding scars still marred his otherwise unblemished, muscular body. He spent three months in the hospital to heal from his injuries from the boar attack and endured multiple surgeries. It was touch and go for a while there. Lacerated internal organs, severe hemorrhaging, months of utter terror for the entire family.

I was *this close* to losing my twin and best friend, the only person on this planet who seemed to understand me without me having to say anything.

A lump formed in my throat as I turned the bracelet over and smoothed my fingers over the sturdy leather. A small inscription decorated the silver clasp:

"Let all that you do be done in love."

- 1 Corinthians 13:4

A burning sensation appeared behind my eyes. I locked my jaw before whispering, "What's this?"

"I got one too." He held up his wrist with an identical bracelet dangling from it. "This is a present for your sorry ass and to tell you,

I forgive you for your stupidity, even though you never believed me when I told you before. Don't think I didn't notice your sulking and performative groveling this past year. I miss my jackass of a brother, the one who gives me no bullshit. You would've done the same thing for me if you were in my shoes. So quit it and forgive yourself. You're fucking annoying me."

I gnawed my bottom lip, my skin suddenly feeling warm for another reason outside of the blistering heat.

"Love you too, bro," I muttered, hiding a grin, before slipping the bracelet on my wrist. I shoved him in the ribs, on his good side, of course.

I shouldn't have yelled at him. He nearly gave up his life for me.

The thoughts echo in my mind, drawing me back to the present. I press my forehead against the window in the quiet office, wishing I were anywhere but here—running in the large fields, surrounded by towering trees, watching colorful birds soaring in the skies, feeling the wind whipping on my face.

Anywhere but here.

* * *

The three sheets of paper weigh heavily in my hand.

The students each take a packet and pass the stack to the next person to repeat the cycle. The chairs are arranged in a circle today for our first JEAP committee meeting. We'll be going over the cases to be reviewed this year prior to funneling our recommendations to the NYUC Ethics Committee for their official disciplinary ruling.

One case is like the stories Mom read to me when I was little—the parables and warnings of the consequences of poor decisions made by weak humans.

Weak humans like me.

Millie sits across from me, but I can still smell the scent of her vanilla and jasmine lingering in the space between us. I can practically feel the heat radiating from her, which has nothing to do with the scorching heatwave going on outside.

She's a picture of radiance again, her thick hair tied in a loose knot on top of her head, with a few wispy tendrils framing her pinkened face, which is blooming like the most beautiful of roses. She's gnawing on her full lip before soothing each bite with a quick swipe of tongue.

I shouldn't look at her. Shouldn't stare at her. Shouldn't notice how perfect the pink of her tongue is.

What's documented in the paper is clearly a warning for me from the fates.

The students flip through the flimsy pages, and I wait for her to get to the third case on the last page.

I know precisely when she reaches it.

Her eyes dart up, her lips parting. She swallows, her gaze flickering back to the black text on white pages—there are really no shades of gray—before returning to me again.

"Tell me, class, what case interests you the most?" I ask, my eyes not leaving hers. I watch the blues darken and a flush creeps up her smooth skin.

"The third case. Professor student affair. I mean, it's wrong, but it's so juicy," someone volunteers, and the rest of the class laughs.

Millie's face pales and I grip my set of case summaries tightly, feeling the thin edges slicing my palms, most likely giving me a paper cut, but I barely notice.

"These are actual cases the Ethics Committee will rule on this year. I must remind you, all of you signed nondisclosure agreements before beginning the quarter. The repercussions will be severe if anyone violates these regulations. It's a privilege to offer our insights and we must not take this responsibility lightly." I tear my eyes away from my biggest temptation and sweep them over the circle of students.

"If anyone at any time feels uncomfortable, you may recuse yourself from the cases and instead, will be given an independent assignment for completion." I swallow, a rope slowly cinching around my lungs. "This is a safe space."

You fucking hypocrite. Maxwell's words during our phone call on my hunting trip almost two years ago ring loud in my ear. Of course he knows me.

My eyes meet hers again, finding her forehead crinkling, those damn perceptive eyes of hers all too seeing. She cocks her head to the side as if reading every thought in my mind.

How I'm the worst possible person to be on this case.

How my mind has already crossed into the realm of the forbidden, erasing every fucking ethical guideline the day a sopping wet water nymph crashed into my class and turned my life upside down.

How, if she didn't cheat and if I didn't have the IPO emergency, which involved switching underwriting banks and boring shit, there was no chance on earth I could've stayed away from her, no way I could've stopped myself from eventually succumbing to this burgeoning need, this ache inside me to touch her, to kiss her, to bury myself deep inside her and purge my darkness with her light, to find out every morsel of every moment in her life.

"Chloe, can you read the case background for the group? The names are pseudonyms." I look at her friend sitting next to her.

She nods. "A complaint has been lodged by Professor Kohl regarding strange noises emanating from Professor Archer's office, which sounded like," she flushes, "the throes of lovemaking. Professor Kohl knocked on Professor Archer's door and after a few minutes, the door opens to reveal Professor Archer with his student, a sophomore named Tammy, in relative dishevelment, defined as messy hair, sweaty face, and flushed skin. Professor Kohl distinctly remembers seeing a red mark, resembling lipstick, on the collar of Professor Archer's shirt. Upon confrontation, both the professor and student denied allegations of inappropriate behavior, claiming they were in a heated debate over a classroom assignment instead. Professor Kohl submitted a complaint to the department chair. The case was submitted to the ethics committee for investigation and review."

My mind drifts back to my office at ULA. When I touched her for the first time and felt the warmth of her skin, the wetness of her tears. When she slid her palms down my chest after she tied my bow tie. When I leaned down, my mind rendered into a useless mush, *this close* to kissing those pouty lips.

This Professor Archer is damn guilty alright.

But we have to undergo the process, the fact finding, before we conclude on the case.

It's only the right thing to do.

I sneak another glance at Millie, finding her staring intently at her paper, her pulse feathering her neck. She swallows and blows out a deep breath. Then another. Her eyes dart up once more.

Two magnets drawn to each other.

Kindred spirits.

The blond friend of hers, Fred Carias, leans toward her, whispering something in her ear, his other arm slung casually over her chair. Heat churns inside me as I witness this tête-à-tête.

Does she like him? Find him attractive with his golden all-American looks? He probably fucks in gentle, missionary style and not like my rough, caveman ways.

Images of them tangled in the sheets have me seeing blood and violence. Heat climbs up my neck and face. I want to tug loose the tie around my neck.

"Ms. Callahan and Mr. Carias, do you have any insight you wish to share with the class?" I bark, my eyes pinning on the fucker with a hard-on for her.

I bet my life he sees what I see.

"We were just discussing how this case may not be as black and white as this summary implies," Millie replies, her jaws locking.

"We don't have all the evidence yet," Fred adds, "and Professor Kohl only suspected something was going on. Strange noises and sweaty faces don't equate to unethical behavior."

"Not to mention, all parties are above the age of consent and no laws were broken." Millie arches her brow.

"But if something nefarious were to have gone on, they'd have broken the university's regulations over inappropriate faculty-student relationships. Their reputations would be ruined, not to mention other potential repercussions. It's unethical, given the power imbalance, the undue influence one party may have over the other." I tap my fingers on the desk, my blood simmering inside me. *Tell yourself that, you idiot.*

"Well, maybe these regulations need to be reassessed. They are both adults and if the relationship was consensual and if there's no favoritism, then there's no harm. Why should we view this as black and white? Who defined those colors and guidelines? Shouldn't the assessment be case by case? Shouldn't there be *exceptions* to the rule?" She raises her voice, her face flushed, her blue eyes blazing like the hottest fire, and I can't help but marvel at her. She's repeating her argument from when I saw her last in LA, when she defended her cheating.

Exceptions to the rule.

And deep down, I know I'm hanging onto the cheating like it's my last shield, my last defense against her when she is *nothing* like Sydney.

Nothing at all.

She's a fucking storm wrapped in a cloak of serenity. A tornado amidst clear-blue skies.

My undoing.

CHAPTER 23

Dear Mom,

He's back, bringing with him his swirling tempest once more. Our connection is so much more visceral than last time. Except now, I know better. I know how fast those winds can turn. But I'm stronger. A fighter. I won't surrender to his dark moods without a battle. I'll tame the storm. Because I see him, the man behind the thousand-dollar suits and icy cold mask, and I know he needs me. He needs an outlet for his dark emotions and someone he can be completely honest with. I can be that person for him. This time, it's my turn to give him my warmth, to shelter him from the storm.

Love, Millie

I BLOW OUT MY BREATH in frustration as I stare at the text on my phone.

Adrian

I know you want to keep our relationship on the down low, but now that I'm back in the public eye, the press has been relentless about digging into my past. They know you're my sister. FYI, there are a few articles up online about you, but don't worry, I'll take care of them.

My pulse ratches up. I wonder if others will view me differently now. Shaking my head, I take deep, calming breaths. *No, Millie. Everything will be fine. You were worried about the girls treating you differently before too and that didn't happen. Don't catastrophize.*

"So, uh, Millie," Fred whispers, his face flushed and splotchy, his eyes darting around the classroom. We're huddled together in the same group, working on drafting our whistleblower policy.

"Corruption hides in plain sight," Ryland said two weeks ago when we started the first phase of our case study. If the recent news headlines of whistleblower allegations frequently gone awry are any sign, these corporate policies—in companies or in schools—leave a lot to be desired.

"Hm?" I cock my brow at him. "Everything okay? You seem nervous."

Fred forces out a chuckle and rakes his fingers over his messy blond hair, rendering into something resembling a nest. "Well...yeah. I actually am."

He leans toward me. "You see, um, I...uh, think you're really cool, Millie. Pretty. Fun to hang out with. Smart."

Oh no. I bite my lip and sweep my gaze around the classroom for Chloe. Dammit. She was right. Where is she when I need her?

"Fred," I begin, trying my best to hold in the grimace threatening to unleash on my face, "I—"

He straightens up and takes my hand in his and squeezes. "Look, I know you're way out of my league, but don't turn me down yet, okay? Just consider it? I like you, Millie. I really, really do. Think about it?" Fred stares at me with those adorable puppy dog eyes of his and I inwardly sigh.

I don't need to consider anything when my mind is filled to the brim with a dark-haired man much older than me, all sharp edges and blistering intensity. Biting my lip, I look at Fred. How can I let him down without hurting his feelings?

"Fred, I like you too." Fred's face brightens. *Shit. Wrong opener. Why am I so awkward with guys?* "I mean I—"

"What's going on here? This is a fucking classroom, not speed dating." Ryland's voice jolts us in our seat. My heart rate skyrockets, and I slap a hand to my chest.

Fred stammers, "I-I'm sorry, Professor Anderson. It's not Millie's fault. I a-asked her a question a-and—"

"I don't *fucking* care, and I'm not talking to you!" Ryland growls, his lips curling up into a snarl.

Those thundercloud eyes dart to where Fred's hand still is clutching mine and I quickly wrench my hand away and tuck it on my lap. I frown. *I did nothing wrong. Why am I hiding?* Cocking my brow, I bring my hand back on top of the desk, trying my best not to fidget.

A vein pulses on his temple and his murderous eyes ensnare mine once more. "Have you completed your policy yet, Ms. Callahan? I thought you were serious about the honors program. That you had grand plans to become an educator for the disadvantaged youth all over the world. To honor your mother? Or was that fucking BS you served to me and the admissions committee so you could get into the program?"

Raging fire chars my insides and burns through my veins. My hands fist on the table. *This is way out of line.* Slowly I get up, not cowering, not bowing down to the storm. The papers on my desk flutter to the ground.

"You. Are. Out. Of. Line. Professor," I hiss under my breath.

Fred pulls my arm frantically before rising to his feet next to me. "Look, this is all my fault. A m-misunderstanding—"

"Shut the fuck up," Ryland commands, his eyes never leaving mine.

His chest heaves up and down and sweat beads on his forehead. There's a madness in his eyes, one I didn't see in ULA. It's like he's a pressure cooker that has been mis-calibrated and is about to burst at any second.

I hear whispering from the other students in the room. We've drawn attention. This isn't the time or the place.

I'm a fighter, and I'll tame the fucking storm.

Forcing out a wide smile, I sit back down in my chair and tug Fred down as well. My fingers poise on my keyboard.

I keep my voice calm even as my pulse gallops, and rage threatens to boil over.

"Apologies, Professor. We're almost done with our draft policy outline and will send it your way upon completion. Until then, Fred and I will need more time to discuss and make sure we deliver our best work to you. After all, we are *serious* students who fought very hard to get into the program."

My lips are frozen in a frigid, teeth-baring smile, and I even throw in a few fluttering of my lashes, just to royally piss him off.

"*Anything else,* Professor?" My voice is sickly sweet, like those artificial hot chocolates I hate with a passion.

Ryland glares at me, his nostrils flaring. His tall frame is vibrating with coiled energy. I see his hands slowly clench and unclench, like he's trying to stop himself from reaching for me, from unleashing himself on me.

My skin feels hot, and the swirling heat is spreading throughout my body. Goosebumps form on my arms, and suddenly, everything feels sensitive.

Taut. Achy.

My nipples bead against my tank top and I see his eyes darken as his gaze slips to what, no doubt, is an indecent display of want on my chest. But I don't cower. I don't flinch. In fact, I thrust out my chest a little bit more just to taunt him. A sharp current of lust flows between my legs and my lips part in an exhale.

His gaze returns to my face, the slate-colored irises darkening to charcoal. His nostrils flare, his breathing sounding labored.

"Anything else, Professor?" I repeat, but this time, my voice is a breathy whisper.

"Whoa, whoa, what's going on here?" Chloe plops in her seat next to me before flashing a light-hearted grin. But I don't let that face fool me. Her eyes are full of questions. She turns to Ryland. "Hey, Professor. We're almost done. We got this." She tosses out a wink.

Ryland tears his gaze away before he pinches the bridge of his nose. His mask of indifference slips back on, and he turns to me again. "I don't want to have this conversation again. Take this class seriously, Ms. Callahan."

Slowly, he crouches down, picks up the scattered sheets of paper from the floor, and gently sets them on my desk.

I'm suddenly reminded of the way he fixed my daffodils that day in ULA.

With a heated glance at me, he walks away, no doubt to terrorize someone else.

"What an ass," Fred mutters.

Chloe nudges me and cocks her brow as if to say, *you need to tell me what the hell that was.*

I shrug, noting Ryland is back at his desk, his attention still searing on my skin. If he thinks he can treat me this way, well, he's in for a big surprise.

CHAPTER 24

HE'S PACING IN HIS glass office, a phone against his ear as he rubs his temples in apparent frustration. His white shirtsleeves are rolled up, his dark navy suit jacket hanging on the coat rack behind his desk. He's the god Jocelyn mentioned back then, hurling thunderbolts in every direction, punishing all those who dare defy him. His Royal Highness, as the press calls him, is very much in his element.

The lava scorches through my veins.

For the last few weeks, his demeanor toward me has been colder than the arctic and I've put up with it because I know he has his misgivings about me. I'm here to prove him wrong, to show him I'm not the cheater he claims me to be. I refuse to be lumped into the same wretched category of human beings who have offended him so.

I've been patient. I've worked hard. Even harder than before.

And to be subjected to his behavior in class earlier today? *I don't think so.*

Gritting my teeth, I stomp toward him. He hasn't noticed me yet. He's facing the floor-to-ceiling windows now, a scowl on his face.

Knock. Knock.

I don't bother waiting for his response before I step into his office and close the glass door with a resounding *bang*.

Chilly eyes meet mine as he slowly turns toward me. His nostrils flare when he sees me standing before him and he mutters something into his phone before turning it off. His lips flatten—nonchalance clearly reflected on his face—as he strolls to his desk and carefully places his phone on top before sitting down in his leather chair.

He steeples his fingers in front of him and lifts his brow at me. "How may I help you, Ms. Callahan?"

I huff out a breath and stride to the other side of his large oak desk. I toss my messenger bag on the chair and don't even bother sitting down.

Pressing my palms on the desktop, I lean over, the fury unabated in my veins.

"Professor Anderson," I grit my teeth, "I want to discuss your behavior in this morning's class."

He sits back and shrugs, his fingers twirling a fountain pen, like he has no idea what I'm talking about. "What behavior?"

"You know what I'm talking about. Fred and I were having a quick, idle conversation while working, and we weren't disrupting anyone. Your words were uncalled for."

"You guys were talking about dating in the middle of a serious project. The classroom is not the time or the place for such conversations." His fingers pause on the pen and his eyes flash with warning.

"Even if that was the case, the comments from you were unnecessarily harsh. They were unprofessional if I were to be honest. I didn't appreciate you using what I told you in confidence regarding my mom and my future plans against me in front of everyone. I've done *nothing* to deserve this treatment from you. I've worked hard, scored well on all the assignments, and am never late to class."

I stab my finger onto the wood desk when I want nothing more than to stab his chest.

"Your censure was completely out-of-proportion, and for an ethics professor, especially, I'd think you'd recognize that."

Muscles twitch in his jaw and a strong pulse pops against his corded neck. He's now gripping the pen tightly in his fist.

"Be careful, young lady."

"Or what?"

Perhaps I'm crazy and out of my mind, because for a moment, I don't care he's my professor and I'm his student.

All I know is, this man has been driving me absolutely *insane* for the last two years. When we were apart, he'd invade my dreams at night. It was his voice I heard rasping in my ear when I grew slick between my legs, with a heavy ache no toys could satisfy. And now, his commanding presence and volatile temper fill my days, driving me crazy.

Ryland presses a button on his desk, and the glass walls and windows instantly turn to solid gray. The room is immediately cloaked in relative darkness, with nothing but the light from his desk lamp offering visibility.

He slowly stands up and leans toward me, his lips parting in a sneer.

"You *don't* want to test me, little girl."

"I know you're disappointed I cheated for Jocelyn," I continue, undeterred.

Perhaps I'm a prey with no commonsense left because anyone will look at his dark expression and know he's seconds from snapping, the dirty bomb inside him threatening to explode at any moment and unleash devastation around him.

But I frankly don't care anymore. I need the lonely man who stood in the rain with a smile on his face, the man with the fiery eyes, rippling muscles, but had the gentlest touch, the man who wiped away my tears and handed me an umbrella so I wouldn't be subjected to the elements.

I want that man back.

"And I'm here to tell you, yet again, in your words, the world is *not* black and white, it's shades of gray. It was the right thing to do for her and I know you agree as well, or you would've reported me. You wouldn't have given her that extra credit assignment. So, don't you dare use this incident against me. I've done nothing to warrant this behavior from you, and I *refuse* to be treated this way. It seems like you have a problem with me."

I lean forward some more and our faces are now a few inches apart. He stands up and towers over me, with the desk in between us, his hot breath caressing my heated face. His intoxicating woodsy scent with hints of citrus lands on my nose and I fight an urge to inhale deeply, to seek its source on his body.

His heavy, large, muscular body.

"Whatever problem you have, it's your problem, not mine. You need to deal with it or tell me what it is. Tell me—"

"What? That you drive me *fucking* insane with need?" he hollers, his rough voice vibrating with tension. His face is flushed, his eyes fevered, pupils dilated.

My pussy throbs and pulses. The blistering eye of the storm. He's so breathtaking. An unforgettable whirlwind, sweeping me off my feet into his madness.

He snarls. "I shouldn't be thinking about how your lips taste. I shouldn't be thinking about how I want to pin you against me and fuck you until you see stars. I shouldn't be fucking attracted to you. You're young. Bright. Fucking beautiful. Your future is untethered. Free. Limitless. I shouldn't have broken my rules for you. You drive me abso-fucking-lutely crazy. A fucking disease, and I...and I..."

He heaves, his chest moving up and down, up and down, his eyes dipping to my parted lips.

I lean forward, drawn to those perfect lips of his. "You what?" I whisper.

"And I," he rasps, "Shit. *Fuck this shit.*"

The tension between us snaps.

He clasps his large hand around the back of my neck and tugs me to him, slamming his lips on mine.

My world spins as he claims me with his mouth, a raging inferno barreling through my body with every swipe of his tongue. He invades and overpowers my senses. His teeth make an appearance, biting on my plump lip as I let out a ragged moan and claw his neck, his back, any part of his body I can reach with the wide desk between us.

He kisses me like I'm an elixir that'll fix his madness.

He kisses me like he's desperate and will die without having his lips on mine.

My heart skydives and free-falls and I meet his passion and heated aggression with clawing hands and raking nails.

With a rough growl, he swipes his arm over the surface of his desk, sending papers, pens, and God knows what else to the floor and hauls me over the desktop in one fell swoop. Like I weigh absolutely nothing.

My core clenches at this outrageous display of masculinity. He pins me to the desk and presses his hot, hard body on top of mine. My legs part of their own accord and I wrap them around his muscular thighs. My fingers dig into his back as he manhandles my face with a roughness that sends me reeling. His mouth claims me over and over again and everything feels feverish, my body on fire. I can't get enough. I want the clothes to disappear between us.

Arching my body up, I rub against the solid steel of his erection, which settles over my jean-clad pussy. He hisses like the motion singes him. He's huge. Long and thick from the large bulge in front of his pants.

"Oh my God, yes," I moan when we part for breath.

"Fuck me. Why is this so good?" he grunts as he grinds against me, his hands trailing down my body possessively, like I'm a feast he doesn't know if he'll ever experience again. He squeezes my heavy breasts over my thin tank top, his fingers pinching my hard nipples, and I let out a mewl.

"I'm fucking obsessed. Out of my mind. You drive me fucking *insane*," he growls against my neck as he bites the tender flesh there, each pinch sending a sharp current of pleasure to my clit.

I gyrate against him, my hand covering my mouth, trying to stifle my moans. His hips thrust harder against me, each slide of his thick ridge hitting my clit at precisely the right angle.

"Ryland," I whimper, my hands grabbing his muscular ass, trying to roll against him as the fire builds in my pussy.

Wetness seeps through my panties. Everything is achy. Needy.

"Yes, Millie, what do you need? You need me to fuck the ever-living shit out of you?" he rasps before biting my earlobe.

"Shiiitt," I mewl as the sensation makes me clamp my legs tighter around him and he lets out a frustrated, guttural moan, his hips snapping faster against me.

The flames climb rapidly, the sparks igniting, our hearts colliding, and the world ceases to be a swath of gray but is an array of incandescent colors instead.

"Yes, oh my God, yes. I need you inside me," I whimper into his ear as more wetness seeps out of my pussy. I need him inside me. I feel like I'll die without him filling me.

Groaning, he ruts harder against me and I feel his cock lengthening.

I thrash on the desk. "Yes, please, please, yes—"

Riiiiiing.

The ringing of the phone lying on the floor is a sudden deluge of icy rain, shattering the alternate world we are in. He freezes for a millisecond before hauling himself off me like I'm a burning hot stovetop, leaving me a melted mess on top of his desk, my pussy throbbing with unslaked need. I can only imagine how I look right now—hair in disarray, bee-stung lips, hard nipples threatening to poke holes through my thin cotton tank, my legs spread and hips arching.

Panting, my lungs rake in desperate gulps of oxygen as reality swiftly sets in.

I almost had sex with my professor in his office. Shit. I almost threw our futures away and crossed a line we could never undo.

Judging from the fury on his face as he scrambles to mute the ringing phone on the floor, he feels the same way.

"Fuck, fuck, fuck," he chants under his breath, his fingers raking through and pulling at his glorious dark hair, his forehead gleaming with sweat.

He turns around and faces the wall. I see the tightness of the muscles bunching on his back, the trembling of his hands as they knot against his sides. I hear the harshness of his panting breaths.

Thump.

He slams his palms onto the filing cabinet, the loud slap echoing in the quiet room. "Fuck. Fuck. Fuck." More frustration. More anger. More...everything.

My limbs finally awaken, and I quickly climb off the desk. I straighten my clothes, my hands shaking as I smooth my tangled hair and touch my heated face. The thumping in my chest is a devastating earthquake and I find myself disoriented.

"Go." His voice is rough. He's still not facing me. "This was a mistake. It will never happen again."

His words are a blade thrust into my trembling heart and the sharp pain wrenches the air from my lungs. *It's the right thing to do*, my mind whispers, trying to make itself heard in the madness and chaos around me.

But I don't care, my heart retorts. *I want him. I want more. I need more.*

"Ryland—" My heart won out.

"Go! We'll never speak of this again."

He whips his body toward me, his finger pointing at the door, and what I see on his face devastates me, the dagger driving deeper and twisting into the bloody wound in my chest.

His anguished eyes reek of self-hatred and self-flagellation. The throbbing vein on his forehead threatens to burst. The overarching regret radiating from his trembling frame unmoors me.

My heart clenches and plummets, a bloody mess at the bottom of my soul.

"Leave, Millie. Please," he begs.

Moisture prickles my eyes and without a further word, I turn around, open the door, and dart out of his office.

CHAPTER 25

"Hey, Ryland. Thanks for coming," a tall man hollers as he strides toward me from the sleek, modern building of soothing teak wood exteriors and pale green trimming. Next to him is a woman with golden brown hair and a beaming smile.

Shit-eating grin. Dimples. Brown hair streaked with gold, which is glinting in the waning sunlight. Dressed like he has stepped out of a Tommy Hilfiger catalog. I smile and wave, ignoring the paparazzi's hollers and bright flashes from their cameras.

"Parker Wellington, as I live and breathe. It's been too long."

Chuckling, I pull my friend to me, giving him a brief hug, before turning to his beautiful wife next to him, whose sapphire eyes are shining with laughter and warmth.

"Liz, nice to see you, too. I'm surprised the two of you came all the way from LA to be here, without the kids, no less."

She grins before wrapping me in her arms as well.

"Well, you know Parker, his firm designed these homeless shelters, so each grand opening of New Beginnings buildings is like giving birth for him. And the New York manager begged us to come out for the inaugural gardening program they're offering here to its residents. I'm excited about it. Homeless and battered women shelters are typically bare bones with basic food and lodging, so it's wonderful they're offering these additional programs."

"And having His Royal Highness, the Prince of the USA, show up and volunteer is totally attracting all the right attention," Parker quips, unleashing another annoying grin as he waggles his brows at me.

"Shut up, fucker," I mutter, unable to stifle the laughter in my voice.

We walk back toward the glass double doors and I can't help but admire the modern sleek lines softened with carefully groomed low-maintenance shrubbery and trees, environmentally conscious materials such as reclaimed wood and locally sourced granite and limestone.

Parker's architectural firm, which he opened with his friend and partner, Dylan Jones, is one of the best in the country. They will work on the upcoming renovation of The Orchid after this IPO business.

"You're doing a good thing here," I comment as we step inside the brightly lit air-conditioned lobby. "I'm happy to support."

Parker slaps a hand on my back. He doesn't need to say much because I already know his story—as a child, he lived in one of these homeless shelters with his mom after his dad died. He has always wanted to give back and now that he's a successful architect and businessman of his own right, he helps to design and build, pro-bono, these award-winning battered women and homeless shelters across the nation.

It's this desire to give back, to leave a legacy in this world which draws me to the man, even though he doesn't make it out to New York often enough.

"So, how's the IPO going? Audit stage, right? Everything is going smoothly, I hope? We haven't seen Jess these days, so I'm assuming she's holed up in the audit cave, pulling her hair out from work." Parker nods to a few attendants bustling around in the lobby. He ushers me up a flight of stairs to God knows where.

"It's going fine. I don't expect smooth sailing. Jess is probably sick of us by now."

Jess, Steven's oldest sister, is Liz's good friend and sister-in-law, since Jess married Liz's younger brother, James. "But she's treating us kindly. You know how Jess is. Even with the stresses of the audit, I haven't seen her blow a fuse yet."

He chuckles. "Yep, that's her. Well, I'm excited about your IPO and will be the first in line to buy myself some shares when you guys are listed on the stock exchange. Have to see what your 'impeccable reputation' will bring us. You know that's what the market is frenzied about—even though we're in a bad economy and folks are pinching pennies, everyone seems to be excited about your IPO because of you. Whatever magic you're wielding, you need to give me some."

Impeccable reputation. The words sound scathing in my mind because everything is smoke and mirrors. They don't see the darkness inside me.

They don't see the ethics professor who almost fucked his much-younger student in his office the other day because he couldn't help himself. They don't realize this unimpeachable Anderson nearly threw away hundreds of years of lauded reputation, endangered the IPO, which would impact the family business, gave up his dream of becoming a tenured professor, smashed through the last ethical wall of being a professor without a second thought.

I'm a disgrace and this is so very wrong.

But my groin twitches as I think of Millie sprawled on my desk, her tits heaving, her dark nipples as sharp as glass, poking out of that little scrap of a tank top, beckoning me to bite them, to suck on them, while I ram my hard cock against her jean-covered pussy. The sounds she made. The moans. The whimpers. How they got louder the rougher I was with her, like she needed my dominance, craved my aggression.

At that moment, all those obstacles disappeared like steam vaporizing in the air.

Everything was inconsequential except for her.

She made me so angry when she rightfully confronted me that day. I knew I was an ass to her. But didn't she know I was barely hanging on by a thread? And now, knowing how soft she is under me, how she yields to me so beautifully, how sweet her lips taste, how can I resist her?

I must—impeccable reputation and everything riding on it. But more importantly, Millie needs a man without shadows, a free man not living in a cage, bound to a family he loves and secretly resents at the same time. She needs to spread her wings and fly, and not to have them clipped if she's enfolded into the Anderson family business.

I need to stay away from her. There's no other alternative.

But the joke's on me, because fate seems to have other plans when we step into the rooftop garden and I turn my head and look toward the front of the space.

She is there.

Like I've conjured her from my deepest desires.

My beautiful lark is in her element, looking every inch an angel fallen from the skies, blessing mankind with her warmth and beauty. She's standing on a small makeshift stage, lecturing to a crowd of men and women of various ages sitting in rows of plastic chairs.

Millie laughs, her voice as sweet as the songbird, and says, "Do you know there are many wonderful benefits to gardening? It's not only a hobby for retired old folks nowadays."

She pauses and quirks her brow. "I see you're unimpressed. Your doubt is written all over your faces."

She leans in, her blue eyes radiating warmth and excitement, and loudly whispers, "I thought the same thing too when I started gardening. Like how lame it was, how tiring, how I could spend my time doing something more fun than watering the soil and pulling weeds."

Light chuckles fill the room as the residents listen to her while she transfers some seeds into the ceramic pots on the table. It reminds me of that day when she came into my office at ULA, holding bright yellow daffodils. The flowers that made her cry when they shattered on the floor.

"My mom loved flowers. She used to spend her free time, what little she had outside of working and taking care of my dad, my brother, and me, on our small balcony, where she'd set up her own garden. Daffodils were one of her favorites."

My heart squeezes, the tears on her face that day in my office suddenly making sense.

Her voice turns wistful, and she forces out a smile. "When I asked her why she spent so much time out there, she told me, 'Millie, do you know plants have healing powers? They're magic. When you get your hands dirty in the soil, feeling nature at your fingertips, nurturing the flowers, vegetables, fruits, or whatever it is you're growing, they'll respond to you.'"

She looks up, her gaze intent on the small crowd. "It's something *you* can control, something you have full power over. When you nurture nature, it'll bloom and blossom under your care. The wonderful flowers and getting your heart rate up as you putter about are just side benefits."

The room is quiet; the crowd sitting with rapt attention. I see a few women shift in their seats and one of them discreetly wipes her face with her hands. Most likely, the lives they ran away from didn't allow them to have much, if any, control.

Millie grins as she pours some soil into the ceramic pot. "Someday, besides teaching, I want to open my own greenhouse to the public for free...so everyone can have these beautiful flowers and gardens at their fingertips, so parents don't have to worry about paying adult ticket costs to take their children to kids-free admission days. Anyone, regardless of status, can enjoy these flowers for free."

Millie swipes her lips with that pink tongue of hers and I feel my cock twitch in my pants. I can still taste her honeyed sweetness, feel the tentative swipes of her tongue as it tangled with mine. I swallow and let out a ragged exhale.

"She's great, isn't she? Captivates the crowd," Parker comments, and I can't help but agree.

She'll be a great educator one day. Empathetic. Passionate. She'll help many underprivileged people from all over the world. *Something she can't do if she is with you and living in the Anderson cage.*

I nod, unable to reply or tear my eyes away from Millie.

"Do you know, there's research showing a certain bacterium in the soil, the *Mycobacterium vaccae*, can act as a natural antidepressant because of its interactions with serotonin, the happy chemical, in our brains? So, Mom wasn't lying to me after all. There *is* magic in the soil..."

"How did you find her?" I ask Parker as I'm transfixed on Millie.

At his silence, I turn to him, finding him gazing lovingly at his wife, watching her flutter around the room, handing out refreshments to the residents who are looking with ardent attention at the goddess on the stage. My heart pinches at the lovestruck expression on his face, like he'd be happy even if his world burned down as long as he had his wife by his side.

For the first time in my life, I wonder what things would be like if I had this kind of love in my life. Would my soul feel less tired, less cold? Would the prison feel more like heaven?

My gaze shifts to Millie once more, and the panging hits harder in my chest, resounding like a gong, and I clench my fists, unwilling to acknowledge the impact or the sound and what they represent.

Love isn't for me. This is physical attraction only. The temptation of the forbidden.

That has to be it. That's all there is to it.

She has dreams—beautiful dreams. Don't take them away from her. You'll imprison her and one day she'll get sick of it. Like Mom did toward the end, when I saw her eyes dimming, how she appeared so sad whenever she talked about the dreams she used to have.

Parker shifts next to me. "Sorry. I got sidetracked for a bit there. Anyway, Millie? She's actually family."

That got my attention. "What?" I stare at him.

He shrugs. "Few people know this because she's down to earth and doesn't advertise her connections. But her brother is Adrian Scott, who, as you probably know, had that epic romance and married Emily, Jess's younger sister, a year ago."

"The Shark? Her brother is The Shark?"

He nods. "It's pretty obvious, right? The dark hair, the elegant features. I can see the resemblance." Parker stiffens, his head swiveling toward me, his eyes narrowing. "Hold on, why do you sound so interested? What's this to you?"

I tug at the pendant hanging around my neck, my skin feeling heated once more. Not only is the forbidden woman my student, but she's also related to one of the most powerful men in the business community, who is renowned for his thirst for revenge to those who have wronged him in the past, the cold billionaire everyone wants to know but is also afraid of. If he catches a whiff of my filthy intentions toward his sister, I can kiss the IPO goodbye. It doesn't matter if my family is old money and more powerful than him. No one wrongs The Shark and escapes unscathed.

"She's my student. I'm just surprised she's here."

"Hm." He stares at me for a few more beats, but I don't look at him. "If you say so."

"Now, we've set up stations here for you to try your hand at gardening. Remember, perfection is unnecessary. Get your hands dirty, feel the damp soil, try to stay present, and focus on your breathing," Millie instructs as the small crowd breaks into quiet conversations and folks move about the space. I hear the scraping of metal spades and trowels against the ceramic pots and muted laughter.

Parker grabs me by my shoulder. He holds up his phone. "Sorry, I have to take this. I'm supposed to help Millie up there. Can you step in instead? I owe you one." He holds my gaze for a moment, registering my nod, and steps away.

My pulse kicks up into a drumming beat and every cell in my body awakens and sizzles with energy. I stroll up to her, the woman who has been featured in every lurid fantasy in the last year and a half, the woman, I suspect, will be my undoing if I don't stop this train wreck in slow motion.

"Millie." My voice is hoarse as I step up behind her. I suck in a gulp of jasmine and vanilla scented air.

She freezes. A pulse flutters in her neck, beckoning me to touch it, to graze it with my tongue. I swallow, watching her turn her blue gaze at me.

"Ryland." My name sounds so damn good on her lips. I don't bother correcting her for using my first name.

We stare at each other as the background chatter and crowds dissolve into darkness, trapping us in this bubble only we can see. My eyes dart to her lips again, which are plump and parted. Her breathing quickens. A blush blooms on her cheeks and I watch those blue eyes of hers darken, the navy striations melting into the black.

I lean in, my willpower quickly losing the battle of what's right or wrong, what's ethical or unethical. Her eyes flutter shut, the dark lashes fanning her smooth skin. *We're not at school today. She's an adult, and it's consensual.* My heart hurls flimsy excuses at my brain, trying anything to see what sticks.

"Millie? I broke my pot. I'm s-so sorry. Please don't be angry at me." A timid voice breaks through our connection and Millie jerks back and turns to the mousy woman before her, who appears terrified of evoking Millie's wrath.

Millie's eyes soften and she clasps her hand on top of the woman's. "Don't you worry about it. This happens to all of us. You can get an extra over there."

The woman scurries away, leaving us in stilted silence.

"You're good with them," I comment as I hand her a new pot.

"I learned from the best." She gives me a teasing wink and my heart hiccups. My lips twitch in an effort not to smile.

Millie waggles her brows. "Well, if you're here to help me, let me put you to good use."

"Where do you want me, *teacher*?" I make an exaggerated bow.

She giggles. God, I want to hear that sound every day. It's like a shot of dopamine in my veins.

"Bring those bags of potting soil around the room and refill the containers at each station. Make sure all the tables have extra supplies and tools. We expect some clumsiness and broken pots, and that's okay. There are extra packets of seeds on the shelf over there in case anyone asks you for more." She points to a few rows of metal shelves in the far corner of the space.

"We want these folks to feel comfortable in their surroundings, to put their energy into the task before them, to make something with two hands."

Millie gestures with her hands, her blue eyes turning animated. "Regaining their lives starts with small steps, and we want them to feel empowered, beginning with growing this little pot of life in front of them."

Her face is flushed, an alluring glow radiating from her. She bites on her plush bottom lip, a flirty glint appearing in her gaze. Slowly, she steps closer, and my heart lodges in my throat, my breath freezing in my lungs.

She trails her fingers up my forearm and my muscles automatically flex. The pink in her cheeks deepens and she frees that fucking lip from her teeth.

Sharp heat shoots south, and my dick twitches in my pants.

Her fingers linger on my biceps. She looks up at me from under her long lashes. "Got to put a *strong, powerful* man like you to good use."

She sounds breathy. I want to hear this voice when I'm tangled in the bedsheets with her at night.

"Oh yeah?"

She's drawing circles on my arm now, and I can feel every stroke on my throbbing cock. I shift my stance.

"Go on, be a *good student* for me," she whispers, her eyes dilating and flickering to my mouth, "listen to your teacher."

My nostrils flare and my cock roars to full-mast.

Fuck me.

CHAPTER 26

THE CLASS PASSES BY in a blur. After our conversation, where it took every ounce of self-control to step away from her, I took a minute to myself in the garden shed and waited for my flagpole to disappear before making my rounds at each table stationed around the large rooftop garden.

It was manual labor, hefting heavy bags of soil and pots of various sizes, and then answering questions people may have or directing them to Millie.

A thin layer of sweat coats my skin but when I stand to the side and look at her, watching her bright smile and calming patience as she bids her students goodbye before they filter out of the garden. I can't help but smile, my cavernous chest flooding with light and warmth.

The afternoon sunlight peeks out from behind the clouds, the rays bathing her in a warm glow, and the traitorous heart of mine jumps and leaps.

This afternoon is a glimpse of what life *could be* like if we were just a normal man and woman, without the shackles associated with my family name and the forbidden nature of our relationship between us.

But we don't live in a land of what-if and could-be. The kiss that day at the office should've never happened.

We can never happen.

I need to tell her that, to tell her not to put her hopes in me.

The crowd thins out and the only folks left are the workers, all diligently cleaning up the space. I walk up to Millie, who is now fiddling with the supplies on her table.

She smiles as I approach her, her beautiful eyes lighting up, but whatever is showing on my face causes the joy to dim in her expression.

I sigh. "Millie, the other day in the office—"

"Tell me, why did you carry my scarf with you that first day in class?"

I freeze, my mind thinking back to that first day when my lungs forgot how to breathe in her presence, when she picked up my things from the floor.

I can't give her myself, but I want to tell her the truth.

"It was a reminder of you. A softness I don't deserve in my life."

When I left LA, I couldn't forget her but I couldn't go to her. And so, instead, I'd resigned myself to carrying around her gift for me, her *handmade* scarf, despite what she told me. Even to my untrained eye, the varying stitches and the uneven widths were obvious.

My fingers would touch the softness in the dark moments, when the pressures of life felt too heavy, and I'd imagine it was a caress from her. And on the frigid winter days, I'd curl it around my neck when I braved the snow, and my heart would feel a little less lonely.

Her eyes soften. "You deserve a lot more than you give yourself credit for," she whispers. Her lips curve into a sad smile.

"Do you know my favorite flower is the pasque flower?" She stacks seed packets into an orderly pile. "It blooms in the early spring when the environment is still recovering from the harsh winter. It may look delicate with its thin, lavender petals and gold stamen, but it's strong. A fighter. Flourishes in the middle of hardship. They say the flower symbolizes rebirth and new beginnings."

Her voice is passionate and strong. Just like her. *A fighter,* as she said. My fingers clench the clay pot in front of me. Anything to stop me from touching her.

I want to feel her vitality, the pulse beating against her throat, bask in the strong rays of her sunshine, and let her chase away the suffocating darkness in my soul.

Instead, I reply, "My favorite animal is the snowy owl."

Her hands pause and I sense her stare. Swallowing the lump in my throat, I continue, "They are rare and beautiful. Their feathers are as white as freshly fallen snow. But despite their beauty, the snowy owls are powerful hunters. They relish in solitude."

"Independent and strong." I hear the smile in her voice. "Just like you."

I scoff. "No, not like me. I'm the facade. They're the real deal."

"Why do you feel this way?" Her voice is gentle, soothing, quietly teasing the wisps of darkness out of me.

"Being an Anderson isn't an easy task. I love my family more than anything in the world, but the expectations growing up, the responsibilities..." My voice trails off as guilt snakes its way inside my chest. I'm privileged, living a life most people can only dream of. And yet, I'm still complaining.

Clearing my throat, I continue, "We're born knowing we need to take a place in the family business and uphold the family's pristine reputation. Ever since I can remember, I've known one day I'll be taking the helm of Fleur alongside Maxwell. There are hundreds of years of unimpeachable Andersons in my lineage. A lot of history and character. It...it doesn't—"

"Leave a lot of room for you to live for yourself," she finishes as she places her delicate hand on top of mine. I freeze at her soft caress, the warmth, the gentleness.

Her magic.

"Perhaps your world isn't as black and white as you think it is. If your family loves you like you say they do, they won't want you to give up living for yourself because of them...because of traditions."

She twines her fingers with mine, every slide feeling like the right key inserted into a lock, a satisfying click, the moment you feel the distinct snap as you turn and realize this rusty old lock finally opens. "They'll want you to be happy, Ryland."

"It isn't done. Generations of Andersons before me and no one has stepped away."

Because the stakes are too high, because everyone will lose every-thing if one of us falls out of line.

"Great Uncle Jameson kept the company afloat during the second world war. Rumors said he even had a rifle in one hand as he was closing the books when the fight got too close. Grandfather once said working for the family business was his greatest achievement."

I have stories, many anecdotes of all the Andersons before me who have done their jobs with honor and pride. "And Maxwell, he gave up so much—" The words are stuck in my throat as the old wound inside my chest festers and aches, the boils spreading throughout my body.

"Family is always first," I whisper. "Always."

I hear her quiet breaths above the background noise, feel the comforting graze of her fingers as they twine with mine. Dancing, whirling, making love to me with her hand. My breath lodges in my throat, a sultry heat moving south, and my mouth waters, wanting to taste her again.

To drink from her magic.

"I think, Ryland," she whispers back, keeping us in this startling intimacy, "life isn't as dark as you think it is. Perhaps you can't see it since you're in the eye of the storm, with rain pouring down your face, blurring your vision. But I can. And I don't care what you say about yourself. You're a beautiful man, inside and out, and letting go isn't as hard as you think it is. One day, I'll convince you. You'll see."

That's what I'm afraid of.

The temptation, my heart fighting a losing battle. That ultimate-ly, I'll disappoint everyone around me because of my selfish desires.

Clutching her hand tightly in mine, I watch her fingers stiffen under the pressure. I increase my grip and hear her gasp. I give her a peek into my darkness and how I want to unleash the beast within.

Don't you see I'm a monster beneath the suit? I can snuff out your life with a pinch of my fingers. I'm not roses and sunshine. I'm lightning and thunder. My thumb swirls a circle on the back of her hand, which is reddening by the second as the blood pools there.

Instead of pulling away, I hear the quickened pace of her breathing and fuck, I can't help but turn and look at her, expecting anger or indignation in her eyes, or a furious command to let her go.

But what I see on her face threatens to burn through the steel chains of my restraint.

Her skin is flushed, her eyes heavy-lidded. Her mouth parts mid-gasp. I see her canting her head toward me, her luscious tits brushing against my arm. I can make out her nipples pebbling with each second of my gaze and the throbbing pulse in her neck.

She looks like my darkest dream coming to life. Submissive, yet both strong and soft for me.

She can take your darkness. She's a fighter.

I want to drag her away to the private gardens on the other side of the rooftop, throw her on the ground, and render her immobile underneath me, her face pressed against the soft grass.

I want to hear her whimpers as she fights to escape, only to succumb to my need for her.

I want to hear her scream my name when she comes undone.

"I see you, Ryland Anderson," her voice is a half moan, half whisper, "I see you and I'm not afraid of you."

Heavy heat—anger or lust or a combination of both—sweeps through me with the power of a flash flood.

Her words shatter the last of my restraint and a low growl tears from my lips. Ignoring onlookers who have turned their heads our way, I drag her to the nearest garden shed, throw open the door, and toss her inside.

Before the door fully shuts, I have her pinned against the wall.

"Not afraid?" I rasp against her neck. *You silly, silly girl.* "If anyone finds out about this, your precious future—the one where you'll go to grad school then travel the world teaching—will be ruined."

The selfish beast inside me takes over, forgetting about the family reputation, the tenure opportunity, the IPO, morals, ethics, everything I'm supposed to stand for.

Illuminated by the faint glow of the sliver of light coming in from the door, I can see her eyes dilating, her hands coming up to where my arm is banded across her chest. But instead of clawing me off her, she wraps her luscious legs around me, the heels of her shoes digging into my backside.

"No," she gasps, her lungs no doubt fighting the burn for oxygen. "I'm not afraid. Not when you're like this, all sharp fangs and talons or when you're giving me your umbrella so I don't have to be cold from the rain."

Her fingernails dig into my taut muscles, and the room feels feverishly hot. "You can't scare me away, Ryland."

"Fuck," I grunt and release my arm across her chest to grip the two cotton-covered globes of her ass.

My hands knead the firm flesh, and I grind my throbbing cock on her heat. She whimpers and thrashes as I rut against her with nothing but my casual dress pants and her little cotton shorts separating us.

"Fuck. Fuck. Fuck." My dick hits her clit, and she lets out a mewl.

Unable to withstand the temptation any longer, I slam my lips over hers and drink the magic at the source, her sweet taste of honey and coffee giving me the highest of highs.

I can't think. I can't breathe. I can't listen to the faint warnings my mind is giving me—to tell me to step away and stop this before we reach a point of no return—I can only invade and take.

Take. Take. Take.

Sweeping my tongue in her mouth, I duel with hers for dominance and she scratches my back like a feral cat in heat.

The fight turns my vision black and overwhelming lust corrupts the last rational thoughts as my teeth scrap over her slender neck, biting the hammering pulse which has taunted me earlier.

"Ryland." She lets out a tiny scream. I try to pause but she won't let me, her legs clamping harder against my back. "More. More. I'm not afraid of you, Ryland."

I lose my fucking mind.

My hand coils around her neck, giving it soft pressure—not enough to cut off her airway, but definitely enough to make her lungs fight for the precious oxygen.

"Still more?" I rasp. I hear the madness in my voice.

Her legs shake around me, her lips forming the words, "*More,*" and I lean in, my breathing heavy against her ear. "I'm not fucking you, Millie. This isn't happening. You can't break me. I'm your fucking professor and I. Am. Not. Fucking. You."

Millie claws at me in earnest now, her eyes defiant as she tries to pull my lips toward her, even as she's gasping for breath.

The fight in her is intoxicating. Addictive.

She succeeds and bites my bottom lip and a sharp pleasure shoots straight to my cock, which hardens to the point of bursting. She soothes the bite with her tongue and attempts to grind her hips over my aching dick.

"I'm not fucking you. But your little pussy needs me, doesn't it? I bet you're dripping wet, needing release. And I wouldn't be a good professor if I didn't take care of my student now, would I?"

Without waiting for her response, I shove my free hand inside her shorts, keeping the other caged around her neck. Swiping her panties to the side, I plunge my finger into her wet hot heat. She lets out a ragged scream and slams her head against the wall.

"You're so fucking wet. So tight. Look at your pussy sucking me in."

I keep my eyes on her face as my finger thrusts into her and my thumb rubs circles around her swollen clit. Her muscles lock with tension, her fingers digging into my hand around her neck, her hips buckling under the onslaught of my fingers.

"R-Ryland," she rasps, "what's happening to me? It has never been like this." Juices sluice out of her and I crave a taste.

The wet sounds of my fingers sawing in and out of her tight pussy have me hanging on by a thread. Pre-cum leaks into my pants, but I couldn't care less.

"Your body wants both oxygen and to come, the needs feeding into each other. But you can't do either until I let you." I insert another finger inside her, fucking her hard and she nearly careens off the wall.

Her moans are loud and obscene as she thrashes against me. Her nails will no doubt leave marks on my skin after this. Her wetness drips all over my hand and her legs tremble. I feel the telltale signs of her pussy throbbing.

"I-I need," she begs, panting harshly, before rolling her eyes back. Her entire body starts spasming in my hold.

"Come for your professor, Millie. Fucking *cream in my hand.*"

I hammer my fingers inside her, and she explodes. I quickly let go of her neck, watching her lungs heave in the much-needed oxygen, her mouth parted in a silent cry of ecstasy.

She's so fucking perfect.

My balls are so heavy, my cock is so hard and throbbing, everything is about to burst, but I don't want to grip it, to give it the few life-giving pumps and unleash my cum because this is the punishment I'm giving to myself, a professor with the hots for his student, dirtying up her innocence, snuffing out her halo.

I will *not* be the one to clip her wings.

I can't.

CHAPTER 27

I'm a fucking coward.

The thought is on repeat as I knock my forehead on the double-paned windows at our reserved room in the gentlemen's club at The Orchid two weeks later. Maxwell used to make fun of how much I enjoyed looking out the windows.

Little does he know it's the freedom outside I crave.

It's one of the most beautiful times of the year in New York City, with summer bidding us farewell and fall welcoming us with open arms, dazzling bystanders with foliage of reds, oranges, and yellows, the weather brisk but not yet chilly. Central Park is sprawled beneath us in the near distance, a beautiful postcard, but I don't really notice.

Because I'm a fucking coward.

After the event at New Beginnings, where Millie came all over my fucking fingers, the image permanently branded into my brain, I've avoided her like a plague.

In the classroom and at the JEAP committee meetings, I've directed my instructions to someone else in her group, including Fred, even though my jaws will ache from clenching every time I see him flirting with her. When she asks a question, I answer it as succinctly as possible. I always leave right after class ends, exiting the room with the throngs of students, using them as protection.

I've canceled office hours, making up some bullshit reason about meetings and conflicts at Fleur for the IPO, and letting students know they can schedule appointments with me via email.

I know she's upset and hurt, judging from the hard glare in her cutting eyes when my gaze inadvertently meets hers in the middle of class. But instead of tears, she sits straighter, her nostrils flaring, her chin tilting higher.

No, she's no longer the fragile water nymph, stammering at my feet. She's a fighter, and I've been mistaken all along. Millie is a predator flying through the skies.

She's the snowy owl. A stealthy hunter. Rare and beautiful. Soaring straight into my heart whether I want it or not.

Letting out a ragged breath, I eye the pedestrians down below, roaming free on the streets, braving the honking traffic and the brisk elements while I sit on my throne, feeling restless, wanting to go to her, to see her, to feel her fall apart in my arms once more.

"Something is on your mind. Don't bother denying it. Now, spill," a deep voice speaks from behind me.

I look behind, finding the imposing silhouette of Steven, decked in his usual three-piece suit even though it's Saturday afternoon. He's early to an evening with the guys. His piercing hazel eyes narrow at whatever he sees on my face, and I straighten up and roll out the stiff muscles on my shoulders.

"What made you decide to go for Grace? You had your obligations at Pietra Capital, saving TransAmerica, not to mention your mom disapproving her. You guys were worlds apart."

He strolls to the wet bar, pours two glasses of whiskey, and walks up next to me before handing me a drink. "There wasn't another choice. My heart wants what its wants."

A heart wants what it wants.

The same sentiments from Sydney all those years ago, the only other woman I've let remotely near my heart, and not even as close as Millie has barged through those barriers.

"But what about right or wrong? Ethics? You know what you're bringing Grace into. Your family is old money like mine, with all the obligations, rules, appearances. The relentless paparazzi. It never ends. Aren't you afraid of suffocating her?"

He chuckles and clasps his hand on my arm. "It's for her to decide, not me, and I'm a lucky man because she chose me. Technically, Grace is part of the old money family now, since she's an Anderson."

I smile inwardly. That she is. Grace and Taylor are wonderful women, but ironically, because their mom wasn't married to Dad when they were born, they are illegitimate Anderson offspring as defined by the terms of the family trust and thus are spared the constraints of our obligations.

Not to mention, they aren't married into the family, nor have they taken our last names, so there isn't an expectation for them to give everything up and join the fold. But Grace, with her plans to open a consulting firm with our family name on it, is already stepping into tradition by choice.

Things don't end well for most of the women in my family, especially the women the Anderson men love. Despite my dad's intentions when he broke up with the second woman he's ever loved in his life, Grace's and Taylor's mom met with a tragic ending as well. She passed away from a car accident last year. Drunk driver crashing his car into her, killing her instantly.

I can't guarantee a happy future for Millie when everything seems to point to an unhappy ending.

How can I let her choose a life like that? How can I let her knowingly walk into a trap? How can I ask her to give up her dreams of teaching, the very thing she wants to do to honor her mom? And if one day she realizes the chains she has been wearing the entire time and how much she misses the skies, how will I survive when she leaves me?

And I can't risk that. I can't risk what's left of my heart, which has a hole in it ever since Mom died, then is overburdened by the weight of the Anderson name and constraints, on top of everything else.

The door opens and in stride my brothers.

Maxwell arches his brow at Steven and me, clearly sensing we're in a serious discussion. I give him a half-smile. *Let bygones be bygones, Maxwell.*

He returns my smile with one of his own and flashes his leather bracelet. *Always, brother.*

"Steven, why the hell are you in a suit again?" Rex grumbles as he slumps into the room, clearly hungover from what looks to be a night of partying.

"Some of us enjoy working," Steven comments.

"I work hard and play hard."

Ethan quips, "Aren't you tired of having different women each night? Haven't you tried out all the kink rooms on the Rose floors already?"

"Tired of pussy? Nah, no way. I like them however I get them. All beautiful—big, small, all colors. There's no such thing as being 'tired of pussy,' old man."

He narrows his eyes at us. "And don't make fun of me embracing my kinks. Heck, Ryland over there likes to chase and pin down women like a savage and you don't see me making fun of him."

"Ryland has one kink, but you have countless. You're a deviant with a capital D."

"Mark my words, Ethan, Mr. Goody-Two-Shoes, I'm going to find out your deep dark kink because I know it's in there."

Ethan smirks and crosses his arms against his chest. "We'll see about that."

"Where's Charles?" Steven asks, looking for the signature blond of our group.

"The fucker is busy. Some meeting in the office. He's a workaholic like you." Rex unleashes a yawn.

"They are contributing members to society," Ethan corrects, waggling his brows at a scowling Rex.

They bicker and I shake my head, a spark of amusement lifting my lips.

Steven squeezes my arm before releasing it with a pat. He leans in and murmurs, "If she's worth losing sleep for, I think she's worth taking a risk for. Let her choose for herself."

The chains bind tighter around my chest, slowly restricting my breath. Perhaps there's a shred of humanity left within the beast. The sliver of conscience in my murky mind.

How can I let her choose when it will hurt her in the end? No, that's impossible.

Rex hollers in the background, "What are you two mumbling about over there? If this is about Ryland's 'I'm not sulking over a woman but it's so obvious he is' problem, dude, no woman is worth losing sleep over. You know what I think? You just need to rip the bandage off and go schedule a scene at Noire. All that celibacy shit is affecting your mind and isn't good for your health, bro."

The guys burst into laughter. A minute later, Maxwell sidles up to me and echoes the sentiment. "This is going to be one of the few times I agree with Rex. The IPO is going smoothly, the press eating up all the information we're handing out, so your surly ass mood can't be about that. If you're trying to get over a woman, perhaps you need to put yourself out there. And if a scene is the easiest thing to start with, then why not? Think about it."

I nod and let out a sigh. Outside the windows, I see a small crowd of people gathering on the sidewalk holding up large signs. There appears to be a protest of some sort against one of the luxury clothing brands nearby. People are braving the crowds, taking time out of their day to fight for change.

Perhaps it's time for me to do something about my situation as well.

CHAPTER 28

IT'S BEEN AN ENTIRE month since he has iced me out. Professor Ryland Anderson, the untouchable Prince of the USA, keeping everyone at arm's length, has been back in full force. He has blocked off every attempt by me to talk to him in private. He's acting like nothing has ever happened between us.

Like anything can erase the fevered memories of me falling apart in his arms, experiencing the most intense orgasm in my life, the way he tasted—mint with a hint of coffee—how he came alive each time he held me against him, all blistering lightning and pelting rain, a tornado sweeping me up into madness.

How can I forget any of this? It's impossible.

The only good thing that happened this last month was receiving my PhD acceptances. The girls were ecstatic for me when the letters came in. Joss even sent me some celebratory flowers and chocolates from LA. My hard work has paid off and I have my pick of programs.

I know I should stay away from Ryland. After all, I'm putting my dreams at risk by being entangled with him. But lately, the argument sounds feeble to my heart, which recognizes in its very core what Ryland and I have. The way our psyches speak to each other is one of a kind, and something I won't encounter again. And I can't bring myself to let this go, to let *us* go. Ultimately, this is a risk I'm willing to take.

Gritting my teeth, I haul ass across the paved pathways on campus, ignoring the chilly breeze of fall. The amber leaves flutter and fall to the ground, a kaleidoscope of colors I usually admire when I'm in a better mood.

Instead, I wrap my red cashmere scarf tighter around my neck and stride toward class, my mind spinning with ideas about how I can get through the heavy layer of sleet to reveal the bubbling lava within the volcano of his soul.

"Who do I need to kill, and will you help me with the body?" Chloe appears next to me, her porcelain skin pink from the elements.

She cracks her knuckles as if she has a black belt in anything, even though the woman can't swat a fly. She'll probably hit herself with a bat while trying to inflict bodily harm on to someone else.

Biting back a smile, I reply, "You don't need to kill anyone. I'm fine."

"You've been sulking the last month and I've noticed something else interesting as well..." her voice trails off as she waits for my reaction.

I roll my eyes. "What did you notice, Chloe?"

"A certain dark-haired professor has been looking extra pissed off this past month too. Like he really needs to get into a good fight or something. I wonder if the two are related."

My heart skips a beat and I fight the urge to look at her, even though I can feel her gaze searing onto the side of my face.

"Who?" I ask nonchalantly.

A gentle shove. "Come on, girl. I won't tell Belle if that's what you're worried about. Well, maybe not everything...but she's been pestering me, so no guarantees. You're seeing her tonight, right? Say hi to her for me."

I let out a sigh. "Chloe, there's nothing going on between Professor Anderson and me. Drop it. I don't want rumors to spread. It'd be disastrous for us both. And yes, I'm meeting with the other girls tonight, you nosy person."

She skips a few steps in front of me before turning around, giving me a saucy, victorious wink. "I said *nothing* about Professor Anderson. You came up with that all by yourself."

Chloe then points her index and middle fingers toward her eyes then at me, the universal hand signal for "I'll be watching you," and waggles her brows. "Hurry, we'll be late soon. And I'm on your side, professor or not!"

Dammit.

The first half hour of class was another frustrating, blood-boiling affair where Ryland would look over my head when talking to me, his hands hidden in his pants pockets. But I felt the heat of his stare when I wasn't looking at him, when he thought I was unaware. And when I'd turn my face toward him, I'd catch the smallest glimpse of his silver gaze flashing away and a vein throbbing on his forehead.

Now, we're in the middle of the JEAP committee meeting, presenting the new information we've gathered on the open cases this past month from hours of interviewing, reviewing footage and emails.

The university IT department has turned over hard drives of emails between Professor Archer and Tammy. There is definitely a personal relationship, but the phrasing has never moved beyond innuendo. There isn't anything definitive to show Professor Archer and Tammy are doing anything inappropriate.

I never knew how extensive these investigations were, but I guess it's a good thing the university is being thorough. I know that's sadly an anomaly and not the norm.

Perhaps the strict, unimpeachable Ryland has something to do with the gold standard here at NYUC.

"Why are we doing this, professor? Aren't we just wasting time? It's obvious Professor Archer and Tammy are guilty of a relationship. Just fire him and expel her. Why continue to spend hours talking to people and wasting everyone's time?" Pete Crosby, a lanky guy with horn-rimmed glasses perched on his nose, asks.

Ryland's face is unemotional as he turns to the rest of us. "Anyone want to answer Pete?"

Looking around the classroom and seeing no raised hands, I speak up. "There's an inherent imbalance of power in the alleged relationship, and the damage to the reputations of both the professor and the student will be severe if the committee rules against them. As advisers, we should do our best to ensure all facts checked out, no rocks are left unturned, and there's unequivocal evidence of guilt before we recommend our position to the Ethics Committee."

I clear my throat. "This might seem like a waste of time when everything seems to point in one direction, but that doesn't mean we get to shortcut the entire process. We owe it to Professor Archer and Tammy to do our due diligence."

Pete snorts and waves his hand in dismissal. "It's easy for you to say, Millie. You are a shoo-in for passing this class with your connections and everything. The rest of us actually have to study and go through the normal process of applying and waiting for PhD program acceptances."

Fred stiffens next to me and Chloe mutters, "What the fuck," under her breath.

My hackles rise and I clench my jaw. "What are you trying to say, Pete? I've earned my academic standing and my early admissions to PhD programs result from my hard work, and those acceptances can easily be rescinded if I don't work my ass off like everyone here."

He rolls his eyes, his lips flattening with displeasure. "Come on, Millie. We live in the real world. I mean, that's what Professor Anderson has been preparing us for, right?"

I sneak a glance over at Ryland, finding his hands behind his back, his muscular forearms straining against his white dress shirt, his lips twitching into something resembling a snarl.

Pete mutters, "You're telling me being the sister of Adrian Scott won't make a difference how others treat you and your acceptances into the top programs?"

He rolls his eyes. "Yeah, *everyone knows.* You want to talk about ethics? Now, that's an ethical violation right there."

The students gasp around me. Chloe shoots to a standing position and points her fingers at Pete. "You asshole. Millie works harder than any of us."

My face erupts in flames as the classroom breaks into chaos. Memories of Lloyd force themselves into my mind. The greedy glint of his eyes when I told him Adrian was my brother. How he'd magically appear at my side whenever I spoke with Adrian on the phone, or how he'd insist on coming with me whenever I met up with Adrian, only to be furious when I rejected him. How he broke up with me because I wouldn't ask Adrian to give him a loan to pay off his credit card debts.

This is what I'm afraid of. Everyone seeing me as billionaire Adrian Scott's younger sister, instead of Millie Callahan. Everyone scrutinizing my achievements under a microscope because of my brother.

My hands clench the edges of the tabletop, a firestorm of fury racing inside me.

"I'm proud of my brother and his achievements, but my successes are my own," I grit out under my breath.

Pete snickers and a few of his friends laugh alongside him. "It must be wonderful to be naïve. If only the rest of us had the same privilege. I just found out I didn't get into the PhD program at Cornell because they only take one student from NYUC and I know you got that spot, you b—"

Slam!

The loud sound of textbooks thrown against the table reverberates in the classroom like a shockwave, abruptly silencing Pete and all the furtive whispers in the room. We turn toward the disturbance.

Ryland towers over his desk, a stack of books scattered over the table and on the floors. A muscle twitches rapidly in his jaw as his dark eyes shoot daggers at Pete, who slowly cowers under his withering gaze.

"This behavior is why you didn't get into Cornell, Mr. Crosby. Not Millie, not anything or anyone else. If you had spent more time studying and working hard instead of forming conspiracy theories and being a general fucking jackass, perhaps you would've had a shot."

He walks away from his desk, his steps slow and measured, a lion slowly approaching his next meal. I shudder at the fury rolling off of him in heavy waves and Pete hiccups in his seat. Ryland towers over Pete and leans down, not stopping until he's a few inches away from his face. I try and fail to ignore the tiny flutters in my stomach as I see him come to my defense.

His voice is low and hoarse, the violence barely concealed within. "Ms. Callahan is a brilliant student, her work speaks for itself, and I don't need to fucking pander to Adrian Scott or to any billionaire because I'm a fucking billionaire myself. If you have a problem with her or with the way this class is run, you come to me. You don't speak to her. You don't look at her. You don't fucking spread rumors about her. Am I making myself clear?"

Those tiny flutters are now a large swarm, flapping wildly and wreaking havoc inside me. My breathing quickens and I feel Chloe putting her hand over mine and giving me a squeeze of support, but I barely notice.

I only see him. My avenging warrior.

He can ignore me for all he wants and pretend everything that occurred between us never happened, but this...this magnificent display of emotion tells me *everything* I need to know.

Ryland's eyes dart to mine and he holds my gaze. My fingers tremble as I press them against my lips and swallow the ball forming in my throat. Words want to escape my throat, but I can't say them here in front of everyone. A burning sensation appears behind my eyes and wetness prickles my vision.

His nostrils flare and his eyes flash, darkening into swirling midnight pools of tar before he turns back to Pete. Ryland's hands are fisted on his desk, clearly trying to restrain himself from physically reaching over and hauling Pete up by the collar of his shirt.

"Am. I. Making. Myself. Clear?"

Pete physically shakes underneath his withering glare and nods. "Y-Yes, Professor."

"Now, apologize to Ms. Callahan and the rest of the class for this immature disturbance," Ryland barks.

Pete jumps in his seat and turns toward us. His eyes are downcast as they briefly skate over me to the rest of the room.

"S-Sorry, Millie. Sorry, class."

My exhales are ragged as I give him the barest of nods. My eyes flicker over to Ryland again, finding him staring at me, the same intense pools of gray right before he hauled me into the shed and kissed the ever fucking daylights out of me. The same eyes boring into mine in my dreams when I'd wake up sweaty with an unrelenting ache between my legs.

Are you okay? His gaze tells me if I answer anything negative, he'll burn the world for me.

I flash him a trembling smile. *I am. Because of you.*

His eyes skim over my features in a gentle caress, even though we're standing several feet apart amidst a classroom full of people. But in this moment, nothing matters. No one matters except for him.

My heart throws itself against my rib cage, wanting to escape and hurl itself toward him. The seconds freeze in time and everything begins to fade around us.

"And you were saying there's nothing going on?" Chloe whispers in my ear. "You guys are having a full-on conversation without words."

I don't respond to her, because my voice is frozen, my breath is stolen by this intimidating man in front of us, and if he is my jailer, I'm willing to walk into his cage.

CHAPTER 29

"So, I just had the most *interesting* conversation with Chloe," Belle comments from her spot on the corner of the sofa as the girls and I lounge in our living room, watching a chick flick playing on the flat-screen hanging over our brick fireplace.

It's another regular girls' night in our apartment where we gorge on ice cream and junk food—chips for the Peyton sisters, gummy bears for me, and cookies for Belle—and movies or TV shows. The logs crackle and pop, a fire burning in the hearth as the temperatures turn icy cold with the heavy rains pouring outside.

While I took care of the rooftop garden, Belle had taken the helm at decorating the interiors of our swanky SoHo apartment using her impeccable fashion sense.

At first glance, it's an overwhelming burst of colors—soothing aquamarine walls decorated with colorful Andy Warhol and other avant-garde art prints, a long, lavender velvet sofa backed up against the wall, a clashing mustard-yellow armchair nestled in one corner and a teal ottoman pouf in another. But somehow, it all works together.

I swallow a sigh and stuff my mouth with a big bite of Choco Madness ice cream to buy myself some time. The explosion of chocolate mixing with swirls of thick, gooey fudge and tiny brownie pieces almost has me forgetting the incident this morning in the JEAP committee meeting.

Almost.

"What did you hear?" *Feign nonchalance, Millie. Don't twist your fingers. Don't even look at her.*

I keep my eyes pinned on the TV, which is showing the classic love triangle between a regular girl, her warm werewolf friend, and the mysterious cold vampire classmate of hers. I've always felt for the girl—she's so normal, just like me, but is stuck in some shitty circumstances and trying to make the best out of her situation. Now, which man to pick...that all depends on my mood.

Right now, my mood is leaning toward stabbing the sparkling cold vampire in the heart with a stake.

After defending my honor, so to speak, Ryland went back to being his mercurial asshole self this morning—ignoring me for the rest of the class and darting out the door at the strike of the hour. I ran after him, not caring I attracted the attention of the students loitering in the halls.

"Seriously, are we back in high school?" I gritted out as I looked surreptitiously around us, the crowds of students moving around us like we were large boulders in rapid waters.

"Ms. Callahan, if you don't have questions regarding class, I need to run to an appointment." Civil, no-nonsense response and tone. Cold, hard eyes. A facial expression chiseled into stone. Unemotional.

"What are you doing, Ryland?" I whispered.

"It's *Professor*. And that's all we'll ever be. Professor and student."

"But, what about what happened—"

"Ms. Callahan." He raised his steely voice. "The past is in the past and cannot be undone. We can only choose to make the right choices for the future. Now, excuse me, I have somewhere to be."

He stalked away, all clenched muscles and coiled strength.

Anger churns in my veins as the events of this morning play for a hundredth time in my mind.

"Just a certain someone has something going on with a certain handsome professor, who is at the helm of a certain famous family, who—"

"Oh my God, Belle, shut it with the 'certains' and tell us who the fuck you're talking about," Taylor, our negative energy "take no bullshit and no prisoners" goddess rolls her eyes, her lips twitching in amusement.

"Do you want to tell them, or should I?" Belle asks me. As if sensing my indecision, she follows up with, "It might feel better if you let it out, Millie. We won't judge."

Setting down my bowl of ice cream, I sigh. The truth is, I've been wanting to say something for the longest time, but I was afraid I'd look like a pathetic little girl with a crush on her older professor. Then, they'd worry about me and would try to talk me out of it as if I didn't already know how this was a very, very bad idea.

Not to mention the professor in question is actually Grace's and Taylor's older half-brother.

A tangled mess of knots.

I look up, finding the girls staring at me expectantly. Grace is leaning forward with rapt attention. Belle lifts her elegant brows in amusement. Taylor is trying very hard to act disinterested in "mundane" gossip, but she doesn't seem to realize she's bouncing her long legs on the floor.

"I am half in love with Professor Anderson, and I think he feels the same way." I bite my lip and wait for the chaos to descend.

The room is quiet for a few seconds. I hear the faint honking sounds of cars at the street level, the squawking of birds as they fly past our partially opened windows.

"You what! Ryland, right? You're talking about Ryland?" Grace screeches excitedly.

I bury my face in my hands and nod.

"No wonder he has been walking around being pissed at the world," Taylor comments before taking a sip of water.

"He has?"

"Sis, if you stop making moony eyes at Steven during our monthly family dinners, you'll have noticed Ryland sulking in the corner. Every time. Everyone is giving him a wide berth, including Maxwell. We all suspected he's involved with a woman, but he has admitted nothing. Well, shit. Now I guess we know why."

I squint through the gaps between my fingers, taking in Taylor's nonplussed recollection of the Anderson family dinners she attends with Grace now that they are officially part of the family.

Ryland has been upset even in front of his family? They think he has a woman?

The thought kicks up my heart rate and my lips twitch.

"Geez, look at her smile. I knew you had boy problems, Millie! I thought it was that Fred guy you mentioned. Now, tell us *everything*," Belle squeals like an excited toddler and sits closer to me.

I don't think I've seen her this excited since she discontinued the luxury clothing line made from real fur shortly after she joined her family's business. She looked like she won the lottery then.

Closing my eyes, I recount the events of the last two years, from how Ryland and I met at ULA, the instant, electric connection, how he comforted me on Mom's birthday, how he almost kissed me the day I helped him with his bow tie, the cheating, our separation, and everything that transpired in the last few months, including our two scorching make out sessions in his office and the shed. The girls' eyes widen, and Grace and Taylor turn a little green when I skim over the details of my amorous sessions with their older brother.

"And now he's avoiding me like the plague," I finish, feeling my chest lightening. Finally, the truth is out, and my girls know. Perhaps they may worry about me, but it's out of my hands now.

Belle's mouth parts, jaw-slacked, Grace has hearts in her eyes, and Taylor's face is scrunched up like she's hurting on my behalf.

After a few seconds, Grace whispers, "What do you want, Millie?"

I shake my head. "I don't know. I know what I *should be* doing. I should stay away, just like what he's doing. It's wrong. It's forbidden. If anyone finds out, we will be ruined, and he has a lot on his plate with the IPO, your family's reputation, his work at school. And me? The schools will rescind their acceptances if they find out I'm involved with my professor, and such a high-profile professor, no less."

"But?" Belle prods, placing her hand on my lap and giving it a soft squeeze.

My eyes burn and I sniffle. "Why is it so hot in here?" I fan myself as heat rises to my face.

"Ah fuck." Taylor stands from her spot on the teal ottoman and sits on the other side of me. She throws her arm around my shoulder and murmurs, "Let it all out, Millie. We're here for you."

Her words trigger the dam bursting inside my chest, and I choke out a sob, then another. "I think I can fall in love with him...if I'm not already there. He sees me, girls. Like no one ever has before. The things I feel when I'm with him, it's so strong. And I want...I want—"

"You want him," Grace finishes, her violet eyes soft with sympathy. "Of course you do. It's not every day you meet someone who feels 'right' in the marrow of your bones. I understand that feeling. What's your gut telling you to do?"

I swallow the lump in my throat and wipe my wet eyes with a tissue. This is the swirl of gray. It's not black and white. I refuse to see it that way.

Straightening up, I look into the girls' eyes and reply, "I want to take the risk and go after him."

Later that night, I fit a sheet of stationery on top of my clipboard and turn on the reading light affixed to it. I sit on the bay window of my bedroom as rain pelts against the glass from the outside, blurring the world in a swath of blues and grays.

I smooth my fingers over the delicate drawing of an owl on the top corner of the paper, its feathers white with specks of gray and brown, its yellow eyes with dark pupils wise. The snowy owl. His favorite.

Uncapping my pen, I write.

Dear Ryland,

It seems fitting the first letter I write to you, one you'll never read because I'll never send it out, is on a stormy night. I'll never forget the day I met you, when I was dripping wet from the rain and absolutely mortified, my mind with one focus, which was to get out of your way so you could continue to teach without my disruption. But even then, you took my breath away.

My mom told me about the whirlwind. The exhilarating feeling of being in love with the right person such that nothing else matters, no hurdles too high, no conflict too deep. I've always wished it would happen to me someday. And when I was at your feet that day, staring up at your angry face, your steely eyes, I could sense the flutters of the whirlwind, an innate connection between us I couldn't explain in words.

And I know you feel the same way because you and I are kindred spirits, both having experienced debilitating loss but are still standing, still fighting. You are my warmth in the harsh rains, and I can be the light in your dark moments, when you feel the weight of the world sitting on top of your shoulders.

I know you're pushing me away because you think that's what I need and I'm here to tell you one word: No.

A resounding no.

What I need is you. The rest is just noise.

Yours, Millie

CHAPTER 30

I FOLLOW HIM. LIKE a deranged stalker.

Stop being so dramatic, Millie. You're just trailing after your professor to his office so you can ask him a question.

Yeah, right.

Class ended five minutes ago. Our teams formulated detailed whistleblower policies and outlined protocols for dealing with complaints. It was surprisingly complex once we delved into laws of various jurisdictions, workplace psychology, and victim mentality.

I can see why Ryland assigned this project to the class. It sheds light on the various factors going into policymaking, and the experience has made me even more excited about the future when I can hopefully make a difference in the world.

Ryland is walking swiftly toward the faculty building, his long legs eating up the distance in no time, and I huff after him, trying to catch up. He's talking on the phone with what no doubt is a scowl on his face, judging by the forceful gestures he's making with his free hand. He has this raw magnetism of a man who knows what he's doing and where he's going, and everyone around him gives him a wide berth.

I'm going to talk to him again. About us. I've come up with at least five reasons he should give us a chance, to give himself a chance, because he's obviously suffering as much as I am. And now, with the Professor Archer and Tammy case, it's almost kismet. It's like the universe is telling me what *not* to do when going after my professor.

One: We can keep it on the down low.

Two: Life is too short not to pursue this chemistry between us.

Three: I'm a big girl and can handle if this doesn't work out.

Then, there are the logistics. We don't want any email trail. Last names only in public. No more sexy times on school property. Or maybe we can wait a few months until I graduate. I'm open to suggestions.

There are a few more reasons and considerations in my arsenal, and I plan to use every one of them to argue my case, since he seems to enjoy healthy debates in class.

After talking to the girls last week, I realize I can't let this go without a fight. I've never felt this way about anyone before, this all-consuming need to know him, to peel back his many hardened layers to get to the softness deep inside, to know the stories behind every scar on his soul, to find out why his striking eyes seem to hold sadness and regret when from the outside, he seems to have everything at his fingertips.

I want his heated gazes, his quiet but meaningful words, his hands and fingers on my body.

I want to live in his storm.

And if this makes me silly, a naïve young woman chasing after her worldly, older professor, then so be it. I'll use my youth and naivety as a weapon, shattering the thick walls of his jaded heart.

My phone pings. A message from Taylor.

Taylor

> You're coming to Grace's celebration at The Orchid this Saturday, right? I know you haven't been inside there yet, and it'll be my first time as well. They're making me dress up. Can you believe it? Me...in some frilly dress?

Snorting, I use the dictation function and reply, all the while keeping an eye on my target, "Of course I'll be there. It's not every day one of your best friends opens her own finance consulting firm. It's such a big deal, and frankly, I'm low-key excited about seeing what The Orchid is all about. I know we won't get to explore the various floors, but I hear the rooftop bar is spectacular. I'll see you there."

Ryland makes a sharp turn into the glass corridor leading to his office. His head is now dipped toward his phone, his fingers pressing a few buttons before he lifts the phone back to his ears. He unlocks his door and strides inside, dropping off his briefcase on a chair before walking to the large windows and staring out into the courtyard.

My steps slow, and I take a calming breath. And another. But nothing seems to slow my heart, which is thumping like a certain cartoon roadrunner running away from a coyote all the while screeching *"beep beep."*

I can do this. Life is too short for regrets. I should know that out of everyone.

Heaving out one big exhale, I walk to his opened door.

"Anytime is fine, but nighttime is preferred." His voice is deep, smooth like chocolate. Of course, he's commanding someone on the phone, my big brute.

I hear faint sounds of the other person responding, but since his phone isn't on speaker, it's impossible to make out the words.

"Monday night at seven works. Yes, Noire at The Orchid."

My brows furrow. *Noire. That sounds familiar.*

"The entire club. No other patrons. I want brunette, long hair, blue eyes, five-foot-four give or take, and..." he pauses for a brief second, as if wavering and pinches the bridge of his nose, "younger, early twenties, can pass as a college student."

What? Is he describing me to someone on the phone? And why does Noire ring a bell?

I take out my phone and text Grace, who knows a lot more about The Orchid than I do, since she worked as a dancer for a brief stint at their burlesque club, Trésor, before she got together with Steven.

Millie

> Do you know a place called Noire?

Three dots appear immediately, then disappear and reappear once more.

Grace

Yeah. It's a club within The Orchid. Why do you ask?

Millie

I was going to talk to Ryland like we discussed, but he's on the phone right now and I heard him mention Noire and then described me to whoever he's calling. What's this place?

A few seconds pass by, the three dots taunting me. I tap my foot on the marble floors as her response comes through.

Grace

Um. I'm just going to tell you straight up. Noire is one of the specialty sex clubs on one of the Rose floors in The Orchid. It's a large indoor space decorated to resemble the outdoors. There's a fake forest, abandoned buildings, and other structures in there.

My stomach plummets and I grip my phone tightly while re-reading her words.

"There are rumors he's a beast in bed and gets off from chasing willing women in their sex clubs. I totally wouldn't mind him hunting me down." My classmate's words on the first day I met Ryland at ULA ring in my mind.

Sex clubs. Chasing. Hunting.

He's arranging for sex with some random woman who resembles me?

My heart stops, the coyote on the verge of finally nabbing the roadrunner, and a scorching heat floods my body. My hands shake, my eyes burn, and the telltale moisture gathering there tells me I'm seconds away from losing it. My mind is filled with images of him pinning another woman down, giving her his lips, his caresses, his bites, and a sharp agony slices through me as I try and fail to control the pain forming in my chest.

How dare he? How could he not give us a chance and instead decide to be with someone else?

How could he?

Swiftly, I turn away and stalk back in the direction I came from. The agony radiating from behind my rib cage squeezes my lungs and wetness blurs my vision. My phone pings.

Grace

> Millie, you okay? Ok, that was stupid. We're going out tonight and will talk about this. I'll text the other girls. We have your back.

Hot tears slip down my face and I'm even angrier now—at him, at myself for crying over him—and I swipe my eyes with my sleeve and hastily type out a reply.

Millie

> Okay.

My emotions are a tornado inside me, with sadness and anger being the front-runners. I want to find a dark hole and crawl into it and bawl my eyes out. Or gorge myself on a pint of chocolate ice cream and chase it with an abundance of alcohol. Fresh tears well in my eyes and I rapidly blink, trying to keep my composure since I'm in public.

Grace

> We'll figure this out, Millie. Don't jump to conclusions. I know some people and will make calls to find out more.

My eyes are so focused on the text, I don't see where I'm going and trip over something. My body pits forward and just as I'm about to make my humiliation complete by sprawling across the floor in the bustling building, strong arms shoot out from nowhere to steady me.

"Whoa. Millie. You okay?"

I look up, finding Fred's concerned gaze on me, his brows furrowing.

Swallowing the ball in my throat, I stare at him, noticing his kind eyes, soft blond hair which seems to gleam gold under the florescent lights, and a kind smile. Tall, fit body. Not as muscular and imposing at Ryland, but still pleasing. He's gentle. A nice guy. Why can't I like someone like him? He won't hurt me like Ryland has. He wouldn't harm a fly.

Why can't I like him instead?

"Millie?" he asks, placing his hand gently on my shoulder. "I'm on my way to visit my TA, but are you okay? You seem sad. Is there anything I can help with?"

His voice is so kind, so comforting, but my heart still yearns for the deep cutting tone of a certain dark-haired someone.

The bastard.

I push my sadness to the back of my mind. Compartmentalize, that's what I'm good at. I excel at hiding my emotions and faking it. After all, I've had years of experience doing the same in front of Dad and Adrian.

Straightening up, I focus on the anger, the fury, the scorched earth in my insides. I curl my hands into tight fists and force out a smile. An idea pops into my mind.

Fred's eyes widen at whatever he sees on my face and I ask, "Fred, are you free on Saturday?"

"Uh...of course. What do you have in mind?" Hope sparks in his eyes. He looks bewildered, but he's smart enough not to look a gift horse in the mouth.

"I'm thinking we can work on our training materials for class," I reply.

He physically deflates. "Oh, of course. Yeah. Classwork, got to find time to do it."

"And then I have an event to go to afterward at The Orchid and maybe you can come with me?" The bastard will be there for his sister and damn if I'll go there by myself and ache over him.

Fred perks up, a bright smile flashing over his boyishly handsome face. "Yes! Of course. I'll go with you, no problem. Just send me the details."

Ryland-fucking-Anderson, I'll make you regret this.

CHAPTER 31

I'm standing in front of a nondescript cement building on the outskirts of Bronx with Belle, who's tugging the worn sleeve of my black shirt, her eyes darting around and looking at the questionable neighborhood filled with colorful graffiti and barred windows. The sun has already disappeared behind the clouds, making the entire atmosphere gloomier and more desolate. A breeze flutters by, blowing up paper bags, random wrappers, and other trash on the sidewalk.

"Are you sure this is the place?" she whispers, even though there aren't many people around us save for a few teenagers smoking weed outside the building and a scary-looking man standing like a sentry at the entrance.

"I think so? I checked the address Taylor sent two times already. She told us to keep an open mind."

Taylor also told us to dress in clothes we can ruin. I have no idea what she and Grace are up to.

Seconds later, the door flies open and Taylor pokes her head out. Her long, dark hair is tied in thick braids, her eyes startling with the grunge makeup she has on.

She waves us over. "Come in, girls. Don't be wimps. This place is safe, trust me."

Belle clutches my hand tightly as I drag her inside the building with me, finding Grace and Taylor standing there, dressed in camo clothing, like they're about to storm into a war zone.

"What are we doing here?"

The place is equally creepy inside, the cement walls decorated with more graffiti, the florescent lighting flickering on and off. The randomness of this location momentarily distracts me from my emotions over Ryland.

Grace waves her hand around. "A few friends in our old neighborhood told us about this place. It's all the rage online these days."

"Ha. Rage. I see what you did there," Taylor snickers.

Grace grins. "This is a rage room, or rage building, to be more exact. We pay a small fee to rent a room filled with crap and you can throw things, damage anything, and just vent out your frustrations in a safe and healthy manner. Better than bottling them up inside."

I gape. "This was what you meant when you said you had my back earlier? I wanted to talk, not inflict violence."

Tay links her arm with mine and leads me to a door. "It was more my idea. I think ice cream and crying are fine and all that, but sometimes throwing a flat screen against the wall really hits the spot. I think this is one of those times. That fucker. We can vent and then discuss options."

My mind reels from everything as we enter the room, which is dimly lit by a single florescent lamp and resembles an indoor scrap yard. The cement walls here are also streaked with paint, hastily scribbled curse words and other artwork. Broken furniture such as a slashed sofa, a small wooden table missing a leg, and other fragile items like vases and bowls litter the room.

Grace hands us each a plastic suit, which can be a costume out of an apocalyptic movie, and a pair of goggles. "Suit up!"

Five minutes later, we're decked out in safety gear, and I look at Taylor. "Now what?"

"Pick up anything, throw it at the wall! Pretend it's Ryland."

I gnaw on my lip and pick up a small ceramic cup. My fingers tremble, but my feet stay rooted.

"Like this!"

Smash.

Glass shatters against the wall as Taylor hurls a vase at a shadowed corner, all the while yelling, "Fuck you, older brother, for hurting my best friend. I can hate you and love you at the same time!"

"Yes!" More crashing and smashing as Grace's eyes take on a feral glint.

She grabs a golf club from somewhere and whacks at a sad-looking table. "And Steven, I love you, but you hurt my fucking heart when you disappeared, leaving me to worry sick about you. Thank God you came to your senses, but I still have residual anger!"

My eyes widen and I gape at the Peyton sisters, who are busy flinging all types of crap at the walls, wreaking havoc and destruction in the tiny room.

Then, next to me, Belle lets out a growl and chucks an old toaster to the floor. "And I hate arranged marriages. It's archaic, it's barbaric, it's fucking ridiculous. I hate it. I. Hate. It!"

Our heads swivel toward our elegant friend, finding her face red with fury, her sleek black hair swinging wildly in the air as she stomps on some broken glass, her chest huffing and puffing from exertion.

"What arranged marriage?" Grace asks, the golf club still in her hands.

Belle freezes like a deer in the headlights and blows out a breath. "Damn, that felt good. And today is not about me, it's about Millie, but long story short, my parents are looking for suitors for me. It's the freakin' twenty-first century and I'm an independent woman, but they won't listen. I don't need a man in my life. I can have a fulfilling career, have babies, save the animals, and do it all on my own. I don't want to talk about it."

I walk up to her and give her a tight hug. "We're here for you too."

She nods and cocks her brow at me. "Millie, you've been holding onto that mug like it's your newborn baby. Let it out. The rage. The hurt. It feels really good."

I stare at the mug in my hand and think about Ryland—his sinful eyes, his growly voice, the way he plunders my mouth like he can't get enough, then how he's acting like an utter asshole and pushing me away, ignoring what we have between us, how he says the damnedest things just to scare me off, and...

How he's going to fuck another woman to get over me.

Tears spring into my eyes and my chest clenches. My pulse kicks rapidly in my ears, my skin feeling hot and feverish. I hurl the mug against the wall, the loud shatter satisfying to my ears.

"You asshole! You think I'm just going to give up?"

I grab a bat and swing it at a TV, shattering the screen.

"I'm not! And you're going to regret this because I'm an awesome person and you won't meet another woman like me, you chauvinistic pig!" My screams echo in the room as the girls cheer and yell out obscenities over the idiotic Ryland Anderson.

"I can make my own damn decisions!" A mirror shatters into a thousand pieces.

"Life isn't black and white!" I tear out an old dictionary, even though my heart pinches with guilt because books are my babies.

Sweat slicks my hair and dampens my clothes as I use all my energy and power to wreak havoc in the room.

"I hate being the caregiver. The nice girl. I want to be angry like Adrian and sad like Dad. I hate how life is unfair." My voice cracks as wetness seeps down my cheeks, and I belatedly realize I'm crying.

My arms are achy and tired, my voice is getting hoarse from yelling. I grab some random object next to me and chuck it against the wall, letting go years-worth of tension I've been bottling up inside, the release so cathartic, so tiring, it's emotionally exhausting in the most satisfying way.

"I don't want to be in control all the time," I sob. "I want to let go and feel what I feel without pretending. I want Mom to come back."

My face is a mess of tears and snot, but I don't care, because my heart is torn open, the ugly poison pooling inside finally pouring out, the corrosive acid spreading to my muscles, my fingers, to every cell of my body.

It hurts. Everything hurts.

My chest feels like it's cleaved in half, my eyes heavy and swollen, my throat on fire. Suddenly exhausted, both mentally and physically, I slide down against the wall, sit on the dirty floor, and curl up into a fetal position before burying my face in my hands.

The girls gather around me, their voices thick with emotions. They too have been crying along with me. I feel their gentle hands and warm hugs, and a few kisses in my sticky hair.

"I'm so proud of you, Millie," Grace whispers. I look up, finding her dazzling eyes bright with tears.

"You're a damn fighter." Taylor swallows, her eyes looking suspiciously red as well.

"A badass. An utter badass," Belle echoes their sentiments as she pulls me to her side.

Minutes pass and the adrenaline ekes out of me. Lethargy sets in. I don't need ice cream or alcohol. I'm all out of tears and energy. I just want to take a hot shower, curl up in my bed, and don't wake up for a very long time.

"You know, I have an idea about Ryland," Taylor murmurs as we stare at the ceiling.

"What idea?" Grace asks.

"I mean, from what Millie told us, he's essentially trying to get over her by finding someone like her to have sex with. So, it's not really going to work since he's using faux-Millie to get over real-Millie."

Taylor sits up, excitement seeping into her voice. "Grace, the scenes in Noire...they're with random people, right?"

Where is she going with this? I stare at the sisters as they look at each other, evil smiles forming on their faces.

Grace nods. "Yes, they are usually anonymous for the primal scenes. You can request people you know, but most hunters prefer strangers. It's part of the high, chasing an unknown prey." She pauses and her eyes take on a sharp glint. "Are you thinking what I'm thinking, Tay?"

Tay nods eagerly. "Is it possible, you think?"

"I'll have to call Sofia, or maybe even Elias. They run the Rose floors, you know, but they liked me when I worked for them there, so they can make this happen if I ask."

I lift my hands up. "What are you guys talking about?" Belle nods beside me, looking as equally confused.

Grace swivels toward me, her voice serious. "Millie, how badly do you want Ryland?"

My injured heart still skips several beats at the mention of him.

"A lot," I whisper, "And I know he wants me too. For some reason, he just won't—"

"If I have a way to get you into Noire on Monday night," Grace begins, a hardened glint in her eyes.

Realization dawns in my mind. "You mean be the girl he's chasing?"

Taylor nods alongside her sister. "He's looking for a random person who looks like you. You obviously fit all the physical requirements. What if you show up instead? He never said that person *couldn't* be you."

"That's genius. Holy shit, that's genius. You're an evil genius, Tay," Belle whispers in awe. "What do you think, Millie?"

My heart, all bloodied and torn up, throws itself around my rib cage, having been resurrected, and my mind is a swirl of thoughts, ranging from *no way this is insane*, to *what if...what if this is what'll finally tip him over?*

I stammer, "I-I need time to think about it. I can tell you on Saturday after your event, Grace."

"There's not a lot of time between Saturday and Monday, but anything is possible at The Orchid. I mean, there will be exceptions to be made, I'm sure. I'll need to call Sofia later to make arrangements and to make sure your brother doesn't find out." Grace scrunches her brows and walks through all the things she'll be looking into.

"Then there are health checks and the blood tests all companions, escorts, and patrons of the Rose floors are subjected to. There's also a detailed questionnaire for you to fill out with your hard limits, safe words, and gestures..." Grace rambles on about the logistics.

And for the first time today since I overheard Ryland's conversation on the phone in his office, the tightness in my chest loosens, and I can finally breathe.

Visions of him chasing me, his focus solely on me, uninhibited, wild, have me clenching my thighs. My pulse ratchets up.

Will he finally understand I very much want this, and I have no regrets?

CHAPTER 32

I SPENT THE LAST few days scouring the internet for more information on primal play, learning about safe words and gestures, and the hunter and prey dynamics. I watched video interviews of people in the lifestyle describing their experiences and the overall empowerment they felt as prey, even in consensual non-consensual or dubious consensual scenes. They could halt the rough sex scenes with a simple word or action. They talked about the freedom they felt when someone overpowered them and took over their body.

My mind flits back to the frenzied make-out session in the shed at New Beginnings, where Ryland gave me a glimpse of his hunter self when he curled his hand around my neck and forced me to orgasm, all the while leaving plenty of room for me to say no, and how he didn't go any further until he heard a moan or whimper of pleasure from me or my urging of him to continue.

Even in the intensity of the moment, I never felt afraid. I felt safe, alive, treasured.

My pussy throbs and my thighs clench with what I've learned about the lifestyle so far and suddenly, Taylor's idea sounds more and more enticing.

But if I go through with this, I'll let him know who I am before he has sex with me. I want him to decide for himself. He needs to be the one to do it, because I'll be no one's accidental fuck. I want him, but I have my pride.

My palms grow sweaty as I finish getting ready for Grace's celebratory event. I'm so proud of her for opening Peyton-Anderson Financial Consulting and taking her dream by the horns.

Eyeing the slinky black dress I've changed into—a simple curve-hugging outfit with two delicate spaghetti straps and a hem ending at mid-thigh—I blow out an exhale before heading back into the living room, where Fred is packing up his laptop and papers after our study session.

He pauses when he sees me, his eyes widening. "You look beautiful, Millie."

My skin heats and I smile before tucking a lock of wavy hair behind my ear.

"Thanks, Fred. And," my fingers clench and unclench, a sticky sense of shame slinking inside me, "I just want to let you know, I'm grateful you're coming with me to the event...as a friend."

Fred stills and his shoulders slump in obvious disappointment. It didn't feel right to lead him on. My invitation to him was out of impulse because I was hurt, and I wanted to make Ryland jealous. But it's not right for Fred, especially if I know he likes me.

"If you don't want to go, I won't blame you," I say softly, watching him shuffle on his feet, his hand kneading the back of his neck.

"Ah fuck. I kinda figured this wasn't a date." He laughs sadly. "You looked so sad that day, so I dunno, I just knew something was up. But I'll still go with you. You look like you need support for this event, and I'm always your friend."

"Thank you. Someday, you'll find someone worthy of you because you're an awesome person. Truly."

He waves me away and motions toward the door. "Shall we?"

A short while later, we arrive at the entrance of the rooftop bar of the towering glass structure on 5th Avenue, right at the edge of Central Park. I've passed by it a few times on the way to the park or when I tagged along with Belle when she visited the luxury boutiques for inspiration for her family's fashion line.

Fred smiles at me and holds out his hand, clearly sensing I need support. We push open the doors and step inside a beautiful fall paradise.

My breath is momentarily suspended when I take in the tall glass ceiling, which lets in all the natural light from the early evening skies. The sunset washes the space in a watercolor of golds and oranges. The delicate crystal pendant lighting gives the illusion of warm balls of fire lighting up the sky. Then, there's the plethora of floral arrangements—the marigolds, chrysanthemums, and other beautiful flowers I want to examine later.

But my focus is shattered when I hear the deep masculine voice of the man of my dreams coming from the far right.

"We don't tell you enough, but we are thrilled to have you and Taylor be part of our family. Father seems so much happier since he reunited with you both and I know Maxwell, if he were here, would say the same. We're proud to have you two as our sisters."

"Thank you, Ryland," Grace replies and they raise their glasses to their lips.

Ryland smiles softly at his sister. He looks so much more relaxed here in this small gathering amongst his family and close friends.

My heart warms at his words to Grace because I know how much she wanted to find her birth father before and how this means the world to her to have the family she didn't know before accepting her into the fold.

Then, those piercing slate eyes snag on me and his tall frame stiffens. He straightens up imperceptibly, looking every inch the prince the public loves in his form-fitting black suit with a gray shirt matching his eyes and a navy tie. His eyes dart to where Fred is holding my hand and the anger simmering in those charcoal pools threatens to boil me alive.

I can't help but tremble under his scrutiny, but after thinking about how he ignored me this past month, his search for an escort at Noire for Monday, blazing hot indignation floods my senses and I grit my teeth before flashing the fakest society smile I can muster.

Fred squeezes my hand, and I look at him, finding him frowning. Then, he fidgets like he's nervous and leads me toward the group. He addresses Ryland, "Professor Anderson, nice to see you here."

Ryland's face does not change, his displeasure clearly shown in his flared nostrils, his clenched jaw shifting from what's obviously teeth grinding. Fred visibly gulps and I tug him behind me as Ryland remains silent and as cold as the Arctic.

I let go of Fred before wrapping Grace in a hug. "Sorry, I'm late." I pull back and level a glare at a seething Ryland. "Fred and I had a study session because our asshole professor gave us a ridiculous project." I'm barely able to contain the hurt and anger in my voice.

Steven frowns, his sharp eyes skating over my face, acting like the protective bonus brother-in-law that he is, since his sister is married to my brother now. But I ignore him and instead take Fred's hand again, lean on his shoulder, and smile at him.

Fred gives me a shaky and confused smile and tugs me closer, like he needs comfort in this strange swirl we're trapped in together.

A low rumble travels through the air, sending shivers throughout my body, and I whip my head toward Ryland.

I can't believe he growled. Like an unsophisticated caveman.

I bite back a grin as a rush of satisfaction flows through me. *You don't get to push me away and then get mad at me for bringing a date, you asshole.*

Glancing at Fred, I give him the sweetest, most adoring smile I can muster before turning back to Ryland.

He steps forward slowly, his hand clenched tightly once more, and rasps, "Millie Callahan, if you don't detach yourself from him at this moment, I'll—"

"You'll what? Flunk me in class? Run away like you did before? Be a coward and avoid me?"

The group is silent; the men staring at each other with shocked expressions on their faces before Charles steps forward with two flutes of champagne. I turn toward him and give him a smile, grateful for the interruption.

Steven comes up to me, his eyes sweeping over my face, his brow cocked in question, and I try not to wince. I'll need to make up some excuse about why Ryland and I are fighting since Steven and Adrian are not only brothers-in-law but are also good friends.

He pulls me into a hug and his head dips toward Fred. "So, does Adrian know about this friend of yours?" *See?* I can only hope Grace will keep her lips sealed.

I shove him and laugh at his protectiveness. "I already have one brother. I don't need another one, but I love you all the same for being a bonus brother."

Standing on my tiptoes, I give him a quick peck on his cheek and I swear I can hear Ryland growling in the background again.

Ignoring him, I turn back to my friends and enjoy the rest of the festivities celebrating Grace and her achievements. The atmosphere lightens after a few more drinks, jokes, and bickering between the Anderson siblings, the group clearly enjoying each other's presence.

After an hour of laughing and catching up with friends, I excuse myself to go to the bathroom, making quick work of completing my business and washing my hands.

Staring at myself in the mirror, I practice a few smiles and am proud of how they look convincing. I've avoided the asshole the entire evening, even though I can feel the heat of his stare tracking me as I walk around the space.

But he's still planning to fuck a random woman.

The fake smile slips off my face and I grit my teeth. I straighten my black dress, which has ridden up my thighs, and step into the quiet corridor to walk back toward the lounge.

"What do you think you're doing?" The deep timbre of his voice from behind me halts me in my tracks.

I don't face him. "Here to celebrate your sister and my friend."

His footfalls are loud as he prowls closer and I fight every impulse to fidget, to run away, or, worse yet, to turn toward him and hurtle into his arms. "You know what I mean."

"Nope. I actually don't."

A tall column of heat radiates from behind me and I feel him pressed against my backside.

His breaths are heavy next to my ear, his voice chilly as he says, "Fred. Why are you here with him? Are you dating him?"

I whirl around, not able to withstand this insanity any longer. "Is it *any* of your business, *Professor*? I thought you and I weren't meant to be and what we did in the past were mistakes. What did you say? 'We should make the right choice for the future?' Why the hell does who I date matter to you?"

He towers over me, his face glowering, his skin flushed, and a pulse throbs rapidly on his temple. His gaze darts to my mouth, then to my chest, and his eyes darken, pupils dilating. He leans in slowly, like he can't help but be drawn to me.

My heart shoots to my throat and my eyes flutter shut. I tilt my head upward, waiting for the moment those soft lips claim mine in a burst of savagery. When he finally gives up this farce we are in and accepts that he and I belong together.

But the kiss never comes.

My eyes fly open and I find him straightening up, glaring at me with lust, want, and a plethora of emotions flittering across those soulful eyes.

"You're right. I don't give a damn." He takes a deep breath and smooths his anguished expression into one of calmness, the face he gives to the press and the public. "Enjoy the rest of the party, Ms. Callahan."

He steps away from me and joins the rest of the group back by the bar.

My body trembles, and I keep in the frustrated scream bottled up inside me. *Big breaths. Inhale for five counts, exhale for eight. Calm the nervous system.*

I close my eyes and fight the mental war against the swirl of negative energy wreaking havoc on my psyche.

Compartmentalize.

Deep breaths. I force myself to release my clenched fists and bunched shoulders, focusing on my breathing, on doing anything other than thinking of him.

He wants me, it's obvious, but for some reason, he thinks he's doing me a favor by stepping away.

The noble idiot.

The infuriating madman.

I heave out a deep exhale and walk to my friends once more. Grace lifts a brow when she sees me stomping toward her.

Reaching her in a few strides, I pause and whisper in her ear, "Set it up for Monday. I'm in."

Let the games begin.

CHAPTER 33

I SPLASH COLD WATER on my face, my gut crawling with dread. The foreboding sensations coil inside me like the ominous wail of a tornado siren.

It's wrong. This scene. Me at Noire. What I'm doing. Everything feels *wrong*.

Blowing out a deep breath, I glance at the mirror and swipe the droplets off my face with my hands. My eyes look bloodshot, but I guess that makes sense since I haven't been sleeping as much, as my dreams are haunted by a certain brunette with blue eyes. Eyes that beckon, tempt, and see too much. Eyes that make me want to abandon my cage and jump into the fire. Eyes that make me forget I am Ryland Anderson, but instead make me believe I'm just Ryland, the man.

I grab a paper towel, wipe my hands, and look at my outfit for the night—a classic gray Henley paired with dark-wash jeans. My usual scene outfit. Easy to run in and to replace if things get rough.

After a long exhausting day of meetings with the finance team at the company and our bankers, getting our ducks lined up in a row for the IPO, which is still progressing well, and a phone call from Jacob telling me he's spoken to the Board about the honorary doctorate, I should be excited for this, getting back out there, as Maxwell put it.

It's been so long since I've stood here in this grand bathroom of black marble and chrome, befitting of a club named after the color. *You haven't been here since you met her.*

When we had our first renovation of The Orchid ten years ago, I suggested adding this club to the Rose floors because I *needed* it. I wanted to chase, to hunt, to overpower a like-minded partner as I slaked my lust with them. I wanted to feel the leather straps around my chest snapping off and be reduced to impulse and intuition, to experience true freedom. Perhaps when I was hunting, I was overpowering all the rules and responsibilities that came from being an Anderson.

But now, standing in the bathroom I helped design, I don't feel an iota of excitement, the emotion I usually feel before I step into the faux outdoors, when I *know* freedom is at my fingertips.

Instead, I think of her, the woman I can't keep out of my mind. I remember how angry I was when I saw her at Grace's event a few days ago, in the arms of another man.

I have no claim over her, but God, do I want her.

Every cell in my body screams for her.

My mind sifts through the email I received from the Noire team earlier today, detailing the information I needed to know about the mysterious woman who's supposed to be meeting me past the sturdy doors separating the restroom and the actual play area.

The physical characteristics and age are one hundred percent matched. She's on birth control, doesn't require condoms, and the Noire team has also sent me her health check results with her name redacted. She's clear. But there's no fucking way I'll forgo protection with a random woman, so I always carry a few condoms in my pants pocket when I'm in a scene.

I know they did the same for her, sending her my information in advance while keeping my identity anonymous—it's part of the usual regulations for entertainment and companions on the Rose floors, to make sure patrons are safe and protected.

She has no hard limits other than urinating and defecating—no thank you, on my end, so we're aligned there.

Fighting, biting, spanking, tearing clothes off, and all that goes into consensual nonconsensual play are fair game. In fact, there's even a note saying she may fight me and she wants me to fight back, let everything out, and not hold anything back.

The safe word is daffodils or three consecutive pats anywhere on my body if she can't speak.

Daffodils. I think back to the small pot of yellow flowers Millie brought into my office two years ago, the ones that made her cry when they shattered on the floor. The first time I felt my heart twist and wench in pain as I saw the agony in those sapphire eyes, and I knew I had to fix it for her.

I had to protect her.

Fuck. I close my eyes and lean my forehead against the cool surface of the mirror. She haunts my thoughts in every waking minute and invades my mind in the dark nights. This is why I'm here tonight, to get her out of my system by surrogate. Maybe my brothers are right. Perhaps not having sex in so long has turned me into some sick, twisted animal.

The profile is perfect for me, like the candidate has been crafted to serve my darkest, most wicked desires. But somehow, the heaviness in my gut seems to increase with each second, and every inhale feels like another slab of weight has been added onto my chest.

Everything feels wrong.

My cock doesn't twitch as it lays lifeless in my pants.

I shake my head to dispel the insane thoughts, but it's no use. I can't muster an ounce of enthusiasm for the scene tonight.

My body doesn't want anyone other than Millie. My lips don't crave anything other than the sweetness of her taste, chocolate mixed with honey. My mind only thinks about her, enthralled by the passion in her voice, the wisdom far beyond her years in her words.

I'm an addict in the throes of withdrawal, a process which seems endless and hopeless.

Maybe I'll just find the mystery woman tonight and call the night off. The gentleman in me can't stand her up and I don't want to let security be the one to find her and tell her the date is off. It doesn't feel right to use an intercom to call the night off, either.

No. I'll find her myself in person. Then, I'll tip her for her troubles. It's the least I can do.

The decision offers me some relief, but the yearning for Millie is relentless, preventing me from breathing freely.

The insidious heaviness follows me as I push open the thick soundproof door and step into relative pitch darkness. It takes a minute for my eyes to adjust to the dim space, which is only lit by the realistic pale light of the artificial moon from the LED screens on the high ceilings. I smell the fragrance of pine trees and feel a cool breeze on my skin.

Everything is set up to my usual preferences.

Closing my eyes, I inhale the scent of nature...a very close approximation, one we've spent hours and dollars crafting with high-end perfumeries in Europe.

I feel the heaviness beginning to melt away in my chest as another gentle breeze sweeps through the air from the undetectable air vents we've installed in this room, one which can generate anything from a balmy breeze to a simulation of a violent hurricane. We don't kink shame on the Rose floors.

My nose prickles as a faint note of something...something familiar registers in my mind. The barely there wisp of jasmine laced with vanilla.

Just barely there.

My heart skips several beats, and my breath catches in my throat. Perhaps my mind is playing tricks on me. Imagining the woman of my dreams is here with me.

I frown at the direction of my thoughts as I hear the mysterious hooting of an owl and the rustling of trees. The hunter instincts inside me rear alive as I take another inhale and walk onto the grass toward the thick cluster of trees ahead, my footfalls sure and silent. After all, I know this place like the back of my mind.

There it is again.

The enticing swirl of jasmine and vanilla. Her scent. The hairs stand up on the back of my neck. *Why the fuck am I thinking of her?*

I'm going mad.

I need to find this woman and tell her to go home. Then, I'll hit the gym and bury myself in work. The files to review for the IPO. The assignments to grade.

The alluring scent taunts me and my blood heats, my heart beginning a war chant in my rib cage. The smell. The fucking smell.

Millie.

But it can't be, can it?

I begin the chase.

CHAPTER 34

MY HEART POUNDS SO loudly, I swear that alone will give away my location. Someone or something is here with me, I'm sure of it.

It has to be him, right? Rational thoughts cease to make sense anymore. My feet pick up speed as I walk faster.

I'm safe. I'm safe. I'm safe.

I remind myself of what Sofia Kent told me when she walked me through the rules of Noire. She looked me in the eye and said I had all the power here. There would be security wearing night vision goggles patrolling the space, out of sight from us but close enough where if I were to scream the safe word or press the button on the sturdy silver cuff affixed to my wrist, they would come and rescue me.

I know I am safe. My mind knows that. Logic tells me that. I'm in a building in the middle of Manhattan.

But my subconscious hasn't gotten the memo, apparently. Because as I'm walking between the towering trees looming over me like monsters in the dark, hearing the rustling of the leaves trembling against the branches, seeing the eerie moonlight casting ghostly shadows on the dark grounds ahead of me, every fight-or-flight response in my body turns on.

Everything feels real.

My breathing is shallow. My pulse is rickety in my ears.

Dark shapes loom in the distance.

More trees? An abandoned building of some sort? I can't quite make out the objects under the inky, gloomy night.

My feet stumble over something on the ground and I let out a screech before my hand flies to my mouth to stem the noise. The underbrush looks dark and foreboding, a devil lurking in the bottomless abyss, its tendrils slithering and swaying, and I knot my hands in fists as the sounds of my ragged breathing escape from my lips.

An owl hoots in the distance, a ghostly echo. I hear faint pitter pattering of footsteps, like some nocturnal animal is scurrying out of my way as I trample on the uneven path before me. *There are no animals, are there? There can't be.* The wind kicks up, a haunted howl tearing through the tall, menacing trees and sweat beads on the back of my neck.

I fight every impulse to run.

But run where?

Crackle.

I freeze, my ears perking up at the sound.

It's an animal. It has to be an animal. Or is it him?

I swallow as my heart pounds against my rib cage. *Ba-dum. Ba-dum. Ba-dum.* I hold my breath.

Snap. Crackle.

Every hair on my body stands at attention and my hands shake at my sides.

It's him.

The lasered focus of his stare at my back. The familiar heat making the hairs on my neck stand at attention. The hunter, the predator, not the man. His footsteps are stealthy, but I can feel each *thump* approaching me. It's like he's taunting me. Fear or excitement claws in my throat and my body burns with jittery energy.

The muscles in my legs twitch, my body choosing flight in his presence.

Logic ceases to make sense and I run.

"Oh shit," I mumble under my breath as I flee as fast as my legs can carry me, my simple striped cotton dress plastered against me. "Oh, God."

I don't know why I'm running, but I'm not a slave to my thoughts right now. I just follow the impulses of my body.

It's freeing.

Everything is a sea of murkiness and shadows and suddenly, the ghostly silver moonbeams fade and I glance up, noticing the moon partially obscured by a thick layer of clouds.

My footfalls are resounding as I pound against the grass and dirt, my lungs burn for oxygen, and the wind feels biting against my face.

But I feel alive, the fear mixing with exhilaration, a high I've never experienced before. Everything is heightened and more intense. My body turns heated, my eyesight sharpening. I hurtle through the trees away from the hunter who's trying to catch me, oblivious to the branches scraping my skin, the brushes digging into my cotton dress.

An unusual energy tears through me, and I swallow the urge to laugh.

The rustling is loud behind me now. Whoever is there is no longer trying to hide his presence.

But I know it's him. I can feel him. His energy. His raw focus. His power. I can feel the distance closing between us, but still, I run.

I run and run and run.

Perhaps we all have a bit of prey inside us, that gut feeling, which keeps us all alive.

The imposing dark shape in front of me, which I can finally make out, is a crumbled wall of an abandoned building. I'm so close; it appears within my grasp. It looks like a sanctuary in this madness.

I can hide behind it and wait until the danger has passed, to see if it's really him chasing me, hunting me, or if it's something else. My skin sizzles, every nerve ending on my body awake and attuned to my surroundings. I no longer feel cold but feel very hot instead as I imagine the man behind the thousand-dollar suits and centuries of good breeding coming undone before my eyes.

I feel the telltale pulsing between my legs, my panties dampening.

I never had this with Lloyd, or even in my imagination during lonely nights.

But now, having experienced it, I can't imagine life without this excruciating high.

The sensations are disorienting. The fear, the lust, the excitement, everything which feels familiar yet distinctly unfamiliar, all magnified tenfold. Unbidden, my lips curve in a smile as I careen toward the tall wall ahead, which is just a few feet away from me. It feels like a victory. If I can reach it, I can—

A hard body slams into me and a muscular arm bands around my waist, lifting me off the ground.

I let out a scream, my body automatically fighting as I claw at my assailant, my nails digging into his forearm, my feet swinging and kicking against his shins.

"I got you. You can't escape me." A low guttural rasp. The familiar scent of the great wilderness with hints of citrus sifts to my nostrils. The hard muscles pressed against my back, rippling with tension.

Ryland.

My mind, a swirl of chaos as adrenaline churns through my veins, registers this pillar of heat as the man of my dreams. The man my heart pounds for, the man whose soul calls to mine. The man who infuriates me to no end.

My clit pulses and my core throbs, my body struggling with the warring urges to fight or to give up, to succumb to the hunter or to give it back to him as good as I get.

Then, I think about this past month. His icy demeanor. His cutting words. And suddenly, my blood boils and the choice is clear.

I grit my teeth and thrash against him, even though my clit pulses for his touch and my body aches for him. My hands deliver solid punches to his body, but it's as if I'm hitting the cement wall ahead. He doesn't grunt in pain, doesn't slow his strides. He's moving, carrying me like I weigh nothing more than a sack of potatoes. The spoils of war.

He's so powerful.

The thought causes me to break out in a fevered sweat. I want to come undone underneath him.

"Ryland." His name is uttered on a ragged exhale as I scratch his arms, his torso, anywhere I can reach.

He freezes.

His arms band tighter around me and I feel his muscles tensing up. A startled breath rips from his lips.

Then, his head dips toward me, his nose skating to my neck, and he takes a deep inhale.

"Fuck," he rasps. "Millie?"

CHAPTER 35

WITH A FEW STRIDES, he turns me around and pins me upright against the cement wall. He grasps my chin and tilts my head up before peering down at me under the faint moonlight. His eyes darken, widening as shock flashes across his face.

I twist harder in his arms, and he tightens his hold on me automatically.

"Surprised, *Professor*?" I spit out. "Didn't expect to see me here, did you?"

Seeing him inches before me, a looming god against the haunted moonlight, his hair disheveled, his muscles flexing, his face twisted in shock, has fury racing through my insides, joining the party. He is fine with fucking a random woman who looks just like me and to deny everything between us.

The chaos. The storm. The whirlwind. Our hearts beating as one.

"You wanted to fuck a brunette who can pass as a college student. Well, here I am."

He flinches at my words and releases his hold around my waist, and I sag against the wall.

He rakes his hand over his hair and clenches his jaw. "I don't know how you got in here, Millie. But I'm not doing this with you. You're leaving."

Ryland reaches out and grabs my wrist and I shake him off. "No. I'm an adult. What I do in my own time is none of your business. You can either stay or *you* can leave. I'm sure there are plenty of patrons who want to have a kinky rendezvous with a college coed in the dark."

He snarls, his eyes turning feral. "You wouldn't *dare*."

I get up on my tiptoes and whisper, "Watch me."

A vein pulses on his temple and his nostrils flare. He pants heavily, his breath fanning across my face, and the air thickens with tension, a heavy accelerant only missing the tiniest spark to combust. I watch his eyes snake to my mouth as my tongue swipes my parched lips. A muscle flutters on his jaw.

"You staying or leaving?" I rasp, my eyes snagging on his beautiful lips.

I feel his body heat enveloping me, blanketing me in warmth. His scent is like an aphrodisiac and with each passing second, my breasts feel heavier, more tender, my nipples beading into hard buds, saluting him, inviting him.

I want him. So much. My heart pounds in response.

He's so still. Quiet. Lethal like the hunter inside him. He doesn't move a muscle, almost blending into the night. The seconds pass by, ticking like a timer on a bomb.

But nothing happens.

It's anticlimactic.

Disappointment snakes through me and I shake my head. *Again. He's saying no, again.* "Coward. You're a coward, Ryland Anderson."

I step to the side to get out from under his grasp, my eyes burning, and I feel the telltale sign of incoming tears. My heart splinters, the frissons widening with each step I take away from him.

I won't beg him to be with me. I have my pride. I've done all that I can.

A shaky sob slips out from my lips as I head in the direction I came from, my steps feeling heavy on the ground. The night didn't turn out the way I thought it would. *What did you expect? Him to give up his morals for you?*

I murmur to the darkness surrounding me, "I'll find someone else. Someone brave enough. Someone who deserves me."

A few more seconds pass by, the forest eerily quiet except for the sound of crickets and the occasional chirping of birds.

With a roar, he reaches me in a flash, grabs my arm, and spins me around to face him. "Don't. You. Fucking. Dare."

He reaches up and curls his hand around my neck before hauling me to him and crushing his lips on mine. His kiss is savage and possessive, each suction and swipe of his tongue melting my defenses, my hurt, my tears. Our tongues duel with each other as I drink in his poison, his antidote, his elixir, all in one. It's violent, it's aggressive.

It's heaven.

I bite his bottom lip, a punishment for what he's put me through, and a metallic taste bursts on my taste buds. He lets out a hiss as he returns the favor, the sharp pinch sending shock waves to my pussy.

"How dare you!" *How dare you sign up to do this with another woman. How dare you ignore what we have. How dare you push me away.* I claw at his chest, digging into his hard muscles, scratching, fighting, unleashing the months of anger I have bottled up inside me. "You *asshole.*"

He growls and spins me around so that my back is plastered against his front. His hand knots mine to my front as he kicks my feet apart. His motions are rough and dominant.

He's unraveling before my eyes.

The thought sends another burst of pleasure through my body and I arch my head back, needing his taste again.

He ignores my silent plea, his other hand reaching under my dress and swiftly wrenching my panties to the side and cupping my wet heat. I'm so slick for him. It'd be embarrassing if my mind were actually online.

Swallowing a moan, I try to head butt him.

"You're so fucking wet for me and your fight is turning me on."

I bite back a whimper as I feel him palm my slit, his finger rubbing circles around my clit, playing with the swollen nub, and I let out a keening wail.

I need more. More. More. More.

I need everything.

Flailing against him, my body is thrashing, battling, refusing to surrender to him yet wanting to succumb to his tempest, his tornado in dark skies. My legs tremble and he tightens his hold on to me so I don't fall to the ground.

"Say the safe word, Millie. Stop this madness," he growls in my ear and with one hard yank, he tears my lacy panties away, baring me to the cold air. "Stop me, Millie. Stop. Me."

I flinch at the burn, but every inch of my body is already on fire. My legs widen and his fingers travel down to my core, teasing the entrance. Sparks alight into a wildfire.

"Safe word, Millie."

My head falls against his hot chest, my panting loud in the night. "No. Fuck me, Ryland. Fuck me, please."

"Shit. Fucking shit."

He releases my hands and pushes me to the ground so I'm face down and pressed against the damp grass. I thrash under him as he covers me with his hard heat and body weight. It's like trying to move a mountain. He dominates me, all raw power and ferocious energy, and I can't help but grow wetter, my body needing him inside me.

"Safe. Word," he grunts, his hands bunching my dress around my waist.

"No!" I arch against him, rubbing my butt over the seam of his pants, my pussy needing more friction. It isn't enough. I feel so empty, so wet and achy for him.

I feel the cool air against my ass, sliding in between my legs. He shuffles and I hear the telltale sound of his zipper.

Then, I feel him.

Every hard, steely inch of him pressed up against my ass. He grabs my thighs and tilts my ass up in the air before pinning me with his body once more. More wetness seeps out of me, leaking down my thighs and my fingers find purchase on the grass, gripping the damp blades, trying to claw on anything that'll allow me to push back against him, to angle that cock of his where I need it to be.

"Fuck. You look so good under me, Millie. On the ground. Helpless. But you aren't helpless at all, are you, little lark? You're the fucking snowy owl pretending to be a lark. You're a fucking phoenix."

He grunts again and I feel his thick cock sliding between my pussy lips from the puckered rosebud to my clit. It feels like a brand. I let out a cry, gyrating harder against his throbbing heat.

It's not enough. Too many clothes. Too much distance. I need more.

"Are you going to be a good student and let your professor stuff his thick cock into your tight little pussy?"

I whimper as he rasps in my ear.

He reaches underneath me and grabs my breast, his fingers pinching my nipples. Plucking, teasing, kneading. I let out a wail from the pleasurable pain.

It's like he knows exactly what I need. Every kiss, every stroke, all sending me toward oblivion.

I can't think. I can barely form words. My mouth is muffled against the grass, and all I can manage is a raspy, "Yes. Ryland. Yes."

He lets out a guttural groan as his hand leaves my aching breast and curls around my neck. Then, with his other hand, he widens my legs even more and nothing can prepare me for the sensation of his steel rod slamming inside me in one full stroke.

I mewl as his hard cock spears me in half. There's no finesse, no soft touches or gentle caresses. This is a rough claiming, a hunter who has captured his prey, dominating her, having his way with her. I moan against the ground as my body widens to accept him, the pain mixing with the pleasure in a heady cocktail.

"Fuck, your pussy is sopping wet for me," he groans as he retreats before slamming in again. His hand holds steady around my neck, his fingers pressing into the tender flesh, like he's marking me, telling me who's in control. "You need this. Just like I do."

I arch under him as he pistons inside me, his thrusts picking up in speed. My knees scrape against the pebbles on the floor and I'm sure I'll have scratches and bruises later, but I don't care. Every nerve ending is in tune with the man behind me and the pleasure he's wreaking on my body.

"Mine. You're fucking mine. Remember that," he rasps, his voice violent and intense.

His words send me into a tailspin, and I grow wetter between my legs.

He completely overpowers me, his hand controlling my breathing, his body restricting my movements. All I can do is just lie underneath him and take it. Take each harsh, punishing stab, accept the sharp pleasure he's giving me stroke by stroke, thrust by thrust.

For the first time in my life, I'm not in control of anything. Not my emotions, not the feelings I show on my face. I don't have to worry about taking care of the people around me or putting on a brave face. I'm a marionette, and he's my puppet master.

Ryland is wrenching everything away from my mind—guilt, worries, doubts, fears—everything ceases to exist other than him and the way he's pistoning inside me, ramming his hard cock in to bury himself deep in me, each stroke hitting the sensitive spot no one has ever reached before.

"No one else gets to fuck this tight little pussy, you hear me?"

I whimper, my body bucking against him, and he growls. "You hear me, Millie?" His cock thrusts deeper, harder and I let out a scream.

"Y-Yes...I'm yours."

"Fucking yes." His motions grow wilder, and I can feel his unwavering focus on my reactions, moans, screams, and whimpers, every movement from him driving me out of my mind with pleasure.

Heat builds in my pussy, and I dig my fingers into the grass, trying to get away from the overwhelming, mind-blowing pleasure. He bears down on me harder, forcing me to accept him, his grunts loud in the darkness. He's an animal rutting in heat.

My moans and screams join the lurid slapping of skin against skin, and a thousand sensations coalesce at our point of connection. My legs throb and tremble, my nipples as hard as diamonds, raking across the rough earth with each slam of his hips on top of me, the scraping adding onto the firestorm brewing and incinerating my insides.

As if sensing I'm close, he tightens his grip around my neck, so I have to fight for each breath. My mind feels hazy, my vision blurry, and every cell in my body is focused on the throbbing building between my legs as my lungs clamor for air.

"Fuck. Take it, Millie. You're taking me so fucking well. You're so fucking perfect. I've dreamed of this and nothing compares to reality. Feel how fucking hard I am for you."

Dirty words spew out of him and I barely register them as my body floats to the precipice between heaven and hell, the pleasure so painful and addictive at the same time.

"Your cunt is clamping down on my hard cock like it can't get enough."

Thrust. Thrust. Thrust. Sweat trickles down my body.

My entire body starts spasming. I'm so close, so damn close. I can see nirvana ahead.

"Milk my cock, you naughty little girl. Come on my cock like my good student." He releases my throat, his fingers reaching down my body and pinching my clit.

I detonate.

My scream echoes amongst the trees as my body splinters into a million pieces, the pleasure overtaking all my senses like an inferno. My lungs rake in greedy gulps of oxygen, the sudden flooding of air prolonging my high, making every sensation one thousand times more visceral.

With a few more punishing thrusts, he slams his body on top of mine and a guttural groan tears from his lips. I feel his cock pulse inside me, unleashing streams of hot cum, sending me into another spiral of pleasure.

The loud sounds of our breathing blend and slowly, he clasps my hand in his, twining our fingers together as the pleasure bleeds out from our pores. He is still on top of me, covering me from behind, his hips gently moving, prolonging our connection, and I don't feel like I'm suffocating underneath him.

I feel treasured. Protected. Safe. I can let go with him and he'll take care of me.

He's still my professor and I'm still his much younger student. Everything is still wrong and yet...nothing has ever felt so very right.

How can we walk away from this?

CHAPTER 36

OH FUCK. I'M SO fucked on so many levels.

The chant is on repeat in my mind as I sweep her up in my arms and stride toward the staff corridors hidden throughout the building after I zipped up my pants and rearranged her tattered clothes. My mind is a mess of rioting thoughts ranging from *how can I ever walk away from her now that I know how it feels to be with her* to *what have I done?*

I'm riding on the highest of highs from the most intense sex I've ever had in my life, and I don't want anyone to see her like this but me. Her knees are all battered and bruised, the hem of her dress ripped and dirty from the damp earth underneath us moments ago.

She emits a satisfied moan, her body softening against mine, and my heart flutters in response. Her warmth, her yielding, her softness in my arms.

It feels so right. Even though this is decidedly wrong.

I didn't even fucking use a condom. And I don't think I can ever have anything in between us now that I know how it feels to be inside her bare.

I push open the hidden doors and step into the corridor, which is flooded with bright lights. My lungs seize when I take in her face and neck—swollen lips, dreamy eyes, a soft smile, hickeys, and scratches dotting her pale skin. She looks thoroughly fucked, used, so thoroughly mine.

Mine. Mine. Mine.

My cock twitches again.

Fuck.

She was so perfect. Exceeded all my fantasies when I fucked my fist in the shower to the thoughts of her, wrenching out one unsatisfying orgasm after another, unable to slake my desire for her.

She submitted to me so beautifully and I still remember every clench of her walls against my cock, the passion in her fight, the anger and strength in her eyes. The connection between us moved beyond the physical. It was a cathartic release of emotions, purging the poison accumulated in the deepest crevices of our hearts.

I've never experienced anything remotely like it.

I came undone, and she didn't run away. She wasn't scared or disgusted. She took it and she bore it so perfectly.

My beautiful lark, a phoenix in disguise.

My heart riots inside my chest, each thump sending an intoxicated warmth through my veins, much like the first sip of perfectly aged whiskey washing down my throat. The heat spreads from my cold chest to my extremities until all my senses are all filled with her—her smell, her taste, her touch.

And if this is a dream, I never want to wake up.

I want to stay in this utopia with her, where the real world doesn't matter, where there are no stakes, no ethics, no morals, no responsibilities, and no unimpeachable reputation to uphold.

No prison.

Just her and me in this heaven, our hearts pounding in unison, our breathing intertwining and in sync. That's all I need in life.

Her eyes blink open, her lush lashes fluttering, and she bestows me with the most breathtaking smile. My heart lurches in my chest. She's the first ray of sunrise to my dark twilight. She's the first sign of life poking through the thick snow after a harsh and dreary winter.

My voice is stuck in my throat, the words at the tip of my tongue. I want to tell her everything; I want to show her all my scars, all my darkness and burdens. I want to bare my soul to her and let her see every ugly corner, every corrupted edge, all the festering wounds and poisonous thoughts.

My selfish, ungrateful thoughts.

"Ryland," she whispers, and lets out a breathy sigh. She presses her hand to my chest.

"Yes, little lark?"

Her cheeks pinken at my endearment. Like that's the thing that'll embarrass her after the savage lovemaking in Noire just now. She's so cute and sexy it hurts for me to look at her sometimes.

But my gaze doesn't turn away from hers as I carry us to the employee elevators. The staff, all taught to be seen and not heard in this exclusive establishment, duck back into the rooms and corridors they came from, everyone giving me a wide berth as they see me carrying the most precious thing I've ever held in my arms.

Normally, I take care of my partners after a scene in one of the standard Rose floors suites designated for aftercare, where I ensure the person has access to the spa amenities in the suite, any healing ointments if needed, or admission to the several full-range luxury spas on the other floors. I don't stay for long, but I'll thank them for their service or participation. There will be a hefty tip waiting for them in the embossed linen envelope after they exit from the bathroom post cleaning up. It'll be civil. Unemotional.

But with Millie, everything is different. The burgeoning feelings inside me are far from civil and are most definitely *not* unemotional.

I'm not taking her to the standard suites. That's not where she belongs. Instead, I press the button to the top floor.

"I'm so happy," Millie says, her dulcet voice curling around my heart, but instead of chains, her voice is a soothing, life-giving balm, an antidote to the corruption inside. "You chose me."

A sharp guilt slices across my chest with the swiftness of a sword, but my heart pounds at her words. I know I shouldn't have succumbed to my inappropriate desires for her. I should've been stronger. I'm the older, more mature person between the two of us. I know what's at stake.

But I can't fight it anymore.

This need for her that is becoming a necessity, like oxygen to my lungs and food to a starving man. Everything pales compared to her—all the responsibilities and shackles, the rules of the family trust, the lure of the honorary doctorate—everything that used to mean the world to me.

And under the cloak of nightfall inside the dark forest, away from NYUC, she and I are just man and woman, two people who are drawn to each other like moths to a flame.

What choice do we truly have?

And now, with her in my arms, it's as if she belonged there all along.

My voice is thick and hoarse as I reply, "I...I feel the same way."

And it's true. The only true thing in my life. The emotion I feel with every ounce of my soul. If I were to die now, I'd be a happy man.

The elevator doors silently glide open, and I stride to one of three doors on the floor before pressing my palm against the palm reader. Instead of staying at the estate like Dad and Maxwell, the rest of our siblings, myself included, have opted to live in our apartments either within The Orchid or elsewhere in Manhattan.

The door automatically opens, and I carry my princess inside my haven of dark marble and reclaimed timber.

"Sir, welcome home." Gretchen, my housekeeper steps into view from her attached en-suite quarters, dressed impeccably in her usual uniform—a navy pencil skirt and a white blouse, her salt-and-pepper hair perfectly arranged in a bun. The elderly woman alternates her hours with others on the housekeeping team employed by The Orchid to serve the apartment owners on the top floors.

Her sharp brown eyes take in Millie in my arms and she immediately asks, "Do you want me to prepare a bath?"

I nod. "Thank you, and yes. In the master bath, please."

Millie gives me a shove, her face flushed crimson as she lifts her head off my chest and smiles at Gretchen.

She whispers, "Put me down! I'm not an invalid!"

"Hush. You're mine to take care of now."

The words come out with no forethought, but they ring very true to my ears. I want to take care of her.

As long as I can. Until I'm not allowed to.

Gretchen smothers a smile as she walks discreetly toward the master suite on the far right and Millie hollers, "Thank you!"

Another little elbow shove from my squirming vixen. "You caveman. I can walk by myself."

I bite back a satisfied grin as I look at her in my arms, her large blue eyes blinking at me with so much heat and tenderness in them, and my heart doubles in size.

"You poked the bear. Now you need to bear the consequences."

Millie snorts and rolls her eyes. "Har. Har. The pun." Then she snuggles back into my chest and emits a satisfied sigh. "I love the way you smell."

Smirking, I stride past the spacious living room, which is dim except for the light from a crystal floor lamp on top of the navy Persian rug, past the chef's kitchen I rarely use, down a wide corridor and I make a sharp left through the double doors of the master suite. I hear the water running and smell the soothing scents of lavender and tea tree oil wafting through the air.

Gretchen gives me a terse nod as she exits the en-suite bathroom, efficient as always, and murmurs, "Everything is set up, sir."

"Thank you."

She hurries away and closes the door behind her.

I stride inside the bathroom, where a bubble bath has been prepared in the deep spa tub. A tray containing a simple fruit platter of watermelon and grapes, something she typically has on hand for me, two glasses of water, and two flutes of what looks to be champagne, is set on the side of the tub, completed with a few sprigs of daffodils.

The same type of flower I've kept in my apartment after Millie visited my office hours in ULA. The ray of sunshine in the dark space and now, its owner will finally see them.

Setting Millie down, I bite back a smile as I watch her gape at her surroundings, even though it's only your standard luxury bathroom with all the furnishings.

"This is bigger than our living room in SoHo." She gasps, her eyes wide with wonder.

"Isn't your brother Adrian Scott? Shouldn't you be used to luxury by now?"

I walk to the bathtub and check the temperature. Hot enough to soothe the muscles, but not scalding. Perfect.

She shakes her head as she trails her fingers over the white marble countertops, skating over the clear glass stall of the two-person jet shower, her mouth parted as she takes in the separate sauna room before glancing at the bathtub.

"Daffodils!" She fawns over the flowers, reminding me of Persephone breathing life into her surroundings, giving warmth to the god of the underworld.

Her hair is a tangled mess cascading over her back, her dress is ripped and covered in dirt.

But she looks perfect. Especially here in my haven, in the space I've taken no woman outside of my family to. I want her to stay here. I want to wake up with her by my side.

And perhaps, for tonight, I can pretend.

"Come here," I command softly, and she whirls toward me.

Her smile slips from her face as she takes in my serious expression. A spaghetti strap slides off her shoulder, and my cock twitches at the effortless seductive sway of her hips, her pouty lips parted as if she's reading every thought in my mind.

Quietly, I trail my hands over her shoulders, relishing the soft gasp and the pebbling of goosebumps gracing her skin. I slip off her dress from her lithe frame, a heady heat traveling south as I see the smooth expanse of milky skin, the way a lacy bra hugs her curvy tits, the red scratch marks, and pinkish bite marks over her cleavage.

Closing my eyes, I pull her toward me and inhale her scent of jasmine and vanilla, now laced with the seductive smell of the forest, and my cock hardens in milliseconds. I press my lips to her neck, my teeth scraping down her sensitive column and she lets out a soft moan, which inflames my senses.

"I'm obsessed with you," I rasp against the pulse fluttering there, my hands unhooking her bra and molding around her swollen tits.

"You're my whirlwind, Ryland," she whispers, tilting her neck back for me as I trail kisses down her cleavage and capture her nipple, a perfect shade of brown, in my lips.

"Oh my God, I feel so sensitive. I ache for you," she whimpers.

A growl sounds from my throat, a curl of possession wrapping around my chest.

I want to be the only man to see her this way.

Hoisting her up, I swallow her gasp of surprise, my mouth tasting those sweet lips once more, my tongue laving the bite mark I left earlier in Noire, noticing the hint of metallic taste from the spot of blood at the corner of her mouth. Gently, I set her in the bath and she lets out a moan of satisfaction.

"This is heaven." She sighs, her eyes fluttering shut, and she leans against the soft headrest at the end of the tub.

Layers of bubbles cover her body, the jets emitting a low hum and Millie moans as the hot water is no doubt soothing her sore muscles.

Lust snakes through me and I quickly shrug out of my clothes and step into the bath with her.

Her eyes snap open, her gaze flaring and trailing down my chest, her mouth dropping open. Her pupils dilate and a pulse flutters rapidly on her neck, an enticing swath of crimson spreading over her pale skin.

Smiling, I lean forward and tug her toward me so her back is flushed against my front. She lets out another breathy moan as she settles in place. I pluck a grape from the tray and feed it to her luscious lips.

She takes in the fruit, her tongue licking my fingers before her mouth closes around them in a lusty suck.

"Fuck," I murmur, my cock as hard as steel again, pressing between the smooth swells of her ass. "I was wrong about you all along."

"Hmm..." She gyrates her luscious behind on my cock, moving up and down my throbbing length, her bottom lip trapped between her teeth.

"I thought you were a goodie-two-shoes, the sweet, bright soul against my darkness...but now I see, there was a slutty schoolgirl inside you all along," I rasp against her ear, my fingers traveling around her waist and reaching between her legs.

She winces as I slide my finger up her slit and gently massage her pussy before reaching up and angling her head toward me. "I'd fuck you, but you must be sore from the scene just now."

I press a soft kiss on her lips as she wiggles her luscious bottom against my cock.

"Stop driving me crazy, my little lark." I punctuate the statement with a thorough kiss, my fingers gripping her long hair, curling it around my hand as I taste her once more.

She sucks and licks, kissing with fervor, and a newfound euphoria pulses through my veins. I soften my kisses with gentle pecks and suctions, tasting every drop of heaven I can reach until I'm dragged back into the real world.

Shifting her in my arms so she's sitting upright, I reach for the shampoo and gently lather her strands, followed by conditioner, then spread body wash onto her body, massaging the tender globes of her breasts, her soft belly, my mouth pressing kisses onto every scrape and wound I can see even though pride streaks through me at the visual claim of ownership.

She turns around to face me and grins at whatever she sees on my face. "Feeling proud of yourself?"

My tongue swipes over my teeth and I smirk before responding, "Very much so."

Her fingers trail over my face, caressing my jaw, my nose, my lips, as if memorizing me by touch. I close my eyes, enjoying her gentle touch on my skin, feeling her light seeping into my body with her healing grazes. Her hands trail down my neck, over my Adam's apple, to my chest, and then she pauses.

I open my eyes, finding her staring at the pendant in her fingers, her thumb grazing the tiny diamond studded key within the silver lock.

"It's beautiful," she murmurs.

Mom's words float to my mind.

"Someday, you'll want to give your heart to someone else. That's what love is, you know? To have your heart live outside of you. It's scary...but beautiful."

Visions of her wearing the key around her slender neck, her eyes reflecting love toward me, flood my mind and the lump grows in my throat.

Dreams. These are dreams within the utopia of today. Only for today.

She's the glorious bird who has just learned how to spread her wings to take on the world. The skies are her limit.

Some birds are too beautiful, their feathers too bright, to be kept imprisoned. I can never be the one to take that away from her, to lock her in a gilded cage, to ensnare her in a trap she can't escape from.

A more selfish man will say fuck it and be with her like this forever. In the shadows until she graduates and afterward, as a man and a woman together in love, no marriage, the ultimate middle finger to the terms of the trust. But the gentleman in me can't. It's not right to string her along if I can never marry her. It's not honorable.

Dad tried this before, with Grace and Taylor's mom. The relationship ended in heartbreak and my half-sisters were raised in poverty. Their mom died years later pining after Dad and the love they lost. It was a tragedy.

It is also a lesson for me. *Don't do it.*

If I can never give her the Anderson name because if I marry her, she'll have to give up her dreams and be trapped in the same prison with me, then isn't the right thing to do is nip this in the bud?

But for today, I can pretend there's no tomorrow, that this one moment will stretch endlessly until the end of the galaxies, until the last grains of sand run out in the hourglass governing the world.

This memory can sustain me for the rest of my life, especially on the lonely days and nights when I'm peeking out from behind my gilded bars and staring at the glorious meadowlark soaring in the endless skies, singing the most beautiful song.

"It was my mom's. She bequeathed it to me before she died."

Her fingers freeze over the pendant, her large eyes lifting and staring at me. Her nose flares and her delicate brows furrow with sympathy. "Oh, Ryland."

"She was the most wonderful soul. Vibrant. Happy. Patient. She had so much love to give and I was blessed to be on the receiving end of it when she was alive." I can drown in the depths of the passionate pools of blue in her eyes.

"This pendant symbolizes eternal love, the key being the only thing that can unlock the padlock of the heart," I rasp, my voice thickening. "I think she had hoped, someday...someday, I'd...I'd..."

I can't speak. The words won't come out of my mouth.

Millie's eyes glitter with unshed tears as she shifts closer and presses her soft lips against mine in a tender kiss. "She hoped you could find someone to love and unlock your heart as well. Of course she would."

She pulls back and clasps the pendant in her small hands. "You deserve to be loved, Ryland Anderson. You deserve to be filled with light and to live for yourself."

I curl my hand over hers so our hands are both wrapped around the pendant, the pendant I desperately want to pull apart and see the key hanging safely around her neck.

Dropping my forehead against hers, I whisper, "How can I when Maxwell won't ever experience the same love? How can I listen to my heart and leave the burdens to my siblings?" *How can I take away your dreams? How can I make everyone I care about lose everything?*

Her forehead pinches. "Maxwell? Won't he want you to be loved as well?"

Closing my eyes, I swallow the breath trapped in my throat. "He will. He's selfless that way."

I sigh. "The men in our family aren't lucky in love, especially the eldest male heir." I can't tell her about the curse or about the family trust. Not yet anyway. It's a heavily guarded secret in our family.

"Maxwell is older than me by seven minutes and he has experienced more tragedy in his life than he deserves. Because of his role in the family, he has trapped himself in our palatial estate, hiding himself from the world, protecting what's left of his heart. But you see," my eyes flicker open and I grab her hand, "he saved my life. Do you see the scar on my eyebrow?"

She nods, her fingers gently touching the faint slash above my eye.

"It was a horrible hunting accident. If it weren't for him, I wouldn't even be here. And because of fate, or whatever you want to call it, my brother spends his time hiding from everyone."

Millie's eyes soften with empathy, and she cradles my cheek in her palm. I lean into her healing touch and whisper, "He'll never find love, nor does he want to. His nature won't let him shoulder the public burdens of the family. If I don't do it, he'll need to step into my shoes. But isn't it cruel to ask him to give up solace, the one thing he has and can control, so I can go after my selfish desires?"

I tell her about the hunting accident and how Maxwell, without a second thought, threw himself on top of me, how he barely survived the boar attack. I mention how he also lost someone he loved dearly, besides our mom.

"But Ryland...you don't need to atone for sins you didn't commit. He won't want you to." She releases a shaky exhale, her eyes brimming with tears. "Don't be your worst enemy."

Tears for me, the selfish monster.

Her warmth wraps around my bleeding chest, stemming the flow of blood from a wound that has never healed. The bandage may be temporary, but I relish every second of her healing touch.

Perhaps she is right, and the devil inside me is myself. But he has my life clenched within his hands, his talons digging, choking, and I can't seem to escape from his clutches.

CHAPTER 37

HIS EXPRESSION IS GUTTED. The devastation in those slate-colored eyes lashes me to the core. His battle is mental, this guilt consuming him, locking him in the prison of his mind. And while I'm grateful he's finally letting me in, I sense more secrets hidden away in those soulful eyes.

"Ryland, I'll be here with you every step of the way. We can do everything at your speed, your own time. And maybe someday, you can let your family know. There have to be other options. It isn't black and white, all or nothing—"

"No."

His grip on my hand tightens. His jaw clenches. I flinch at the sudden chill on his face, completely at odds with the swirling heat of the bath waters.

His face softens. "No," he repeats. "Millie, you and I...we can never be together. Your dreams are far greater than what I can offer you. You deserve to travel the world and teach, help others as you've always wanted to."

"I can do all that and still be with you—"

"No, you can't. Don't you see? The women in our family are trapped with us. Once they're involved with an Anderson, their dreams and lives before cease to exist. It almost killed my mom before she died from the accident. This is," he pauses, his eyes conflicted, *the tradition*. Over four hundred years of impeccable reputation, our business managed only by people within the family. You'll never be able to change me, Millie. I have my role in my family, one that was decided for me before I was born. It's my cross to bear. I won't have you shoulder my burdens with me."

"That doesn't make any sense. I don't understand."

He lets out a ragged sigh. "Maybe someday I can tell you everything. Then you'll understand. But I know I can't give you the forever you deserve, Millie. I just...can't."

He presses a kiss on the tip of my nose, his eyes red and clouded with moisture. "I've felt the burdens of being an Anderson. Seen the sacrifices up close. Mom, when she was alive, loved us with all her heart. But I'd see how sad she was whenever she talked about her hopes and dreams when she was younger."

"Ryland, I'm not your mom. I can still be me while being with you. It's not all or nothing."

I clutch his arm, imploring him to understand. Taking a deep breath, I tamp down the frustration ramping up inside me. I feel like I'm staring at a complicated puzzle and missing one last piece. But he's opening up to me and I recognize this is hard for him.

Ryland shakes his head. "You know, I'm sure she felt the same way as you at one point. She wanted to do so much, to be a professor, but she couldn't once she became the woman behind my dad. Then, the sadness in her voice when she talked about him, her husband who was working more than he should, was not home often enough. She was trapped. I know it now as an adult."

Ryland swallows, his voice hoarse. "You deserve to be free. You're young, your future is endless. You have an abundance of light to share with the world. Don't snuff it out by being with me. Trust me, there are things I haven't told you, but I know I can't be with you in a way you deserve."

Anger churns through my veins and I push at his chest. "You don't get to decide for me! If you have feelings for me, which you clearly do, and I have the same for you, we deserve a chance."

"I won't be able to stand it if one day you're tired of being chained. Please don't ask this of me." His fingers tremble as he swipes a tear sliding over my cheek.

"Even without everything else, we aren't supposed to be doing this. I'm your ethics professor," he scoffs, his voice dripping with derision at himself. "If we get caught, your future will be ruined. And so will my family's reputation. I can't be the one to cause the downfall of the Anderson name."

My nose twitches, and I clench my hands into fists. We've come this far already. I refuse to give up, especially after knowing how good it can be between us.

"My answer is no, Ryland. I don't care what you say, I don't care about the future. You can call me immature or naïve, but I want the now. The present. You and I both know tomorrow is not guaranteed." I hurl myself against him, burying my face in his neck.

"Please don't tell me no," I whisper before pressing a soft kiss on his heated skin, "If you care for me at all, please...please don't break my heart. I don't want to think about the future. Please, just g-give me tomorrow." My voice chokes up and I shudder.

Maybe I can convince him, one day at a time, like Scheherazade spinning her stories night after night to entice her husband, the king, to keep her alive in *One Thousand and One Nights*.

His rough breathing fills the bathroom, the steam from the bath enveloping us in a tender, heart-wrenching embrace as I hug him tightly, feeling the righteous rhythm of his heartbeat pounding against mine.

"Please, Ryland. Give me tomorrow," I whisper once more. *Please don't give up on us before we start.* "I can take your darkness, your burdens. I'm the lark masquerading as a phoenix, remember? Please trust me. Give me tomorrow. Give *us* tomorrow."

A few moments pass, and slowly his muscular arms envelop my back and he presses a kiss on my hair. He releases a tortuous sigh.

"Tomorrow. We still have tomorrow."

She bounces on her feet, her back is turned toward me as she bends over the stove. After our bath, she heard my stomach grumble, and she donned one of my dress shirts before darting out of the bedroom. Now she's in the kitchen doing God knows what.

Millie is humming under her breath, spreading warmth and happiness throughout my apartment.

She looks like she belongs here.

In another life, I can imagine her filling my apartment with laughter, moving around the space as she entertains friends and family. Maybe there will be a dog or two or perhaps a little one screaming for mommy in the living room.

My heart clenches at the vivid image.

In another life.

She pauses her movements and looks up at my black kitchen cabinets.

"Hmm...if I were you, where would I be?" she whispers. My lips twitch. I can imagine the cute little frown on her face.

She opens the cabinets one by one, her hands rummaging through the various containers and boxes, clearly looking for something. Then, a few seconds later, she exclaims, "Aha!"

Millie places her hand on the granite countertop, using it as leverage as she tries to reach the contents on the upper shelf of the cabinet in question, her hand missing whatever she's trying to retrieve.

"Dammit."

She tries again, fails, and lets out the most unladylike growl I've ever heard. My heart skips several beats.

Chuckling, I walk up behind her, my hand automatically sliding around her slender waist, and murmur, "What are you trying to get, my little lark?"

She spins around and points to a bag nestled in the back of the shelf. "That bag of dark chocolate hiding over there. Gretchen mentioned she had some in the cabinets before she left, but this kitchen is not made for short people like me."

Biting back a smile, I reach up and grab the bag for her. In another life, I'd demolish this kitchen and remake everything to her specifications.

"You're the perfect size." I punctuate my words with a kiss on her forehead.

She flushes before turning back to the stove.

"What are you making?"

"You're in for a treat. I'm making Mom's hot chocolate." She glances at me and winks. "Maybe that's the secret sauce to melt your heart."

No. You're the secret sauce, Millie.

I lean against the counter, my heart racing inside my rib cage. "I'll have to see if it tastes as good as you make it sound. I see you drinking hot chocolate all the time."

She grins as she stirs a mixture of chocolate and other powders into a saucepan filled with steaming milk. She shakes her luscious ass as she hums once more.

The warm overhead light casts her face in a beautiful glow and her hair cascades down her back in waves. She doesn't have a stitch of makeup on.

But she's perfect. Breathtaking.

"The key is the vanilla and the espresso powder." She stirs the contents of the saucepan.

"When I was a kid, Mom, of course, left out the espresso powder, because she didn't want me amped up on caffeine." She laughs, her eyes taking on a faraway glint, clearly reminiscing about the past. "But later, I found the real recipe in her stuff."

She looks at me and waggles her brows. "Trust me. The espresso acts as an intensifier, making the chocolate richer."

Turning off the stove, she wafts her hand over the saucepan, closes her eyes, and inhales the rich scent of chocolate permeating the space. She pours the contents into two mugs and adds whipped cream and a few pieces of tiny marshmallows on top.

Millie hands me a mug, her eyes widening as she watches me take a sip. The richness of the chocolate hits my tongue in an explosion of flavors. It's creamy and thick, the texture luxurious, but the taste is not too sweet. There is a small thread of bitterness as an aftertaste, keeping everything from becoming too overpowering, followed by a lingering hint of vanilla.

It's delicious. A liquid warm hug.

I stare at the marshmallows floating on the surface. Am I supposed to eat them or wait for them to melt?

"So? Do you like it? It's the best, right?" She adds, "The marshmallows are fun, but you don't need to eat them."

Of course she knows what I'm thinking.

I stare into her eager sapphire eyes and watch her tongue peek out and swipe at her enticing lips before she takes a sip. The whipped cream lingers on her upper lip.

My breathing stutters as an all-encompassing warmth fills me. Gently, I wipe the cream from her lip and whisper, "It's perfect. *You're* perfect."

Millie holds my stare, and I set down my mug to the side before slowly bringing my lips to hers, tasting her sweetness at the source. She clutches my sweatpants as she melts into my arms.

Breaking apart to take a breath, I take in her upturned face—her beautiful eyes closed, lashes fanning her pale skin, a rosy glow on her cheeks, her plump lips parted as if she wants another kiss.

In another life, this will all be within reach.

The refrain echoes in my mind and a lump forms in my throat. "So, can I help with anything?"

Her eyes open, and she gives me a sweet smile. "You bet you can. Come on, my big, strong hunter, man the grill. We are having post-coital burgers and hot chocolate."

She shoves me with her hip and throws out another saucy wink. I laugh, watching her wiggle her butt once more as she shifts out of the way. If I were by myself, I'd ask Gretchen to fix me something before she left or order food from the restaurants downstairs.

But with her, this is what I want.

The normal life. Ryland and Millie. Just simply us.

She walks around the kitchen like she owns the place, taking out other ingredients we need for our late-night meal. A desperate yearning coils inside my chest.

In another life.

The tomorrow she's asking for.

I want every single tomorrow with her.

CHAPTER 38

Millie

Dear Ryland,

I don't care what the rest of the world will say about us. The older professor with his forbidden student. I don't care about the centuries of traditions you think you're bound to. I refuse to believe fate allowed us to meet only for us to be passing ships in the night.

I think your mom in heaven brought me to you because she couldn't bear seeing her sensitive son torturing himself, because she knew your cold heart needed warmth, needed sunshine, and I want to be the one to give it to you.

Be brave, Ryland.

And until you get there, I'll be brave enough for the two of us. I won't give up. I want more tomorrows with you until one day I won't need to ask anymore because they'll be a given.

Love, Millie

I WIELD MY PRUNING shears like a weapon and trim the dead or weakened branches from the barren trees in the rooftop garden. An icy wind lashes my skin and I burrow myself inside the warmth of my down jacket and wool scarf, the thick wintry clothes doing little to ward against the chill of a New York December evening.

Snip. Snip. Snip.

The motion is cathartic, and I imagine the fallen branches are my worries, and with each cut, my problems disappear.

Problems like him and his conflicting behavior.

It has been a few weeks since our night at Noire, where Ryland revealed a part of his soul I suspected had been long buried under the weight of his responsibilities.

We spent a beautiful night in his penthouse apartment, talking about our childhoods, eating overcooked burgers because the man couldn't grill anything to save his life, and drinking hot chocolate. He curled me in his arms afterward, wrapping me in his strong, warm body as we sat on the sofa on the heated balcony and gazed at the stars.

He kissed me like he had been starving for the press of our lips together, like he hadn't had anyone love and care for him in far too long. He tucked me tightly against him as we fell asleep, holding onto me like a drowning man would hold on to a piece of driftwood in the deep, dark seas.

I whispered in his ear, "Tomorrow. We still have tomorrow," and that seemed to settle him and calm the restlessness in his tense frame.

Then, the next day at school, his demeanor turned into ice again, his expression a sharp blade to my heart. But when class ended and I lingered behind after everyone left, he snaked his arm around my waist, pressed me against the closed classroom door and kissed the ever-living daylights out of me, and the fatal wound in my heart would miraculously heal again, revived by the passion in his kiss.

That day, as we parted for air, I once again whispered, "We still have tomorrow," and he gave me a solemn nod, the barest of acknowledgments.

And for the last few weeks, we'd fall into this strange routine—a chilly reception in class, one where I'd start doubting his feelings for me, followed by the occasional make-out session when I loitered behind after everyone left.

My mind would warn me we shouldn't be doing this on campus. After all, look at what happened to Professor Archer and Tammy. But I couldn't bring myself to deny him, to deny us, when these fleeting moments were all that he'd offer me.

The kisses were bone melting, his possessive touch setting a fire in my veins, but he wouldn't go beyond that. His fingers or mouth would bring me to a sopping mess as I'd cover my screams with my hand, but he wouldn't have sex with me. His cock would be hard as steel but he'd ask me to leave, or he'd make up an excuse about an appointment he had to go to or a call he needed to take.

He was holding me at arm's length.

My heart clenched every time I saw the longing ache in his dark gray eyes, the throbbing pulse against his temple, and I just knew one day he wouldn't nod anymore. He wouldn't give me the tomorrow.

I lied.

I told him I'd be fine. I told him I was strong enough to handle his darkness. To handle him walking away from me whenever this ended, because he made it clear this wouldn't be permanent.

We are living on borrowed time. One tomorrow after another.

And when that day comes, and I know it will, he'll set me free, even though I want to be chained to his side forever. My heart will break into a thousand pieces, the pain eviscerating, and the organ will never beat for anyone else again.

Moisture prickles my eyes as I take a step back and look at my well-tended garden, half blanketed in snow, with the more delicate plants and flowers covered in a large tent constructed with a clear weather tarp.

Closing my eyes, I lift my face toward the skies, hoping somewhere up there, a higher power will take care of my fragile heart, which has been sliced far too many times.

The plants will survive the harsh New England winter, but will my relationship with him, if we can even call it that, survive?

A lump lodges in my throat and I heave out a heavy sigh, watching my breath crystallizing in a white plume before dissipating, a transient whisper, much like the love I'm trying to hold on to, only to watch it helplessly slip through my grasp.

"Dang, it's cold out today," Belle says from behind me, her footfalls soft on the ground. "Are you almost done?"

I blink, trying to dispel my morose thoughts, and turn around, giving her a shaky smile. "Yes, just finished. The tarp is holding up well and the plants look healthy."

Belle frowns, her light brown eyes narrowing. She sets two cups of steaming hot drinks on the outdoor coffee table and walks up to me. "What's wrong, Millie? Don't lie to me. You look like you're about to cry."

I swallow and look away. Sniffling, I shake my head. "I-I'm fine."

"Bullshit. Don't hide from me, Millie, or from any of us. We're always on your side. Nothing you say or do will chase us away. You don't need to take care of our feelings or be worried about how we'll respond because," she steps closer and takes my icy hands in hers, "you'll never get rid of me or the other girls. Ever."

My face scrunches and I take in the concern in her kind eyes.

I let out a sob and throw my hands around her neck and breathe in her faint scent of lavender. Old habits die hard. I'm so used to putting on a front with everyone, I keep forgetting I can be vulnerable in front of my girls.

"Shhh..." she hushes me and rubs soothing circles on my shuddering back. "I'm here, Millie. You can tell me everything."

Tears slip down my face and I nod wordlessly. After a few minutes, she gently pulls away and leads us to the wooden bench, which is protected from the elements by the canopy we had set up at the beginning of the season.

I take out my latest knitting project—a small blanket I barely started—from my tote and stare at it. The stitches look uneven and wrong, like everything else in my life. I pull at the yarn.

"Hey, hey. Tell me what's going on." Belle stops my hand with hers, puts my project back in my tote, and hands me a mug.

Staring at the hot chocolate in my hands, I whisper, "Thank you."

Belle shrugs and gives me a wink. "I see you drinking your hot chocolate like how I inhale my coffee, but be warned, I don't know how to make them fancy like the way you do. This is just an instant mix."

My heart warms, the earlier pain fading away slightly as I take a careful sip. The drink is much too sweet, but my soul feels soothed. It's the thought that counts.

"So tell me, why are you so sad? I thought the plan worked and you and Ryland are together now?"

I stare at the colorful twinkling lights of the tall buildings surrounding us. The city is a veritable Christmas snow globe, with buildings around us glowing in red and green lights, and adorned with festive decor—a sparkling Santa atop a sleigh and his team of reindeers on the rooftop garden in the next building, a light dusting of snow atop any shrubbery or flat surfaces.

The honking of cars and faint melodies of Christmas songs travel through the air from our surroundings. The city is very much alive and bursting with the excitement one normally expects for the week before Christmas.

But my heart doesn't feel the elation, the thrill of the season.

"Do you know that feeling in your gut when you think something bad will happen? That uneasiness swimming around in your chest making it hard to breathe?"

I blow out a deep breath. "That's how I feel every time I'm with him. He has never made me any promises. Our interactions are intense but fleeting. A stolen kiss here, a make-out session there. I feel like I'm trying to hold on to him, but he wants to let go, if that makes any sense."

Belle curls her arm around my shoulder, giving me a squeeze. "Aww, Millie. That sounds so rough. I was hoping things were going well for you two, since I'd seen that smile on your face more this past month than I did before."

I stare at the cup in my hand, a wistful smile on my lips. "I can't help but wonder, is it better not knowing how it feels to be loved by him, to feel his warmth and kisses, than to have experienced it knowing it won't last? I feel him pulling away, Belle."

"If this doesn't work out, will you regret it? Or will this be a beautiful memory?" she murmurs, her eyes taking on a pensive gaze as she stares at the buildings in front of us. "I'd like to think, if I were to have a choice, it'd be better to have experienced something earth shattering, to have an empty heart be filled with love, than to never feel it before. If there was a choice, that is..."

Her voice trails off, and she sounds sad.

I look at her just as she turns her head toward me, her eyes dimming. I remember what she said back in the rage room all those weeks ago and how her parents were looking to set her up in an arranged marriage. "Are you okay, Belle?"

She pauses for a second and shakes her head. "Not really, but I will be." She pauses and I wait for her to continue. "I'll tell you girls everything someday."

Belle takes a sip of her drink as she looks far away, a wistfulness in her expression. "And maybe you'll hate me for saying this, but honestly, I'm jealous of you sometimes, Millie. You're strong. A go-getter, going after your dreams of becoming an educator, chasing after your man, allowing yourself to get hurt. And while you might feel your future is uncertain, you're living your choices, Millie. You *have* a choice. You get to decide what to do next."

Belle tips her lips up, but the smile doesn't reach her eyes. "Don't you think that's a powerful thing? To *have* that choice? To choose if you want to risk it all? To let yourself get hurt in the process? To experience love?"

She swallows and sighs. "Not all of us have that choice and for some people who do, they aren't even brave enough to take a step into the unknown, and that's how I know you'll be okay, Millie, regardless of what happens. Because you'll always get back up. You may cry, you may get hurt, but you'll stand back up and fight."

Tears well in my eyes as I look at one of my best friends, who's clearly troubled by problems of her own, who sees me in a different light, and I'm reminded of what Ryland told me once. Something I once told myself, but have conveniently forgotten.

I'm a fighter.

Squeezing her hand, I whisper, "Thank you, Belle. And you're a fighter too, just like me, just like Grace. Just like all of us. And I'm here for you."

She stays silent as we take sips from our drinks, allowing the hot liquid to warm our insides in this frigid cold. After a few moments, she asks, "Want to learn something interesting?" She sneaks a glance at me and grins.

I chuckle, my chest feeling lighter now that I've unloaded some emotions weighing me down for the last few weeks. I nod.

"In my mom's culture, or I guess, my culture too since I'm half-Chinese, there's a saying, 'when a woman pursues a man, they're separated by a silk screen, but when a man pursues a woman, they're separated by a mountain.'"

She waggles her brows, the spark appearing back in her eyes. "What that means is, it's much easier for a woman to get to a man. She just needs to poke through the thin silk screen to reach his heart, but it's much harder for a man to get to a woman. So, you have a distinct advantage."

"Probably because the idiots are ruled by their brains down below." I snort, motioning to my groin.

"Bingo. *Exactly*." She sits up, her soothing voice picking up in volume, and says, "If I were to pretend to be our evil genius friend, Tay, what would she say?"

I laugh. "She'd probably be hurling F-bombs and other expletives at Ryland and men in general."

Belle chuckles. "Yes, she would, but then she'd probably say," Belle's face twist in a comical scowl resembling Taylor, "'If you like him so much, Millie, then grab him by the balls.' And she'd be right. Obviously, you guys have an emotional connection and it sounds like on the physical side, things are combustible too."

My skin heats as I think of his scorching kisses, his deep growls in my ear making my panties wet, the orgasms he tears out of me in the few make out occasions that are too few and far between.

"Ugh. That flush on your face totally answers my question and I'm really jealous, girl," Belle comments, a knowing smirk on her face. "If he's pulling away but still giving you those 'tomorrows' as you call them, he's obviously torn inside and definitely still wants you but doesn't know how to get out of his head...or this brain on top," she taps her index finger against her temple. "I say, let's take it up a notch and engage his brain down there and kick off 'Operation Vixen.'"

"Operation V—What?" I can't stop the incredulity from seeping into my voice.

She sits back, a smug grin on her face, her fingers twirling around a thick lock of silky black hair. "You know how we just launched McKenzie's Little Secrets?"

I nod. Her family's new luxury lingerie line has taken the fashion industry by storm, rivaling some of the bigger brands like Agent Provocateur or La Perla. The cute, lacy designs are sexy, available in a wide range of sizes to embrace the unique body shapes of women, and are made to empower the wearer, to flatter and make them confident in their own bodies.

"Well, we've partnered with the famous sex toy company, Femme Fatale, and are beta testing a few lingerie products with built-in toys."

My eyes widen. "I mean, that sounds exciting and all, but how does that have anything to do with Ryland or this 'Operation Vixen?'"

Belle twiddles her thumbs. "Well, he always comments how he's much older than you and more experienced and all that. Let's show him how worldly you are...unleash your inner vixen, if you will."

She leans forward eagerly and whispers, "We have this prototype you can wear...you can be our beta tester, and I think he will go crazy over you. Absolutely insane. Let's bulldoze over those mental hurdles he has. Have him lead the march with his brain down there for once."

Curiosity sifts through me, and I clutch the hot chocolate tighter in my hands, finally feeling its warmth spread from my skin to my insides.

"Tell me more."

CHAPTER 39

I BLOW OUT A deep breath before I step through the classroom door.

I'm late today. On purpose. A dramatic entrance, if you will. But part of me is nervous because of what I'm about to do. I'm pulling out all the punches, throwing everything at the wall to see what sticks.

Taking a risk.

Knowing him, he won't let it get too far in public. And because I have faith and trust in him, I know this is a risk worth taking.

Silence sweeps through the room as heads swivel in my direction. I feel his heated gaze on me almost immediately.

Holding my head high, I stride inside. My face twitches, and I bite back a smirk at Chloe's jaw dropping open. Tossing my thick hair, meticulously curled into loose waves, over my shoulders, I turn toward Ryland, meeting his intense stare, his stormy eyes flashing, but this time, instead of anger, I see a mixture of lust, admiration, and frustration swirling in those murky pools.

Under his unwavering attention, my skin feels sensitive. The wide neck sapphire sweater wrap dress, the color matching my eyes, feels rough against my skin, even though it's made of cashmere.

Belle dressed me up this morning to kick off Operation Vixen, lending me one of her brand's luxurious wrap dresses, which highlights the swells of my cleavage, tapers around my waist, and lands mid-thigh, showcasing my lean legs clad in thigh-high leather boots, with an enticing sliver of skin showing between the tops of the boots and the hem of my outfit.

She also helped me with my makeup, a gray smoky eye that doesn't look over-the-top for daytime but makes my eyes pop, three coats of mascara, a perfectly done cat eye, all paired with an orange-red lipstick. The seductive outfit is unusual for me, someone who's more comfortable in jeans and a T-shirt, but now watching him staring at me, his eyes tracking each sway of my hips as I make my way toward him, all the preparation has been worth it.

But what's most unusual about today, outside of the care I put into my makeup and dress, is the little scrap of lace between my thighs. *Amore* is what McKenzie's Little Secrets calls this innovative underwear—an open-back panty made from the sheerest lace with delicate floral designs, two barely there straps crisscrossing over the cheeks of my ass, which is bare all the way to my puckered rosebud.

But that's not all. Under the tiny scrap of cloth covering my slit lies a thin vibrator with two nubs, one nestled comfortably against my clit, and another, longer one, which resembles a mini dildo, inserted inside my entrance. I can barely feel it any more than I can feel a tampon, but the fact I'm wearing *that* under this sexy dress has me wanting to clench my thighs.

As if he senses the wayward direction of my thoughts, Ryland's dark eyes flare and a pulse flutters in his throat. His hands curl into fists on top of his desk as I step closer, reaching inside my tote to take out an analysis that is due today.

Leaning toward him slightly, I whisper, "Sorry, Professor, for being late today. It won't happen again."

I hand him the stapled packet, watching his eyes drift from my face to my cleavage, his throat rippling as he swallows, then the pinch of his brows when he realizes I not only gave him my assignment, but also a tiny, thin remote, small enough to curl inside the palm of your hand.

"Take a seat, Ms. Callahan." His voice is rough, the deep timbre sending a shiver down my body and my nipples prickle into hard points, saluting him through my soft dress.

I give him a saucy wink and he frowns as I step away and saunter to my seat in the first row, sliding into the cool chair gingerly, my pussy throbbing when I jostle the vibrator in the process.

"You look amazing, Millie! What's going on? Hot date?" Chloe whispers and nudges me.

I glance at her, finding her curious eyes darting between me and Ryland, who's staring at me like he's marooned on an island, famished for his next meal, and I'm a scrumptious buffet.

"Something like that," I murmur noncommittally.

Ryland is glaring at my assignment now and I see him discreetly looking at the remote I gave him before his eyes flicker up and find mine. I arch my brow. I taped a small label to the top of the device: *Press me at your own discretion.*

His brows furrow even more before I see him slide the remote into the pocket of his dress pants and address the class. "We were going over the latest evidence in the Professor Archer case. Fred, continue."

Fred clears his throat, his eyes darting away from me, his skin flushed, as he responds, "A social media post from another student showed Professor Archer and Tammy in an embrace in front of the Christmas tree at Rockefeller Center. Upon further interviews, Professor Archer admitted he knew Tammy before she was a student in his class, but nothing untoward happened."

"Why would they be hugging if nothing is going on?" Chris, another student, asks.

"The university ran a deeper background check on Professor Archer, which was allowable per his employment contract, and they found out Tammy was actually his stepsister. Professor Archer claimed that was why they were hugging, because they were family."

"But that makes no sense..." A few other students chime in, but I barely pay them any attention as my gaze pulls backs to Ryland, who is studying me again.

I think back to what Belle told me—drive him crazy using his other brain...get him out of that beautiful, complicated mind of his.

Holding his gaze, my tongue darts out and makes a leisurely swipe over my lips before dipping under my teeth in a seductive lick. I arch my brow again, my head cocking to the side. *Press the remote, Ryland.*

His nostrils flare, a muscle twitching in his cheek, and I see his hand sliding under the desk toward his pocket, and I hold my breath.

A few seconds later, a vibrating sensation appears between my legs, the sound quiet and unnoticeable amidst the conversation in the room. A sharp pleasure shoots from my core straight to my nipples and other erogenous regions, and a sharp exhale escapes from my lips as my breathing quickens. My thighs clench together involuntarily as the rolling sensations tease my swelling clit, the mini dildo moving in a small rotating motion.

Heat quickly gathers below as the pleasure rises like a tidal wave. I grip the edge of my desk, my knuckles stark white and my eyes flutter shut from the onslaught of sensation.

I'm not sure if Operation Vixen is getting him out of his mind, but it's definitely driving me crazy.

Snapping my eyes open, my mouth parted, my gaze finds his again and what I see on his face sends a renewed flush throughout my body.

His eyes are stark. Fevered. So dark I can't see the grays from where I sit anymore. His undivided attention feels like a caress as he takes in my struggle to contain my shudders, his eyes darting from my face to my tits, to under my desk, where my legs are twitching and I squirm in my seat.

A second later the vibration grows stronger and I pitch forward on my desk, my shaking hands feeling my fevered skin.

Sweat beads on my upper lips and I hear Chloe murmuring, "You okay, Millie? You don't look so good."

I shake my head. "I think the milk was bad in my hot chocolate this morning. It'll p-pass," I rasp.

My eyes snake toward Ryland again, and he looks like the hunter I saw at Noire that night, the muscles tight on his shoulders, rippling in his corded throat, the throbbing vein on his temple looking like it'll burst at any moment. His eyes flash with voraciousness. He looks murderous.

A few seconds later, the sensations quiet again and I breathe a sigh of relief, my wetness already drenching the panties. I know he'll stop before it gets out of hand. And I know he's turned on. I thank Belle's wisdom for making me wear a dark-colored dress in case any mishap happens today.

If I even survive today.

"So Professor Archer and Tammy are step-siblings? Why did they hide this from everyone?"

The discussion in the classroom draws my attention away from Ryland.

"Apparently, there were circumstances leading to an estrangement, and they didn't realize each other was at NYUC until the quarter began and they found themselves in a professor and student capacity," someone answers.

"But shouldn't they have disclosed their relationship the moment they found out?" Fred asks.

I take a calming breath and raise my hand, watching the students turn their heads toward me.

"P-Perhaps they didn't want there to be any prejudice against them—his reputation or hers. Nor do they want their private matters opened for public discussion among the university staff," I answer. "Just because they have a relationship doesn't mean there'll be favoritism. Life isn't black and white. Plus, Tammy's class is a prerequisite to graduation. If she drops out, she'll need to stay behind longer to graduate. That hardly seems fair to her."

My classmates mull over this response, and the next thirty minutes pass by in a blur, the JEAP committee clearly invested in the case.

Soon, the end of the class is upon us, and Ryland instructs, "Good discussion today, class. Remember your required reading for the next class and also bring your interview notes."

The students filter out of the room and I slowly pack my things into my leather tote, my pussy still slick and tender with a relentless, unsatisfied ache.

"If I didn't need to run to a group project meeting right now, I'd wrangle the answer out of you and find out why you're dressed up like you're out to bamboozle the hearts of anyone with an XY chromosome," Chloe says, smirking at me, "But I like the look on you."

She leans in. "If this is for a certain broody professor who looks like he's seconds away from a having a heart attack, then I think you were very successful."

My face heats and she laughs before giving me a friendly shove and darting out the door.

After the last of the students walk out of the room, I hear the quiet click of the door shutting behind them, and suddenly, the vibrations flare back to life, more intense than before.

"Ryland," I moan, clutching the hem of my dress, the throbbing between my thighs strong in rolling waves, the vibrator hitting my clit at precisely the right way and the dildo pulsing in my pussy in steady bursts. Wetness seeps through my panties and my breasts swell as I look up, the sounds of my heavy breathing filling the air.

"Come here, my dirty girl."

Ryland's voice is a low growl and I rise to my feet, my legs trembling, barely keeping me upright as the sensations grow into an inferno between my legs.

"Fuck," I whimper.

I stop after a few steps, a fresh wave of pleasure freezing me to the spot. I grip my tender breasts and bowl over. The sparks coalesce into a sharp pressure and the walls of my pussy start to flutter.

God, I'm so close.

"Oh my God," I moan, my thighs clenching, my hands involuntarily kneading my puckered nipples, and I try to ride out the sensations.

The vibrations lessen and I heave out a ragged exhale, my mind turning into mush, my vision blurring at the edges.

These panties will get a five-star rating from me.

A second later, a strong pillar of heat hoists me up and carries me across the room before slamming my back against the closed classroom door.

"How dare you jeopardize your future with a stunt like that?" His eyes flash with lust and anger.

"I-I knew you wouldn't take it too far because you'd protect me."

His nostrils flare and I repeat, "You'll protect me. I'm safe around you."

Ryland delivers a toe-curling lick from my chest up my neck to my ears as his hands wrap my legs around his butt. He tugs open my wrap dress, baring my tits.

"I should be angry, but fuck, I can't bring myself to be mad at you," he growls, his breath fanning over my breasts.

"Fuck me. No bra today." He palms my tits before sucking a beaded nipple into his mouth, his tongue flicking over the hardened tip and I slam my head back against the cool door, his suctions sending pulses of sensations to my clit.

His other hand snakes up my thigh and cups my wet pussy. "You naughty, dirty girl. Looking so fuckable in that dress. Your nipples beckoning me to suck them in front of everyone. Giving me a vibrator remote, you vixen. Making your professor so hard for you in class, he couldn't even stand up from his desk because everyone would see the steel rod in front of his pants leaking pre-cum for you."

He thrusts his erection in between my thighs and saws his pant-covered dick up and down my wet pussy.

Shards of heat build between my legs at a rapid speed—the moments before a volcano eruption. This is what I've been missing these last few weeks. Him letting go. Him embracing me. Us coming together.

The doorknob rattles and we freeze.

Knock. Knock.

"Professor Anderson, you in there?" an older masculine voice asks.

Our breathing is loud against our ears, my heart threatening to give out behind my rib cage as my gaze flies to him.

Ryland's eyes are grim as he slowly grinds his erection on me, fanning the flames of my lust while panic tries to interrupt the party.

Digging my nails into his back, I whisper urgently, "Let me down, Ryland. Someone is looking for you. We can't get caught."

Shit. I shouldn't have tempted him publicly. What if he loses everything because of me?

I claw at his arms, my eyes widening, pleading with him to let me down. He can't get in trouble because of me.

Instead of answering, he dips his sweat-covered forehead toward me, his voice deep and raspy in my ear as he says, "Perhaps they should catch me. Punish me for being a bad professor. For violating every ethical line there is. For trying to capture the beautiful lark in the skies."

Knock. Knock. Knock.

"Anderson, you there?"

My legs flail against his body, my body still hovering above the ground. "Ryland, please. Don't do this to yourself. If anything, this is my fault. I tempted you."

The doorknob rattles next to me as cold panic sweeps through my body like an avalanche, dulling the embers of lust coursing inside me moments ago.

He renews his gyrations, his cock hitting harder against my clit, and I can feel the flames burgeoning once more as he grunts in my ear.

The sparks intensify and I bite my tongue to leash down the whimpers threatening to tear out of my throat.

"Let go, Ryland. P-Please," I sob, my arms still clutching him as my legs try to touch the floor. It's as if my body can't decide if I want us to burn together or to save him from immolating himself. "You'll protect me, right? You always do."

He swallows, steps back, and lifts his head. His breathing is labored, and an aching anguish is reflected in his soulful eyes. With trembling fingers, he wipes my face, and I belatedly notice a panicked tear has slipped out onto my cheek.

"Always," he rasps.

Ryland nudges me to the corner of the room and straightens up before adjusting himself. His pants are dark colored, masking the wet spot that's no doubt there. He rakes in a deep breath and runs his long fingers through his hair before smoothing on his cold, apathetic expression again. He opens the door and steps outside.

"Sorry, I was on a call. The door was a bit stuck. I need to call maintenance to fix it."

"No problem, I want to get your thoughts on this research I'm doing..."

Their voices soften as I hear their footsteps treading away from the classroom.

I sag against the door, my dress sticking to my sweaty body, my skin still feeling feverish and sensitive, and wholly unsatisfied. My heart twists as I remember the forlorn expression on his beautiful face moments ago, when he was prepared to give everything up, to get the punishment he thought he deserved, stopping only when I reminded him I may get into trouble.

Oh, Ryland.

Five minutes later, my phone buzzes.

Ryland

Eight o'clock tonight at Noire. Same outfit.

CHAPTER 40

IT'S A STORM TONIGHT inside Noire.

That alone should've warned me of his mood.

High winds whip against the towering trees, rain falling in sheets from what must be sprinklers on the ceiling, plastering my wet dress to my body. An occasional squawk of a bird echoes in the space, followed by a screech of some other nocturnal animal. The skies are pitch black, with only a sliver of the moon in sight, the faint light blurred by the pelting rain.

A burst of lightning flashes across the sky, followed by a blast of thunder and I flinch as my boots trample on the sodden puddles in the ground a few feet away from the abandoned building.

Closing my eyes, I inhale the scent of wet earth and saltiness in the air.

The mercurial moods of the great nature. Much like the man who has stolen my heart.

This reminds me of the day we met, when I stared at his lonely silhouette, his face tipped toward the stormy skies, letting the rain wash over him, his lips curving in a bittersweet smile. I remember my heart seizing, a visceral pain stabbing me in the chest at the haunted loneliness in his imposing frame, the way every atom in my body clamored toward him, wanting to chase away the darkness in his soul, to see him smile, unburdened and untethered.

Unbothered by the wetness cloaking my skin, soaking my clothes, I step inside the abandoned building, which is only a shell of cement walls and steel frames. I know he'll eventually find me, then I'll—

A hand clamps over my mouth as a muscular arm ensnares my waist, lifting me high in the air.

My biological response automatically kicks in and I dig my nails into the hand over my mouth, my teeth biting at the fingers I can reach, my elbows shoving backward, landing on the hard slabs of his muscles.

I hear a faint *oomph* from under his breath and my nostrils fill with the familiar scent of woody citrus.

"Stop fighting, my little lark." A deep rasp followed by another grunt when I elbow him once more.

A sharp pinch slices through me when his teeth clamp over the sensitive whorl of my ear.

"Give up," he mutters.

He unleashes another bite. "Give *up.*" *On me.*

The words are unsaid but hang between us, morbid like the blade of the guillotine moments before it's used.

But my body doesn't want to stop. I want to show him I can overpower him and absorb every tendril of his darkness. I want him to know I'm a fighter and I can destroy his mental enemies for him. And so, I buck against him, my elbow connecting with his abs again, this time harder, stronger, and he winces. His arm loosens around my waist and his hand dislodges from over my mouth.

Spinning around, I face him, noting his shocked eyes, his mouth parted in an anguished groan, and I shove him with all my strength, backing him toward the wall.

"Never!" I scream as I push him again. "I'm a fighter, Ryland Anderson, and you can't beat me."

I give him another hard shove and he lands against the cement wall beside the door. His chest moves up and down rapidly as he stares at me advancing toward him. His eyes turn into molten iron, scorching and flaring.

"I'll never give up on you, on us."

With that, I hurl myself on top of him, his hands automatically catching my hips, and I slam my lips on his.

She bites me, my ferocious little lark, her fingers clawing the back of my neck, and I let out a hiss of pleasurable pain as she soothes her bite marks with soft suctions.

Every nerve in my body wakes up as I become a slave to sensations. Feeling the storm raging around us and having the woman of my dreams fighting for me have effectively murdered the remnants of my common sense.

The monster inside me awakens, the bottomless dark hole threatening to swallow her whole, and a low growl rips from my lips.

I can't think. I can't speak. I can only feel the basest impulses driving my every movement. The need to conquer. The need to dominate. The need to decimate.

My teeth collide with hers in a war of dominance and her fight feeds my bloodlust in a way I've never experienced before. The chains binding me to reality snap and clatter to the ground.

I spin her around, pinning her against the wall as my tongue dives into her mouth, sweeping through her intoxicating sweet taste, my brand of addiction, a unique high tailored for me.

Millie scratches my back in her hasty attempt to take off my dress shirt. She lets out a moan as my teeth rake over the sensitive spot where her ear meets her neck and with a roar, I yank my shirt off my body, sending a few buttons pinging off the cold floors.

The storm rages on, befitting the turmoil overtaking me. The gentleman inside me dissipates into smoke and the caveman hiding within steps to the front and center.

With a guttural growl, I set her on the ground and render her immobile against the wall with my body weight. One rough yank later, her wrap dress pools at her feet. She stares at me, her tits glistening with rainwater, heaving like the water nymph who changed my life two years ago. My jaw clenches as my eyes devour her seductive figure, the creamy skin, her soft belly, curvy hips, and that scrap of black lace hiding the tightest little pussy I've ever felt.

I take off my jeans and underwear and stand before her, suspended in this strange alternate universe where she and I, two fighters with scars over our souls, stare each other down. A violent burst of lightning streaks across the skies, flooding the space with a flash of white light, and the crackle of thunder following echoes within the walls.

Her eyes are glazed, the alluring blues in her irises nowhere to be seen. Our chests heave in unison and a sharp energy sizzles up my spine, jolting the clamoring heart behind my rib cage, spreading to my entire body.

Another flash of lightning blinds the room, and she hurls herself at me as we come together.

Man and woman. Fighter against fighter. A huntress and her prey.

We're a mess of scratches and kisses, tangled limbs and gyrating torsos, our bodies like flint stones sparking with every graze and every scratch.

I swallow her cries with my lips, my mouth parched and needing her sweetness to quench my never ending thirst, my hands clamping and kneading the round swells of her ass, my fingers skimming over the delicate strings of her panties until my fingers reach the forbidden hole in the back.

"Fuck. You've been walking around campus practically naked under your dress."

My hand comes down hard and slaps one cheek, and she whimpers before gyrating her hips over my cock, which is so hard it's practically plastered against my abs.

"That's for tempting me, Millie. For driving me insane, so I forget who I am and what I stand for."

Slap.

"That's for making me break my rules. For making me want to be selfish."

Slap. Slap. Slap.

My hands rub the globes of her ass after each strike. She moans against my mouth, and I feel her juices dripping on my cock.

"Safe word, Millie. Stop this." *Please, stop me.*

My fingers move to the front and slide under the delicate lace. "Dildo in your underwear, you naughty girl."

I dislodge the toy and plunge two fingers inside her soaked channel, and she lets out a loud mewl, her lusty sounds echoing in the room.

"I'll never say the safe word because I feel the safest when I'm with you, Ryland," she whispers, her eyes heavy-lidded, her lips swollen, her voice drunk with pleasure.

"Fuck." I saw my fingers in and out of her pussy, curling it at an angle so it hits her g-spot with every pass. She cries out my name, her pussy getting impossibly wetter.

"My dirty student. A good girl on the outside, but a whore on the inside. Just for me. God, you're so fucking tight. You need more, don't you, baby?"

"Yes," she moans. "More, Ryland, more. I want *everything*."

My mind is hazy with pleasure, not able to form any more words and with a hoarse grunt, I tug her underwear to the side and slam myself into her tight cunt, groaning as her pussy takes every inch of my throbbing cock.

"Yes!" she screams, bucking against me, and my vision turns red.

I bite her neck as she claws my shoulder blades, my hips hammering against her, my balls smacking her ass.

The wet sounds of our skin slapping against skin accompany the rumbling of the thunder, and we're overtaken by the tempest in our souls. The hurricane. The tornado. A tsunami obliterating the last defenses of my heart.

My balls grow taut, the pleasure climbing into unbearable euphoria. My eyes only see her, my Millie who is strong enough to take the challenges the world gives her, my ears only hear her sweet voice, capturing every moan and cry into memory, my lips only taste her sweetness, the honeyed chocolate drug I'll never get enough of, and my skin only registering her warmth, her vitality.

The walls of her pussy tremble and throb. "You're strangling my cock, little lark. Your greedy pussy wants every drop of cum from me." I pant, my dick thickening and lengthening unbearably so, and sweat drips down my forehead. "Come for me. Be a good girl."

Millie arches her back, her eyes rolling back as her muscles lock before trembling.

Her lips part and she lets out a harsh cry as her pussy clenches my cock in the tightest vise and wetness sluices out of her. "Ryland!"

Black dots cloud my vision, the pleasure sharpening until I reach the point of no return, and with a few more punishing thrusts, I clamp my teeth on her shoulder and white-hot heat shoots up from my balls to my shaft. I follow her into bliss, my cock throbbing, and I unload spurts of cum inside her.

My monster roars inside me, satiated for the first time in his life, and I tighten my arms around her, our hearts racing next to each other, the thudding adding to nature's symphony.

I cover my lips with hers, needing the connection. A burst of heady warmth floods my chest, and it's then I know.

It's too late.

My heart has escaped my rib cage without me noticing. It has been living outside of me all along, nestled against hers.

Every beat. Every thump. Every flutter.

Only for her.

CHAPTER 41

Millie

Dear Ryland,

The last few days have been some of the happiest days of my life. I know our circumstances haven't changed. You still have your responsibilities to your family and we are still forbidden in the eyes of the public. But I feel you softening with every warm gaze you give me in class, the trail of your fingers over mine as I hand my work to you. The way you kiss me and hold me in your arms like I'm your peace.

I know you'll have moments of uncertainty and I'm prepared for it. After all, it's hard to overcome years of upbringing, tricking you into thinking a certain way.

But life is not limiting and has many avenues and possibilities.

Someday, I'll convince you we have all the tomorrows in the world, and the skies will not fall because we are together.

You're not my prison. You're my heaven.

Love, Millie

PRESSING THE HEAT PAD above my lower abdomen, I wince and fail to keep a neutral face during my video chat with Belle and Taylor.

"Dude, you look kinda green, Millie," Taylor unhelpfully supplies as she takes a sip of…is that carrot juice? My stomach turns at the revolting sight.

Grace slides her arm around my shoulders and answers for me, "It's that time of the month for Millie, poor thing, and she ran out of painkillers. I've sent Steven for some of those extra strength ones. He'll be back soon."

"Do you want anything to eat? Hot tea or your favorite gummy bears?" Taylor frowns.

I shake my head. I've lost my appetite completely.

"Are you sure you're still up for The Ball, Millie? You don't have to go." Belle brushes her hair to one side as she takes a sip from a ceramic cup.

The glittering lights of the Eiffel Tower are in full view outside the window of her hotel room. Her family has opted to go to Paris for the holidays, to celebrate her grandmother's eightieth birthday instead of attending the infamous Christmas Ball at The Orchid.

I nod as another flash of pain carves through me, and I take in deep breaths. My periods have been horrific since my early teens, and there were days when I used to be so sick I could barely get out of bed because I'd be too nauseated and dizzy, the throbbing in my abdomen too unbearable. Those were horrific days. Later, after a checkup with my gynecologist, I learned I had dysmenorrhea, the medical term for painful periods.

In the recent year or two, after I got on birth control, the pain has lessened to a point I can resume normal activities provided I take extra strength ibuprofen and don't over-exert myself, but I didn't realize I ran out when the pain hit this morning, and I'm once again reminded how awful it is to be a woman.

"I'll be fine, girls. I promised Adrian I would show up and mingle with a few folks for him now that my relationship with him is out in the open. He's taking Emily to the Maldives. He never takes any time off and so this vacation means a lot to him. I just need to show up for a few hours, put on a smile, and chitchat. I'll be fine once Steven comes back with the meds."

Plus, *he'll* be there.

Ryland mentioned a few days ago, after he doled out another intense orgasm in the back of his town car when we headed back to his apartment after class, he'd be at The Ball with his family, as usual, for Christmas.

He held my eyes, his gaze softened after the throes of sex, and whispered, "I'm sorry I can't spend Christmas with you."

He didn't need to say anything more. I understood. After all, he couldn't really invite me to The Ball with him or introduce me as his woman to his family.

We belong in the shadows. An illicit secret. The brightest flame shining in the darkest hours of the night, always threatened by the brightness of the encroaching dawn.

My heart clenches at the thought. *I want more. So much more.*

But if I'm going on behalf of my brother, that's a different story, right?

"You need to tell me how The Ball is," Belle says, drawing my attention back to her.

"Why have you never been before? For me, I was trying to keep my relationship with Adrian under wraps, but your family is in high society."

Belle rubs a delicate hand over her elfin face and shrugs. "I'm never one for all those fancy shindigs, fake smiling, and brownnosing. That's what The Orchid is to me, anyway, before you girls—a lot of rich people trying to outshine each other, gossiping, and everything. The amenities I'm sure are nice, but I don't really need them. I prefer to spend time doing things I truly enjoy."

She leans in and looks around furtively before whispering, "I guess you can say it's my tiny act of rebellion. It drives my parents crazy how I don't fall in line like most of the socialites in our circles."

"Hell yeah, I dig the rebellion," Tay comments.

Belle grins, a spark shining in her warm eyes. "But now that Grace is with Steven, and you're stepping into society...maybe I'll tag along next time, and we can have a girls' night at that Japanese medspa I've heard much about."

A noise travels from her laptop. She suddenly looks to her side and swivels her head back at us. "Sorry, girls. Have to run. We have tickets to the Moulin Rouge."

Grace sighs. "I'm so jealous of you, Belle. I love Paris." Her violet eyes take on a wistful gleam.

Taylor snorts. "Of course you do. Steven proposed to you there and gave you the trip of a lifetime. Look at that ice skating rink on your finger." She smirks at the love-drunk expression on Grace's face.

Steven proposed to Grace this past Thanksgiving in one of those straight-out-of-fairytale's plot lines by whisking her off to the city of love, the one place she wanted to visit for the longest time but never had the funds to do so when she and Taylor barely kept afloat growing up.

My heart pinches at the dreamy smile on Grace's face, and an unexpected rush of sadness curls itself around my rib cage. I'm truly happy for my friend, someone with a heart of gold and kindness.

But I can't help but want the same with Ryland. Wishing I could stroll hand in hand with him in public, my head nestled against his strong shoulder, him smiling warmly at me as he wipes off the whipped cream stuck on my upper lip after I drink a big sip of hot chocolate; him bending me backward in front of the Rockefeller Center and giving me a passionate kiss to rival those we see in movies.

The little, everyday vignettes of a life full of love and brightness. That's what I want with him, a desperate tugging, an aching yearning.

I don't need the luxuries of The Orchid or the wealth of being with an Anderson.

I just want him.

The thought adds to the heaviness in my chest as another wave of agony tears through my abdomen. I close my eyes, breathing through the layers of pain threatening to unmoor me.

CHAPTER 42

"SAY HELLO TO YOUR brother for me. It's such a shame he couldn't make it tonight."

I smile at the portly gentleman standing in front of me. "I'll let him know for sure. And he told me to tell you he'll call you after the holidays."

He nods, clearly pleased at the idea of Adrian calling him later, before striding away toward the sea of blue and white, no doubt to say hello to other important people.

I let out a soft sigh as I admire the beautiful scenery before me.

The theme this year is Crystal and Frost Soirée. I've heard from Grace that every year, there's usually a unique theme and the decor will be impressive in a way a multi six-figure decoration budget can produce.

I must admit, I was taken aback when I stepped through the double doors of the ballroom tonight and was immediately transported into an otherworldly atmosphere of glittering winter decor, where I could be dancing alongside the Sugar Plum Fairy in *The Nutcracker*.

The large space is a vision of white, with gauzy silk draping over the walls, backlit by pale blue lights. The floor is covered in artificial snow, and not the kind that melts, and with every movement of passersby, small flutters will kick up at their feet.

Thousands of crystals in the shape of icicles hang from the towering ceilings. I raise my hands to the air to reach toward the fake snow drifting down from vents up high, giving the illusion we're amid a beautiful snowfall, but the white flakes disappear before they reach my hands, never falling too far as to ruin the thousand-dollar gowns and tuxes of the patrons.

Elegant Christmas trees, tipped in white and adorned with elegant gold and silver ornaments, decorate the corners of the room, complete with large, wrapped presents carefully arranged over gold-spun tree skirts.

Attendees were asked to dress in black, blues, or whites to match the theme. I walk toward the refreshments area and admire the breathtaking centerpieces of hydrangeas and peonies. Everything is so beautiful and perfectly done.

People mingle and laugh, dressed to the nines, with efficient waiters and waitresses circling the room, carrying trays of hors d'oeuvres and refreshments. A full orchestra sits to the side, strumming elegant melodies. I take a small glass of water from a waiter passing by and listen to the musicians' performance.

The Christmas Ball at The Orchid is the most sought-after social event of the year for the upper crust of society. Invitations are secretly extended and can't be purchased.

It's *the place* to show you've made it in society. All the headlines of newspapers and gossip rags tomorrow will feature recaps of this infamous event, with the media coverage overtaking The Met Gala or any of the Hollywood awards ceremonies.

It's also the only time the press is allowed through its hallowed doors. All the usual antics of the paparazzi are forbidden here. They can take photos but can't ask questions or disturb the guests. Any funny business and they'll be dragged out of the building and blacklisted at all high society events across the country in the future. This usually means a career death sentence for the paparazzo in question.

No one escapes the wrath of the mighty Anderson family.

"Almost done with the obligatory schmoozing?" A deep voice says from behind me before I feel a hand gently brushing against my back.

"Yes, thank God. I said hello to the folks Adrian wanted me to touch base with, Steven."

I turn to my friend and bonus brother, who looks dapper in his black suit molded over his tall figure.

"I don't think I'm cut out for the business world. I don't know how you do this all the time. My cheeks are about to fall off from all the fake smiling."

He laughs, his hazel eyes twinkling as he surveys the winter wonderland before us, his gaze no doubt sweeping for the love of his life.

"You get used to it. Plus, once you're powerful enough, you don't need to go to them. They come to you."

"It's still exhausting. I'm ready to call it a night and the dancing hasn't even started yet."

Steven furrows his brows. "You feeling better, Millie? Are the meds helping?"

I flash him a tentative smile. The pain in my belly has lessened after taking two extra strength ibuprofen, but the occasional lash of pain, which breaks through all medication, still threatens to rob me of my breath.

"I-I'm fine. Thanks. I'll probably stay for another hour and head out."

"Don't over-exert yourself. Adrian won't want that for you."

I nod. "I won't. Don't worry."

Plus, I haven't seen *him* yet.

And I can't leave without seeing him, my dark prince reigning over his realm.

"I see Grace over there. I'm going to whisk her away for the first dance," Steven says softly and my heart warms at the happiness shining on his face.

He was a workaholic in the past, the cold King of Wall Street, as the press nicknamed him, like he was walking around with a half-functioning heart. But ever since he's been with my friend, he has come alive, like he finally knows his purpose in life.

"You look lovely tonight, Millie...and Merry Christmas." Steven gives my arm another squeeze as the orchestra strikes up a light melody.

I murmur my thanks, but his attentions have already turned toward Grace, who's clad in a curve-hugging black silk dress with delicate spaghetti straps, her eyes dancing with so much love inside them as she smiles at her fiancé.

A twisting sensation hits my chest as I watch the king whisking off his queen to the throng of dancers twirling on the dance floor. The faux snow spins in the air around them as they join the fray. Grace throws her head back in laughter at something Steven says while he looks at her with utter adoration in his eyes.

To be dancing with the person you love in public, the wistful thought slips into my mind.

My hands smooth over my baby blue tulle gown, which is a gorgeous confection of the McKenzie brand with its wide, off the shoulder neckline adorned with crystals, the bodice cinched at the waist, and a long, flowy skirt with a thigh high split. The sleeves are sheer and delicate, adding an element of whimsical to the ensemble.

Grace helped me with my hair today, expertly curling the thick strands before pinning a simple crystal hairpin resembling a feather on one side of my head. My makeup is a simple sweeping eyeliner and ruby red lips.

I feel like a princess today...a woman who should be standing by *his* side, the magnificent prince the public loves.

Just then, a sudden hush descends over the room, and everyone glances toward the double doors, with me following suit.

My lungs seize when I see the unmistakable silhouette of Ryland striding into the ballroom with his siblings behind him. They are a striking group—all elegant lines and sharp features—each one of them can grace the covers of fashion magazines.

His deep navy tux with black lapels clings to his muscular frame, his dark hair artfully swept back, his slate-gray eyes glittering with confidence and power, and his lips are tilted up in a small smile, like he knows a secret we aren't privy to.

The face of the Andersons. The Prince of the USA.

And I'm nothing but his dirty little secret.

Ryland strides inside, nodding to a few folks he clearly recognizes, passing by several ladies who look like they're about to swoon. He stops along the way and shakes their hands, murmuring a few words before moving on, addressing his subjects who are clearly paying tribute to him.

I stay frozen in place, the ache in my abdomen simmering in the background and my fingers twist in front of my dress.

Should I greet him? Say hello? Or pretend I don't know him? What is the protocol of addressing the much-older professor you're carrying on an affair with?

Just as I'm mulling over my options, Ryland's eyes sweep over the room, past where I'm standing by the refreshments table before his gaze springs back and locks onto me.

His confident strides falter and he stops mid-step. His gray eyes darken impossibly so, and his nostrils flare. I can see his corded throat rippling as he swallows, and his hands slowly fist at his sides.

A quiet murmur breaks through the crowd at his sudden inaction and a beautiful, aching melody sweeps through the room as the orchestra begins a waltz.

Ryland's intense gaze is searing, warming up my skin, the heat and awareness sizzling from the base of my spine, radiating to my hands and feet. I feel a blush blooming on my face as my heart tries to escape from my rib cage and hurl itself toward him. My breathing quickens, and I wet my parched lips with my tongue.

His eyes smolder at the motion, and just as abruptly as his stopping in the middle of the room, he starts walking once more.

He's coming to me.

This time, the leisurely stroll in his gait disappears, replaced with urgency in his long strides. He reaches me in a matter of seconds, ignoring the passersby calling out to him, clamoring for his attention.

My breath freezes, my drumming pulse nearly eclipsing the music in my ears, and I stare up at him as he stops a foot away from me.

"Millie," he whispers, his chest heaving like he ran a few miles to stand before me. His voice is filled with awe, warmth, and so much penetrating intensity it threatens to melt me on the spot.

"Ry—Mr. Anderson," I reply, my eyes darting to the sides, keenly aware of the interest from the large crowd around us.

Ryland doesn't seem to notice, his undivided attention intoxicating, it feels like a spotlight shining on top of me in a dark room. I can't see anyone else as they fade into the shadows. In this moment, I don't feel like his illicit secret, and my heart flutters with elation.

Slowly, he dips into a bow and I can't help but curtsy, the action involuntary, and he unleashes a glorious, lethal smile.

"May I have this dance, Ms. Callahan?" He extends his hand.

Swallowing, I nod wordlessly, my hand reaching into his. A sharp current sizzles through me when his hand touches mine. His eyes snap up to my face, a fire burning brightly in them, and I know I'm not alone in this swirling inferno we find ourselves mired in.

Ryland leads me to the dance floor, places my hands in the proper positions, and sweeps me into the swells of the music.

My heart swoops and falls with his practiced movements, my body yielding to his dominance, the surety of his hand pressing on my lower back, the confidence in his footwork on the dance floor. I've only waltzed a few times before, the last time at my brother's wedding. My movements felt stilted then, my hands and feet not quite coordinated.

But here with him, I'm gliding. Flying. Whirling. I feel as graceful as a swan.

Our bodies move as one as he twirls and dips me into expert moves to the romantic strains of the music, the velvet strings serenading the room in a poignant, heartrending melody.

My eyes never fall away from his, and he seems equally entranced with me.

The rest of the room simply falls away. Vaporized. Inconsequential.

Maybe this whirlwind can be permanent, and I can be in his arms forever.

His chest heaves, and he swallows, his eyes burning with tethered emotions and unspoken words. He pulls me tighter against him, far closer than the usual respectable distance of a waltz. I find myself not caring, the heaviness in my chest finally dissolving in the intimacy of his embrace.

"Millie," he rasps, his lips almost grazing my ear, "You're breathtaking. I...I can't take my eyes off you. You're my beautiful meadowlark, singing your sweet melody for me to hear, gifting me with your presence. *You set me free.*"

My eyes flutter shut and I whisper, "I didn't take you for a poet."

"Only with you, Millie."

A burn gathers behind them while I lean into his embrace. There's heartbreak behind the hoarseness in his voice and the sentiments behind his words. The soulful man still doesn't believe he deserves the happiness he's experiencing right now.

I pull him closer, my touch conveying everything I want to tell him but haven't yet. I feel so treasured. So loved. My soul is entrenched in his tempest, and I never want to leave.

In this moment, the sadness of hiding in the shadows, the frustration of desiring more, all fall to the wayside. When I'm basking in his attentions, a flower angling toward the rays of the sun after a long storm, I feel loved and I realize, much to my dismay, my heart would much rather have these fleeting moments with him than have nothing at all. And what does this say about me?

"I'll only sing for you, Ryland. Only for you," I whisper as he whirls me into another spin before pulling me tightly against him once more. "You may feel you're chaining me down, but it's because of you I feel safe enough to fly. Higher than before."

I pull back and smile at the man I love—my feelings as clear as the sun shining brightly on unblemished skies—moisture coating my eyes because nothing in the world feels righter than this moment, more perfect, than being wrapped up in his arms.

"I don't need saving, Ryland. I've been free all along. Don't you see? I don't want an audience for my song. I just only want to sing for you."

His nostrils flare, a sharp exhale slips from his lips. His fingers dig deeper into my back, but I don't feel the pain. His lips part, his eyes turn into molten obsidian as they lock onto my lips, and he dips his head down.

Kiss me, please. Claim me in front of everyone.

My eyes flutter shut.

Applause rings out in the room as the strains of the music fade into silence and a few flashes erupt around us from the paparazzi.

He pulls back, and the room comes into focus. I'm suddenly aware of the furtive whispers and curious gazes, the very public nature of our almost kiss.

A sharp pain pierces my chest as I'm relegated to the shadows once more.

A denial. A rejection. *Again.*

My heart, which foolishly dared to leap moments ago, sinks back down in my chest. I realize I want him to choose me, to throw caution to the wind. Damn the consequences and the optics.

But I live in the real world and that'll be selfish of me, won't it? It'll be stupid to throw everything I've worked for away for a man.

And don't I deserve more?

My pulse is thready, the pain radiating inside my chest, and I feel breathless as I dip into another curtsy, the answer to his curt bow. He leads me back to the crowds gathered around the dance floor, doling out his usual public smiles to the people seeking his attentions.

Before letting go, he steps close and whispers, "Meet me in The Orangerie in ten minutes."

Stepping back, he flashes me his impersonal smile, but his brooding eyes reveal the storm brewing within, and he strides away.

I press my hand over my fluttering heart, a riot of conflicting emotions flowing inside me as I stare at his retreating figure, a towering beacon in the sea of fancy dresses and pristine suits.

Ten minutes later, I find my way to The Orangerie, which is nestled in a far corner on the same floor as the ballroom. It's one of the many courtyards and gardens hidden in the labyrinth inside The Orchid.

The moonlight shines through the clear glass ceilings, casting shadows on the leaves of the citrus trees, the sweet, honeyed scent of the small white blossoms yielding an intoxicating perfume in the air.

I walk toward the trickling sound reaching my ears, and find an intricately designed copper water fountain, the exterior already oxidized into a pale green patina. Leaning closer, I examine the exquisitely carved flowers and delicate little birds flapping their wings.

Then, the air shifts, and a presence fills the room.

I smile, not turning around.

He's here.

Despite my complicated emotions toward this man, my soul feels settled in his presence.

"I thought you'd enjoy the fountain." His quiet voice sends shivers up my spine as I straighten up and finally turn toward him.

Ryland stands before me, his face half-cast in the shadows from the pale moonlight, his lips tipping up in a small smile.

He looks dashing in his evening attire. A long time ago, I thought he resembled a villain from the romance novels I read, but I'm clearly wrong.

He's a prince in disguise.

My prince. The man I've been waiting for my whole life. If only he feels the same way about me.

He reaches out and cups his large hand around my face. I lean into his caress and let out a satisfied sigh. Perhaps these stolen moments in the shadows are all we have, but I won't trade them for the world. Even if my heart yearns for more.

"I should've known you'd be here tonight, since Adrian couldn't come."

I smile. "I wanted to see you at Christmas. I hope that's okay." My fingers trail up his silk lapels, enjoying the way his muscles bunch and ripple under my touch.

His hand captures mine and he pulls me closer to him, pressing my body tightly against his chest. I look up and the overwhelming love shining from his eyes steals my breath.

"I'm so happy you're here. I've been missing you the entire day," he whispers before pressing a soft kiss on my lips.

"When I saw you in there, I wanted to haul you out of the room because you looked so beautiful. I didn't want any other men looking at you." He swipes his tongue over my bottom lip before sucking on it, sending sparks to my belly.

He rasps, "If this makes me a terrible professor, so be it."

I grin and lightly bite on his bottom lip, enjoying the sharp hiss of lust slipping from his mouth. He palms the curves of my backside, tugging me flush against him so I feel his hard erection digging into my stomach.

"You're a wonderful professor." I grind myself on him and he groans as I move up and down the outline of his cock. The pulsing between my thighs intensifies, nearly distracting me from my period pains. "So much...hands on instruction."

"You dirty little minx." His panting breaths are hard against my ear. "If I didn't need to be at my own event, I'd set you down on the fountain ledge, flip up your dress, and fuck the impertinence out of you."

Biting back a grin, I step back, knowing he can't stay here for too long before his absence is noticed. I wink. "Merry Christmas, Ryland. I hope the magic of the season brings happiness to your heart."

His eyes darken to inky pools of tar, a muscle pulsing in his jaw. His lips part and tremble, one hand reaching into his pant pocket, retrieving something he has tightly curled inside his palm.

"*You* bring happiness to my heart," he whispers.

Ryland takes a step back, a flush creeping up his neck as his lips curve into a shaky smile. He blows out a rough exhale before unclasping his fist.

A silver chain dangles from his fingers. A delicate silver key, encrusted with tiny, sparkling diamonds.

Half of his mother's pendant.

My mouth parts in a gasp, my eyes darting up to his face.

With unsteady hands, he unclasps the fastening and reaches around me before gently securing the necklace around my neck. He heaves out another breath as his fingers trail over the chain to the delicate key nestled over the cleavage of my dress.

"I knew it'd look beautiful on you. Like it was supposed to be around your neck all along," he murmurs, his voice hoarse, his attention focused on the key.

My heart spins in a dizzy rhythm, my lungs ceasing to work.

"Thank you for allowing it to have an owner, Millie." Slowly, he drags his gaze up to mine and the passionate ardor in those bottomless pools robs me of all words. "Merry Christmas, my little lark."

My eyes brim with tears and with a choked sob, I pull his head toward mine and seal my lips with his. Maybe I won't get his public kiss today, but I have his heart in my hands.

And that has to be okay...for now. It has to be.

My fingers grip his thick hair, my kiss ardent, desperate, my entire being needing to taste him more than I need oxygen in my lungs. He groans as he tightens his clasp around my waist, his tongue invading my mouth, swirling, savoring, ravishing me.

The kiss is intoxicating, an emotionally drunken affair of rioting storms and tethered thoughts and my heart feels full even as uneasiness threads inside me, so insidious, I almost don't notice it.

Desperately, I cling to him, meeting him kiss after kiss, suction after suction, the maddening bursts of pleasure sparking over my body, tuning every cell inside me to the vibration that is him.

He loves me.

He doesn't need to tell me the words. I can feel it in the pressure of his kisses, the weight of the pendant around my neck.

That has to be enough. The refrain echoes in my mind, stemming the blood loss from my heart and yet, not enough to seal the wound.

Our kiss turns heated, his mouth trailing down the sensitive column of my neck as I lean back and let out a moan.

"I'm tired of fighting, Millie." He rakes his teeth over the pulse point near my collarbone.

"Nothing has ever felt so right. I need you more than I need sustenance, more than I need to feel the harsh elements of Mother Nature on my skin." His hand caresses the sensitive swell of my breast and kneads it as I let out a keening cry.

I feel the same way, Ryland. Please, take the leap with me.

Someone clears his throat loudly in the distance and we quickly spring apart, my breathing coming out in harsh exhales.

"Sorry to interrupt, but we need to make a speech."

Maxwell stands at the entrance, his quiet, brooding presence reminding me of his brother, yet different all the same. He has a colder, more unemotional edge, a refined elegance about him, but his dark eyes are penetrating all the same as they sweep over us.

A soft smile appears on his lips as he strides over. He's leaner and taller than his brother, equally handsome in a different way.

He extends his hand, his charcoal eyes sharpening when they land on the pendant on my chest. "I'm Maxwell. And you are..."

My eyes dart to Ryland's, finding him clenching his jaw, a myriad of emotions appearing on his face with each tic of muscle, each throb of the vein on his forehead. He gives me a subtle, almost imperceptible nod.

I turn back to Maxwell and reply, "I'm Millie Callahan, Adrian Scott's sister."

I don't want to say I'm Ryland's student, so I settle for the identity most people recognize.

Maxwell's eyes widen a fraction as he shakes my hand and glances at my necklace once more.

"A pleasure, Ms. Callahan. Thank you for taking care of my brother."

His words are laden with meaning as the brothers share a look, communicating messages bystanders can't possibly understand, and Ryland's lips tilt up in a soft smile.

Maxwell grins, the smile transforming his face into something much more approachable, and he slaps a hand on his brother's shoulder before stepping away.

"I'll give you two a few minutes." He nods at me and walks out of the garden.

I wince as a sudden flash of pain unmoors me and a whimper escapes from my lips. *Time for another round of meds.* My hand curls over my belly as the roiling stabbing steals my breath. Sweat forms at the back of my neck and I close my eyes.

"Millie?" Ryland leans down, clasping my face in his hands, his voice urgent. "Are you okay?"

"I..I'm f-fine." I curl into myself as another wave punctuates the calm.

"No, you aren't. Do I need to call the doctor?" His arms move to my back and effortlessly, he swings me up in his embrace and heads toward the door.

I groan and lean against his chest, listening to the reassuring thumps of his heartbeat, focusing on the lulling sound, trying to time my inhales and exhales to the movements of his chest.

"It's that time of the month and I was probably standing too much earlier tonight. I just need to lie down and take some medicine. I'll be fine."

He hoists me closer to him and presses his lips over my forehead, which is glistening with a thin layer of sweat. "Let me take care of you."

I grab his arm and shake my head. "You have The Ball and the speech."

"Nothing is more important than you."

My heart can't help but skip a beat at his words.

CHAPTER 43

I THOUGHT IT'D BE terrifying, giving her the pendant. *Having my heart live outside of me.* But instead, I feel a strange sense of calm, because now she knows what she means to me. Even if we can't be the end goal, at least I can give her this bit of honesty.

It's the least I can do, and she deserves so much more.

A few people stare at me as I'm sure I stand out like a sore thumb in front of the feminine products aisle, their whispers drawing me out of my thoughts.

I ignore them as I survey the rows of colorful packages in front of me at the pharmacy one block away from The Orchid, a shopping basket in one hand and my cell phone in the other.

My phone pings, a new message from the chat group, "The Orchid Shenanigans," with my siblings and my good friends.

Lana

> You want to get maxi pads of various sizes. If she's in a lot of pain, she's probably in the beginning days of her period. So, you want some overnight ones, some heavy ones and maybe a few regulars. Get the ones with the wings.

A few seconds later, another text follows.

Lana

> Ah shit. Sorry, I meant to privately message you but accidentally replied in the group chat.

Then my phone lights up with a deluge of messages. I called Lana after I carried Millie upstairs to my apartment, changed her out of her gown and into one of my T-shirts, and tucked her into bed with a heating pad I got from Gretchen.

Millie looked so pale, her slight frame shaking with tremors every so often, her body drenched in sweat. Desperation flooded my insides at the misery I saw on her face.

What I would do to take that pain away from her. I'd rather someone slice off my hands than to see her writhing in agony on my bed.

I could've asked Gretchen or the other staff to purchase the supplies for me from the pharmacy, but somehow, that didn't feel right.

I needed to be the one to pick out the items for her, to ensure she has the best of the best. I wanted to be the one to care for her, even though I couldn't love her in the public manner she deserved.

The Ball, the speech, and everything else faded into the background, my priority first and foremost, her.

Then, I arrived at the pharmacy and realized I had no idea what I was doing and had to enlist Lana for advice on what items I should get for Millie.

I roll my eyes as I read the other texts hitting the chat group incessantly.

Rex

Whoa, whoa, whoa. Stop the presses. What on earth is going on? Why is B asking about…pads? Wings? What the fuck is happening?

I smirk. I can see his grimace all the way from over here.

Ethan

Because B is a mature man who is comfortable with his masculinity. Because his woman is obviously suffering from that time of the month. And Ryland, for the record, I knew you had a woman.

Rex

> What makes you the expert, Ethan? And no shit. We all knew he was hiding someone this entire time. It's as obvious as the sky is blue.

I guess I haven't been very good at hiding my feelings. But I'm actually relieved my family and close friends know how I feel about Millie. They won't tell anyone. I trust them with my life.

The texts continue to light up my phone.

Ethan

> I'm a mature man myself, unlike someone.

Lana

> Morons. All of you. Except Ryland. I think it's sweet what he's doing. Even if everyone at The Ball is asking me about his whereabouts now. I'll handle the PR side of things, B. I have your back.

Maxwell

> Don't worry about The Ball. We got you covered. Go take care of Millie.

My breath freezes in my throat as I realize the attention I've drawn to us by dancing with her. Of course, people will notice. I should've known. Fuck. I hope this doesn't cause problems for Millie later.

The three dots appear on the screen, and I see the statuses noting multiple people are typing at the same time. God, I love my siblings and friends, but they are a fucking nosy bunch.

Rex

> Millie Callahan? That's the girl you're dancing with? The one you look like you were seconds away from devouring on the dance floor? You're dating The Shark's sister?!

Seconds pass and another text comes through.

Rex

Paging Grace and Taylor… Where are you at, dear sisters? How come you kept this interesting tidbit from me? I thought I was your favorite brother.

Grace

Because you're the worst gossip in the entire world, Rex. If we told you anything, the world would know about it half a second later.

Taylor

Ryland is restoring my faith in the opposite gender, but then that's offset by you, Rex. So, my opinions of the male species have remained unchanged.

Steven

What about me, Tay? I'm a good soon to be brother-in-law to you.

Taylor

Fine. I'll give you a pass. Thank you for sending over that citrus carrot cake from Estrelle's. They are to die for.

She sends over a photo of herself dressed in some fuzzy pajamas, her mouth stuffed with cake. She said she'd rather die before attending a stuffy ball with the rest of us.

Charles

Get off your high horse, Tay. If I were to judge women by you only, I'd have different opinions as well. And seriously, carrot cake? It's disgusting.

Taylor

> Say that to my face, Charles. I dare you. *Knife emoji*

Charles

> *Audio message of him calling Taylor a brat.*

She and Charles have been at it since they met, and I have no idea how she pissed off my blond, good-natured friend. He's the man everyone likes to hang out with, the guy who constantly bemoans his single status because he actually wants to settle down but hasn't been able to find *the one.*

Lana

> Oh jeez. I should've called Ryland instead, but I didn't want to talk on the phone while I was schmoozing with everyone. Ryland, after you get the pads and the ibuprofen, get some snacks that she'll love. Chocolates, chips, the yummy and not-good-for-you stuff. I always crave them during my time of the month.

Grace

> You're a good man, Ryland. At first, I was worried about you two, but now I'm glad she has you.

For now.

Guilt stabs me in the chest and I put my cell phone back in my pocket as I pick the most expensive pads of the sizes Lana suggested and put them in the basket. I don't know which brands are the best, but going with the priciest can't be wrong.

Deep down, I know Millie and I can't last. Despite her whispering, *"we still have tomorrow,"* in my ears every time we are together, our circumstances haven't changed. We are still forbidden in the court of public opinion, and even if we get past that temporary situation, there's still the family trust, the iron-clad rules that'll force her to give up everything if she were to stay with me.

Even if I want to be selfish, even if I can take the risk of our relationship blowing up in our faces, ruining my family's much lauded, centuries-old reputation, killing our IPO plans, which is going well at the current moment, and saying goodbye to the pipe dream of becoming a tenured professor, there's no way I can take her dreams away from her.

I can hurt myself a thousand times over, but I can never let her give up everything to be with me. And I can't do what Dad did to Grace and Taylor's mom and be with Millie without the promise of marriage in the future.

She deserves that and more from a man.

This is my act of love for her, to set her free to find someone else, someone who can love her unequivocally and give her *everything*.

And so, this time we have together is a beautiful dream I'm giving to myself. One where I know I'll need to wake up from at any moment and face reality. But my selfishness drives me to give myself one more tomorrow, one more moment with her, to delay the inevitable.

Striding over to the snack aisle, I pick out a few bars of Swiss chocolate, some gummy bears from the German brand she loves, a bag of mini marshmallows, and a few bags of potato chips. Then I grab a bottle of ibuprofen and quickly pay for the items before hurrying back to The Orchid where Millie is waiting for me.

Minutes later, I arrive back at my penthouse.

Gretchen greets me as I open the door. "She's resting but not asleep, the poor thing."

"Thank you for looking after her. I'll take it from here."

She dips her head and disappears back into her quarters.

I carry the shopping bag and tread quietly into the master bedroom in case she managed to fall asleep.

The whimpering sounds from the small lump in the middle of my bed are the sharpest blades carving into my heart. I'll fight the world to relieve her of her pain.

"Millie, I'm back."

She shuffles on the bed, sits up, and gives me a wobbly smile. Her face is glistening with sweat as she tries her best to hide her pain.

My brave girl. My fighter.

"You didn't have to," she says as she looks at the bag I set on the bed.

Sitting next to her, I take her clammy hands in mine, my fingers rubbing some heat into her. "Of course I have to. I need to take care of you." *While I still can. While we still have our tomorrows.*

I smile, my fingers tucking a damp lock of hair behind her ear before I press a soft kiss on her forehead.

"I hope I got everything you need."

Carefully, I retrieve the packets of sanitary pads, the snacks, the medicine, and the water. I uncap the water bottle, shake out two tablets of ibuprofen from its container, and hand them to her.

"Take this first. It'll lessen your pain."

She follows my instructions and brushes her hand on my cheek. "This is more than enough. How did you know?"

Heat rises to my face and I mumble, "I asked Lana."

Her lips curve up in a dazzling smile, clearly pleased I consulted my sister on her ailment. She throws herself on me and buries her face in my neck.

"I love you, Ryland."

Millie presses a kiss on my skin. I shudder as a hot ember sparks to life inside my chest at her soft touch and further fanned by her words.

She loves me.

I don't deserve her love. My voice is trapped in my throat, and I clutch her tightly to me, my fingers digging into her slender back. My mouth opens and closes, trying to get the words I feel so strongly out, but I've lost the ability to speak.

"You don't have to say anything, Ryland. I know how you feel," she whispers before pulling back, her hands clutching the key pendant tightly.

As Christmas approached, after every scorching and heartrending kiss between us, after our bodies coming together time and time again, our souls merging into one, I felt an undeniable urge to give her half of Mom's pendant.

Maybe my story doesn't have a happy ending, but selfishly, I want her to carry a piece of me with her always. After all, my heart already resides with hers, where I know she'll take good care of it.

My vision blurs as I curl my hand over hers. Maybe I can't get those three words out, but I want to tell her the truth. I want her to understand why I can't live for myself, why I can't be with her.

Why our tomorrows are limited.

"Millie, my family is under the regulations of a family trust formed long ago." I caress her fingers in mine, relishing the soft skin, the strength laced in the delicate digits.

I tell her about the rules of the trust, which I hinted at that evening in the bath. I tell her how I can never leave Fleur or everyone else in the family will lose their fortune. I tell her how anyone joining the family has to give up his or her dreams and how I can't do this to her. I tell her about the family curse, how the woman the firstborn male of the family loves and marries always dies from a premature death under suspicious accidents.

The words pour out from inside me, the poison so dark, I can't help but feel it's corrupting her just by listening to my thoughts, absorbing my selfishness.

How I want to risk everyone's happiness to live for myself. How I'm resentful of everyone around me, even though the guilt always comes in strong after these thoughts like a tsunami. How I'm a privileged asshole, a hypocrite who preaches ethics but is violating these very moral obligations every single day by thinking about her, by kissing her, by being with her.

Millie's eyes cloud with tears by the time I'm finished, and she quickly blinks them away.

"You're the farthest thing from selfish, Ryland. The fact you've leashed down all your thoughts and desires because of what you think is good for the people you love tells me what a selfless person you are." She reaches out and swipes her thumbs on my cheeks.

I belatedly realize tears have escaped from my eyes.

It feels cathartic, baring my soul to hers, letting her see the darkness inside me.

And she hasn't shied away.

"I did the same thing to Adrian, Dad, and my friends for the longest time. Hiding myself. Pretending to be happy and fine in front of them when I was angry at the world deep inside, when I wanted nothing more than to lash out and tell them I was tired of being their anchor or being positive." She presses a kiss on my lips.

"It turns out my friends didn't abandon me when I cried in front of them and I never needed to pretend all along. I still make the mistake and hide inside my shell sometimes, and I think you're the same. After all, it's been years of training and practice to be the caregiver you are."

Her voice is urgent and ardent, her blue eyes flashing with ferocity. "But you know what? Sometimes we are wrong. Sometimes, when we think we *must* do something and there's no way out, there's usually a hidden window or door that's cracked open, but we don't notice until we let other people in, and they lead us out of the chaos."

She adds, "Have you considered, I might be willing to give up my dreams for you? Or maybe my dreams had changed after I met you? Or perhaps I'm okay with not being married as long as I can stay by your side?"

My breath stalls in my throat, and I grip her hands tightly in mine. "Millie, you *can't* give up your dreams for me. I've seen this happen to my mom. The resentment that builds afterward. You deserve a man who can offer you his name and put you as the top priority. I can't let you sell yourself short. You deserve so much more than me."

She holds up the key around her neck, the jewels sparkling under the dim light. "You gave me the key to your heart. Trust me with it. Trust that there's also a hidden key to unlock your problems. *There has to be.* And the people who love you will want to find it for you. And they will."

She looks up. "*We will find it together* because if we can't solve it today, we always have tomorrow."

A pressure forms in my chest and spreads like wildfire as I take in this fighter in front of me. The rarest of songbirds. The most powerful of hunters.

And she loves me.

"Tomorrow," I echo her words, my voice hoarse. *Tomorrow.*

Wordlessly, I cradle her face with my hands and seal my lips to hers, needing to kiss her, to love her with every suction, every lave of my tongue.

The words finally find me.

"I love you, Millie. I love you so damn much."

CHAPTER 44

HE HELD ME TIGHTLY in his arms that night and I vaguely remember waking up in the middle of the night, my mind groggy, my abdomen on fire, with him already sitting by my side, his arms gently hoisting me up before handing me more medicine and a cup of warm water. It was like he was in tune with every inch of my body and was intent on taking care of me the best way he could.

Like no one has ever taken care of me before.

My family loves me, I'm sure, but I've never had anyone put me in the front and center of their unwavering focus, like the way Ryland has.

I can cry, laugh, say anything in front of him, and it'll be okay.

Oftentimes, I don't even need to say anything and he seems to know what I'm thinking or what I need.

My nose crinkles and a ball forms in my throat. I gaze at the large expanse of Central Park below us, which is covered in a thick blanket of snow. The waning sunset provides a stunning backdrop to the enormous park, the warm light casting a soft glow on the snow-tipped trees.

I blow out an exhale, watching the condensation vaporizing in the air, melting with the purplish red striations in the evening skies. It's beautiful. Mother Nature is giving us a swath of hope and color amid the dreary gray and white winter.

I'm sitting on the heated patio outside the sliding glass doors of his spacious living room, which is a statement of masculine luxury with dark wood paneled walls and the occasional pop of colors from the vases of daffodils around the apartment.

He's taken to ensuring every room in his place has those bright yellow flowers.

He said they reminded him of me.

It's been a week since Christmas, with today being New Year's Day. Except for a few work calls and meetings, Ryland has never left my side. We haven't talked about me going home or how we'll deal with his problems in the future. This one week has been a break for both of us.

Living out the what-ifs and what could-bes like a dream.

And tomorrow, we have to return to reality, where other tomorrows aren't certain once more.

I wish I had a cup of hot chocolate or even a bag of gummy bears. Maybe that'll distract me from my melancholy thoughts.

"Did you enjoy dinner?" Ryland asks from behind me and I turn around.

He's holding two large red mugs in his hands, the thick scarf I knitted him before placed over his arm. His hair is slightly disheveled in that sexy, I just rolled out of bed, way. He's wearing a blue T-shirt that's molded to his body like a second skin, showcasing all those muscles that have been used to pin me down in the past. My pulse kicks up a new rhythm.

I'll never get used to the sight of him.

"It was wonderful. The chili was delicious and perfect for this weather. Please tell Gretchen thank you for me."

"She'll be pleased. She doesn't cook for anyone you know. But I've always loved her chili...even more than some foods the chef prepares or from the restaurants on the floors below."

A flash of red in my peripheral vision distracts me.

A little bird lands on top of the railing—a cute little thing with a white body flecked with brown on his back and startling red patches on his head and his chest. He's warbling a light melody as he shakes his feathers.

I lean toward the bird, not wanting to spook it, but I've never seen anything like it before.

It cocks his head and stares at me like it's deciding if I'm a threat. Then, with another flap of his wings, he sings another trilling melody before flying away and becoming a tiny dot against the brilliant skies.

Its presence may have been fleeting and minuscule, but it left a lasting imprint.

"That's the *acanthis flammea*, otherwise known as the common redpoll," Ryland says as I turn back around. He's staring into the skies, a yearning in his eyes.

"Despite the name, they are rare in New York City. Perhaps it was stopping by for a bit of rest before heading back north. A sighting can be considered a jackpot in the birdwatching community."

I bite back a giggle. "You told me you like birdwatching before, but I didn't quite believe it until now."

He chuckles. "It takes a certain mindset and patience to admire birds. They're unpredictable and yet there are patterns you can rely on. Even so, you never know what you may encounter. You also need to stop and focus on your surroundings to see them because they are so small, so unassuming, they typically blend into the background."

His head swivels toward me. "But the best things come in small packages." His eyes hold mine for a few seconds, leaving no doubt what he's referring to.

My face heats and my heart triples in size.

Giving me a quick wink, he traipses over and hands me one of the mugs.

I look inside.

Hot chocolate with tiny marshmallows and a hint of whip cream, just the way I like it.

Of course he's a fast learner.

He then carefully wraps the scarf around my neck, making sure I'm warm in the cold elements.

My nose twitches, a heat spreading inside my chest, and I stare at his grinning face. His lips are tugged up in a boyish smile, and I bite back a smile of my own before taking a sip and setting the mug back on the table.

It's perfect.

"Just the way I like it. How did you know I was craving hot chocolate right now?"

The grin slowly slips away and his gray eyes turn darker.

He murmurs, "I notice everything about you. The three freckles right underneath your right ear. Your love for jalapeños even though you can't tolerate the spiciness. How you spend the first ten minutes in bed facing the ceiling, but you can't fall asleep until you shift to your right side. You prefer natural essential oils over perfume, but I haven't figured out the exact combination yet."

He chuckles under his breath and shakes his head. "I've tried multiple combinations of vanilla and jasmine with other scents, but it's still missing something."

My heart thumps in a victory lap in my chest.

"It's chamomile," I whisper. "You're missing the chamomile. I get stressed easily, and it helps me relax."

"Chamomile," he repeats, his voice serious, and gives me a nod, like he's memorizing the password to his bank account.

My heart hiccups again. How can I *not* love him? It's impossible.

Ryland sits down next to me on the long wicker sofa and places his mug on the table in front of us. He tucks the thick blanket tightly around my shoulders.

His brilliant gaze is intent on mine. "It's normal to want to know everything about the person you love."

He takes my hands in his and gently rubs the chill away from my fingers. Then he cups them to his mouth and blows a warm breath before continuing, "It's like second nature, Millie. Wanting to know everything about you, the woman I shouldn't be involved with yet desperately needing, like my body requires oxygen and sustenance."

The ache inside my chest resurfaces. It hurts to hear him beat himself up. I want to shake him and yell, *you deserve happiness and so do I. Why shouldn't we be together?* But I don't because he's not ready yet and if I press him too hard, I'm afraid he'll end what we have.

"You have no idea how much I need you, my little lark." Ryland's eyes flicker up, a wet sheen appearing in those deep gray pools.

"You give me life. You give me oxygen. You're the sunshine to my storm. You're my freedom," he rasps, his voice hoarse.

"Ryland," I whisper. I shiver, but it's not from the cold.

Climbing on top of his lap, I hold his face in my hands, my fingers trailing over the hard edges and rough planes, his five o'clock shadow longer than usual. I press my lips to his, savoring the taste of hot chocolate in his mouth.

My pulse is a heavy drum in my ears, my heart bursting with emotions as a sultry heat flows through my body, warming me up instantly.

Our kiss turns passionate. He clutches the nape of my neck, his tongue invading my mouth, taking, giving, tasting, each swipe an aphrodisiac to my veins.

Letting out a moan, I press closer, needing this man more than I need anything else in the world. His alluring scent of the woods inflames my senses. Nipping his lip, I relish in the guttural hiss from his mouth and the digging of his fingers on my back.

His erection hardens beneath me and my nipples bead in answer. I rub my body against him, every scrape of his chest against mine sending shivers to my belly, every gyration of my hips over the outline of his cock hitting my clit at a tortuous angle, dragging moans from both of our mouths.

Ryland groans and hoists me up as he stands, his hands palming my ass. He pulls back briefly and cocks his brow, our harsh breathing sounding loud in the air.

"It ended yesterday. I'm good now," I reply, answering the unasked question in his eyes.

His nostrils flare and he seals his lips with mine again, his nips, licks, and suctions growing more desperate and wilder with each step he takes toward the bedroom.

By the time he tosses me on the bed, my pussy is wet and achy, my body seconds away from combusting.

Using one hand, Ryland tugs off his shirt in a smooth motion, his defined pecs and abs rippling with the motion.

My mouth dries.

His gaze is incinerating, a dark flame in his eyes, like he wants to devour me whole.

The pulsing between my legs intensifies. I scoot back on the bed and rise to my knees, my hands automatically taking off the large sleep shirt I have on.

"Fuck," he rasps, his gaze traveling over my heaving tits, my belly, my hips clad in a pair of black lacy underwear.

My tongue swipes my parched lips as I keep my focus on him and slowly drag the lace down my legs before tossing it to the floor.

He swallows, his chest rising and falling rapidly, his eyes turning fevered. Wild. The hunter in the woods. With one swift motion, he tugs off his pants, his long, thick cock bobbing against his stomach, and he climbs onto the bed.

My pulse flutters, every inch of me wanting to submit to this predator before me.

"You're so fucking breathtaking," he whispers, before tugging apart my legs. "Look at this pretty pink pussy, dripping wet for me."

Ryland leans in and inhales, his breath causing tremors to flow through my body. I arch my hips toward his mouth, but he keeps me immobile with his hands.

"Ryland, please," I beg.

Dark chuckles fill the room. "Where does my little lark need me?" He presses a kiss on my inner thigh as I writhe on top of the sheets.

"Here?" A kiss on my lower abdomen, followed by a toe-curling lick.

"Or here?" He laves a sensitive spot on the inner crease of my thigh.

I pull his hair, trying to angle his mouth where I want it most.

"Tell me what you want, Millie. I want to hear those dirty words coming from your mouth."

Moisture gathers between my legs at the dominance in his voice.

"Ryland, I need your lips on my aching pussy. I need you to play with my clit, suck on it, taste it, make it flutter." The words are shaky, and my mind turns hazy as his fingers dig into my thighs.

He trembles. He's moments away from snapping.

A fire burns through me. "Then, I want you to put your fingers in my tight little pussy and ass and fuck me while you eat me out until I come all over your face."

Ryland growls. "Fuck yes. Your wish is my command."

The restraints fall away and he dives in and feasts.

A scream tears out of my mouth as he sucks on my clit like his life depends on it. The wet licks sound lurid in the quiet room.

"Fuck, you taste good. Sweet chamomile. All fucking mine."

He inserts a finger inside my channel, and I clench around it, my body arching up as the sparks gather at the base of my spine at a blistering speed. Out of self-preservation, my hips try to shift on the bed, away from his onslaught, but he holds me down and ups the ante.

"Yes, yes, yes," I chant, my legs twitching.

He grunts and doubles down, his tongue swirling around the hardened nub before his mouth sucks on it like a delicacy. He takes his finger out from my pussy and swipes the wetness down to my ass and rims the tight rosebud.

"Look at my slutty little lark, twisting on my bed, needing to come. Play with your nipples, baby. Tug them into hard buds for me."

I moan, my fingers trailing to my swollen breasts and circling my hard nipples, each twist and pinch sending me closer and closer to the edge.

"God, I could eat your pussy every day. I'm fucking obsessed," he rasps while he feasts on my clit.

Then, he inserts two fingers into my pussy and one in my forbidden hole, the sensations so sudden, so sharp, I let out a hoarse cry as my fingers clamp around my hard nipples.

His slurping grows loud, his fingers sawing inside me, curling in just the right way, building an inferno.

I feel so full, his fingers filling me up. My mouth falls open, the sparks gathering between my legs, a dark heat spreading to the rest of me. My breath freezes in my lungs and dots appear in my vision.

My mewling is loud and the sounds seem to drive him wilder.

"God, I'm so hard for you. The way you feel, the sounds from your mouth, the way you taste."

He finger fucks me in earnest and I nearly careen off the bed.

"Yes, little lark. If only you can see what I see. Fuck. Your walls are strangling my fingers. I can't wait until they're clenching around my cock. Come, baby. Scream my name."

Then his teeth clamp down on my clit.

I explode, the fireworks lighting up my entire body. "Ryland!"

Liquid gushes out of me and he licks it all up, each swipe of his tongue prolonging my orgasm.

"Fuck, that is the most beautiful sight I've ever seen," he says, and he climbs above me.

My eyes blink open, my vision hazy as I take in his flushed face, wet with my essence, the male satisfaction shining in his eyes.

I reach up and kiss him, tasting myself on his lips, and he grinds his large cock on my stomach, leaving a trail of pre-cum on my skin.

With a strength I didn't know I have, I flip him around and straddle him. His eyes widen in surprise at the reversal of our positions.

I want to fuck him, to dominate him this time. I want to drive him crazy like he has done many times to me.

I want him to let go.

Wordlessly, I grab his hands and place them on my breasts, my hips lifting so his tip notches against my sensitive entrance.

My hair tumbles over my face as I stare down at him, finding his gaze heavy-lidded, a banked fire inside his eyes. He kneads my breasts, his thumb flicking my nipples.

I slide home.

"Fuuuuck," he groans and shakes beneath me.

I answer with a whimper, his hard cock nearly spearing me in half, the sudden pain blending with the sharp pleasure in a heady cocktail.

Tossing my hair back, I arch up and move over him, gyrating my hips in a maddening rhythm.

I clutch his hands on top of my breasts, our fingers interlacing as I increase my speed, every glide of his dick hitting me deep inside, in the sensitive spot no one has ever reached except for him.

The pleasure wraps itself around my heart and burrows deep inside.

The headboard thumps rhythmically, and the bedsprings squeak as I increase my speed.

My fingers tighten against his as the walls of my pussy tremble around him once more. Wetness seeps out with each glide.

He lets out guttural moans and my eyes fly open, finding his gaze pinned on me, his mouth parted like he's desperate for oxygen. He grips my fingers and tits to the point of pain, but I barely notice as I bounce harder and faster over him.

Ryland's face turns red, sweat dripping down his forehead, his breathing harsh as he shakes beneath me, and I know he's close.

"Yes, baby. Your hard cock is ramming so deep inside me," I murmur, my voice shaky. His cock twitches and lengthens even more.

His lips move, but no sounds come out. His eyes glaze over.

"I'm addicted to you and your fucking cock. *Professor.* You want to come in my hot, wet pussy? Because I want your cum. All of it. I want you to stuff me full of yourself so I'll leak whenever I walk."

A roar tears from his mouth and his head falls back, the muscles in his neck flexing.

His beast comes undone.

He grips my hips tightly, his hips snapping up like a battering ram. "Fuuuck," he growls.

His cock throbs and pulses as he unleashes ropes of cum inside me, the hot liquid pushing me off the cliff. I scream and collapse on top of him, my orgasm hitting me like a ton of bricks and we ride the high together.

"I love you so fucking much, Millie." He sounds winded moments later, and I rest my head on his chest.

I hear the reassuring thumps of his heart. The sound of safety.

My eyelids grow heavy, and I shift against him, our bodies still connected, but we make no move to disentangle ourselves.

His hands rub over my back in gentle circles.

"I love you too," I whisper. Sleep threatens to overtake me. *Forever. I could love this man forever.* "Tomorrow, Ryland. We still have tomorrow."

"Tomorrow," he murmurs.

Right before I drift off into a deep sleep, I hear the deep timbre of his voice again.

"I wish we had more time."

CHAPTER 45

"MR. ANDERSON! MR. ANDERSON! Who was the woman you danced with at the Christmas Ball?"

I'm standing behind a podium inside the Kensington Hotel next to The Orchid. It's one of the many hotels Fleur Entertainment owns. The press conference was going well moments before, when I updated the crowd of reporters on the progress of the IPO. The stock listing date is set and we're scheduled to be at the New York Stock Exchange to ring the opening bell.

Then they started asking about Millie.

These fucking vultures are at it again.

Lana tried to warn me before this was going to happen. *Shit.*

I have to protect Millie. I can't let her get hurt because of me. *You hypocrite. You caused this mess by dancing with her, by being with her.*

But when I saw her standing by the refreshments table at The Ball, my heart literally stopped and I wanted to be selfish. I wanted to claim her as my own. I was carried by impulse, the need to hold my ethereal angel in blue in my arms.

It was the only thing that mattered at the moment.

And now, I'm paying the price for my stupidity.

Maggie, our friend from CBC, speaks over the ruckus. "Sources say she's Millie Callahan, Adrian Scott's sister?"

She shoots me an apologetic look, her shoulders lifting in a shrug as if to say, sorry, but a girl has a job to do, and this is riveting gossip.

The group erupts in chaos and folks leap up from their seats as The Shark's name is brought up. The questions are incessant, pelting down at an unsuspecting victim like a sudden hailstorm on an otherwise warm day.

"Is she someone special, Ryland?"

"An anonymous source said you disappeared from The Ball after the first thirty minutes. Where did you go?"

"A Bromwell Pharmacy employee mentioned seeing you shopping on Christmas evening. Is that where you went?"

"Who's she to you?"

"Isn't there a significant age gap between the two of you?"

My veins turn to ice, their questions echoing in my ears, the sensation like I've caught a right hook to my face.

I was too reckless. I should've stayed away from her.

Scenario after scenario flashes through my mind. What if they find out she's my student? What if they find out about our illicit affair? What will happen to the IPO, to my family's reputation, to my position at NYUC, *to her*?

The room swirls, and I close my eyes for a brief second. *Get a grip, Ryland. Anything you say or do right now can turn the tides. Get your fucking act together.*

Pasting the fakest smile on my face, I stare at the crowd, a blur of gray and black suits, flailing hands, and bright flashes. Nausea roils in my stomach, and I clear my throat.

"It was simply a dance between acquaintances. I dance with multiple people at events at The Orchid. No need to make a story out of nothing. Any other questions regarding the IPO?" Sweat trickles down the back of my neck.

They aren't satisfied with my response. I see it in the shrewd glint of their eyes, the harsh scribbles on their notepads, the fervor in their follow-up questions, which are decidedly not about the IPO.

My heart thuds an ominous beat in my ears.

Ba-dum. Ba-dum. Ba-dum.

The ticking of a timer on its final countdown.

"You know, if you want me to help you with this, all you need to do is ask."

The quiet man sitting in front of me appears nonchalant, like he doesn't have a care in the world.

His dark navy suit unbuttoned, a silver metal chain hanging from his tailored vest to his vest pocket, one ankle propped up against his other knee.

But it's his eyes that give him away. The vivid green, a lethal sharpness in them, which pairs well with the long scar spanning his entire cheek.

Elias Kent is dangerous, and his help comes at a price.

I stare at the man who handles the personnel for our Rose floors, which straddles legality with the companionship services of a more amorous nature. But he makes sure the employees working there are well protected and have agency in their jobs. The infamous crime boss has his own set of moral codes, after all.

Elias rakes his fingers over his dark hair and smirks.

Of course, he'd love to get a favor from me.

"No, I think I can handle this."

The damn smile remains on his face, and he cocks a brow. "You sure? Considering you and Maxwell brought me on all those years ago, I owe you one. I can handle this for you for free."

He reaches into his vest pocket and takes out the antique gold and silver lighter attached to his vest chain and fiddles with it. I see him carrying that damn thing everywhere.

Tossing back the rest of my century-old MacGregor single malt whiskey, the smooth taste barely registering in my mouth, I stare beyond him through the glass walls of the private room we're sitting in inside the MacGregor's Whiskey Library within The Orchid.

Turning my attention back to him, I respond more firmly. "Appreciate the thought, Elias. But no, I don't think we need to pull out the big guns yet."

With Elias, his methods will most likely involve some sort of blackmail or strongly worded "suggestions" to the press to persuade them to pull their attentions away from Millie and our waltz on Christmas.

I set my tumbler on the table. "I think any intervention will fan the flames right now."

"Fair enough. But I have to ask, is there any truth in their speculations?"

"You too, Elias?"

He laughs. "I admire you and your brothers, Ryland. It seems to be a shame you all are perpetually single. I have to think the Anderson family needs to think about heirs."

Elias holds my gaze for a beat and adds, "Especially with your family trust and the requirements for legitimate heirs."

My nose twitches. Of course he knows about the trust. The man can unearth secrets from the dead. "I'd ask how you found out, but I don't think I want to know."

"Frankly, I hate seeing you being such a loner. You seem happier lately." This time, his eyes warm up a smidgen. Concern. I should be touched the master of the shadows is concerned about me.

"Some things aren't meant to last, Elias. It'll just be a beautiful memory to hold on to later."

And that *has to* be enough.

My heart clenches at the thought and I draw in a harsh breath.

"You know, if I never took risks in my life, I wouldn't have gotten to where I am right now," Elias replies. "I'd still be in the slums, running weapons for lowlifes. Maybe I'd be dead."

He stands up and clasps a hand on my shoulder, giving it a firm squeeze. "Think about it, Ryland."

Like a phantom breeze, he slips out the door as my phone vibrates.

Steven

Tread carefully. Adrian called me, asking about the rumors between you and Millie. He's protective of his sister.

My fingers type out a quick response.

There comes a time when you encounter a fork in the road, and you know your next decision will have lasting impacts.

I'm at the fork now.

My phone vibrates again. This time, it's an email from the dean lighting up the screen.

Ryland,

The research the JEAP committee has conducted on the Professor Archer case has been very thorough. The Ethics Committee is impressed with your work. You make a compelling argument against disciplining Professor Archer and Tammy Simmons based on the evidence so far, but the optics aren't good. Several conservative members of the Committee are still concerned about the clandestine nature of the alleged sexual affair, even if the evidence leans toward no favoritism. While they recognize your viewpoints, there are significant reservations about the JEAP recommendation.

The Committee will reconvene in a month but continue to send information our way.

Your honorary doctorate also looks promising.

I know I didn't hire the wrong person.

Regards,

Jacob

My tie feels more and more like a noose around my neck as I reread the email. A sticky heat travels up my spine, landing on top of my chest.

I've been in the business circuit for a long time—politics, optics, they are all the same whether it's in *Fortune 500* companies or in large universities. Everyone is in it for themselves. Selfishness, cover-your-ass actions always win.

The Ethics Committee will side against Professor Archer and Tammy. I'd bet my net worth on it. He's a younger professor, hasn't earned his stripes yet to be irreplaceable by the university. He'll lose his career, his reputation will be tarnished, and his prospects to teach in the future will be dismal because others will treat him as a predator.

As for Tammy, her reputation as a student who has slept her way to the top will precede her. When people run background checks on her in the future, this black mark will come up first, even before people review her work and contributions. Opportunities will be lost. Admissions to graduate school will be rejected or rescinded.

That's how the world works.

It's all about optics. No one really cares about the truth.

No amount of wishful thinking will change that fact.

Visions of Millie float to the forefront—her soft smiles, her intoxicating kisses, the way our bodies move together as one, and how I've never felt freer than when I'm with her.

My beautiful lark who has just learned how to fly. She has so much to give, many more beautiful songs to sing.

She hasn't seen the world yet or felt the wind beneath her wings.

And my family? My siblings may be a rowdy bunch, but what have they done to deserve to be dragged through the muck with me? They are fulfilling their obligations as unimpeachable offspring of a centuries-old dynasty.

If being an Anderson is such a burden, why would I want the woman I love to suffer the same fate?

How can you be so selfish, Ryland?

I bury my head in my hands, the pangs in my chest more incessant, a thousand knives slicing my heart.

"We still have tomorrow," Millie's voice whispers in my mind.

Eventually, all tomorrows have to end.

CHAPTER 46

Millie

Dear Ryland,

Tell me, why are you pulling away again? I feel the distance growing more between us; I see the walls you're trying to build back around your heart. When I ask you to meet, you say you're busy. You say it's the IPO, the effects of working two full-time jobs. The shadows under your eyes worry me, but you tell me everything is fine. But you forget, I can read you as well as you read me.

Don't you know you're hurting me? I lay awake at night missing you and angry at you at the same time. I'm not a quitter, but you make it so damn hard for me and it frustrates me to no end.

Don't you see? We are meant to be. And perhaps I'm as stubborn as you, because even though you make me furious at times, I'm going to change your mind, because I know you love me. After all, you gave me your mom's pendant.

We may not have all the answers yet, but with a love like ours, we are written in the storms, and I'm sure at the end of it all, there'll be a beautiful rainbow and sunny skies.

I miss your kisses. I miss your touch. I miss you.

Love, Millie

"CLASS, IT HAS BEEN an absolute honor teaching you this year. I know it's only the beginning of February, and we still have spring quarter left, but I just want to get that off my chest," Ryland says, his voice sullen, in front of the classroom at another JEAP committee meeting.

His shoulders look extra rigid today, and a heaviness blankets his frame. He runs his fingers through his tousled hair, rendering it into an unkemptness rarely seen from the Prince of the USA. The man I love is miserable and struggling, and I'm helpless to stop it.

He has been avoiding me after class now, and I can count with one hand how many times I've had his lips on mine in the weeks that have passed since New Year's Day.

An anvil sits on top of my chest, and I sit up and twist my lips in what I hope is a convincing smile. *I will not let him break me.*

His eyes catch mine, the intensity in them almost stifling, and the only acknowledgment to my reassuring smile is a harsh swallow, his muscles rippling in his throat.

"I've submitted our final recommendations to the Ethics Committee for Professor Archer and Tammy's case. You've made a sound argument against punishment for them. After all, they appear to be victims of unfortunate circumstances."

His penetrating gaze is unwavering on mine. "Whatever happens, know that you've tried your best, and *in the end*, that's what matters. The committee will make a decision soon and it's out of our hands now."

Ryland walks around the podium so he's standing closer to us. To me. His shirtsleeves are rolled up, and he releases a haggard sigh. I smell the familiar scent of his cologne and a piercing want spears through my chest.

In the classroom full of people, he still appears as alone as that first day when I saw him standing in the rain.

A lonely silhouette carrying the weight of the world on his shoulders.

But I am here, Ryland. You aren't alone anymore.

The weight sinks deeper inside me, and I bite my lip to contain my emotions. I wonder if my efforts are useless, hurling pebbles against a steel wall.

But my heart won't let me quit him. *But do you really want to quit him?*

Deep down, my answer is no. But I also know I deserve more, like he told me before. I deserve to be loved without reservations.

But seeing him so anguished in front of me, I want to hold him in my arms and hear the reassuring thumps of his heartbeat. I want to whisper in his ear he no longer needs to carry his burdens by himself because I can share the weight with him. If only he'll just let go of these invisible chains he has clasped tightly in his hands.

His gray eyes linger on me before his jaw flexes, and he looks away.

"In the past year we've spent together, I've seen you grow. I've witnessed the brilliance in your theories and arguments, the thoughtfulness in your responses. And I'm proud of you for being part of *my legacy*. Perhaps this is one final lesson—sometimes, the real world doesn't see our efforts and the truth in our arguments. Politics, optics, and many other factors are in play. But remember your heart even when the real world closes in, even when you're forced to accept reality. You've tried your best and sometimes," he pauses, his eyes meeting mine. *"Sometimes, some things aren't meant to be."*

Ryland's passionate gaze brims with unsaid emotions. His words reverberate in my ears and I feel a burning sensation behind my eyes.

No, I refuse to accept that.

The classroom is silent. I shake my head.

No, I don't accept this reality.

I don't—

Bam!

The doors swing open and suddenly, we're blinded by flashing bright lights, followed by a stampede of random outsiders into the room.

"There she is! Over there!"

By the time the dots disappear from my vision, I find several men and women crowding in front of me, cameras and microphones thrusted at my face. *What the fuck is going on?*

"Ms. Callahan, what is the nature of your relationship with Mr. Anderson?"

"We just received a photo from an anonymous source showing Mr. Anderson carrying a woman who resembled you in the halls of The Orchid. You had scrapes over your legs and arms. Was he abusing you?"

"Ms. Callahan! Ms. Callahan, how long has this been going on?"

"I have it on good authority you two were in a scene at a primal kink club. Is that true?"

"Weren't you already his student at the time?"

"Do you think you're above reproach because you're Adrian Scott's sister?"

My heart drops to my stomach as nausea roils inside me. *No, they found out. Despite all our efforts, they still found out about us. I had hope... God, I was so stupid. Shit. What do I do?*

My pulse races in my ears as I angle my head and try to find Ryland past the wall of people in front of me, only to see more paparazzi gathered around him. He throws a swing at a reporter in front of him, his eyes frenzied as he tries to break through his barricade to reach me.

"Let go of her, you creep!" Chloe tries to peel off a reporter who has his hand clamped onto my forearm.

Chaos erupts in the classroom, and I hear chairs dragging over the floors, shouting as classmates come to my aid. I hear Fred yelling something like, "Security is coming, assholes. Get the fuck out of here!"

"Ms. Callahan!"

More bright white flashes. More noise. More everything. I want to move, to escape, to fight back, but panic claws my insides and I'm frozen in fear.

"Ms. Callahan, answer our questions! Are you trying to sleep your way to an A?"

My breathing quickens, the seconds feeling like hours, and I find myself mute, unable to speak, unable to move, a literal prey frozen in front of the dangerous predators in front of me.

Move, Millie. Get out of here. What are you doing?

But my body won't cooperate and sweat trickles down my back as desperation kicks in. I need to get out of here. I need them to leave me alone.

I need him.

My breathing turns rapid, my lungs trying but failing to get in the much-needed oxygen. I curl over my desk, my hands covering my ears. There's a loud ringing in my ears that won't stop.

Too much noise. Too many lights. Too many questions.

The door swings open again and campus security marches in with batons and handcuffs. Someone yells something about this being a private institution and the press is banned on campus.

The next moments are a blur of fragments and echoes.

The paparazzi being dragged out of the classroom and dealt with.

A tall man saying he's the dean and class is dismissed.

Chloe shaking my shoulder, asking me if I'm okay.

My mind is sluggish, my brain still trying to catch up to the insane events. My lungs attempt to draw in air, but it feels like I'm drowning in front of everyone.

Suddenly, a strong hand clamps my wrist and drags me up from my chair. My muscles finally wake up and I fight and claw at my assailant before the whiff of pine trees and citrus wafts to my nose.

Looking up, the ringing in my ears slowly subsides until all I can hear are the sounds of my heart racing.

Ryland looms before me. Tall, strong, powerful.

He's not even human. He's a god.

Jocelyn's words float to my consciousness and an inappropriate giggle bubbles up my throat. *I'm losing it.* Everything fades away. I rake in a ragged inhale, my first full breath since our world fell apart.

I'm okay, Ryland. I'm okay. It was only a panic attack. I'm fine.

My lips tremble before tipping up into a smile.

He lets out a low growl, as if he doesn't believe me. His red tie is askew, his face flushed, his hair even more disheveled than before. A vein pulses angrily on his forehead. His eyes are wild, fevered with anger, desperation, vengeance, and more emotions than I can name.

Before I can say anything, he crushes me against him and wraps me in the safety of his embrace.

My body relaxes as I burrow myself automatically into his warmth and surround myself with his masculine scent.

"Ryland," I whisper into his chest.

Wordlessly, he drags me out of the room in full view of everyone.

CHAPTER 47

RED HAZE FILLS MY vision and violence laces my blood. I want to maim and destroy, to shove every single one of their cameras and microphones up their asses and watch them writhe in agony on the ground.

Logic and rational thoughts fled my brain the moment I saw the paparazzi surround her like fucking vultures. The desperation I saw on her face, her complexion as white as a sheet of paper, her lithe body trembling in her seat as the motherfuckers attacked her with questions.

And I couldn't reach her.

I couldn't protect her.

My surroundings blur around me in a sea of white. The only common sense I have left is to let go of her hand and instead, usher her toward my office with my fist lightly grazing her back. I hear the harsh sounds of her breathing as she quickens her strides to match mine. I know I should slow down. I should ask if she's okay.

But I can't.

Because all I want to do is find those bastards and force feed them several servings of knuckle sandwiches and right hooks. I vaguely register people leaping out of the way, no doubt wondering what has gotten into me, the unimpeachable Prince of the USA.

Impeccable reputation.

A delirious laugh slips out of my mouth.

"Ryland?" Millie huffs after me as we approach the office. She sounds concerned.

A sharp pinch of guilt stabs me in my chest.

I did this to her. I should've stayed away. I knew what would happen, and I did it anyway.

You fucking selfish, greedy bastard.

I don't deserve my dream, to be a professor, to have her in my life.

I don't deserve anything.

Ignoring her, I unlock the door and step inside. I wait for her to enter the room before I close the door and secure the lock.

I stride to the desk and press a button on the remote to turn the walls from clear to gray, blocking the view from the prying eyes outside.

Heated blood rushes in my ears, the sounds akin to the roaring wind in a hurricane. The madness I've attempted to rein in slams through the metal chains. I feel the metal giving, little by little.

A losing battle.

Millie stands before me, her luscious hair in disarray, a light sheen of sweat on her face, her pale skin pinkened from exertion.

Her beautiful, startling blue eyes stare at me in concern, her pouty lips curving down into a frown.

My little lark looks so beautiful. My heart, already bloodied inside my rib cage because of the last few weeks—my tortuous attempt at withdrawal from what surely would be a lifelong addiction—swells in her presence.

It clamors for her. It beats for her. It hungers for her.

And I don't know how I'll survive without her.

"Oh, Ryland," she murmurs while stepping toward me. "I'm okay. They didn't get to me. For a moment there, I froze because I was shocked."

She chuckles, her sweet voice sounding hesitant. "Who wouldn't, right? But I think it's time I get used to them. I'm Adrian's sister after all, a public figure now. So, don't worry abo—"

The chains snap and fall at my feet.

I grip the nape of her neck and crush my lips to hers. I'm voracious, desperate, frantic, an addict getting his last hit.

She whimpers as I thrust my tongue inside her mouth, tasting her sweetness of honey and chocolate, the elixir of life I need but will no longer have. She leaps into my arms and my hands automatically catch her by the round swells of her ass.

Stumbling back, I drop into my chair all the while devouring her with each swipe of tongue, each sharp bite. My hands travel up her body and pull up her T-shirt to expose the heaving swells of her tits.

Millie's fingers dig into my neck as I wrench her bra out of the way and clamp my teeth on her pebbled nipple, the beaded peak thrusted out like eraser buds, and I suck.

She cries out before slapping a hand over her mouth to stifle the noise. My mind can't compute how we shouldn't be doing this in my office moments after the press made accusations against us.

I don't care anymore.

I just know I need her. I need to taste her, to be inside her and to feel her heart beat against mine as our souls take one last flight together.

I want to feel her pussy strangling my hard dick one last time.

My free hand kneads her other breast before I switch sides. Millie grinds her hips on my cock like she needs this as much as I do. My suctions turn harder, stronger, each drag urgent, and I'm sure I'll leave marks on her beautiful skin later.

"Ryland, oh my God, please fuck me. Fuck me, fuck me, fuck me," she chants under her breath, her head bent toward the ceiling, her back arched as her movements turn frenzied.

"Millie, my lovely little lark," I rasp, and we pull apart just enough for me to wrench off her leggings and underwear and toss them to the ground.

Her fingers shake as she unzips the fly of my pants, reaches inside, and takes me out. My throbbing cock is seconds away from erupting, the tip red and dripping with pre-cum.

Her eyes are wild, dilated, her lips swollen, and we reach for each other again as she slams herself on top of me and I thrust home.

"Fuuuuck," I groan, the sharp pleasure almost unbearable.

She lets out another keening moan as her body struggles to accept me, but I push through, too far gone to slow down. I'm in my own version of heaven...or hell. Tremors spread through her body. Inch by inch, I invade, and she submits.

So fucking beautifully. So fucking perfect.

"Yes, yes, yes," she mewls, her words inflaming every part of me, and I clamp my fingers around her hips and thrust into her with the anguish of a dying man enjoying his last meal.

My lips find hers again, tasting her once more, telling her without words how much I love her, how I wish things were different.

But then again, words are never necessary between us.

She knows.

A burst of saltiness reaches my tongue and my eyes open, my vision blurry, and I realize tears have escaped me.

Millie shakes as she kisses me back ardently, her lips trailing over the wetness on my cheeks as if she wants to take away all my pain.

My cock slams into her repeatedly from below, my chair squeaking under the harried motions of our bodies as we're carried away by this tempest we never want to leave.

A heated burn gathers in my thighs as the thrusts turn into pistoning. The sounds of skin slapping against skin mixes with the clinking of the metal pieces of my belt buckle.

Her legs shake and her pussy grips my cock in a vise and I know she's close.

"I love you," she whimpers as I ravish her thoroughly.

Her gasps turn louder and pitchier. My balls draw up and contract as unbearable pleasure gathers below. *I love you, too, Millie. I love you so fucking much.*

Thump, thump, thump.

"Anderson, open this door right now! We need to discuss some things." Jacob's command travels through the door.

Millie pulls back, her body frozen on top of mine, her eyes widening in panic.

The sounds of our breathing are loud in the room. I stare at her, my breathtaking soulmate, someone I was blessed to love, even if only for a short period.

I don't stop.

Instead, I grip her waist tighter and slam her harder on my cock.

I need her. One last time.

Thrust. Thrust. Thrust.

Her nails dig into my arms as we stare at each other, my mind memorizing every feature of her—her doe-like eyes, her plump bottom lip, her heavy-lidded gaze as she's close to orgasm—every cell of my body imprints with hers, committing to memory how our bodies join and merge into one.

Her lips fall open as her eyes glaze over. The trembling of her legs starts up once more and I feel a fresh torrent of wetness gushing out of her.

"Anderson! Open this door right now or I'm calling security."

She freezes and shakes her head, but I hold on to her.

"Safe word, Millie, say the safe word."

My words come out as low grunts. I'm delirious with want, with the need to be with her this final time because this will be the memory I'll revisit over and over when I lay awake at night, sleepless to the thoughts of her.

"Never," she replies, and she moves harder against me, like she wants to impale me deeper inside so I can never leave her.

Thrust. Thrust. Thrust.

"They decided against Archer and Tammy," I rasp, locking my arms around her back. "The committee made their decision this morning. I didn't have the heart to tell you."

She shakes and claws at my back, her head thrown back. I reach down and pinch her swollen clit, and she comes undone.

Her mouth parts and I swallow her cry with my lips as the pressure breaks inside me, shooting through my hard shaft. My vision blackens.

I fall into oblivion with her. My cock pulses inside her trembling pussy, the orgasm never ending.

Our kiss turns fevered, suction against suction, swipe against swipe, hunter against hunter as we slowly climb down from our high.

My perfect match. The right person, but the wrong time and the wrong circumstances.

Losers in a game of fate.

Slowly, the room comes back into focus, and I can hear the commotion outside.

Hastily, I pull out of her and help her back into her leggings before righting the rest of her clothes and zipping up my pants.

The office reeks of sex and she looks well and thoroughly fucked.

She looks like mine.

But I don't know how to save her. I don't know how to protect her from the shitstorm. It's the final nail on the coffin.

Moving around her, I stride to the door, unlock it, and my fingers close around the doorknob.

"Ryland, I love you, *please*. Please don't do this." Her voice is pleading. I can hear the tears she's holding back and my heart splinters into a million pieces.

I falter, just briefly, my eyes flickering shut for a moment before I open the door and face my fate.

I don't answer her.

Millie

Tears spring into my eyes as I watch the dean storm into the room, his countenance dark and foreboding. He slams the door shut behind him.

Ryland steps aside, his head hung low, his shoulders slumped, devastating defeat clear in his frame.

He has given up on us. That was his goodbye.

Perhaps I never had him at all.

Heartbreak spears through my chest, the pain so unfathomable, it eclipses the fear, the anger, and all the other emotions coursing through me.

It was goodbye.

"What the *fuck* is going on, Ryland? What did you do?"

The dean stabs a shaky finger into Ryland's chest, but the man I love remains silent, his eyes still looking at the ground.

"How could you do this? Your reaction alone spoke volumes. You didn't need to say anything to the press. What you did back there and now," he glares at both of us, "signed your death warrant and quite possibly mine! And to think I was putting you on the tenure track!" The dean paces the room, his fingers gripping his hair.

Tenure track? His lifelong dream that he thought he could never have? He put that at risk...for me?

My lips tremble as sobs threaten to unleash. *Please look at me, Ryland. Please.* I will him to acknowledge me, to stand next to me, to do anything other than staring at the ground and ignoring me.

"Ms. Callahan."

At my name, I swivel my head toward the dean, who's looking at me with both pity and compassion.

"I have campus security waiting for you outside to escort you back to your apartment while we figure everything out. Please leave this office." The firmness in his voice doesn't allow for arguments.

"Dean, please, it's not what you think, don't punish—"

"Everything is my fault. What happened, didn't happen, what the press thinks, what you think, *everything is my fault*," Ryland interrupts, his head lifting, his desolate charcoal eyes finally meeting mine.

His voice is thick as he continues, "Please don't punish Ms. Callahan. She did nothing wrong. I take full responsibility for anything from this scandal."

"No!" My feet hurtle forward, wanting to go to him, but he halts me with a chilling glare.

"Please leave us, Ms. Callahan," the dean repeats his command. "I'll be in touch."

My hands fist around my sides and I step toward the door. Pausing before opening it, I look back, finding the dean facing the window and Ryland's impassioned gaze on mine.

"I love you," I mouth, my eyes pleading with him to not give up on us. Despite everything, to keep fighting. My heart is in my hands, wishing he'll take it and keep it safe.

His nostrils flare and a muscle pulses in his jaw.

He looks away, leaving my heart a bloody mess on the floor.

Chapter 48

I scroll my phone, my fingers pausing on a photo of Ryland staring into the camera, his lips twitching into a smile as I pressed a kiss onto his cheek.

It was after one of our scenes at Noire and Ryland had just placed a special order for omelets and pancakes in a restaurant downstairs because I told him that was what I was craving, even though it was in the middle of the night. I leaped into his arms like a koala hugging a tree, one hand holding a cell phone.

"Say cheese," I whispered after going in for my sneak attack.

He chuckled, his arms automatically wrapping around my waist. "What's gotten into you?"

I took my photo and pulled back, smiling at him. "You're my snowy owl, you know? The powerful bird rarely seen but a sight to behold. I'm the lucky hunter who found one in the wild and I'm keeping him. Forever!" I peppered more kisses over his face.

"Is that right? A hunter, you say? What type of hunter kisses his prey instead of killing it?"

He hoisted me up and stared at me with so much love in his eyes, I could get drunk on his gaze.

"The smart kind, Ryland. A hunter who kills will have a meal or two, but I know better."

Leaning in, I kissed the corner of his lips, followed by a quick lick, relishing the way his breath hitched.

"My method is no less lethal. Death by a thousand kisses. That way, I have your heart and you'll never, ever leave me. My soul will always be full."

He slanted his head and sealed his lips with mine, his tongue swiping at the seam. "That sounds like one hell of a way to go," he rasped.

Curling my arms around his neck, I deepened our kiss, my hips moving over the outline of his hard cock pressing against his stomach.

"Again." I moaned.

"Are you sore?"

I shook my head, and he groaned in approval.

"Who's the best hunter, Ryland?" I whispered as he grunted between our fevered kisses, his feet already moving toward the master bedroom once more.

"Always you, little lark. Always you."

Tears cloud my vision as I trace his face in the photo. We were so happy then.

So happy.

My fingers fiddle with the jeweled key pendant around my neck. He hasn't asked for it back.

But he also hasn't contacted me since *that* day two weeks ago. All my calls, texts, and emails have gone unanswered. He has been placed on immediate administrative leave and disappeared without a trace. Another adjunct professor, a Professor Smith, is taking over the class and JEAP committee for the rest of the year.

The silver lining in this mess is, my classmates have been supportive, staunch defenders of me and Ryland to whoever approaches them. Even Pete Crosby had tried to comfort me earlier in class, and the damn bastard doesn't even like me.

The media have been reporting nonstop on the alleged illicit affair between the Prince of the USA and his much younger student. Sources come out of the woodwork, from classmates who have defended us, saying they have never seen Professor Ryland being anything other than professional to random Joes making up stories for a quick buck. Then, there's the news of Fleur Twilight's IPO being temporarily delayed for unknown reasons.

I swipe to another photo, this one of Ryland sleeping, a thick lock of dark hair covering his eye. The lines of his face softened; his lips curved into a small smile. He looked so much younger then, like the weight of the world was temporarily lifted off his shoulders.

God, I'm so worried about him. Everything he cares about—his family's reputation, the IPO, his dream of becoming a tenured professor—all up in smoke now.

He must be devastated.

I'm also angry at him. The boiling rage flares up at random moments in the day, invading the all-encompassing sadness. *How dare he leave me after everything we've been through? How dare he leave me to deal with the fallout alone? How can he say he loves me but run away at the first sign of trouble?*

I deserve more. I know I do.

Knowing him, he's probably blaming himself for everything, even if I was the one to push him into this relationship, the person who stupidly thought I could best the system and defeat the odds like Mom and Dad did a long time ago. But still, we entered the relationship together and we should deal with the consequences together.

The breeze from the opened windows of the apartment sifts to my face, and I belatedly realize my cheeks are wet.

But I still miss you so much.

My heart is heavy, the organ barely eking out the life-sustaining thump in the widening hole in my chest. The last two weeks have been a dark blur, one where I'd move through life like a robot, trying to put on a brave face so others around me wouldn't get worried.

I guess old habits die hard.

Ding dong.

Ignoring the doorbell, I stare at the clear blue skies outside our windows. A bright yellow bird flies by, singing a sweet song.

Ryland will know what bird this is.

Tears spring into my eyes again. Dammit. I swipe my cheeks, angry at myself again. I shouldn't miss him so much—he has walked away from this so easily. Why can't I do the same? Why won't my heart listen?

Ding dong.

"Open up, Millie! Tay is with me. Belle told us before she went to the office for her meeting that you had nothing scheduled today. She's on her way back now."

Thump. Thump.

They're knocking on the door now.

"Don't make me pick the lock, because I know how!" Taylor yells.

Staggering to my feet, I smooth my hands over my wrinkled pajamas and eye the empty bags of gummy bears in front of me.

I ran out of my stash of happiness.

A sharp pain lances my insides. Whoever said heartbreak is a physical affliction is correct.

"Coming," I holler before the girls really break down the door.

After fumbling with the lock, I open the door and Grace leaps across the threshold in a blur of white and wraps me in her arms. The backs of my eyes burn once more.

"We're here, Millie. You aren't alone." She holds me tightly while I shudder against her. "Cry it out."

"I'm going to ruin your sweater," I wail.

"Screw the sweater! I'll just get another one if it doesn't wash out."

"Aw, fuck." Taylor joins the group hug. "You look as shitty as *him*."

That got my attention. I pull back, not caring if tears and snot are all over my face.

The girls walk me back to the sofa and Grace gasps in apparent horror as she looks at the pigsty of snack wrappers and soda cans on the coffee table.

"Oh no, you poor thing." She flutters around the apartment, a determined glint in her eyes, and begins cleaning up.

I grab Taylor's wrist after we sit down. "You've seen Ryland? He won't pick up when I call. How is he doing? Is he okay?" Amidst the anger and pain inside me, my concern for him still apparently takes priority.

Taylor lets out a ragged sigh. "He has handed all his work to the others and doesn't leave his apartment. He hasn't shaved and is barely eating. I've talked to the others, and no one has ever seen him like this before. I think Gretchen and the staff practically have to force-feed him sometimes. And whenever we try to talk to him, he'll say everything is his fault and how he's the one to bring down our family."

She bites her lips and clasps my hands in hers. "But he misses you. I know it. He doesn't say anything, but whenever Grace and I talk about you, his eyes will brighten for a moment, like a spark flaring to life."

Grace traipses around the room, stacking loose sheets of papers into piles, placing all the wrappers, cans, empty cup noodle containers into a plastic bag before setting it on the floor. She hurries over and sits on the other side of me as the front door opens.

"How is she? If I didn't have that stupid meeting at the office today, I wouldn't have left her." Belle hurries over, shrugging out of her peacoat along the way.

"I'm fine, girls. Just heartbroken," I whisper, my voice unsteady. "Grace, now I know how you felt when you went through what you did with Steven."

"It was only a day for us, not weeks and not with the press breathing down our necks!" Grace mutters.

"I just miss him s-so much," I cry, my voice thickening, "and I'm so worried about him and so damn angry at the same time. Do you know teaching is his dream? That's the one thing he wants to do more than anything else in the world. It gives him purpose. And now, it's taken away from him."

I shake my head. "I should've stayed away. I don't know what I was thinking, believing we wouldn't get caught. And now, he lost everything because of me." I bury my face in my hands.

"It's not on you, Millie. How can anyone stop true love? That'd be cruel," Belle murmurs.

"I didn't know teaching was his dream," Grace whispers. "I always thought it was like volunteering for him. He never told us."

Sniffling, I look up and stare at the Peyton sisters. That stupid man. Keeping everything in his heart. Always the one to sacrifice for others around him.

"It is. He would've done it full time, and he had the opportunity before I came along and messed everything up. But the family trust..."

Grace and Taylor share a knowing glance. I guess their siblings have clued them in on this secret.

"He told you about the trust?" Grace asks.

I nod. "He didn't want everyone to lose everything because of him. But teaching is his lifeblood, the fuel driving him out of bed each day, his legacy, and now that's gone."

"What trust? What's going on?" Belle frowns, and I shake my head sadly at her.

"Sorry, Belle. That's not my story to tell." I've already said more than enough.

She nods, her eyes softening with understanding.

"So, what do you want to do?" Taylor asks. "Do you want us to take you to him? Or make him answer your call? 'Cuz I'll do it."

"No, I can't keep fighting for us anymore. I can't be alone in this, like how he has left me to deal with everything by myself." I look at Taylor, my hands fisted on my lap. "God, I'm *so pissed* at him, Tay. He just left. He didn't give us a chance to talk this through. Even if we were supposed to end, didn't I deserve closure? *What the fuck is this?*"

Taylor's face darkens and her eyes narrow. "That's it. I'm going over there and kicking his ass." She stands up and I pull her back down.

"You know, he knew this would happen, but I wouldn't listen to him. So, if he wants to pull away, it's his right. But still, couldn't we have at least talked about this? That's what mature people do, right?"

My heart pounds, each thump painful in my chest, and I struggle to get the next words out. "If w-we are meant to be together, he *has to* choose me for himself this time. I won't force him anymore."

I shake my head and Taylor folds me in her arms. Closing my eyes, I whisper, "But I can't let him lose his dream over this."

My lips tremble and I let out a rough exhale.

I need to set him free.

It's the right thing to do. I feel it deep inside my soul. Despite my fury toward him, my love for him is too deep and I can't bear to see him languishing away after watching everything he cares about getting destroyed in front of him.

I pull back from Taylor's embrace and look at my girls, my hand gripping my shirt. "He has been living for everyone else around him, but he's dying inside. Ryland deserves to have his dream. He deserves to be happy. Despite his issues, he's a good man."

"Ryland is so lucky to have you." Grace's eyes mist with moisture.

"Fucking lucky bastard," Taylor agrees.

We fall silent as I blot out my tears with a tissue. I've had two weeks to mope around in my apartment as my life burns up in flames around me. It's time to stop and get my ass back up from the floor.

As much as I know the hole in my chest will never heal, the waves of agony destroying everything in its path, I need to put one step in front of the other, to move toward a future that now seems so uncertain and gray.

Mr. Roberts's words echo in my mind. *Even if the road is hard and the skies are gray, you're bravely walking forward, one step at a time, and one day, you'll find yourself on top of the mountain, the sun shining on your face, and you'll look down and be amazed at how far you've climbed.*

Yes, I'll scale this mountain if it's the last thing I do.

"Don't you have the meeting with the dean soon, Millie? What are you going to do then?" Belle asks.

"I'm going to save Ryland from himself."

CHAPTER 49

THE STARES AND WHISPERS are rampant, and I pull the lapels of my wool coat tighter against my body as I focus my attention on the cement path, wet from this morning's dew.

"That's her, Adrian Scott's sister, right?"

"Do you think she really fucked Professor Anderson?"

"What does *he* see in her? She looks so average."

I try not to pay attention to them, to the students huddled in groups, their cell phones pointed at me, no doubt trying to take photos to post online or sell to gossip rags. Nausea swirls in my stomach and I feel an urge to cast up the cup of coffee I had this morning, the only thing I could stomach before I had to go to the appointment.

To meet with the dean. To tell my side of the story.

Security has increased in the neighborhood. The four campus gates are now locked down to prevent undesired visitors. Adrian sent me a driver and told me under no circumstance was I to walk or take public transportation anywhere. He wanted to assign me a bodyguard too, but I told him no. The press is vile, but not violent. And I don't want my life to change even more than it has already.

My phone vibrates in my coat pocket, and I take it out and stare at the incoming message.

Not him. *Of course, not him.*

Grace

> We'll get through this, Millie. Hang in there. We're always in your corner. You're a fighter, remember that. You got this.

Belle

> This will blow over soon. I know the media. Once the next scandal breaks, they'll forget all about you.

Taylor

> The damn vultures. If you let me, I'll give them a piece of my mind. And by the way, I have more goodies. I've stocked up in case you run out. Just let me know. Five pints of ice cream and all the gummy bears you could ever want are waiting for you.

I sniffle as I stare at the texts from my girls. Their unwavering support and love. I don't think I would've survived the last two weeks without them.

Just as I'm about to put away my phone, another text comes through.

Adrian

> I've taken care of the major newspapers. They won't be running stories about you anymore because I've promised that they will be the first to know once we're ready to give a statement. Gossip Times is next on my shit list.

Adrian

> I know you've told me not to fly over there, but that's not going to happen. After I get back from my business trip to London, I'm coming over to New York whether you like it or not. I worry about you, Millie. Let me see you, okay?

I was afraid Adrian was going to fly off the handle when the sordid stories came out, but he was surprisingly calm about everything, going first into damage control mode, which was what I'd expect The Shark to do. It's what makes him good at his job.

But I know my brother. He's no doubt beating himself up for not preventing these events and is probably seething over Ryland. It's better I see him in person before he does something to Ryland.

Millie

I'm fine, I promise. But if you want to come, I won't stop you. I miss you too, Adrian.

Slipping my phone back into my pocket, I quicken my pace to the tall white building. The Ivory Tower is what we call it amongst the students. Ignoring more pointed stares and whispers, I make my way to the dean's office.

His assistant, a redhead with sharp eyes who looks not much older than me, gives me a quick nod and says, "Dean Emery is expecting you inside. Good luck."

Swallowing the lump in my throat, I knock on the door.

Knock. Knock.

"Come in."

I blow out a deep breath, square my shoulders, and push open the door.

Dean Emery sits behind his large desk, a pair of glasses perched on his nose. He glances at me and closes his laptop before clasping his hands on top of the table. "Have a seat, Ms. Callahan."

Nodding, I sit down across from him. "You wanted to see me?"

"Yes, I think we have things to discuss, don't you agree?"

My pulse is thready in my ears. "I-I'm assuming you want to talk to me about Professor Anderson."

He dips his head in acknowledgment. "I know you've already spoken to a few of my staff members, but I want to hear the story from your side. But before we speak, please note everything we say here will be reported to the Ethics Committee. There's an open case based on the alleged accusations made by the press."

I twist my hands on my lap. I know what I say next will have far-reaching effects on Ryland's future. Teaching means so much to him.

It's the little slice of freedom he gives to himself. To take that away from him will be the worst cruelty, and he's such an excellent professor.

Despite everything, I need to protect him. Because I know the man won't protect himself. He is punishing himself enough as is.

"What do you want to know, Dean Emery?"

"Is there any truth to their allegations? Are you two involved?"

Fisting the hem of my sweater, I force myself to look up and stare at the shrewd gaze of the dean. My heart pounds inside my chest.

The world isn't in black or white. It is in shades of gray.

"Professor Ryland and I are good friends. Our families run in the same circles. My brother-in-law, Steven Kingsley, is engaged to Professor Ryland's younger sister, Grace. I think because of this relationship, the press may interpret certain actions as…"

"Unseemly?" The dean straightens up.

"Yes."

"So, you deny any romantic relationship between the two of you?"

Nausea coils inside my stomach and I clench my fists on my lap. "Regardless of what the allegations are, Professor Anderson has never given me preferential treatment in class. In fact, he was quite antagonistic with me at the beginning of the honors program. I think others in the class can attest to that."

Sweat beads on the back of my neck. Not lies, but not the whole truth.

"That's not what I'm asking you. Are you or are you not involved with Professor Anderson?"

"Do I admire him? Like him? Yes, I do, along with plenty of people at this school. But who wouldn't? That's why you hired him, right?"

"How do you explain the photos, then?"

"I've looked at this so-called proof before and the photos are so blurry, they may or may not be of him carrying a brunette. We did dance together at The Orchid, but like I said, our families run in the same circles."

He narrows his eyes at me and I hope he doesn't call me out on my evasion.

I forge on. "We've done nothing wrong and impacted no one. Forgive me for being rude, but these last two weeks have been extremely stressful for me, but I am *not* admitting to any wrongdoing."

"So, you are saying there's nothing untoward between the two of you?"

I stand up and look him straight in the eyes. "I'm saying there's nothing inappropriate in terms of the guidance I've received in class, nor has there been any preferential treatment."

"How do *you* know that? How can you guarantee that not to be the case?"

Heat rises to my face and I lean forward, a courage I didn't know I had coursing through me. "My grades speak for themselves, Dean Emery. You can review my academic performance before his class. They are all stellar because I've worked my ass off to achieve them. So no, there has been no preferential treatment, and my successes are my own."

Dean Emery remains silent, his face pensive.

My blood boils in my veins, and the next words pour out of my mouth. "The university would be making a big mistake by punishing Professor Ryland for any alleged relationship."

Tilting my chin up, I stare at the man who has the ability to crush the dreams of the man I love.

And I can't let him do that.

I *will* protect his dreams.

"The Andersons are an influential family and are known for their philanthropy and charitable donations, *especially* in their funding toward educational institutions." I hold his stare and his eyes widen at what I'm not saying aloud.

"Any family that famous is bound to have unsubstantiated rumors from the press every now and then. Professor Anderson is an excellent businessman and an even more brilliant professor. Please tell the Ethics Committee that. I like to think they'll make the right decision."

A knowing glint appears in the dean's eyes, and his lips twitch. "So, you are saying, Ms. Callahan, you deny all the allegations."

"Nothing untoward has happened in his role and guidance as my professor. He's an excellent professor, and if you don't believe me, you can poll the class or check out his ratings on the Rate My Professor websites. I have nothing further to add."

Dean Emery contemplates my answers, and the room is silent except for the sounds of my breathing and the ticking of my watch, but I force myself to remain still.

"You're in love with him," he murmurs. This is a statement, not a question.

My eyes burn as tears threaten to break free. A lump forms in my throat.

"He doesn't love me back." I let out a shaky sigh. "And that's what matters."

Because if he loves me, he wouldn't be doing this to me. He wouldn't be leaving me to deal with everything alone.

But I'm a fighter, and I'll fight for him, even if he doesn't deserve me.

"Very well, Ms. Callahan. You may go now."

— ◆ —

Adrian buries his face into his hands, his fingers tugging his thick dark hair as Emily, his wife, and Steven's older sister, comes back from the kitchen with a tray of hot tea. We're in Dad's apartment on the outskirts of the city for a long overdue family meeting.

Emily smiles and mouths, "You got this," before retreating to the kitchen, no doubt to give us some privacy.

"God, I'm such a colossal failure," Adrian groans into his palms. "How the fuck did I miss all of this? I thought you were stressed because of school because I know how hard you push yourself to get the best grades possible."

He lifts his head and stares at me with those startling sky-blue eyes of his. "And the entire time you were out here, dealing with this all by yourself? Falling in love, getting your heart broken by that bastard," he seethes, his eyes flashing in anger. "I'm going to break every fucking bone in his body."

"Adrian, no, that's not what happened. I told you before, if anything, I was the one who pursued him."

"He should've said no! He's my age! He should've known better!" Adrian stands up, his jaw clenching. "Why didn't you tell me, Millie? Why didn't you talk to me?"

"I knew what we were doing was wrong...so I kept it a secret," I whisper.

I clasp one trembling hand on top of the other and look at him and Dad, who is sitting silently in the armchair near us, his head hung low.

I've disappointed them.

A weight settles on my chest. It's the feeling I've tried to avoid for so long because I want everyone around me to be happy.

But then I think of what I told Ryland when he confessed about his guilt toward Maxwell. I told him the people who loved us would want us to be happy.

And I realize I've been preaching something I don't practice, and I'm the worst culprit out of everyone.

The heaviness increases, smothering my lungs. I want to deflect, to paste on a fake smile, to do everything I used to do, so I can see the smiles of relief on the faces of my loved ones.

But I won't hide anymore. Perhaps the whirlwind is over between Ryland and me, but I'll live. I'll survive and be stronger. A fucking damn fighter.

And I'll be honest for once.

"And frankly, I've gotten used to holding in everything for most of my life. I couldn't tell you or Dad because I couldn't stand to see either of you being worried about me!" The words rush out from my lips, smashing open the box holding all my secrets inside for so long.

My nose crinkles and my voice is hoarse, but I continue, "After Mom died, neither of you have been the same, and I don't expect you to be."

I look at the kind man who has tried his damned best to raise us as a single father while navigating an unfathomable loss. "Dad, you were buried in your cups for those first few years and Adrian and I were worried sick about you. We lost one parent, and we couldn't lose you too. So, I had to be good. I had to be happy. I had to come home and tell you only the good things and never the bad."

Dad's eyes shine with tears and his lips tremble. I want to take back the things I'm saying because I know they're hurtful, but I persist.

"And then one day you started getting out of bed earlier. You ate breakfast with me. Sometimes, you'd take me to the park. I'd hear your laughter. And I knew I needed to do whatever I could to keep that smile on your face. Don't you see? I *couldn't* tell you anything! I was so afraid you'd slip back and be depressed again."

Swiveling my head toward Adrian, I choke out the next words. "And Adrian, you were so angry at the world. You couldn't see the beauty of *anything* around you. You only saw darkness. You were driven by the need to take revenge against our grandfather for abandoning Mom, leaving her with no means to get the proper health care. And you had broken up with Emily at that point and were just in such a dark spiral."

I let out a ragged sigh. "You couldn't even help yourself. How could you help me? A little girl so much younger than you, someone who needed her mom as well! And now, you've finally found your happily-ever-after with Emily."

Placing my hands on his, I say, "I've never seen you so happy before. The light in your eyes. Your smile. I love you, brother, and I never want you to feel guilty about the past because you didn't cause it. It was just a tragedy. A shitty game of dominos. You've been through enough. You've taken care of us the best you could. I don't see the need to burden you anymore with things you can't change."

The room is silent, and the mahogany grandfather clock, still marred by the long scratch I carved into the wood accidentally as a ten-year-old, ticks loudly in the corner.

I blow my nose in a tissue and turn toward them again.

"I know now I should've told you guys because we're a family and families support each other. I'm sorry."

Adrian growls and crushes me to him. His voice is rough as he rasps, "No, I'm the one who should be sorry."

He exhales. "I'm so sorry, Millie. So sorry you had to deal with everything alone because you thought we weren't strong enough to handle it. I should've done more. I should've gotten my head unstuck from the sand and looked at you. I should've noticed."

His eyes are glassy as he swipes a tear from my cheek. "From now on, promise me, if you encounter problems—work, academics, men," he scoffs at the last one, "you come to me, okay? I promise you, I'll listen. You *never* have to hide from me."

"Francine would be so proud of you, little Millie," Dad says, his eyes red. "Your strength, your positivity, your fearlessness are all from her."

He walks over and wraps us both in a hug. "I love you so much, and like your brother said, I'm so sorry for neglecting your feelings for so long. I should've done better and I *need* to do better. Please forgive me." He presses a kiss on my temple.

I let out a wobbly smile and stare at the two men I love. The two men I know will always be on my side, no matter what.

Perhaps romantic love won't work out, perhaps the whirlwind has ended, but true family will always stay with you.

That night, in the peaceful quiet of my childhood bedroom, I sit on top of my twin bed and stare at the dark skies outside the window. There's a blanket of smog in the air tonight, hiding the stars behind an inky backdrop.

I wonder what he's doing right now.

A fresh torrent of blood seeps out from the open wound in my heart, a wound I suspect will never be healed.

Placing a sheet of stationery on top of my hardcover copy of *Wuthering Heights*, I stare at the floral design with a tiny yellow bird perched on a branch. I uncap my pen and write.

Dear Ryland,

There's not a day that passes by without me missing you. Sometimes, it'll be seeing the fresh yellow daffodils at the florist or even something as mundane as smelling the scent of oranges. I walk around campus and imagine the dark shadow of you storming down the courtyard or in the halls, your energy sucking the oxygen out of every space you occupy. The other day, I saw these curious birds, a blue one with a purple sheen, and I thought of you then.

Do you think of me? Do you miss me like I miss you?

Despite everything—the press, the gossip, the finger pointing and furtive whispers from strangers on the streets—I don't regret anything.

Being with you was the happiest time of my life. It was the only time I truly felt seen, heard, and understood. And I realize I'm also culpable to our circumstances because I haven't been honest with the people around me as well. And it's time to change that, to be true to myself for myself and also for the people who love me.

My only regret is, because of me, you may lose everything you care about.

A relationship takes effort from both sides. Both of us have to be invested in our tomorrows and perhaps, because I'm so madly in love with you, I haven't realized the imbalance in our relationship. I always wanted more, and yet, you were always more reserved.

I won't ask you to give me another tomorrow anymore. I won't force you to make this decision for my sake.

I only wish for your happiness because you deserve to live for yourself. Freedom is at your fingertips. You just need to reach for it.

Love always, Millie

Clutching the letter close to my chest, I stare into the starless night, thinking of him, the man I'll miss with every breath I take.

CHAPTER 50

"That's it. Get your sorry ass dressed and we're taking you out. You've been at this for the entire day, and you look like a fucking mountain man."

Rex tosses a towel at me as I throw punch after punch at the heavy bag in the boxing gym inside The Orchid. He and Ethan are standing at the sides of the padded mat, staring at me with concern.

It's either this or holing myself up in my apartment and thinking about her.

Which I have. Almost non-stop for the last few weeks, and I realize the pain isn't going away. I miss her with every atom in my body, every ounce of my soul. The pain festers and spirals in the middle of the night as my mind is filled with images of the sweet woman with the softest kiss and keenest eyes. The woman who loves every inch of my corrupted soul.

I've tossed and turned in my bed each night, desperately trying, and failing, to fall asleep. Whenever I manage to doze off, I'll wake up with my face always buried in the pillow she slept on, my lungs trying to breathe in a whiff of her jasmine, but the scent is fading by the day, the once warm bed is now another lonely, cold prison for me.

My family has visited. Steven and Charles have attempted to knock some sense into me, saying Millie wouldn't want to see me like this. Lana has taken over cooking meals for me, saying a home-cooked meal from a loved one is always better than food from Michelin restaurants or meals prepared by my personal chef, because it contains her love for me.

After being placed on administrative leave, Jacob has left me multiple messages on my phone that I haven't listened to. I've taken time off from Fleur. The less attention I draw to the company, the better right now. From what I know, there is a temporary pause on the IPO because of the scandal, but my family is working to get it back on track.

My mind drifts to the tenured professorship, another beautiful dream now vanished into thin air and the loss feels visceral, like my arm being carved out from my body. Emails ping incessantly from my laptop, but I haven't had the fortitude to go through them.

And Millie—I see her texts and missed calls and each time, I have to fight every impulse to call her back. Because I know if I do, I'll succumb to my desires once more. Because my soul needs her more than anything. As if I haven't caused enough damage to her already.

I've asked Grace to keep an eye on her for me, to make sure she's all right. I've also requested one of the men from our security team to look after her from afar in case the press gets rowdy.

But I need to stay away.

I've tried hiding my sorrows from everyone, but the pain and remorse are relentless, a strong riptide carrying me back into the turbulent seas. I've created a mess my family has to deal with now, and it's all because I didn't have better self-control.

No one would've been hurt if you had just stayed away, Ryland. You're undeserving of the people you love.

And so, since eight this morning, I've been at the gym, hitting the punching bag in front of me like it's my worst enemy.

Like it's myself.

After taking off and tossing my black boxing gloves to the ground, I towel off the rivulets of sweat dripping down my face. I'm sure I look like a disaster with my beard untrimmed and untamed, my skin fucking pale because I haven't stepped into the sun in the last two weeks.

But I can't bring myself to care.

Wincing, I slowly unfurl the hand wraps, revealing blistering red knuckles, swollen to almost twice their normal size.

"Shit, Ryland. Why are you doing this to yourself?" Ethan murmurs, eyeing the sores on my hands as we walk toward the locker room. "Come on, it's the press. They're ridiculous. That's nothing new. We'll weather this. We're the Andersons. A little tarnish on our name won't hurt us. It's not your fault."

Loathing. Hatred. Guilt. Anger. Worry.

And pain. So much fucking pain.

The storm never ends.

"I'm a fuck-up. If it weren't for me, everything would go along fine. Our reputation, our legacy…everything is now at risk because of my selfishness. I don't deserve you guys or the family and grandfather is probably rolling in his grave."

"Bullshit!" Rex retorts, "That's fucking bullshit right there. I get it, I really do. The pressures of being part of this family is enough to drive anyone crazy sometimes. Maintaining the stiff upper lip and upholding our family name. You've tried your best, but you're human too. Everyone is allowed some mistakes."

He points to himself. "I'm the family fuck-up, and you can't take that title away from me, B."

With that parting comment, he pushes me into a shower stall and turns the water into the temperature of the Arctic. "Now get your ass cleaned up and come back out. We're taking you somewhere."

✦

Half an hour later, Ethan pushes me into the backseat of his SUV and even tries to fasten my seatbelt for me. The damn guy acts like he's a suburban dad when he's the youngest male of our family. Rex gets into the front passenger seat as Ethan starts the car and exits the underground parking garage.

"Where are you guys taking me?" I place my forehead on the cool window, watching the golds and reds of streetlights and taillights streak past me.

"Floyd Bennett Field. There's a race tonight and Maxwell and the other guys are meeting us there," Ethan responds.

"You sure you want me behind a wheel tonight?" I snort.

"For Christ's sake, you aren't going to drive. Not over my dead body," Rex retorts, his eyes meeting mine when he twists over in his seat and glares at me. "We at least have to get you out of the building, B. Small steps. I hate to see you like this."

I don't respond. I just stare into the night and watch the wind swaying the trees, my eyes eventually closing as I drift off into an uneasy sleep where I'm running in the endless fields, the breeze caressing my face, a sweet voice laughing in front of me, a flutter of long brown strands in my peripheral vision.

"Wake up, we're here."

Rex shakes me in what feels like a few minutes later, but I know time must have elapsed as I hear the loud cheers from the crowds gathered at the abandoned airfield outside.

The smell of burned rubber is acrid as flashy cars swivel onto the large stretch of land then screech to a stop at the end of the airstrip.

Girls in short leather skirts and even skimpier tops, like it's the middle of summer as opposed to the beginning of spring, wave around flags as people rush toward the drivers getting out of their cars.

I can smell the excitement, the fear, the adrenaline in the air, but I can't feel an iota of...anything.

Following my brothers toward the vehicles, I ignore the hollers of the crowd, who no doubt recognize me even though I look like a caveman with my facial hair and T-shirt and jeans attire.

Maxwell's familiar silhouette steps out of the winning car and is met with shrieks and cheers. He's walking in our direction with the swagger of someone who has just won the street race we organize quarterly for other rich people who have no care for their lives. There's a sharpness in his eyes as they sweep through the crowd and land on the three of us.

A muscle twitches in his jaw, and he quickens his strides. I see the black-haired, tall silhouette of Steven and the unmistakable blond hair from Charles right behind him.

He reaches me a few seconds later.

"Good. You came out." Maxwell cracks his knuckles.

Smack.

His fist flies to my face, knocking the air out of my lungs, and my vision swirls.

"Maxwell!" Steven gasps in horror and he leaps forward to hold back my twin, who looks like he wants to follow that punch with another hook.

"Your painting hand!" Ethan's eyes widen in shock as Maxwell shakes out his right hand, which he's usually careful with because the man loves his art.

"What the fuck, dude? You said to bring him out so he can get some fresh air, not to beat the shit out of him," Rex yells.

The sharp pain spirals from my jaw to the rest of my body, and I heave in mouthfuls of oxygen. The black dots clear from my eyes. I wipe my mouth and find my hand streaked with blood from a cut on my lip.

"Keep them coming." I motion to Maxwell. *I deserve it.*

His eyes flash, and he shucks off his leather jacket in a swift motion. The crowd is converging on us now; some folks with their cell phones held high.

"If any of you *dares* to film anything, your membership to The Orchid will be revoked and you'll be looking over your shoulder for the rest of your life," Ethan growls and hulks toward the nosy interlopers. "Now *get out of here.* There's nothing to see."

"I'm standing here, Maxwell. I won't fight back."

Maxwell charges me and slams into my chest, knocking me onto the pavement. He straddles my torso and rains his fists on my chest, each jab and hook hitting directly on target.

My body flinches at each punch, the pain sending tears to my eyes, but my body and mind must have disconnected, because I find the strangest urge to laugh.

Delirious chuckles rip from my lips as I flinch under him, my hands not blocking his assault.

"Fuck. You guys, stop it. What are you, fifteen? This doesn't solve anything," Charles hollers while prying a furious Maxwell off me.

Maxwell shakes Charles off, stalks back, and stands over me, his penetrating eyes boring into mine.

He shakes his head in derision. "You know, Ryland, I'm not upset you fell in love with a woman. Someone who happens to be a student. I'm actually fucking happy for you, because you get to do something I want to do but *can't!*" His eyes are wild, his chest stretching the confines of his black T-shirt.

He spits on the ground and continues, "What I'm so fucking disappointed with is how you handled this situation. Instead of facing the problem like a man, you chose to hide. You left the crap for all of us to clean up instead of coming to us for help. You left *your woman* to deal with the press all by her fucking self! That is *not* how Anderson men are raised!"

Maxwell leans down, his teeth flashing in a snarl. "We are your family. There's nothing you say that'll make us think anything less of you. Yes, our reputation and the company are important, but nothing is more important than the *people* in this family."

His nostrils flare, the anger pouring out of him in torrents. "I knew you were going through things. I tried giving you space so you'd come talk to me. I tried pleading with you to tell me what was bothering you. But no, you decided to mope and become this martyr...*for what!*"

He heaves out a deep breath. "I don't pity you. I've never resented you for being the second-born, never once blamed you for that stupid boar attack. I've always, *always* wanted you to live your best life, your *happiest* life because I love you, brother."

Ethan sighs, his hand clasping my shoulder and giving it a quick squeeze, as if to support me.

Maxwell shakes his head. "I had to learn from Grace and Tay how you felt about working at Fleur. How you were suffocating because you hated your job. How you were desperate to be in academia but never had the guts to tell us. And now, with the scandal and the press breathing down our backs, the IPO hanging by a thread, you chose to hide. You're a fucking coward, Ryland Anderson, and I don't feel sorry for you. At. All!"

He leans down and grabs the collar of my shirt. "Do you know the woman you love is suffering too? I've kept tabs on her because she doesn't deserve this anymore than you do. Grace and Tay have been keeping her company. Do you know she cries herself to sleep and yet, she's strong enough to face the whispers, the murmurs, the questions from the press each day? You don't deserve her, Ryland."

I don't. That much is true. "I had to leave her, Maxwell. Let the press think I'm the bad guy. Eventually, this will blow over and she can continue with her life and achieve her dreams and—"

"Who the fuck made you the arbiter of her hopes and dreams? Who gave you the right to decide for everyone else?"

His chest heaves from exertion as he stabs his finger at my chest. "When you decide to be a fucking man about all this, come find me. Until then, I'm so *extremely* disappointed in you."

Without another word, he turns around and stalks back toward the car he exited from.

Rex lets out a low whistle. "Damn. I wouldn't want to be his kid when he becomes a dad later. He's got the whole parental disappointment thing down pat."

My lips twitch in an effort to smile, but everything just hurts like hell.

Steven motions to Maxwell. "I'm going with him to make sure he doesn't do anything stupid." He looks at me. "Ryland, we love you, man. He loves you. I think the stress of the IPO stall has been getting to him. Things will be okay. Hang in there. We'll fix this."

He hurries toward my twin.

I slowly sit up, my head feeling very much like the punching bag from the gym earlier today, an incessant ringing reverberating in my ears.

Be a fucking man. Maxwell's words echo in my mind.

I look at the guys to find Ethan's brows pinched, his lips curving in a small, reassuring smile, Rex pulling at his hair, his devil-may-care attitude nowhere to be seen, Charles letting out a deep sigh and patting me on my shoulder.

They may be disappointed. They may be angry. But they haven't left. The family is still intact. The company is still running without me.

Be a fucking man.

CHAPTER 51

"THANKS FOR MEETING WITH US, Millie," Lana says before wrapping me in a hug, her rose perfume wafting in the air. "I know it was last minute."

This morning, Lana texted me out of the blue, asking if I could meet with her and a few others at The Menagerie within The Orchid in the afternoon to discuss strategy. We've met a few times after Grace and Taylor found out their connections to the Anderson family.

As of this morning, the Ethics Committee still hasn't ruled on the case yet and I have no idea if my conversation with Dean Emery did any good, so it makes sense the Anderson family wants to play offense in this situation.

I squeeze her back as she ushers me through the intimate lounge decorated like a scene from the rainforest, with lush greenery and delicately painted gold vines on wallpaper, luxurious velvet sunken seating, pendant lighting that can double as artwork.

Pausing before I step through the open door of a private room, I say, "Lana, I want to apologize to you and your family for causing so much heartache for you all. I know a relationship takes two people, and this is not all on me, but the fallout has impacted everyone."

"Nonsense," a deep voice murmurs from inside the room.

Maxwell stands at my arrival with the same impeccable Anderson manners I've seen his brother display before. His bearing is tall, his hands behind his back, looking very much like the mysterious frigid king the press calls him, because he guards his privacy like Fort Knox protects its gold, and he never lets photos of him be published. Another tall, dark-haired man with a scar on his face stands next to him.

"My brother is damn lucky to have you. Judging from your actions and how you're handling everything, he's a fool to let you go."

He flashes me a wry smile and in a split second, he looks like Ryland with the same sardonic tilt of the lip as if he can't believe he's experiencing a positive emotion.

"Thank you."

"Please come in. This man," he motions to the person next to him, "is Elias Kent. He handles the personnel for the Rose floors, among...other things."

My mouth drops open and I quickly shut it. I may be a sheltered college student, but *everyone* knows of Elias Kent, the alleged crime boss who rules the underground.

Elias grins, no doubt an effort to make himself appear less threatening, as if anything can shake off the lethality in his green eyes and the alertness in his frame. It's pretty much like staring at a lion attempting to smile at you.

Lana and I take our seats as Maxwell presses a button on the round table. A minute later, an attendant appears, bringing us a cart filled with various refreshments, from hot coffee to juices, bottled water, and trays of fruits and nuts.

Maxwell quirks a brow at me.

"W-Water is fine."

Wordlessly, he uncaps a bottle before handing it to me. Then he pours coffee from a carafe into a cup.

"Black, like your soul." He smirks, handing the cup to Lana, who rolls her eyes.

After everyone is settled, he begins, "We want to form a strategy to deal with the press and save Ryland from himself. Elias is here because he has information for us and insists on butting his nosy self into our business."

"You'll thank me later," Elias murmurs while stirring the coffee in his cup.

"On the IPO front, we have a statement prepared to be released on Monday. Dad will come out of retirement to face the press. He is a much-loved member of the Anderson family and is a powerful leader, so his presence will soothe the waters," Lana says.

She tucks a curl of dark hair behind her ear and continues, "Not to mention, we've just received a clean audit opinion we can share with the public as well. With our statement and Dad's support, the IPO should proceed without issue. Then, in a week or so, after the dust settles, we'll get Ryland in front of the cameras again."

"I'll be working in the background with the investors and assuaging any concerns they may have," Maxwell adds. "What we need from you, if you agree, is to issue a statement of your own to the press as well, because they are waiting for you. And if you're open to it, we can prepare that today with Lana's help."

I nod. This makes sense. I've been dodging the press left and right since the scandal broke a few weeks ago and I know I'll eventually need to say something to get them to drop the subject.

Elias is quiet until this point. He clears his throat and leans forward. "I'm here today because I may have done something without your permission, but I can't stand by and let that idiot lose everything because of some bullshit. I owe him and you, Maxwell, one."

Maxwell lifts one brow. "What did you do, Elias?"

Elias turns to me and asks, "Millie, I've seen your transcripts. Straight-A student, very impressive."

I don't even want to ask him how he got his hands on my records.

His lips curve up into a soft smile. "How do you feel about graduating earlier?"

"Huh?" *What on earth?*

"I may have paid a visit to Jacob Emery. It seems like you have enough credits to graduate in the fall if it weren't for the Education Honors Program."

I nod. *Where is he going with this?*

"And you're already accepted into the Cornell PhD program, which is the best in the country. I assume you want to go there?"

"Yes, but they can rescind the acceptance if I don't finish the honors program. It's one reason I've worked so hard in the program this year."

He waves me away. "Millie, if I may...the real world is seldom black and white." *Tell me about it. Better yet, tell Ryland about it.*

His voice deepens, his tone serious, and he says, "Having power and influence are gifts to be wielded sometimes. It may not be fair, but then again, the world isn't fair. Use the influence for what's right and there's no shame in that."

My heart thumps rapidly in my rib cage. I stare at the enigmatic man in front of me and want to shrink away from his perceptive gaze. It's like he knows my ambivalence and avoidance of using my connections when facing the world, and how I've attempted to hide my identity as Adrian's sister to those who know me.

Elias smiles in a self-assured way, a chess master calmly moving the pieces on the board and anticipating his opponent's next move.

"And we know what's the greater good here and what's right. So, finishing the honors program before or after a small little piece of paper is issued...all semantics. The dean has agreed that with your impeccable grades, stellar volunteering and extracurricular activities, exceptions can be made. The exception being...your graduation certificate will be dated December fifteenth of last year."

"What does this have anything to do with anything?"

Elias leans back and takes another leisurely sip of coffee, his posture relaxed as if he's talking about the weather and not my future.

"Well, as of your graduation, you're no longer under the university's regulations. So, let's say you have a good relationship with a family acquaintance, a certain man who was your professor in the past. You graduated with honors and over the holidays, you and this professor became acquainted even more so outside the confines of a classroom. Then things sparked, and you entered a relationship in the spring. Even though you had already graduated, you still audited the honors program in the winter and spring quarters because you are voracious about learning. Interesting timing? Perhaps. Breaking any rules? No."

I blink a few times. Remind myself to take a breath. Blink a few more times.

His words echo in my brain. Is he saying—

"Yes, you can have your cake and eat it too," Elias answers my unasked question. He adds, "You have a bad poker face. Do us all a favor and don't gamble."

"B-But, Cornell? And what about Ryland's tenure?" My mind struggles to catch up with all this new information and strategies that have never even crossed my mind.

"The dean had a chat with Cornell, and your acceptance will remain standing. Just make sure to finish...or...audit the rest of the class in the honors program. Accumulate the knowledge," his startling green eyes glint as he stares at me, "for intellectual curiosity's sake."

"And Ryland's tenure?"

"Well, if you've already graduated, I don't see why his honorary PhD and path to tenure will change. Ryland Anderson is an exceptional member of society and, frankly, a damn good man. Also, an excellent professor, from what I've heard." Elias's voice thickens at the end. "If any of this goes back to him, I'll deny saying that to my dying breath."

He stands up, slips on his suit jacket, and pulls out a gold and silver object from his vest pocket. A lighter?

He flicks in on and off. On and off. The clicking sound is loud in the quiet room.

Then he slides it back into his vest and buttons his jacket.

He stares at Maxwell and murmurs, "Don't worry. You don't owe me any favors. This one is on the house."

Then, without another word, he strides out of the room quietly and efficiently, a phantom disappearing into the shadows once more.

"Fuck, of all the things he was going to say, I didn't expect that," Maxwell mutters.

"And he found the employee who took the photo of you two as well. That's been dealt with," Lana murmurs, her eyes still gazing at the closed door.

She turns back to us. "I swear, we've known that guy for a long time and I still can't ever figure out what he's going to do next."

She heaves out a loud sigh and looks toward the ceiling. "Ryland. He's such a stubborn asshole sometimes. I swear, his biggest enemy is himself. Why can't he see he doesn't have to do everything by himself? There's no challenge too big for us to solve together."

A burst of warmth seeps through my chest and spreads to my limbs. I stare at the siblings before me, all clearly worried about their brother and love him with all their hearts.

You're so damn stupid, Ryland. What were you so afraid of? Asking for help? Disappointing the people who love you?

I murmur, "He's so lucky to have all of you in his corner."

Lana smiles, her gray eyes twinkling under the pendant lighting. "Ryland is lucky to have you, Millie."

My heart twists. *But it wasn't enough, and all dreams have to come to an end.*

"Thank you for taking care of him and giving him the shelter he needs," Maxwell adds. "Let's hope he gets the stick out of his ass soon."

———— ✦ ————

"And that's all there is to it, Ms. Callahan?" a blonde reporter from CBC news, Maggie O'Farrell, asks as she clasps her hands over the small marble table at a coffee shop near campus.

The cameraman pans his equipment toward me, and I try to ignore him. The room suddenly feels stifling, and I feel my face heating. They have the entire coffee shop reserved and locked down for this exclusive interview Lana secured for me.

I blow out a slow and even breath and smile at Maggie in front of me. The weight of his pendant sits reassuringly under my blouse. *I got this. I've rehearsed this with Lana a few times already.*

"Yes, that's all there is to it. I graduated from NYUC back in December and Ryland and I are close family friends. He was extremely upset when he saw the other reporters accosting me that day in class, as he has younger sisters of his own, and he is also friends with my brother, Adrian Scott."

I sit up straighter. *"Having power and influence are gifts to be wielded sometimes. It may not be fair, but then again, the world isn't fair. Use the influence for what's right and there's no shame in that."* Elias's words reverberate in my mind, and I realize I can't live life being afraid of how others may perceive me because of my connections to my brother. The right people will be with me because of me. My brother is an important part of my life and I refuse to hide this any longer.

"That's understandable. From the footage I've seen, it was very rowdy that day in the classroom," Maggie prods.

"It definitely was. I'm a very private person, so I didn't know what to do when the paparazzi converged in front of my face. Needless to say, my brother was furious when he heard about what happened."

Maggie pales a smidgen. No one wants to piss off The Shark. She forces out a chuckle. "Well, can't blame the older brother for being protective. I have one myself."

"So you understand why Ryland stepped in that day."

"But what about the photos?"

I shrug my shoulders. "I don't know anything about them. They were so grainy—I could barely recognize Ryland if the press didn't mention it to me."

Maggie nods. "So, to clarify, are you saying you and Ryland Anderson aren't in a relationship?"

A heaviness settles over me and sinks its talons into my chest. At least this is the truth. I swallow and reply, "No. We're not in a relationship."

The rest of the interview goes as smoothly as Lana predicted. Maggie is thorough in her questions, but never too overbearing. The copious notes Lana provided covered all the interview questions and then some.

That night, as I sit on the bed with a paper and pen at the ready, I write my last letter to Ryland.

Dear Ryland,

I don't blame you for pushing me away. If I were you, perhaps I'd make the same decision. But I'd never lock you out.

The last few weeks have given me a lot of clarity. I realize I'm stronger than I thought I was. Facing the press, the rumors at school, the comments by trolls online, and I haven't broken. They haven't clipped my wings. Don't you see? Isn't this what you were afraid of, Ryland? Trapping me in a prison with you? Having me be a shell of my former self?

Whether you believe me or not, I'm capable of making my own decisions. I'll never let a relationship become all of me and kill me inside. I'll leave you without hesitation if it means I'm going to lose myself. I'll survive and thrive. That's who I am at the core.

You've carried the weight of the world on your shoulders, afraid of sharing your burdens with the people who love you—your family, friends...me.

But if there's anything I've learned in the last few weeks—you don't need to. You have so many people in your corner wanting to help you, to free you from the prison you've trapped yourself in. Sometimes, it's easier to stand in the shadow of guilt and fear, but you don't need to.

All you need to do is leave the shelter of your gilded bars.

Take a leap of faith.

I love you and I don't think there'll be a day when the feeling will ever cease. You're my whirlwind. But I realize I don't only want to stand in the storm and feel the pelting rain and harsh winds with you, I also want to stand in the sunshine, smelling the scent of flowers blooming in the spring with you by my side.

And if you can't do that, then I'll be on the sidelines cheering for you on your journey. But I'll continue to chase my dreams, climb the summit, and fight for my future, because I deserve that.

And I think you do too.

Spread your wings and fly, Ryland. Go chase your freedom. May my love be with you always.

Love, Millie

My fingers tremble as I set down the pen and climb out of bed. I walk to my desk and open my drawer to retrieve the packets of letters I've accumulated in the last two years—words sincerely written to my mom and him. I place this letter on top of the stack, take out a large envelope, and carefully place the stack inside.

Flicking on my phone on my desk, I swipe at the screen until I reach Grace's name, and I press call.

"Millie? How are you?" her sweet voice comes across the line seconds later.

My fingers graze the envelope, my heart pounding in a nervous rhythm because it knows pieces of it are stowed carefully inside this unassuming package.

"I'm fine, Grace. But can you do me a favor?"

CHAPTER 52

Ms. Callahan is doing well this week. Nothing unusual to note. The paparazzi calmed down after she gave an exclusive interview with CBC.

I STARE AT THE weekly update Matt Barnes provides me as part of his security surveillance of Millie to ensure she's safe. He also attached a link of Millie's interview with Maggie. This set up has all the markings of Lana's handiwork on it.

Jitters flow through my veins and I press play.

"Thank you for being here today, Millie. Do you mind if I call you Millie?" Maggie asked, her hands curled around a ceramic cup.

"No, I don't mind," Millie responded.

Her blue eyes snared me through the screen, her luscious locks curled and arranged over one shoulder. Her hands were on top of the table, her fingers twisting and pulling at each other.

She was nervous, but from the way she sat with her shoulders straight, she tried to appear brave. She also looked tired, like she hadn't slept well in ages. Her smile didn't reach her eyes.

A sharp stab of guilt scores through my insides and Maxwell's words hurl themselves against my consciousness.

I left her to deal with this alone. I did this to her.

What the fuck was I thinking? How could I have been so stupid?

I thought I was doing right by her by staying away, but in retrospect, the right choice shouldn't leave everyone feeling miserable.

I should've felt relief and not this constant pressure on my chest, this relentless yearning for her which has only grown in time. In the last few weeks, I realized my desire to teach, to escape my prison, all faded to the background compared to my need for her.

She's my other half, and I threw her away because I didn't trust her enough to respect her decisions. I didn't respect her enough to work through our problems together.

I didn't fight for us.

My hands clench into fists as regret flows through my veins. Fuck, I don't deserve her. Maxwell was right.

Be a fucking man.

I'm going to get back up and win her back. I don't know how I'm going to do it yet, but if she is brave enough to face the world with her head held high, then I'm strong enough to do the same and ask for her forgiveness.

And if she refuses, then that's what I deserve.

A loud whirring noise disrupts the quiet of the cabin. The unmistakable sound of a helicopter. After a few minutes, the ruckus abruptly cuts off.

Knock. Knock.

Pausing the video, I look toward the door and frown. There shouldn't be anyone out here in my cabin in Bitterwater Valley, California. I'm not expecting any visitors.

Rolling up the sleeves of my gray Henley, I walk to the door and look through the peephole.

Quickly, I swing open the door.

"Maxwell and Steven," I murmur, stepping aside to let them in.

A third man strides into view. Dark hair, almost black. Sky-blue eyes. Chilly features. Animosity dripping from his gaze.

Adrian Scott, The Shark. I've met him a few times in the past and consider us casual friends. He has even infused some capital into our business, but now, I wonder if the friendship has come to an end.

Probably, Ryland. You'd do the same if someone broke Lana's heart like what you did with Millie.

Wordlessly, he enters the cabin and I close the door behind me.

"You look better, at least. Shaved your beard, made an effort to wear decent clothes," Maxwell comments from the leather sofa in the middle of the room by the stone fireplace.

Steven helps himself to a drink from the wet bar and offers the others refreshments. After a few minutes, the four of us sit in the large rustic living room, the silence sounding louder than thunder.

My laptop pings from the dining table off to the side and Maxwell's eyes dart to it before he furrows his brows at me.

"I'm replying to some overdue emails. Getting back into the swing of things. It's time for me to get my shit together," I reply.

He nods, clearly satisfied with my response.

"What the hell are you planning to do with my sister?" Adrian stands up abruptly and hauls me to my feet, his hand fisting the collar of my shirt. A vein pulses in his forehead and his lips twitch into a snarl.

"Millie asked me to leave you alone, but fuck it, I'll be damned if I don't find out your intentions myself."

He tightens his hold on me and gets in front of my face. "Do you love her? Or have you been playing games with her all this time?"

I must have a death wish because I snort and reply, "What? Are you going to call me out at dawn? A duel? Pistols or swords?" *Ryland, why are you being an idiot?* I can hear Millie whispering at me.

"Fuck, Ryland. Stop with your bullshit. I want to know too. Millie is a sweetheart and is like a sister to me as well," Steven says, his voice impatient.

Adrian's grip tightens and the collar of my shirt digs into my neck. My lungs fight for air, but I refuse to look away, refuse to back down and cower before him. If I get to wish one thing on those stupid shooting stars Steven prattles on about—something he got from Grace—I wish I could be with Millie, reputation and everything be damned.

I won't have Adrian doubting my feelings for her.

"I fucked up. I thought I was doing the best by her, but I was wrong." My answer comes out in a choked gasp and Adrian growls.

"Before you two kill each other, I want to let you know there's a way out of your dilemma...well, part of your dilemma," Maxwell murmurs from the sofa.

Adrian and I stare at each other for a beat. He abruptly lets go and stalks off to stand by the fireplace, his glower firmly attached to his face.

I heave in the much-needed oxygen and sit back down. "What?"

Maxwell cocks his brow. "If you weren't hiding out here, you'd have found out sooner."

"I was working, getting back on the horse, getting my shit together like you said." *And trying to figure out a way to atone for the colossal mistake I made.*

"I was hoping you'd be getting your shit back together closer to home."

"Does it matter where I am and what's this news you're talking about?"

"Millie graduated in December and because you and her are practically family courtesy of Steven's relationship with Grace," Maxwell motions to Steven, who has the audacity to look as smug as shit, "you spent time together in holiday gatherings and naturally, you two grew closer then. That's what those rumors are all about."

He takes a sip of his drink and continues, "Millie, being someone who loves to learn even after she graduated, decided to audit your class for the last two quarters for her own intellectual curiosity. No professor student regulations were broken because she had graduated before your relationship grew close and because no violations occurred, your honorary PhD and tenure track plans are still intact."

My mind spins. *What in the ever-loving bullshit is this?*

"What the fuck are you talking about?" My heart leaps to my throat and I pinch my wrist to see if this is some sort of crazy dream. A sharp but fleeting pain spears me.

Still hurts.

"And to think, last year, you changed the name of our chat group to 'Save Steven from Himself.' Well, I say it should be 'Save Ryland from Himself' this year." Steven chortles in the background.

Maxwell fills me in on the events from the last few weeks—Millie holding her ground with the dean to protect my reputation, Lana, him, and Elias meeting up with her, Elias's intervention behind my back with the dean, something I'm immensely grateful for even if I'll never tell him that or else his ego will grow bigger.

I stare unblinkingly at my brother, who is conveying problems and solutions like he's reciting the number of digits in pi, completely unruffled and the opposite of the livid guy who gave me a beating that night at the airfield.

"What about this trust issue I heard about?" Adrian asks, his eyes narrowed at me.

I blow out a breath. "Aside from catching up on work here, I've also been in contact with our lawyers, and they're researching solutions to unravel the trust as we speak."

Staring at him, I murmur, "I messed up. Big time. And I don't know if Millie will ever forgive me. But I figure I'll start by looking into the trust because it's about time I do something for myself and for her, if she'll ever take me back."

Adrian's eyes soften. "And you think you can unravel this shit?"

"They think it's possible, but it'll take hours of research and we'll need to work with Steven and Pietra Capital to move the trust assets around. But they're optimistic."

Maxwell leans forward, his voice thickening with emotions. "Don't you see what I've been trying to tell you all along? We're the Andersons and we look out for each other. You *never* had to go about it alone. I have faith in you figuring out the trust. And now, with the school situation settled, you can teach and do whatever you wanted to do all along."

Steven murmurs, "And if you choose to quit Fleur and the company needs a COO, I'm more than happy to step in. I've been at Pietra long enough. It's time for a change in scenery. Plus," he smirks, the arrogant King of Wall Street in full force, "I'm going to be family soon."

Maxwell lifts his wrist, the leather bracelet flashing under the daylight shining in through the windows.

"Let all that you do be done in love," he murmurs, reciting the inscription I've long since memorized.

"Maxwell. Steven." My throat tightens and my vision blurs.

This is what he said all along.

This is also what Millie said long ago as well.

I was too stubborn and set in my ways to see. Until now. And God, I hope it's not too late.

A shadow appears in front of me, and Maxwell hauls me to my feet. He pulls me in for a hug and slaps his hand on my back.

"You would've done the same thing for me," he whispers.

These are the same words he said when he was lying on the ground bleeding after he threw himself in front of the boar on the fateful day forever emblazoned in my mind.

Blinking rapidly, I clasp my twin tightly in my arms, my heart heavy and full at the same time.

After a few moments, he lets me go, gives me a wink, and saunters back to his seat.

"So, what are you going to do about Millie?" Adrian asks, his countenance much calmer than before. He rakes his hand through his hair, disheveling it, and lets out an exasperated sigh.

"I have one sister, and I've failed her too many times already. But I love her so much. She deserves the world."

He stares at me, his eyes narrowing. "She deserves to have a man willing to risk everything for her. A man who puts her first. Can you be that man?"

I look at him, my chest heavy with regret. "I *want* to be that man. If she'll ever forgive me for my stupidity."

Steven reaches behind him and retrieves a manila folder. "Grace got this from Millie. Millie wanted you to have it. Read the contents. Maybe they'll help you win her back."

He stands up and the other two men follow suit. The impromptu intervention is over. Steven opens the door and walks out into the sunlight toward the helicopter sitting a few feet away.

Adrian pauses when he reaches me. "Don't disappoint me, Ryland. Or else you'll feel the wrath of The Shark for the rest of your life."

I nod, giving my friend a squeeze on his shoulder. His eyes soften and he steps outside to join Steven.

Maxwell lingers behind and slaps me on my shoulder.

"Maxwell, the other night at the race, I'm sorry for being a disappointment—"

"Not all of us can be smart one hundred percent of the time. I may be cursed, but I clearly am the brains of the family." He grins. "Don't worry about it. Let bygones be bygones. I have your back...always."

After the guys leave, I carry the manila envelope to the wooden lounge chair on the porch. Taking a seat, I quickly unravel the fastening and reach inside to pull out a stack of letters bound with a binder clip.

The feminine swirls and beautiful penmanship. My breath lodges in my throat as I realize Millie has handed over pieces of her soul in these carefully written letters.

While my heart lives outside of me, residing next to hers now, she's returning the favor.

My pendant over her heart, her letters in my hand.

Dear Mom,

The skies are crying today and perhaps it's because I'm near you again, I feel its tears most intently. I don't think there's a timeline for grief or a way to fill the hole in my chest.

My eyes greedily absorb her words, my chest wrenching at the pain and heartache in those heavy presses of her pen, the depth of emotions in her sentences.

I flip to another letter.

Dear Mom,

I think he's the special someone for me, the man I told you before whose gaze sets me on fire. He's someone I feel an undeniable connection to. Someone worthy of the word "whirlwind." I think he hides his tattered heart behind a suit of armor, but he's hurting, just like me. And for the first time in my life, I want to heal him, because I think I understand him.

He sees me. The real me.

The words blur together and a burning sensation appears behind my nose.

She has seen my heart, scars and all, since the beginning.

Then, there are the letters she wrote to me.

Dear Ryland,

It seems fitting the first letter I write to you, one you'll never read because I'll never send it out, is on a stormy night.

The passion in her writing, the steadfastness in the black ink on white paper, no shades of gray to be seen.

I know you're pushing me away because you think that's what I need and I'm here to tell you one word: No.

A resounding no.

What I need is you. The rest is just noise.

Yours, Millie

I never heard her. I never listened. *The rest is just noise.* I allowed the noise to overtake the righteous beating of my heart, the surety and peace I felt in my soul whenever I was with her.

I flip through the letters like a madman, reading every single one of them, all the tears, the pain, the happiness, all little fragments of her laid bare at my feet. My little lark. My fighter in the skies.

Then I reread them again. And again. And again.

The woman I don't deserve and yet love with every cell in my body until my last breath on this earth.

A small flash of yellow flutters in my peripheral vision, and my attention snares on the unmistakable bright chest—the color of the daffodils she loves—with a stripe of black feathers in the middle.

The western meadowlark perches on the railing and scrutinizes me, much like that day long ago before everything began. It opens its beak and sings a beautiful, heartrending melody, one that snakes its way into the newly beating organ inside my chest.

His name is Ryland...and I think...he's my whirlwind.

This time, I'm the fighter, and I'll fight for us.

An hour later, I trek on the grass, my rifle slung over my shoulder as torrents of thoughts muddle my mind.

Regret is such a useless emotion.

Sweat drips down my forehead from exertion and I follow the set of tracks before me, belonging to the beast I know very well and have tried to conquer time and time again. I've found clarity when I hunted in the past, and I hope to do the same once more.

How can I make myself deserving of her again?

A twig snaps in the distance and leaves gently rustle in the breeze, which carries the fragrant scent of wildflowers blooming in spring. Clusters of orange poppies dot the grasses, swaying to the wind like dancers twirling on stage. In the distance, I see shadows sifting through the trees, most likely deer and other wildlife scattering away as they sense me in the midst.

The tracks on the ground are deeper and fresher now, and I slow my strides and crouch low, sensing the animal nearby. A rustle of the bushes pierces the calm, and for a moment, everything falls eerily silent.

Seconds later, an animal darts out into the open.

I freeze, my muscles coiled in tension, and time slows to a crawl when I see the imposing black shape of the beast.

The wild boar.

I slide the rifle down my shoulder and take aim.

For a brief millisecond, time freezes, the seconds suspended in an alternate dimension, and my heart seizes, my breath lodging in my throat as goosebumps prickle my forearms.

My finger perches on the trigger, but for some reason, I hesitate.

The boar munches on something on the ground before he stills, as if aware his life is hanging precariously by a thread. He shifts his legs and charges toward me before stopping a few feet away, his beady, black eyes staring into the barrel of my rifle.

And so, the hunter and prey square off once more, but this time, when I look into his eyes, I realize one thing with startling clarity.

The need to conquer the boar isn't there anymore. It belongs in the past...to a past version of me, someone who was much too hard on himself.

My heart slams itself against my rib cage, the prey inside me struggling to break free. My shoulders tighten before I expel the breath trapped in my throat, my rifle shaking in my unsteady hands.

As I stare at the boar mere feet away from me, a reflection of myself, I realize one thing.

It's time to let go. *Let bygones be bygones.*

The hammering of my pulse roars in my ears and slowly, I lower my rifle to the ground.

The boar kicks and digs its foreleg into the grass. It emits a loud grunt, then turns around and darts back into the thick bushes, disappearing from view.

I slowly stand up, my vision finally clearing, my surroundings coming into sharp focus. I finally feel the warmth of the sunlight hitting my skin, the comforting breeze wrapping me in a gentle embrace. I close my eyes and inhale deeply, letting the air seep into the deepest crevices in my lungs.

The smell of true freedom.

To conquer or be conquered.

This time, I know, not only am I still standing, I'm also free. And I know what to do next.

CHAPTER 53

CHEERS AND APPLAUSE ERUPT on the trade floor as Rex presses the green button to ring the infamous bell on the bell podium of the New York Stock Exchange. I smile, watching the live streaming of this monumental event on my phone as I sit in my town car heading toward Millie's apartment. This marks the successful initial public offering of Fleur Twilight as our stock goes live in markets, the goal we've been working toward for the last several years.

Rex laughs, excitement rolling off him in waves, and hugs my other siblings, minus Maxwell, because, true to form, he's avoiding the crowds and celebrating in the privacy of the estate, no doubt surrounded by paintings and listening to opera. My mind flits to the conversation I had with Rex last night.

"You aren't going to the ceremony?" Rex asked, his eyes widening in shock. "And you want *me* to ring the bell?"

I nodded. "I'm going to Millie's. I always go to her place every morning, and tomorrow will be the same."

"But it's the IPO! The thing you've worked your ass off for the last few years!"

I swallowed and shook my head. It was a pity how this realization came much too late. "Nothing is more important than her."

Rex looked at me with sympathy in his eyes. "Got it. Go get her. I hope she opens the door this time." He suddenly grinned and pumped his fists in the air. "Yes! Finally time for Mr. Sexy Anderson to shine."

I chuckle under my breath as I turn off the screen of my phone and look outside the windows, watching the throngs of tourists walking excitedly on the sidewalks.

The city brims with liveliness—from hot dog stands lining up street corners, couriers breezing by on their bikes. Businessmen frown at their phones as they stride down the sidewalk, weaving through crowds of people like second nature.

The city has a pulse of its own and for the first time in a long time, I feel the resonating beats inside me. But there's a gaping hole nothing can fill.

Millie.

I miss her so damn much.

As Lana predicted, once I flew back to New York after my brief hunting trip last week and met with Maggie for a follow-up interview to reiterate pretty much everything Millie had told her before, the paparazzi moved on to other topics and scandals.

Then, I got swept up in the madness of last-minute IPO preparation—board meetings, investor conferences, discussions with the underwriting banks and other top executives in the company.

But despite that, when I wasn't working or putting out fires, my mind was filled with memories of her. The woman who saved my career, my path to tenure, my dreams, my family's reputation, everything I thought I cared most about but now realize pales compared to her.

I've called Millie every night after dinner, but she hasn't picked up. My messages are left unanswered. I've visited her every morning before work, but each time, Belle will open the door, give me a sad smile, and say, "She needs some time. I think you owe her that, don't you?"

It's fitting—to experience a small fraction of what she must've endured the last month, when I thought I was saving her but was hurting her instead.

My phone chimes and my hand flies to my suit pocket to take it out, eager to see if it's her.

But it isn't. It's only an email from Jacob.

Ryland,

Because of the high profile of your family, the Ethics Committee expe-
dited your case and after reviewing our multiple interviews with Millie
Callahan and yourself, examining her transcripts and work products
from your class, and also considering the public interviews you both
made, they decided no transgressions occurred and your honorary
doctorate and tenure track would still stand.

However, it may take you one to two more years of exemplary behavior
before you're officially nominated for tenure. Take the summer off and
we'll talk before fall quarter begins.

Regards,

Jacob

His email is quickly followed by a text from his personal number.

Jacob

I can't say this over university email, but son,
please, for fucking sake, if you decide to pursue
a relationship with Ms. Callahan, wait another
month, will you? Let's put this to bed before you
give me another headache.

My lips twitch into a smirk as I imagine the number of new white
hairs I've given the poor man. Then, an anchor drops on my chest.
Regret, my new best friend, makes a reappearance.

I know apologies are insufficient as I make amends with everyone I've disappointed. But I'm no longer a coward, no longer only mired in my misery so much I'm blind to other people's pain.

I'm going to face the consequences—the good, the bad, and everything in between.

A sigh escapes my lips and I swipe to the social media post I uploaded to my account last night. It's a photo of the western meadowlark perched on a branch.

I can't name her or broadcast my love for her so blatantly, because it'll unravel everything she, my family, and the dean have done to save my career. But I hope she sees my daily posts and knows they are for her.

I'm no longer hiding, and she won't be in my shadows anymore...if she'll still have me.

Thump. Thump.

Clutching the small pot of flowers in one hand, I knock on Millie's door with the other and steel myself for another rejection, but I'm not giving up. Not anymore.

Muffled sounds of the IPO press conference on the television travel through the door. Someone is home.

Thump. Thump.

I knock again in case whoever is in there doesn't hear me the first time.

The television turns off and a heavy silence blankets the air.

She's there. I can feel her. I'm as sure of it as I am of my name.

"Millie?" Leaning my forehead on the cool door, I close my eyes. Sorrow lances through my insides, and my chest twists in pain. "Little lark, you're there. I know it. I can feel you."

More silence greets me and the vise around my heart tightens. I place my palm on the door, wishing I could turn back time, undo the damage I've done, and take back the heartache I've caused her.

"Please don't tell me I'm too late," I rasp. "Please, Millie. I was an idiot. A miserable, pathetic idiot. I know I don't deserve a second chance from you, but I'm asking for one, anyway. Please don't turn me away."

A few seconds pass by—a heavy, aching silence. Then, a soft sob travels through the door and I hear the clicking of the lock disengaging. The door slowly swings open and Millie stands before me, her eyes bloodshot, her nose tipped red, her hair haphazardly piled in a bun on top of her head.

She is still the most breathtaking woman I've ever beheld.

Gripping the flowers tightly in my hands, I stand before her and fight every impulse, every clamoring and desperate need inside me to haul her into my arms, to kiss her a thousand times, and to apologize for every tear I've caused her to shed.

Then, I want to repeat the process again.

"Ryland." My name comes out in a breathy whisper. "Aren't you supposed to be at the IPO press conference?" Her lips wobble and I feel her agony like a gut punch.

"Nothing is more important than you, Millie. What can I do to win you back?" My nose burns and my voice thickens. "P-Please. I'll do anything."

Her shoulders slump, and she shakes her head sadly. "I don't know. I-I'm scared, Ryland. My heart hurts so much because you left me when things got rough. You didn't talk to me; you didn't give us a chance to decide together. You took that decision away from me."

A sharp flash of pain strikes me in the chest at her words—too much regret and far too late to matter.

"I love you, Millie."

She flinches and wraps her arms around herself. Taking a deep breath, she looks up and stares at me with those beautiful, startling blue eyes. "I love you too, Ryland. I don't know if I'm even capable of falling out of love with you."

My heart stirs and my fingers dig harder into the ceramic pot as my body fills with desperation and trepidation.

"But how do I know if this isn't another impulse for you? Like how it was when we first got together at Noire, when I all but *f-forced*," her voice chokes up, "you into that position. I made an offer you couldn't refuse. What if things get rough again? How will I know you won't run away once more?"

"Millie, that's different, that's—"

She shakes her head vehemently. "Perhaps for you, it's different right now. After all, the obstacles you were so afraid of before were cleared...just as I predicted all along. But life is full of hurdles. Tomorrow, it may be something else. And my heart," she jams her index finger to her chest, "can't take any more of this pain. I've already lost too much, and I don't want to love another person just to lose him again later on."

She shrinks back into her apartment and my pulse clamors inside my ears. *I'm losing her.*

"Millie, *please*," I plea, my voice hoarse. I reach for her, but she holds out her hand to stop me. "*Please* give me another chance."

"I-I...I need to know you're sure of this, of us this time. Right now, my heart is filled with doubt."

She lets out an anguish-laden sigh. "I know that's not what you're looking for, but I can only tell you the truth. I'm sorry, Ryland."

Glancing away, I blink my eyes rapidly, attempting to dispel the burning sensation behind them.

I turn back to her and say, "Time will tell you the truth. You'll see. This isn't an impulse for me. You and I...it's the only thing I'm sure of, right down to the marrow of my bones."

Millie gives me a sad smile and backs into her apartment. "Goodbye, Ryland."

She begins to shut the door, but I stop her. I hand her the flowers. "At least take these. Pasque flowers. Your favorite. Maybe you can keep them along with the daffodils I got you yesterday. They'll thrive under your care, just like my heart beats only for you. I won't ever stop. I'll be back tomorrow."

She glances at the pot of purple flowers, her eyes shining with tears, and closes the door behind her.

The vise around my heart cinches and tightens, the pain so eviscerating I lean against the door for support. But minutes later, a renewed energy courses through my veins as I realize I have a lifetime to prove my love to her. If she still loves me, I still have a chance, and this time, I'm not letting her go.

I'm going to show her the surety of us, our destiny written in the storms, blossoming under the sun.

This is not a goodbye. You'll see, Millie. You'll see.

CHAPTER 54

IT'S BEEN ONE MONTH of Ryland coming by my apartment each morning like clockwork. Every time, he'll leave a small pot of flowers, or a bag of my favorite gummy bears, or premium cocoa for my hot chocolate, or other little knickknacks he knows I love. Some days, I'll answer the door, wanting to see his face, even if we don't say more than a few words. Other days, I don't.

But I feel my heart softening, the chains around it melting under his persistence.

Then, there are the messages he'll post online, the ones that have the media in a fervor because of the romantic nature of his words.

I pull out my phone and swipe to his post from two days ago, a photo of daffodils on his nightstand.

Ryland.Anderson.Official: Dear Little Lark, I miss your sunshine and your bright light. You are the best part of me. Without you, my life has lost meaning. You are my whirlwind.

He didn't come yesterday or this morning. Nor has he posted on his social media.

Has he given up on us?

A heavy melancholy blankets me, dulling the colors of my world to dreary shades of gray.

I sit at my bay window and stare at the streets below. Pedestrians walk around construction workers climbing on scaffolding placed over a red-bricked building across the street. A small group of people line up in front of a new art gallery around the corner. The late afternoon sun shines brightly on this beautiful New York spring day and the skies are clear of smog, the rain from two days ago having washed all the grime away.

My "auditing" of the spring quarter is ending. Projects are completed, final presentations will be in two weeks, then graduation ceremony in early June. I'm slated to start at Cornell, my dream school and my brother's alma mater, for my PhD program in the fall.

Everything is working out the way things should be. My dreams are coming true, one by one.

But there's an empty, dark hole in my heart, a cavern that seems impossible to fill. My mind wanders back to my last conversation with Ryland, and I wonder if I was too harsh on him, and if I should've given him a chance. It's funny how your mind works against you sometimes. But I know I made the right choice. After all, he gave up on us so easily before.

I have to protect myself.

And if he does the same thing again this time, then, as painful as things are right now, my heartstrings being yanked and nearly severed whenever I think of our memories together, it'll be the right decision.

After all, I deserve more.

My phone chimes and a text message flashes on the screen.

Chloe

> Millie, did you hear about the new exotic plant exhibit at Central Park? Want to go? I'm not that much of a plant girl, but I want to cheer you up. I can text the other girls. We can make a girls' day out of it?

I smile. I had heard about a new exhibit being built somewhere in Central Park. The grand opening isn't for another week, but I plan to pay a visit once the crowds have thinned out after the initial excitement.

Millie

> Sounds good. Maybe in a few weeks when things ease up? Don't worry about me. I'm doing well.

I hit send, then reread my words. My fingers hover over the keyboard and I type another message.

Millie

> I lied. I'm not doing well, but I will be. One foot in front of the other. I'll get through this. Thank you for thinking of me.

I won't hide anymore. Not to the people I love and the people who love me back.

Chloe

> Love you, Millie. I'm a call away if you ever want to chat.

Another message comes through, and I smile, seeing the name of my roommate from ULA.

Joss

> Long time no chat! I'm coming to NYC next month, let's hang out?

Millie

> Definitely! Keep me posted.

Clicking shut my phone, I set it to the side and stare at the light blue sky again. I close my eyes and let the warmth of the early afternoon sun wash over my face. Moments later, I hear the faint sounds of the front door opening.

"Is she asleep?"

"I don't know, but if she is, we're waking her up."

Giggling and furtive whispers reach my ears. My eyes snap open.

The sounds of footsteps echo in the hallway, and three heads pop through my opened bedroom doorway. Belle, looking as trendy as ever in her sleek white sundress, is beaming. Grace, in a colorful getup only she can pull off, is bouncing on her feet, her violet eyes barely containing her excitement. Taylor, dressed in black leggings and a crop top, purses her lips and waggles her brows.

Something is up with these three.

"What's going on, girls?"

Grace prances over and hauls me off the window seat. "Get dressed, we are going out, and we aren't taking no for an answer."

She looks at Belle and issues a command like she's a general in the throes of a war. "Go through her closet and pick out something appropriate for her to wear."

"Aye, aye, madam." Belle mock salutes and dashes to my walk-in closet.

"What's going on?" My brows hike up to my forehead.

"That's for us to know and you to find out." Grace eyes me from top to bottom. "Okay, at least you've taken a shower in the last day or so. I can work with this. I'll do your makeup and hair."

She ushers me to my chair, takes out my makeup, and gets to work. I catch Taylor's sly grin in my mirror.

Rolling my eyes, I ask, "And what are you going to do, Tay?"

Tay winks and takes out a bag of carrots from her bag and munches on one. I don't know why she's so obsessed with them. "Emotional support animal. That's me."

"*You?* Emotional support?" I can't help the incredulity seeping through my voice.

"Totally! I'm a breath of positive energy today. See my nose stud today? It's a smiley face."

I let out an exasperated sigh. "Do I get *any* say in this? Anything at all?"

"No!" A resounding chorus.

What on earth is going on now?

—— · —— ——

"Why are we here?" The girls are dragging me down 5th Avenue toward Central Park.

The crowds are bigger today—a beautiful weekend in spring after a dreary rain has drawn out locals and tourists alike. The sun is low in the skies, twirling a final pirouette before dipping into a curtsy and disappearing behind the veil of the night. The girls spent an hour primping me, dressing me in an elegant white sundress with pink roses, arranging my hair in loose waves, then applying light makeup on my face.

Despite my complaints and questions, none of them have told me what on earth is going on. And now, they are pulling me into one of the main entrances of Central Park and dressed in this getup, I feel completely out of place with the other people wearing jeans and T-shirts.

"Eeek! I'm so excited." Grace claps her hands with the enthusiasm of a toddler.

"Calm your horses, Grace. I'll reserve my approval until I see it. And even then..." Taylor sounds skeptical.

"You two. Zip it. Don't ruin it for her." Belle whips her head toward the sisters, who look down sheepishly at the ground.

A few minutes later, I see the Conservatory Garden Center Fountain in the distance. The gentle breeze rustles the leaves in the carefully groomed trees and shrubbery, the lush, vibrant green of nature calming to the senses after a long winter. A light scent of wildflowers permeates the air, especially from the sweetness of the peonies and lilacs in bloom.

As I stroll through one of my favorite places in Central Park, the Conservatory Garden, I feel the heaviness in my chest lifting and my spirits lightening. Perhaps the girls are onto something by taking me here.

Before long, we stand in front of a new building on the sprawling lawn of the Italian-style Central Garden, one of the three unique gardens in this area.

The new exotic blooms exhibit.

"What are we doing here? The exhibit doesn't open until next week. Chloe said she was going to text you guys to see if we should all go together," I murmur while I stare at the impressive structure in front of me.

The tall building sits on a raised concrete foundation and is constructed entirely of glass and copper frames, which will oxidize to a wonderful pale green in the years to come. There are intricate carvings on the windowpanes, reminding me of the palaces in Europe.

The architect and interior designer must have taken great pains to blend the building into its surroundings, because it looks like it belonged there all along. A blue cloth drapes over a large sign by the entrance. I assume it's the name of the building, which will be unveiled at the grand opening.

"Okay. Watch this. This popped on my newsfeed this morning." Belle shoves her phone in front of my face and clicks on a link which redirects to a trending video on the *Gossip Times* website.

"What?" I frown.

"Shh!" Belle hushes me.

My breath freezes in my throat as I see Ryland standing behind the podium, answering questions about his company's stock performance.

I look at the girls in confusion. Taylor shrugs. "Grace and I didn't know about this until Belle sent it to us this morning. Ryland didn't tell us anything either. But even I have to say I'm touched. Just watch it."

I turn my attention back to the video.

"Mr. Anderson, can you tell us why you're posting romantic messages online?" a blonde reporter asks.

Ryland stills, a muscle twitching in his jaw. The room is silent.

He slowly adjusts his gray tie and leans forward on the podium. Clearing his throat, he stares straight into the camera.

"Little lark, if you're watching this, know that you're the best thing that has ever happened to me."

Gasps erupt in the room and he holds up his hand for silence.

"If I could take back everything I've done, every tear you've shed, I would. I'm so sorry for hurting you and my days are miserable without you. The only reason I'm not screaming your name at the top of my lungs is because you've sacrificed a lot for me, and I don't want to unwind your efforts. This time, my heart is laid bare at your feet. This time, the choice is yours. I love you and I know I don't deserve you. I can only hope one day you'll forgive me, and you'll give me a chance to love you once more."

He lets out a shuddering exhale, his penetrating eyes full of regret, heartache...and love.

"That's all I have to say." He stands up and walks off the stage.

"Mr. Anderson!" Reporters holler at him as the room descends into chaos. "Are you talking about Millie Callahan? Is she your little lark?"

He pauses at the foot of the stage and faces the camera again. "I'll be waiting for you," he mouths, ignoring their questions, and disappears into a back corridor.

He is a private person and I know this is a way for him to declare his love to me publicly while respecting my privacy.

He hasn't given up on us. He's telling me he chooses me and is giving me a choice this time. He's putting everything on the line...for me.

Tears spring into my eyes as I hand the phone back to Belle.

"What is this?" I whisper.

"Don't kill us, okay? Trust me, it'll all make sense later." Belle gives me a hug and a wink before backing away and the trio head back in the direction we came from.

"Wait! Where are you guys going?" I move to follow them, but Grace raises her hands to stop me.

"Ah crap! I forgot this." She rushes forward and hands me a small envelope. "Stay here and read it! Trust me! Thank us later!" With a squeal and a giggle, she spins around and hurries after the others, quickly disappearing from view.

My mind is a swirl of emotions, filled with images of him and his words to the reporters. I'm in a daze as I make my way to the graveled path up the steps leading to the entrance.

A fresh breeze blows through the garden. My fingers tremble as I tear open the envelope and take out the letter inside.

Dearest Millie,

It seems fitting the first real letter I write in my life is to the one woman I love with every beat of my heart. To be honest, I don't know how to begin—I've never written a love letter before and the small captions on social media don't quite count. But I've been told it's best to write your truth.

Life without you is not a life worth living. These past few months, without you by my side, my soul has been bereft, my world has lost its shine, and my freedom has lost its enticement.

I realize what a coward I've been in the past, disguising my fears as a cloak of responsibilities when deep down, perhaps, I'm still the little boy who has never moved beyond loss, the person who has experienced death and decided never to love again. But having met you and seeing how you live your life, taking one hard step at a time, carving out your future even when the odds are stacked against you, I understand one thing.

You are the hunter, the fighter. Your spirit will allow you to conquer and soar no matter where life takes you. You are an inspiration. You make me want to become a better man. You make my freedom have meaning.

I hope you'll find it in your heart to give me another chance to show you being with you is not an impulsive decision. It's my one craving, my true obsession.

I hope you'll give me all your tomorrows, starting with today. I hope you'll step into the sunlight with me.

Love, Ryland

My hand flies to my mouth as I re-read every passionate word, every fervent promise. His public declaration at the press conference echoes in my ears.

The thumping in my chest intensifies, and I look up.

I see him.

I'm rooted to the ground as I see the tall, powerful man stepping out of the building and walking toward me with determination on his handsome face. My heart pounds rapidly in my chest, frantic and ecstatic to see its other half nearby. His pendant feels heavy around my neck, and every cell of my body comes to life.

He still steals my breath and robs me of speech.

My fingers automatically clutch the jeweled key in my hand, and I blink several times, wondering if he's a hallucination. But he's still there, striding toward me in his perfectly tailored navy suit, crisp white shirt opened at the collar. His dark hair is swept up and perfectly tousled.

Ryland's dark gray eyes are pinned on me, the penetrating intensity reminding me of the first day I met him when he berated me in front of class for being late.

I knew it then and I know it now. This man has left an indelible print on my heart and my life will never be the same after him.

My lips part as my breathing quickens, and he quickly makes his way down the steps and reaches me in a matter of seconds.

"Millie," he whispers my name reverently, his eyes warming with so much love, my chest actually hurts from being so close to him. "You look beautiful."

"Ryland, you planned this?" I hold up the letter in my hand.

Another gust of wind blows by, and a few loose curls of hair fall over my face. Ryland reaches out and hesitates for a second before tucking the strands behind my ear. Then he lightly trails his fingers over my cheek.

My skin lights up. And all it took was a simple, fleeting touch.

"I read every single word you wrote in your letters, Millie. I don't have a way with words, not like you, but I need you to know how much I want you, how much I need you. Please forgive me if I haven't given you enough time." His words are hurried, urgent, as if he's afraid I'll deny him.

He continues, "I want to show you I'm serious about us. I'm not going to hide our relationship from the world. I was lost in the maze inside my mind for the longest time, but you, Millie," he gently clutches my hand, the one holding the pendant around my neck, and curls his palm around it, "you showed me the way out. You showed me how I'm not alone anymore and I have people to lean on, people who'll never leave me."

He cups my cheeks in his hands, his eyes taking on a wet sheen. "My heart has lived outside of me ever since I met you. I foolishly thought I could live without my heart, and I would save you from my prison...from me. But I was wrong, and I hurt you. I wish I could go back in time and take all the pain away, but I know I can't. I can only ask you to let me make it up to you for the rest of my life, starting with today."

My eyes well and my words are stuck in my throat. He looks so sincere, so desperate, so irrevocably in love with me. My heart teeters at the edge, wanting desperately to leap into his embrace once more.

As if sensing my hesitation, he presses a soft kiss on my forehead before gently interlacing his fingers with mine and tugging me up the steps toward the main entrance of the glass building.

"I would've brought you here sooner, but there was a lot of red tape to get through—permits, board meetings, designs, construction. I even tried to help with some of the manual labor. That was why I didn't stop by your apartment the last two days—last minute issues to take care of here." He stops in front of the large plaque covered in cloth.

Ryland glances at me, a pulse feathering his cheek, and he swallows nervously. He takes a deep breath and pulls the cloth away.

My heart flies to my mouth and my lips part in a gasp.

The Millie Callahan Exotic Botanical Greenhouse Conservatory.

"The admission will be free all year round, so people in all stages of life and all income levels can access beautiful flowers because...nature should be free." His voice is thick, impassioned.

"The upkeep is funded by a new endowment set up by the Anderson family—specifically out of a portion of my funds. It's perpetual. The funds will continue after my time on this earth. A press release is slated to be published tomorrow."

He heard me that day at New Beginnings. My words—he remembered.

My lips tremble as I reread my name carved into the granite for the world to see. Then his words register in my mind.

"P-Press release? Then everyone will know you built a greenhouse for me. And what about what you said at the press conference this morning?"

His eyes widen. He's clearly surprised at my mention of the press conference. He didn't know I saw it.

I clutch his arm. "There'll be gossip again. They'll connect the dots with what you posted on social media and your responses to the reporters. What about your reputation, your fam—"

He presses his finger softly on my lips, his touch reverent. "I don't care if the world knows. I want the world to know you've captured my heart and brought me back to life. You've freed me from the prison of myself. I want everyone to know how I'm desperately, madly, and irrevocably in love with you and that will never change, much like this building will be here forever."

"Ryland." I press a kiss on his finger, my arms looping around his neck automatically, my body no longer able to hold itself back from him. All the lingering doubts vanish from my mind and I don't want to be separated from him any longer.

He groans and rasps, "Does this mean you'll give me a chance? Does this mean you'll forgive me for my idiocy?"

My lips tremble before splitting into a wide smile.

"Well," I let out a shaky breath, "that was a very good grovel, I must admit."

He laughs, his smile lighting up his entire face.

"Thank fuck," he murmurs before swooping down and sealing his lips to mine.

CHAPTER 55

THE MOMENT OUR LIPS touch feels like the first rainfall on the parched desert. Electricity crackles between us and every atom in my body vibrates with intensity as his kisses turn heated, his lips licking and sucking mine like he's desperate for me just as I am for him. He groans and hauls me closer, one hand clutching the nape of my neck, his fingers digging into my skin just the way I like it, the other hand curling around my waist.

"Ryland," I moan as we part for air, our breaths mingling in the tiny slither of space between us.

"Fuck, I've missed you. So fucking much."

He swoops down for another soul-shattering kiss. I lean closer so I'm flush against him, all hard muscles and restrained power.

He growls when I move my body over his, grinding against the erection tenting his pants. He dips out his tongue, teasing the seam of my lips before thrusting in.

The world swirls around me, my skin heating like I'm in the throes of a fever. Every inch of me is sensitive, craving his touch, and there are far too many clothes between us.

Ryland deepens his kiss, his tongue plundering my mouth as mine duels with his, every inch his equal. My teeth make an appearance as I bite down on his bottom lip and he lets out a hiss of pleasure.

"Not enough," he rasps, "not enough."

Without another word, he swoops me up in his arms and stomps toward the entrance, taking us inside.

I vaguely notice the towering glass ceilings letting in rays of light, the kaleidoscope of warm reds, oranges, and pinks of the sunset streaming indoors, bathing the lush foliage in an otherworldly glow.

Tearing my lips away briefly, my mouth drops open at the rows and rows of carefully curated plants on various planters, trellises—there are trees of all sizes, ropes of vines arranged in artful, yet natural displays.

And the flowers, oh my God, the flowers—I see a room to the side dedicated to orchids, areas where the ethereal lavender-colored wisteria hangs from the ceiling, a scene straight out of a fairytale. Then, there are the unique orange and reds of the birds of paradise, roses, peonies, and so many more blooms I can't wait to examine and name.

My eyes well with moisture as I behold the breathtaking beauty around me and I turn back to the man who has barged into my heart like a whirlwind and has made a permanent home there.

His dark eyes glitter, and he whispers, "Nothing here is as beautiful and as precious as you."

My heart soars to the skies, and my heart burgeons in size.

I hurl myself at him and kiss him until I can't tell where he ends and where I begin. His breathing turns harried, and he carries me somewhere, but it can be anywhere for all I care. He sheds his clothing on the floor and we're a mad tangle of limbs and passion as we come together, needing each other more than anything else in the world.

Soon, I find myself naked, my arms twining over his shoulders as pleasure shoots down to my core when he rakes his teeth down the tender column of my neck. Every pinch from his bites is followed by a heated suction and a tortuous lick. Wetness seeps out between my thighs and I curl my legs tighter around his ass, angling my clit to rub against every hard ridge of his cock.

"Fuuuck," he grunts.

Setting me down on a settee, his mouth travels down to my breasts and takes one beaded nipple between his lips, suckling it, laving it, making love to it.

I moan and I arch my back. My eyes snag on the familiar yellow daffodils and the beautiful purple pasque flowers in the surrounding displays, and I realize he's making love to me amongst the things I hold dearly in my heart.

"Ryland, I need you."

I grip his hair and pull him up, but he growls and moves his attention to the other nipple, his hands traveling between our bodies and palming my wet pussy.

My cries of pleasure echo in the glass halls. "Please, please fuck me, Ryland. Please. I need you so much."

"No," he grunts before thrusting two fingers inside my tight channel and I nearly careen off the seat. "Fuck, you're so wet for me. I've missed this so fucking much."

He doubles down and rubs my clit with his thumb—light flickers and firm circles—and the shards of pleasure gather in my core at the speed of light.

It's been too long and I'm too primed for him. I can't hold on.

My legs shake under him as he moves his fingers harder, angling them just right, so they hit my G-spot with every pass.

"Please," I beg, "I want you inside me. I want you to fuck the living daylights out of me."

His cock hardens even more, and he lets out an animalistic growl. "My dirty girl, my little lark."

He takes his fingers out and slides them into his mouth, his tongue swirling around them like he's tasting the most delicious delicacy in the world. More slickness seeps out of me, and I feel my pussy throbbing, my body needing the barest friction to topple over the cliff.

Ryland leans down, his eyes so dark they're almost black, and he rasps, "I'm not fucking you today. I'm *making love* to you, my sweet little lark, because I love you so fucking much."

With that, he slides his cock inside me to the hilt and I let out a long mewl.

He intertwines his fingers with mine and stares at me while he moves, his thrusts alternating between deep, slow gyrations to quick parries. My eyes fall shut as the pleasure builds to an unbearable point.

"Keep them open. Keep your eyes on me. I want to see you come apart in my arms."

Ryland's breathing is heavy in the air and the wet sounds of our bodies coming together are lurid, but I don't care.

My lips part as I meet him thrust after thrust, the *smacking* sounds inflaming my senses. I tremble underneath him, my body so desperate for release I can practically scream.

"Yes, your pussy is squeezing me so tightly. Ah fuuuck, this is so good." He pumps faster, his fingers clutching mine harder.

It's a merging of souls, our hearts beating and soaring in unison.

"I love you, Millie Callahan. I love you so much." He angles his hard cock so it rubs against my clit. The pressure breaks, and I tumble into oblivion.

"Ryland!" I scream, my legs uncurling from his ass, my body shaking as my body breaks apart into a thousand pieces while he moves harder, his cock grinding against my G-spot, prolonging my orgasm into endless waves.

Thrust. Thrust. Thrust. "Yes, fuck yes. I'm going to come so hard into your tight pussy."

A few seconds later, a guttural roar rips out from his mouth and a burst of warmth floods my insides. His cock unloads streams of cum in rapid spurts, the hot liquid unleashing another surprise orgasm from me as I fall into the abyss of pleasure once more.

"I love you, Ryland," I sob, my body fluttering against him, our movements softening, our hearts slowing, and we come down from our high.

Sweat glistens on our skin. My pussy is sore in the most delicious way. He settles himself on top of me but props his weight up on his arms so he's not too heavy.

Ryland gazes at me, his skin flushed from exertion.

But his eyes, his brilliant slate-gray eyes, are spilling with love and warmth. He looks at me with such reverence, I can get lost in his gaze forever.

"You're my love, Millie, my forever. I've been yours since the moment our hearts collided."

With that, he presses his lips on mine once more, sealing his vows with each kiss, each touch, and each breath.

He holds me tightly in his arms after we make love three more times, once in the hallway when we return to his apartment at The Orchid, another time in the shower, where he teaches me how useful the jets can be, and in his bed, when he twists me like a pretzel and has his way with me.

After taking care of business in the bathroom and donning one of his oversized shirts, I take out a pad of paper and a pen from his nightstand. Perhaps it's a habit or a way for me to document my feelings at the end of each day, but I climb onto the bed and uncap the pen to prepare to scribble another letter.

"May I?" Ryland asks from my side, a teasing grin on his lips.

My heart skips a beat at his genuine smile, one no longer holding the bittersweet sentiments I saw when he was standing in the rain two years ago outside the classroom, staring into the stormy skies.

I hand him the paper and the pen.

His brows furrow in concentration as he angles the notepad away from my line of sight and begins writing. The pen scrapes against the paper in a soothing rhythm. He pauses and gnaws his bottom lip, his eyes darting to my face for a beat before he smiles and resumes scribbling.

A few minutes later, he hands me the notepad, and I read.

Dear Mrs. Callahan,

My name is Ryland Anderson, and I'm the man who loves your daughter very, very much. I believe she has told you about me before. Thank you for giving birth to such a wonderful woman with a beautiful, pure heart. Thank you for setting her in my path and allowing us to meet.

She told me how you once described true love as a whirlwind.

Perhaps that's true.

But I believe my love for her far exceeds the transient wind. My love for her is an ocean—bottomless and deep, strong and enduring.

If you are looking down from above, please don't worry about her anymore, because I will be by her side and I will look after her.

I love her, now and forever.

Eternally grateful, Ryland

A lone tear slips from my eye and I set down the letter, wishing Mom were here and could meet this wonderful man by my side.

He shares a bittersweet smile, no doubt thinking of his own mother, and I curl myself into the crook of his shoulder and close my eyes, listening to the reassuring *thumps* of his heart.

Ba-dum. Ba-dum. Ba-dum.

Strong and enduring.

Epilogue

One Month Later

"Suck it. Take it down your throat."

I grunt, fisting her hair as she kneels before me, her mascara running down her face in streaks of black, her lips swollen as she gags on my cock. Hickeys mar her creamy tits—thank God she's wearing something with a high collar later for the graduation ceremony this afternoon.

She's beautiful and so fucking perfect. Brilliant and kind-hearted. She fucking humbles me.

Millie sucks harder as the artificial daylight shines brightly upon us. I have her backed against a tree inside Noire, her clothes shredded in a pile a few feet away and she's servicing my cock like she's famished for it.

Gagging sounds reach my ears and I swell even more as her tight throat wraps around my head in an embrace that has me seeing stars.

"Fuuuuck, you're so good at this."

I piston my hips, tunneling myself deeper inside her as tears stream down her face. "You want my load, little lark, every single drop? Are you going to be a good student for your professor?"

Millie moans and her hand travels to her breast, her fingers kneading the hardened nipple as her thighs squeeze together.

"You're so hot for it, Millie. Damn, you look good on your knees—ah fuck!"

My hips spasm as the sharp pleasure shoots straight from my balls up my shaft and I try to hold back, but a telltale spurt of cum escaping tells me I'm close.

My mind turns hazy and I tear my cock out from her lips and haul her back up to pin her face forward against the tree.

"I'm going to come in this tight little rosebud today, Millie. I'm going to own it like I own every inch of you," I growl in her ear, my front flushed against her backside, my fingers teasing the forbidden entrance we haven't breached yet.

Millie whimpers and trembles but sticks out her butt more and gives it an enticing wiggle.

"Safe word, my little lark? Because once I start, I'm going to finish."

I fist my dick once...twice, dragging the sensitive swollen head between the crack of her smooth cheeks, my pre-cum dripping over the surface.

"Never." Her voice is a breathy whisper but strong...a fighter through and through. "I want you to stick that cock up my ass and fuck an orgasm out of me."

My mind blanks as a noise echoes in the quiet forest.

And I realize that animalistic growl is from me.

My fingers reach to her front to play with her slit and I drag her essence to the back, inserting one finger into her little hole.

"Aaaah," she screams, her ass shaking against me.

"Safe word?"

"More!" She rolls her backside against my fingers, her hand moving downward to play with her clit. Millie writhes and lets out a few frustrated moans.

"Can't get off, you filthy girl?" I bite the lobe of her ear and she melts against me, her body moving desperately against my finger. "Let me show you how it's done."

I insert my ring finger into her hole to join my middle finger and thrust my index finger into her tight pussy. My other hand reaches to her front and my fingers flick little circles around her clit.

"Ryland!" she screams when I hammer my digits inside her, listening to the slurping sounds of her body accepting my invasion.

"F-Fucking shit, o-oh my shit," she chants, her body thrashing in front of me.

"You're strangling my fingers like a good little slut. Are you ready for the main event?" I rasp, my cock moving up and down her backside, eager to join the party below.

"Y-Yes." Her legs tremble and I press my body tighter against her, holding her up.

My breathing is ragged as I take out my fingers and replace it with my cock. I press a kiss at the sensitive whorl of her ear and whisper, "Tell me if it's too much."

Slowly, I thrust home.

My pre-cum drips over my dick, which, combined with her wetness I spread to her rosebud earlier, act as lubricant, and her tight little asshole swallows me up eagerly, inch by inch.

She whimpers but pushes back, her hand grabbing my fingers and tugging it toward her clit.

"Shit, you're so tight. Yes, that's it. Relax. You're doing so well, such a fucking good girl."

I let out a guttural moan as I move against her. My fingers tease her clit, flicking and plucking the hardened nub the way she likes it, and she shakes violently against me.

"Yes, baby...you're mine. All of you," I groan, the pleasure clouding my senses and I move faster, strumming her clit to the rhythm of my cock in her ass. Then I slide two fingers into her wet pussy.

She shrieks, her screams echoing in the forest, and her head lolls back against my chest. I see her eyes glazed and unfocused, her lips parted. She looks delirious and fuck if that doesn't make me even harder.

My other hand wraps around the slender column of her neck and I squeeze, watching her pale skin, glistening with sweat, turn pink.

Her thrashes turn into kicks—my little lark gets off in the fight, but she knows a simple three taps anywhere on my body will stop everything. I hold on tighter, watching her breathing stutter. Scalding pleasure gathers in my loins, and my vision blackens at the corners.

"You have no idea what you do to me. How much I fucking love you…to the fucking ends of the earth," I growl. "Feel my fingers on your clit and pussy, baby? Your pussy is trembling and weeping for me. Do you know how tight your ass feels all wrapped up around my cock? God, you're spectacular."

My hips move faster, my body completely dominating hers. All rational thoughts leave my mind, and I'm only left with my core instincts, my need to conquer, to run, to be free. My cock thickens and swells, the squelching sounds a soundtrack that'll be imprinted in my mind forever.

Millie's thrashes turn erratic, and her gasps for breath become short drags, her skin flushing into dark pink.

"Now, be a good student and come for me. Squeeze out all my cum from my throbbing dick."

I give her clit one last swirl and release my hand around her neck.

She screams and liquid gushes out of her pussy, where my fingers are hammering inside her, curling against her G-spot, and my cock is tunneling in and out of her ass.

"Yes. Yes. Yes!" I roar, her orgasm triggering mine, and electrifying pleasure rushes down my body like water bursting through a dam. I hold her tightly and empty myself inside her, my lips peppering kisses wherever I can reach, my eyes seeing stars.

Slowly, I roll my hips and massage her pussy, dragging out our high as our breathing slows and cries turn into moans and mewls.

"You're an animal," she whispers minutes later, a dreamy smile on her face.

"Only for you." I tug my bottom lip between my teeth and bite back a grin. I swat her curvy bottom. "Come on, let's get ready for your graduation and the celebrations later. We don't want to be late."

*

Pomp and Circumstance plays loudly on the speakers as I stand below the stage, waiting for my name to be called to receive my diploma. My fingers smooth over my black graduation gown before adjusting my cap.

Jitteriness flows through my veins as I look at the throngs of people sitting in the crowded auditorium, my eyes sweeping through the audience until they land on Adrian, Emily, and Dad. Next to them are my girls.

They're standing up. Adrian is cheering even though it's not my turn yet. Taylor flashes me a peace sign, Grace jumps up and down while clapping, and Belle hollers something sounding like my name. Joss is next to them, her visit coincidentally lining up with my graduation ceremony. She cups her hands over her mouth and lets out an excited screech.

"Millie Callahan," the MC announces, and the shrieks and cheers rise in volume.

My heart throws itself against my rib cage as I climb up the steps of the stage and walk toward Dean Emery, who is standing in front of the two rows of chairs occupied by the faculty.

"Go get them, little lark!"

My head swivels toward Ryland. He has risen from his seat in the first row of faculty seating on the stage, clearly not caring his colleagues are staring at him. He grins, his smile unleashing a new swarm of butterflies in my stomach, and he claps loudly, pride shining in his eyes.

It has been a month since he unveiled the greenhouse to me and, as expected, the press went crazy when the story broke about how he funded a greenhouse in perpetuity and named it after me.

But true to his word, this time, he didn't shy away. He bravely took my hand in his as we strolled the streets of Manhattan, ignored the paparazzi when they screamed questions at us before we walked into The Orchid for some peace and quiet. The official story was because of the alleged scandal earlier on, we spent even more time together and fell in love—he even thanked the reporters for getting us together.

I bite my lip and give him a wink before striding to Dean Emery, who briefly rolls his eyes heavenward, no doubt at Ryland's public display of affection.

"Congratulations, Ms. Callahan. Well deserved," he murmurs as he takes my hand in his, gives it a firm shake, and hands me my diploma.

I did it. The thought echoes in my mind as elation churns through my veins. I'm one step closer to my dream.

I can't believe such happiness exists.

After taking the obligatory photo, I walk off the stage, my smile permanently plastered on my face. I clutch the ceremonial diploma tightly in my hand as I make my way back to my seat. After all these years of working hard and studying nonstop, I'm now a college graduate.

It didn't really hit home until I crossed the stage moments ago, even though my official certificate is dated half a year ago.

I look toward the ceiling and whisper, *Mom, if you're watching over me, I hope you're proud.*

The rest of the ceremony passes by quickly, the excitement from the crowd palpable. Joss rushes up to me and envelops me in a hug.

"I'm so happy for you, Millie! You did what you told me you were going to do at ULA."

I grin. "Thank you, Joss."

"Congratulations, Millie," a raspy voice murmurs and I turn, finding Charles grinning as he saunters up to us, his blond hair gleaming under the overhead lights. "Sorry, I had a work meeting I couldn't get out of, but I'm glad I caught the tail end of it. You look beautiful today."

"Seriously, dude, hold back on the charm, will you? She's taken," Taylor mutters while picking at her nails.

Charles glares at her.

I shake my head and laugh. "You two, seriously." I'm not sure if they'll ever get along.

The next half hour is filled with laughter as we take photos—so many, my smile seems permanently etched on my face—and catch up with friends and classmates.

Soon, everyone leaves the building. Charles has to run to a work dinner, and Joss is meeting up with other friends across the city. Ryland and I return to his apartment at The Orchid to get ready for the next event of the day, a celebratory graduation dinner with our families.

"Do I look presentable? I tried my best with the makeup, but someone was a *savage* this morning at Noire."

I eye my reflection in the mirror inside the master bathroom to check if any of his love marks are showing through. I fiddle with the lavender boat-neck dress I have on as nerves threaten to break free.

It'll be the first dinner between my family and his—officially, that is.

Ryland steps up behind me, looking like my wet dream come to life in his sharp gray suit, carefully arranged hair, and a sexy five o'clock shadow. A heat creeps up my skin as he stares at me in that sole unwavering attention of his, his gray eyes darkening to obsidian.

He murmurs, "You look perfect. You look like mine."

My heart skips several beats, and a heady warmth washes over me.

A few minutes later, we take the elevators down and walk to one of the private rooms at Carlisle's, one of the award-winning restaurants inside The Orchid. It's the love child of two married Michelin-starred chefs, each specializing in steak or seafood, thus making the restaurant a unique place where one can have the best surf and turf in the country.

Steven and the rest of the Anderson family, including Grace and Taylor, are sitting at the large circular table in the elegant room decorated in creams and whites. Adrian is smiling at Emily as she chats with Dad, who is sitting next to them. The men stand up automatically when we walk in and don't sit down until I take a seat next to Lana.

"The person of the hour!" Rex winks before striding over and pulling me into a bear hug. "The better half of my brother. Please keep putting up with him because he was a surly ass when you weren't by his side."

I laugh. Rex is the clown of the family, which already has too many serious men, and I kind of dig that.

Rex looks at Maxwell, who is sitting near the entrance with a satisfied smile on his face, a king clearly pleased with his subjects.

"It's your turn, Maxwell. Find yourself a woman. You aren't getting any younger, you know. Those swimmers of yours may be defective if you wait any longer." Rex doles out a shit-eating grin.

Maxwell arches his brow, clearly unfazed.

"Oh, for fuck's sake." Ethan's eyes roll heavenward.

"Rex Cassius Anderson!" Linus glares at his middle son, no doubt angry at his topic of choice in front of the ladies, if the aristocratic upbringing I've seen from their family is any indication.

"Your middle name is Cassius? Seriously? Like some dead Roman emperor? That's why you never want to tell us, huh?" Taylor grins gleefully and Rex shoots her a baleful look, which makes everyone laugh.

The group settles into their seats and Maxwell chats quietly with Ryland.

Taylor frowns and waves at me to get my attention. "Is Belle coming? I thought she couldn't go to the ceremony today because of her work trip, but she's coming to dinner. Did that change?"

I shake my head. "I think she's on her way. Things might get dicey with the traffic from the airport. Maybe she's—"

Something clatters to the ground with a *clang*.

Maxwell mouths, "excuse me," as he bends to the floor. I think he dropped his cell phone.

"I'm so sorry I'm late!" Belle dashes in, her face flushed and very much out of breath, but she still looks every inch the fashion goddess dressed in her black couture tweed dress.

"Don't worry about it. New York traffic is no joke," I reply, turning back to Belle. I point to the empty seat by Maxwell. "We haven't started yet. Sit next to Maxwell."

She nods and gives everyone a sheepish smile before pulling out her chair.

Maxwell stands back up and straightens his suit. He holds up his phone and murmurs, "Apologies again." Then, he turns toward Belle. "Hi, I'm Maxwell, Ryland's older bro—"

He freezes as he takes in Belle for the first time. His nostrils flare and his jaw clenches.

Belle looks equally shocked as well. "I thought you weren't going to be here."

"You guys know each other?" Taylor asks. As far as I know, the two have never met before.

Maxwell turns toward us, his face grim. The frigid king doesn't look cold at the moment, with his hands gripping his tumbler tightly, his forearm trembling with tension. His jaw locks as he stares at Belle with something akin to fury in his eyes.

"Yes. She's my fiancée."

"What?" This time I think it's Rex, but I can't be too sure because I'm reeling with this surprise. *She's engaged?*

"Did you know about this?" Ryland interlaces his fingers with mine and squeezes. I shake my head. *What on earth is going on?*

I whip my head toward Grace and Taylor, seeing their equally astonished expressions on their faces.

Grace scrunches her brows. *Did you know about this?*

I shake my head vehemently. *Did you?*

"No," she mouths.

Taylor sits frozen in her seat in apparent shock, her mouth dropped open, and Grace gently nudges her.

"*What the fuck?* Belle?" Tay whisper-shouts, all too unsubtly.

Belle's gaze swivels toward us, her brows furrowed, her eyes shining with guilt.

"It's very new," she mumbles.

I give her a soft smile, letting her know I'm here for her and we will talk later.

Maxwell clenches his jaw as he stands there rigidly, his hands fisted and white-knuckled on top of the table, and waits until Belle takes a seat before he follows suit.

Linus clears his throat. "Well, this is unexpected, but I guess the news will come out soon enough. Our Maxwell will be marrying Annabelle in an arrangement beneficial to all parties involved. We can discuss this later, but tonight, we are here to celebrate our dear Millie for her accomplishments."

Chairs squeak as folks shift in their seats and silverware clatter against the plates. A strange tension hangs in the air from Maxwell's exceptionally hostile reception, much icier than his usual demeanor. Someone coughs and another person clears his throat.

"If I may." Ryland raises his glass, his gaze shrewd as he surveys the room, no doubt taking in the discomfort.

He turns to me, his eyes warming and his lips tilting into a smile. My pulse flutters in my ears as butterflies swarm in my stomach. I don't think I'll ever get tired of the way he looks at me, like I'm all that he needs in the world.

His eyes dip to my lips before returning to my gaze. "I want to thank everyone for coming to celebrate with us. Congratulations to Millie for graduating at NYUC and embarking on her journey to become one of the finest educators the world will ever see."

"Yes! Millie, I'm so happy for you!" Belle cheers, her lips splitting into the dazzling smile I know so well—a genuine smile this time.

"You got lucky, Ryland. God knows why she picked your sorry ass," Rex comments, earning another smattering of chuckles.

"Trust me, I know," Ryland murmurs wryly before leaning down and pressing a brief kiss on my lips.

The tension in the room melts as cheers and laughter fill the space. My skin feels warm, and I throw him a saucy wink. "As long as you remember that."

He barks out a laugh and pulls me flush against him, clearly not caring about the audience in the room. He dips me back into a more thorough kiss and suddenly, all questions, rational thought, and embarrassment disappear as I'm swept up in his embrace.

I'm disoriented and breathless by the time he pulls away and turns toward the others.

"I also want to announce I'll be stepping down from my position as COO at Fleur in the fall," Ryland says.

My hand flies to my mouth in surprise. I know he's been contemplating leaving his job to pursue academia full-time, but he has been waiting for the family trust to be dissolved before making the change.

He turns to look at me. "The lawyers called this morning. They found a way to dissolve the trust."

Tears spring into my eyes, and I throw myself into his arms. "Ryland! I'm so happy for you."

The room breaks into more cheers and applause, everyone clearly happy for him to pursue his dreams.

"Who's going to do your job, then?" Taylor asks.

Ryland grins and cocks his head toward Steven. "The King of Wall Street over there."

Steven rolls his eyes and mutters, "Oh shut up. If you don't let up, I'll be calling you Your Highness along with the rest of the folks here." He smirks and tugs Grace to his side.

Lighthearted laughter and quiet conversations carry on around us when he tilts my face toward him, his eyes heating, his breath quickening. A pulse flutters his jaw, and I feel the same racing beats in my chest. Perhaps he's turned me into an insatiable beast as well.

"I think this calls for some more celebration, Ms. Callahan." His deep voice sends shivers down my spine.

"Noire tonight again, Professor?" I whisper under my breath so no one can hear. I watch his eyes darken and flare and he leans in, his mouth inches away from my ear.

"Run. I'll catch you...always."

Thank you for reading WHEN HEARTS COLLIDE. Hope you've enjoyed Ryland and Millie's story as much as I did writing it.

Bonus Epilogues: Want to know if Ryland ultimately gets tenure and what surprise he has up his sleeves? These are the bonus epilogues you don't want to miss! Sign up for my newsletter to get **TWO EXTRA BONUS CHAPTERS**, new release alerts, exclusive bonus material, and more. Just click on the "When Hearts Collide Bonus Epilogues" on the website: https://www.victorialum.com/bonus

Read Maxwell's Story Next: Do you know Maxwell and Belle's story is next? This is one angsty arranged marriage/marriage of convenience billionaire romance with gothic vibes, family secrets, and a curse. Don't miss WHEN HEARTS SURRENDER. Read it here: https://geni.us/whenheartssurrender

Please Review: Please consider leaving a review on the retailer website and Goodreads https://www.goodreads.com/book/show/206026147-when-hearts-collide. Your reviews will really help this author out and will allow for more readers to find this book.

THANK YOU

ONE OF MY FAVORITE tropes to read about is professor/student. There's something uniquely forbidden and seductive about knowing you cannot fall for this person and then doing it anyway. So, I've read a lot of books in this genre and I was a bit nervous to write Ryland and Millie's book because I wanted to do justice to their story and the trope I love so much. So, to date, this has been the most difficult book for me to write. Not to mention, Ryland pretty much ignored me for half of my writing time (but I got his thoughts out of him eventually). Perhaps because I spent a lot of time with these characters, they are also the ones I've fallen really hard for. I hope you love them as much as I did.

Without my team, I know I won't be able to put out these amazing stories. Thank you, in no particular order:

My family: You are my strength, my joy, and I'm blessed every moment with you in my life.

My editors: Theresa Leigh and Amy Briggs, thank you for your help with this book! I love our chats as always!

Proofreader: Thank you to Michele Ficht for turning this around so quickly.

My PA: Nikki, without you, I'll always forget my deadlines. Thank you for busting my balls.

Cover designer: To the awesome LK Farlow of Y'All That Graphic, thank you for bearing with me as I nitpick on colors, fonts, and making the most beautiful covers.

Beta readers: Malia, Jenn, Jess, Fiona, and Isha, thank you, ladies, so, so much! Your feedback is gold!! And Malia, the rage room scene is for you.

My ilLUMinati girls: you know who you are! Thank you for being the best girls an author and fellow reader can have.

Fellow authors: There's a wonderful community of authors out there – thank you to each and every one of you.

PR Firms: Thank you to Truly Yours PR and Literally Yours PR for your promotional efforts and helping me get the word out!

My Fellow Readers: I love you guys so, so much. I still can't believe you guys love and read my books. Thank you from the bottom of my heart.

With love,
Victoria

Also by Victoria Lum

Catch up on Victoria's backlist! Don't miss these swoony, romantic stories with all the sizzling spice and angst. All stories are standalones and can be read out of order.

LA Hearts:
The Sweetest Agony (James and Jess)
The Coldest Passion (Parker and Liz)
The Harshest Hope (Adrian and Emily)
The Brightest Spark (Jack and Sarah)
The Orchid:
When Hearts Ignite (Steven and Grace)
When Hearts Collide (Ryland and Millie)
When Hearts Surrender (Maxwell and Belle)

About the Author

Victoria is a lover of all things romance, including movies, books, and television shows. A hopeless romantic since childhood, she is always dreaming up stories and happily ever afters. Caramel lattes are her fuel in the morning and she can usually be found reading anything she can get her hands on. She lives with her family and a beautiful Siberian husky in sunny California.

Keep in touch!
Sign up for her newsletter below:
Newsletter
Follow Victoria on social media:
Victoria Lum's Luminaries Facebook Group
Facebook Page
Instagram
Tiktok
Bookbub
Amazon
Goodreads
Scan the QR code below for all the links!